Also by Michelle Douglas

Billionaire's Road Trip to Forever
Cinderella and the Brooding Billionaire
Escape with Her Greek Tycoon
Wedding Date in Malaysia

Also by Ally Blake

Brooding Rebel to Baby Daddy
Dream Vacation, Surprise Baby
The Millionaire's Melbourne Proposal
The Wedding Favour

Discover more at millsandboon.co.uk.

RECLUSIVE MILLIONAIRE'S MISTLETOE MIRACLE

MICHELLE DOUGLAS

WHIRLWIND FLING TO BABY BOMBSHELL

ALLY BLAKE

MILLS & BOON

ISBN: 978-0-263-30228-8

10/22

MIX
Paper from
responsible sources
FSC C007454

This book is produced from independently certified FSC™ paper
to ensure responsible forest management.
For more information visit www.harpercollins.co.uk/green.

Printed and Bound in Spain using 100% Renewable Electricity
at CPI Black Print, Barcelona

RECLUSIVE MILLIONAIRE'S MISTLETOE MIRACLE

MICHELLE DOUGLAS

MILLS & BOON

To Sue, for raising two fabulous children and
putting up with this crazy family with humour and grace.

CHAPTER ONE

CHLOE SWORE AS she slipped and skidded across the cobblestoned courtyard from the converted coach house to the back door of the big house, the heavy dew making the trip perilous. Her feet started to slide out from beneath her and she windmilled her arms wildly, catching hold of the door handle at the last moment. She held on for grim life until she was sure she'd regained her balance, and then pounded on the door with more vigour than grace, muttering a slew of equally inelegant curses under her breath.

Welcome to Devon, Chlo.

Pulling her coat around her, she tried jogging on the spot, her breath frosting the air, as she tried to prevent the cold from creeping into her very bones. It was *freezing*! And it wasn't even December yet. How was it possible to be this cold?

She knocked again—though it was more of a beating of her fists as her extremities started to lose all feeling—and then fumbled in her pocket for her phone and hit redial. She'd had to ring the number of the big house earlier after she'd got so lost from the directions the locals had given her that she'd become convinced that the people who lived in this part of the world had no sense of direction *at all.*

Deep inside the house she heard the phone ringing, just as the back door opened.

She tried to turn her phone off, but her hands were shaking too hard.

'Chloe, what happened to you? You're soaked!' Stephanie Gladstone, the housekeeper she'd met briefly earlier this evening, pulled her inside and closed the door, before taking her phone and turning it off. 'Come with me, quickly! We need to get you warm.'

Yes, please.

In next to no time, she found herself sitting in front of a heater in the kitchen, her hair up in a towel, and her wet things removed in favour of a thick fluffy robe that Stephanie had seemed to magic out of the air. She accepted the mug of steaming cocoa Stephanie held out to her, with a grateful, 'Thank you.'

She blew on it, the steam lifting to warm her face, and momentarily closed her eyes to savour that very first sip. She touched the mug to her lips, eager for that first hit of hot sweetness, but before she could take a sip a large wolf of a man stormed into the kitchen with the kind of ferocious scowl that in ordinary circumstances might make her quail. But not today.

'What in the name of God is all this infernal racket?'

He bristled all over, the rangy frame crackling with energy and outrage and temper.

His gaze zeroed in on her and his brows lowered even further over his eyes. 'And who the hell are you?'

She recognised him immediately. Setting her mug down, she shot to her feet. 'I'm Chloe Ivy Belle Jennings, and if this is the way you usually speak to your employees, Mr Beau Diamond, you can shove your contract where the sun doesn't shine and find somebody else to be your damn lackey.'

She wasn't sure why she used her full name, only it did sound more impressive. *And* it made him blink. At least, she thought that was what made him blink.

To her right, Stephanie huffed out a laugh. 'That'll tell you, Beau. Stop bellyaching. A water pipe in the flat has burst. I've got George onto it, but you're going to need to get the plumbers back.'

'And probably someone to fix the soggy wall. And the carpet will be ruined as well,' Chloe added for good measure. Water had gone everywhere at a ridiculous rate of knots.

He swung back. 'Why on earth didn't you turn the water off at the mains?'

He stared at her as if she were stupid and she didn't bother trying to put a lid on her temper. Today had been trying on so many levels and this was one straw too many. 'If I could've found the mains, I would've! If we're asking searching questions, why the hell did you give me such substandard accommodation?'

Accommodation had been part of the contract. She didn't require much, but warm and dry were non-negotiable.

She'd been told before that she had ferocious eyebrows and she did what she could to use them to best effect now, frowning as fiercely as she could. But then she realised what a sight she must look, in this enormous fluffy robe and her hair wrapped in a towel, and had to fight an insane urge to laugh.

Not funny share-a-joke laughter, but the kind that held a hint of hysteria. Turning her back on the grump of a man, she lifted the cocoa to her lips and took a big sustaining gulp, closing her eyes and feeling it warm her all the way through.

'Well, you can't stay here.'

She swung around. 'If you think I'm leaving in the dead of night to find accommodation in the village then you're going to be rudely disappointed, Mr Diamond.'

His eyes widened as she advanced on him. At the back of her mind she noted his rumpled appearance and the too-long hair that was sticking up all over the place as if he'd just jumped out of bed. Which, of course, was exactly what he had done. But at least he hadn't had to slosh through icy water!

She stopped in front of him. 'Do you know how long it took me to get from my door to yours?'

He shook his head, eyeing her as if she were some rogue wildebeest from the plains of Africa.

'It was thirty-four hours from the time I left my house in Sydney to when I stepped off the plane at Heathrow. It took an hour on the Tube to get to Paddington train station and then it was a four-hour train journey to Barnstaple. At that point there was a problem with my hire car booking, which delayed me for the best part of an hour, but then according to my satnav it was supposed to be a simple seventeen-minute Sunday drive to the apparently idyllic but tiny village of Ballingsmallard and a further two minutes to Dawncarden Court.'

He cleared his throat and nodded. 'That's correct.'

'Hallelujah, I said to myself.' The words left her on a growl. 'But the satnav was wrong!' She shook her head so hard the towel on her head unravelled and her wild mane of hair fell down below her shoulders, which probably made her look more and more like that rogue wildebeest by the minute. It wasn't an image that improved her temper.

She stabbed a finger at him. 'The people in this part of the world clearly don't know their left from their right or… or which way is even up! So I wasn't sent on just one, but *three* wild goose chases. Nobody warned me that I'd lose satellite signal, so I didn't bother printing a map out. Why didn't *you* warn me?'

He adjusted his stance. 'How long did it take for you to find Dawncarden Court?'

'Three hours eighteen minutes and thirty-three seconds!'

He winced and glanced at Stephanie. 'I thought you'd—'

'And I thought you had.'

She ignored them. 'And now I don't know whether I'm coming or going! I'm jet-lagged, tired, cold, wet and hungry. And if you think I'm going back out there—' she pointed in the vague direction of the road outside '—to try and find a room at the inn, then you're more wrong than you have ever been.'

They eyed each other across what seemed like some invisible divide, and to her amazement he eventually shrugged. 'Well, I'm sure we can at least do something about you being hungry, can't we, Steph?'

'Already on it,' Stephanie said, cracking eggs into a frying pan.

Chloe stared and her entire frame drooped. 'Oh, but I didn't mean to put you to any trouble.' She moistened her lips, fighting a wave of exhaustion. 'I just wanted to get warm and dry and…'

'And to have a rest,' the older woman finished for her, 'and that's entirely understandable. Sit down and finish your cocoa. I'll have this whipped up in no time and you'll feel all the better for it, I promise. Would you like some as well, Beau?'

'Why not?' With a shrug he hooked out a chair at right angles to Chloe. She buried her nose in her mug, and squinted slightly to blur his outline, tried not to wince. Had she really just ranted at her employer like a fishwife?

Holding the mug in both hands, she stared into its contents. 'I think I probably owe you an apology for, um… going off like a firecracker just now.'

'Not at all.'

She didn't believe him. In her mind, she replayed what she'd just said and heat flooded her face. She stared all the more doggedly into her mug. 'Tomorrow, when my brain is hopefully in decent working order again, I'll try and apologise properly and…' Try and find a way to prove to him that normally she had the most level of tempers.

'You are allowed to look at me when you speak,' he snapped.

She did what she could to smother the yawn that threatened to split her face in two as she turned towards him. 'What?'

'I won't bite.'

But his voice had lost its venom and a furrow appeared between his eyes. She huffed out a laugh, too tired to try and work out what any of it meant…too tired to even care if she'd still have a job in the morning.

Don't be daft. You need this job.

'So you're saying your bark is worse than your bite, then?'

'I'm glad to see you've got his number.' Stephanie set plates of scrambled eggs and toast in front of them. 'Stop pestering the poor girl, Beau, and let her eat. She's too tired for your nonsense.'

She decided then and there that she loved Stephanie.

'Where were you thinking of putting Ms Jennings, Steph?'

'Chloe,' Chloe said around a mouthful of egg. 'Please call me Chloe. Ms Jennings is my mum.' She gestured to her plate with her fork. 'These are the best scrambled eggs ever.'

'In the daffodil room.'

'But—'

'Oh, that sounds lovely,' Chloe murmured, finding it a sudden effort to chew and swallow…to even lift her fork. Now that she felt deliciously warm again, she wasn't sure she ever wanted to move. 'Daffodils are the happiest flowers, don't you think? So warm and yellow and everything. Daffodils and wattle and sunflowers and Billy buttons…'

'Oops, we're losing her,' she heard Steph say at the same time as a warm strong hand wrapped around her upper arm.

She jerked back into immediate wakefulness. Even through the thickness of the towelling robe, she could feel the unmistakable strength of Beau Diamond's fingers and it made something weird stir to life inside her.

She jerked upright. 'Sorry!'

'No problem.' He removed his hand.

'I don't know what's wrong with me. I feel drunk. But I've not had any alcohol since…' She shook her head. She wasn't a drinker. 'It'd be weeks.' Maybe months. 'And my balance is off.'

'That'll be due to the air travel. The balance thing,' he clarified. 'As for the rest, Chloe, basically you've been travelling for two days with very little sleep and probably not a whole lot of food either. You need to finish your eggs.'

He gestured at her plate, so she forked more egg into her mouth and then ate half a slice of toast for good measure.

'And you need to keep hydrated.'

He poured her a glass of water and she drank it—greedily. She hadn't even realised she was thirsty.

'And now you need to sleep and sleep until you don't feel like sleeping any more.'

How divine that sounded. 'Don't we have a meeting tomorrow?'

He reached out a hand to prop her up when she started to list again. 'The day after. Tomorrow you rest.'

She made a half-hearted effort to straighten up again. But it was kind of nice to feel that firm strength—all warm and reassuring through the towelling robe. So it was only half an effort. She found a smile. 'Do you know how good that sounds?'

One side of his mouth hooked up. 'I've got some idea.'

For a fraction of a moment something in his eyes danced and a sigh fluttered out of her. 'You have the loveliest eyes.'

They were the colour of a deep blue sea. 'I never noticed that from the telly.'

His smile vanished and she forced herself to straighten. 'While I apparently, or so I am told, have fierce eyebrows.'

He blinked.

'And I do believe they stopped you barking at me earlier, so I'm rather grateful to them.'

She found herself frowning. 'And why are the two of you letting me rattle on with nonsense like this?'

Stephanie laughed. 'Because it's refreshingly direct and I like it. But you're right. It's time you were in bed. Come along and I'll show you your room.'

Grateful, she pushed to her feet. 'Goodnight, Beau. I can call you Beau, can't I? Or do we have to do the awful formal Mr Diamond and Ms Jennings thing?'

'Beau will be fine.'

With a salute, she turned and followed Stephanie from the room. 'I think I'm going to die a thousand deaths when I remember all of this tomorrow,' she whispered.

'Nonsense.' Stephanie laughed. 'You're exactly what the doctor ordered and I can't tell you how glad I am to welcome you to Dawncarden Court, Chloe.'

Chloe crossed her fingers as hard as she could and hoped that Beau Diamond was nowhere to be seen before stepping into the kitchen the next morning. She gave an audible sigh before leaping across to fill the kettle.

Coffee. Please. Now.

'Good morning, Chloe.'

She whirled around with a yelp when a deep voice sounded behind her. 'Oh, Lord! Lordy lord. You just took ten years off my life.' She patted her chest and tried to find a smile. 'Good morning… Beau.'

One rather commanding eyebrow rose. 'Were you just *tiptoeing* through my house?'

'You bet your sweet patootie I was. I figured I'd disturbed you enough last night. I wanted to prove I could be as quiet as the proverbial mouse when occasion demanded it.'

He didn't laugh. He didn't even smile.

She swallowed. 'Is it okay to grab a cuppa before I head into the village to find alternative lodgings?'

He might have an enormous house, but it was clear he didn't want to share it. And as someone who valued her privacy too—though coming from as big a family as she did, privacy was a relative term—she didn't blame him.

'Help yourself to a decent breakfast. It'll help your body clock adjust.'

'Thank you. Coffee?'

He shook his head, but he didn't leave. He just stood there and watched her.

In the cold light of morning—*late* morning and, yes, it did look cold—last night's impression of height and breadth hadn't been misleading, and the energy he'd once projected onto the television screen from his natural history documentary series was still present, but any humour she might've once imagined in that face had well and truly disappeared. Unfortunately she hadn't dreamed that bristling, brooding undercurrent thing that he had going either.

Swallowing a sigh, she made a coffee and eased into a seat at the table. 'Do I still have a job?'

He moved across to the kitchen bench. 'Yes.'

She closed her eyes. *Thank you. Thank you. Thank you.*

Winning the contract to make over Dawncarden Court's walled garden had been a lifesaver, and about the only thing standing between her and losing the house she and Mark had saved so hard for. She'd put so much work into her submission. Had brushed up on all things associated with English country gardens until her brain had been in danger of exploding. She'd wanted to wow him with her knowledge of the local climate, of local plants and soil types, of English native trees. And it had paid off.

Don't mess it up.

Forcing her eyes open, she sipped her coffee and glanced back up at him. Even though it was a good twelve months since he'd been on TV, she'd have still recognised him. Even given the accident and his scars, and she wasn't sure why, but that felt like a relief. 'Would you like me to attempt a proper apology now or—?'

'I'd really rather you didn't.'

He didn't turn back, and she craned her neck to see what he was doing. Oh, he was making tea! Why hadn't she asked him if he wanted tea? 'Well, for what it's worth, I *am* sorry. I'm not usually so bad-tempered.'

'Jet lag.' He set a large teapot to the middle of the table along with two mugs before lowering that tall rangy frame to the seat opposite. Despite the mellowness of his tone, when he glanced at her the blue of his eyes was oddly piercing. 'How are you feeling today?'

She gulped more coffee. 'Like I'm hung over, but without the headache. You've been a globetrotter, what are your tips and tricks for overcoming jet lag?'

Before he could answer, Stephanie came tripping into the kitchen. She'd been dealing with the plumbers she'd called first thing to look at the burst pipes in the flat.

'You need to start eating your meals in this time zone, rather than when you feel hungry, as well as drinking lots of water, and getting out in the sun for a walk,' she said with her usual crispness.

Chloe choked on her coffee. 'Sun?' She pointed towards the window. 'You're calling that weak excuse for a bit of light the sun?'

He found himself wanting to laugh. Just as he'd wanted to laugh several times last night. But just as he had last night, he suppressed the urge. He didn't trust it. 'Getting out into the daylight will help your body clock reset itself.'

She stared at him, dragged in a breath and then nodded. 'Okay, but… I had no idea how cold it'd be here.'

He and Stephanie exchanged glances but didn't inform her that there was nothing particularly cold about the current weather. She'd flown in from an Australian summer to an English winter. It'd take her a few days to acclimatise.

'Once you're properly rested, the cold won't seem so bad,' he found himself assuring her.

Stephanie glanced at him with a raised eyebrow, but he studiously ignored it, pouring them mugs of tea instead. Thankfully, she fetched the cake tin and cut them all a generous slice of Madeira cake.

'Oh, but…' Chloe started.

'Eat,' Stephanie ordered. 'I have a proposition for you both and the cake will help sweeten it.'

His gut instantly clenched. He knew immediately what this proposition of Stephanie's was. She was going to suggest that Chloe *Ivy Belle* Jennings stay here in the manor for the duration of her contract, and while he knew it made sense everything inside him protested. He'd rather the expense of having to put her up in the village.

Damn it! It was *his* house. *He* made the rules.

Stephanie fixed him with an eagle eye as if she'd read that thought in his face. She didn't challenge him, though, didn't say it wasn't his house yet and that it was his grandmother who made the rules. Not for the first time he could see why his grandmother had engaged her as housekeeper twenty years ago. He expected the two women would see eye to eye on most things.

From the corner of his eye, he saw Chloe take a bite of cake and a momentary expression of bliss crossed her face—as if she hadn't eaten cake in a long time and had forgotten how good it could be. She captured a crumb at the corner of her mouth with her tongue and things low down in his belly suddenly clenched, taking him off guard.

What the hell...?

Scowling, he took a huge bite of cake. All he could say was that he was glad her ridiculous hair was pulled back in a thick plait this morning. When the towel had worked its way loose from her hair last night and all of that gingerbread-coloured hair had tumbled halfway down her back, he'd not been able to do anything for a moment but stare.

His scowl deepened. It was ridiculous hair for a gardener to have!

'You can get that expression off your face right now, Beau Diamond,' Stephanie told him in no uncertain terms. 'And you *will* hear me out.'

'As I've yet to find a way to stop you from speaking your mind,' he returned just as swiftly, 'then I expect you're right.'

That made her laugh. Very little disturbed Stephanie's equanimity.

'What did the tradesmen say?'

'The plumbing is old—that renovation was done back in the sixties. To be on the safe side, they want to replace all the pipes. According to George, it's just as well someone was staying at the time as that pipe could've gone at any moment.'

Stephanie turned to Chloe. 'George is our general handyman. When he's not busy mending fences and replacing tiles in the rooves of the various outbuildings, he cuts the grass, keeps the vegetable patch in order, and prunes what he can, but the gardens here are too much for one person. He lives in the village, but I'll introduce the two of you later.'

Chloe nodded and went back to her cake.

Stephanie swung back to Beau. 'Because it was found

early the water damage isn't too extensive. But I expect some painting and new carpet will be necessary.'

He sighed. It wasn't the expense that bothered him—there was plenty of money for repairs—but the thought of tradesmen in and out of Dawncarden had his hands clenching.

Well, Stephanie could deal with them. It was one of the things he paid her for after all.

'I spoke to Julia last night.'

Hearing the concern in her voice, he set his mug down.

'Julia is my daughter,' she explained to Chloe. 'And she's pregnant.'

'That's lovely news. Congratulations.'

He didn't want to like Chloe Jennings. He didn't want to have any feelings for her whatsoever. But he couldn't deny that she had a nice smile. And when she wasn't in a temper, her eyebrows didn't look the least bit fierce.

He shook himself. 'Is everything okay?'

'The morning sickness hasn't passed and she's sounding tired…a little glum.'

'But she and the baby…?'

'They're both fine. But I'm worried about her, Beau. She wants me to spend Christmas with them.'

But Julia lived in Newcastle! That was a six-and-a-half-hour drive away. It wasn't exactly a hop, skip and jump to go and have Christmas dinner with her daughter and then get back to Dawncarden Court to cook his supper.

Not that he needed her to cook his supper. He knew his way around a kitchen. But—

'I want to take some leave, some proper leave. I've not had a holiday in years. I've not spent more than a weekend away from the estate in two years.' She folded her arms. 'I've earned some time off.'

He wanted to argue, but she was right. He couldn't begrudge her the time off. Especially if she was worried about

Julia. And it *was* coming up to Christmas. Not that he gave two hoots about the season for himself, but it seemed to mean a lot to other people.

None of that stopped a scowl from settling over his features, though.

'Don't look at me like that,' she ordered, clearly not the least put out. 'I've come up with the perfect solution.'

It was his turn to cross his arms. Across the table he was aware of Chloe's gaze on his arms. His lips twisted. Checking them for scars no doubt. The entire world was hungry for news—and photographs—of his scars.

He forced his focus back to Stephanie. 'The *perfect* solution?' He suspected that as far as he was going to be concerned it would be far from perfect.

'If Chloe here is amenable, she could fill in as temporary housekeeper for a few weeks.'

Chloe straightened. 'Oh, I...'

She swallowed and he sympathised. Stephanie could be hard to withstand.

'What would it entail?'

'Not a lot. Cooking the evening meal and a little light cleaning. We have a house-cleaning service that comes in once a week to do a comprehensive spit and polish, but they're banned from Beau's rooms, so whipping through those areas with a duster and giving them a quick vacuum is about all you'll be asked to do. The supermarket in the village will deliver whatever you need...and—'

'And nothing,' Beau cut in. 'I can deal with all of that myself. I know how to cook and clean as well as the next person.'

Steph raised an eyebrow. 'And are you also prepared to deal with the tradesmen and the house-cleaning service?'

Hell, no.

'I thought not,' she said, evidently reading the answer in his face. 'And before you suggest it, you're not cancelling either. This is your grandmother's estate, and, while you'll inherit it one day, she's my employer and this is the kind of property that can get away from a body if they let it. I'm following her instructions, not yours.'

Damn it!

'How long are you planning to be away?' he demanded.

'Until after the new year.'

'But that's *six weeks*!'

'I've earned it, Beau. And I need a break.'

He dragged a hand down his face. Across the table, Chloe watched them with eyes the colour of treacle.

Steph gestured towards her. 'You saw Chloe in action last night. She's not the kind of girl tradesmen *or* the press will be able to walk over.'

He glared at Stephanie, wanting to bellow at her that she wasn't allowed to go anywhere. But he didn't have the right. And he couldn't begrudge her time away with her family.

'If neither of you like that idea, then I can organise a temporary housekeeper from a reputable agency.'

'That is *not* going to happen.'

He wasn't having yet another person in his space. Strangers couldn't be trusted. That had already been established.

This Chloe Jennings probably couldn't be trusted either, but her garden design had been the best, and her knowledge of the local flora and ecosystems had impressed him. And he *had* made her sign a watertight privacy clause. If she tried to leak photographs of him to the tabloids, he'd sue her for every penny she had and utterly destroy her professional reputation while he was at it.

'Are you seeing sense yet, Beau?'

'Chloe hasn't agreed to the arrangement, Steph, and I don't see why she'd want to.'

'Of course she will, won't you, Chloe? For one thing, you'll receive a generous stipend on top of what you're already being paid for the garden makeover.'

Chloe's eyes brightened, and things inside him hardened. Was he going to need to lock the family silver up while she was here?

'I don't have any objections to the plan.' Chloe glanced at him uncertainly. 'I'm a passable cook and can certainly cope with a bit of light cleaning, but you don't seem the least bit keen. And as my gardening contract comes first…'

Stephanie spread her hands. 'So can I go and pack my bags yet, or do I need to call the agency?'

He bit back an oath and swung to Chloe, knowing his face had turned ferocious, probably scary, and certainly ugly. It was what he saw whenever he looked in the mirror these days—ugly, jagged scars. To her credit, she barely blinked. But that was probably because she was still jet-lagged.

'I want us very clear on one thing.' He stabbed a finger to the table so hard it jolted his entire arm. It took a force of will not to wince.

Serves you right for trying to be a tough dude.

'That privacy clause you signed in relation to the garden will also extend to this temporary housekeeping gig too. Do I make myself clear?'

'Perfectly.'

'And I'll be making you sign a document to that effect.'

'Okay.' She glanced at Stephanie. 'Privacy is a big deal around here, then?'

'Absolutely.' Stephanie started clearing the table. 'His lordship here has a real bee in his bonnet about it. If it were up to him, he'd never leave this place and would refuse to see anyone. Hence the reason you'll need to be the one to deal with the tradesmen and anyone else who might come knocking on the door.'

'Does anyone come knocking?'

'Not so much any more, but we do still get the occasional journalist looking for a story and hoping to catch a glimpse of Beau.'

Those not so ferocious eyebrows shot up.

'Apparently the price of an up-to-date picture of Beau is now rumoured to be upward of the twenty-thousand-pound mark.'

Chloe shot forward on her seat. 'You have to be joking! That's…it's—'

'Hence the privacy clause I insisted you sign.'

She slumped back and his every instinct went on high alert. Given a chance, would this girl try and sell him out?

'And if you break that clause, I will sue you for every dollar you have and more, do I make myself clear?'

Her eyes widened, and then those brows did become ferocious. 'I've no intention of breaking my contract with you, *Mr Diamond*, but if you're worried that I might, then you're free to make other arrangements for your housekeeper and I'll find accommodation in the village. I'm more than happy to speak to the housekeeper about the garden rather than you.'

That certainly wasn't going to happen. The garden was too precious to him. Too *necessary*.

He shook his head. 'The more I think about it, the more Stephanie's plan makes sense. It also makes sense to have you right here where I can keep an eye on you, rather than staying in the village where you might be tempted to gossip. The fewer people working at Dawncarden, the better, and the less the likelihood of the press getting a picture of me.'

Stephanie clapped briskly. 'Excellent! The lord and master has spoken.'

Chloe drooped in her chair like a flower in dire need of water and he winced. He'd become a bad-tempered beast since the accident, but he hadn't wanted her misunderstanding the gravity of that privacy clause.

You all but accused her of wanting to sell pictures of you to the press.

No, he hadn't! He'd just made it plain where they stood.

She shook her head. 'And yet you don't look happy about the arrangement.'

'Since the accident that's been his permanent expression,' Stephanie said. 'If he's not careful, the wind will change and he'll be stuck with a face like thunder forever.'

Given his scars, what did it matter? 'When did you say you were leaving?' he growled.

Chloe gurgled out a laugh. 'I'm going to miss this sniping. Is that part of the job description?'

'Absolutely,' Stephanie said.

At the same time as he said, 'Don't even think about it.'

But some of the blackness of his mood lifted.

'Are you really a lord?' Chloe asked.

'No, that's simply what passes as a joke to Stephanie.'

'I like her sense of humour.'

So did he but he wouldn't admit it, not even under threat of torture.

'If it's any consolation, the remuneration package will be very generous,' he found himself saying.

'Consolation for what—your bad temper?' She stood. 'I guess time will tell. If today is my last day of leisure, then I'm going for that walk and praying you're right about it helping me beat the jet lag blues.'

When she'd gone, Stephanie swung to him. 'If you ever spoke to me the way you just spoke to that young woman, I'd resign on the spot. She doesn't deserve your nasty suspicions or your rudeness. You're turning into a bitter, bad-tempered man, Beau, and you need to do something about that.'

'Why?'

'Because this is no way to live! You shut yourself away

here and what good is it doing you? You're letting your talent go to waste—'

'The world no longer wants my talent!'

Soon, though, he'd have his garden and perhaps his world wouldn't look quite so bleak. Maybe then he'd find the resources to manage a semblance of politeness and civility.

CHAPTER TWO

'OH, MY GOD! You ought to see Dawncarden Court, Mum. It's amazing!' Chloe gushed before her mother could start fussing and worrying again about Chloe not spending Christmas at home.

This year she was determined to not wreck her family's Christmas. She'd been the kiss of death to the last two and that was more than enough. This year her family deserved to celebrate the season with joy and laughter. She was determined to give them *nothing* to worry about.

She had promised to video-call regularly while in England, though. She was hoping it'd be easier to fake Christmas cheer from ten thousand miles away than it would be if she were still in Australia. In her lap she crossed her fingers.

Her mother's face moved closer to the screen as if she was trying to peer into her daughter's soul. 'You're not brooding, are you, love? You know it's time to move on and—'

'Absolutely not! This is all such an adventure. I'm planning on enjoying every moment of it. And seriously, when I show you pictures of this place, you're going to see exactly what I mean.'

She did her best to describe the house and gardens. Not that she'd yet seen the walled garden. Oh, she'd found it—the wall at least. That had been impossible to miss. But the door had been locked. When she'd mentioned it to Stephanie, the other woman had shown her the hook behind the door where the key was hung. 'Next time I call, I'll do it from the baronial hall so you can see it. It'll knock your—'

She blinked when a large hand reached across and snapped her laptop shut. Glancing up, she found Beau straightening from the other side of the table. 'What—?'

She choked back the rest of her words at the expression on his face. He looked as if he wanted to throttle her, and it suddenly occurred to her that she was alone with a man who, for all she knew, could be a Bluebeard in his castle. Why hadn't she asked Stephanie more about him?

She should've asked for a character reference or something. At least an assurance that the man was in his right mind. Her heart thudded. She'd so badly needed the contract she'd been more focussed on proving her own credentials than checking his.

'Already selling me out, Ms Jennings?'

She frowned. Hold on, he thought…?

'What is wrong with you?' she found herself shouting. He'd cut off her call to her mother because he'd thought she was talking to someone from the press? *Seriously?*

And seriously, had she just *shouted*? She never shouted.

Thrusting out her jaw, she glared. Beau Diamond's nasty suspicions deserved to be yelled at. Besides, her rations of 'nice and polite' had been severely depleted prior to arriving here—burned out, in fact, hence the need for the strategic retreat from her family. Now that she'd relaxed her guard she was finding it impossible to get even a semblance of 'nice and polite' back into place.

She tipped what was left of her now tepid coffee into the sink. Was she going to have to put up with this mentality for the next two months? 'Have you thought about therapy? Because you're starting to sound ridiculously paranoid.'

His jaw dropped. '*Paranoid?* You were giving detailed

descriptions of the lie of the land so a photographer would know the best vantage points to lie in wait and hopefully get a picture of me. *And* you were promising pictures of the inside of the house! There's nothing paranoid about that. You can pack your damn bags and—'

'You *idiot*! I was talking to my *mum*, not some sleazy journalist. God! When are you going to get it into your thick skull that I'm not interested in selling you out?'

They stared at each other, both breathing hard. Beau eventually swallowed and rolled his shoulders. 'Your mum?'

'My mum,' she repeated, flipping open the lid of her laptop.

He didn't move, not a single muscle.

'And now you're going to meet her.'

That galvanised him again. 'I don't *do* face-to-face interviews with *anyone*.'

She curled her lip in his general direction. It seemed better than calling him a rude name. 'This isn't an interview.' She planted herself in her chair in front of her computer again and punched a few keys.

'I'm not—'

'If you don't, I'm leaving.' She leaned back and folded her arms. 'I need this gardening contract—more badly than you can possibly know—but I won't be bullied. And I won't be treated like this. It's not fair and I've had enough unfairness in my life to last a lifetime. More to the point, I won't have my family treated like that. My mum is already worried enough about me as it is. I'm not having you adding to it.'

She hit the camera icon and her mother came back into view. 'What happened, honey?'

'I think the connection up here is a bit…*dodgy*.' She glanced at Beau over the top of her laptop, letting him know that the only thing dodgy here was him. 'Hopefully, it's righted itself again now. And I expect I ought to get back to work, but I thought you might like to meet my employer, Beau.'

She sent him another pointed look and, with a scowl, he slouched over into view, but she noted he kept the scarred side of his face away from the camera.

'Hello, Mrs Jennings, it's nice to meet you.'

'Oh, it does put my mind at rest to meet you, Mr Diamond. And here you are looking so hale and hearty too!'

He stiffened and Chloe had to swallow a groan.

'You will keep an eye on Chloe for us, won't you, love? When she gets out in the garden she forgets all about the time and eating and whatnot.'

A slow—and she suspected somewhat reluctant—smile tugged at his lips, making her blink.

He crossed his heart. 'I promise to make sure she has three square meals a day. Besides, for the next few weeks she's also my housekeeper so she's going to have to learn to be a better timekeeper.'

'That all seems to have come a bit out of the blue.'

'It did, but my housekeeper's daughter is pregnant and suffering from morning sickness, and she wanted to be there for her over the holidays. I was grateful Chloe was able to step into the breach. I'm discovering that your daughter is a woman of...many talents.'

A cunning look came into her mother's eyes and she glanced at Chloe. 'Honey, why don't you get to work and leave me and Beau here to have a little chat?'

'Not a chance, Mum.' She pulled the computer back around to her and tried to push Beau away, but he proved immovable. 'I'm not letting you chew the poor man's ear off and give him a ton of instructions about what he ought to be doing and what I ought to be doing.'

'Oh, but—'

Beau turned the computer back towards him. 'Was there something specific you wanted to ask me, Mrs Jennings?'

'Yes, love. It's just…we're that worried about Chloe spending Christmas away this year.'

Chloe groaned and dropped her head to her hands.

'Christmas is a really big deal in our family. I mean, Chloe was even named for Christmas.'

'Ivy Belle,' he murmured.

'Exactly! Look, Beau, I know you must be a busy man, but can you find it in your heart to look out for our Chloe? Like I said, she'll work herself into the ground if you let her. And I understand her need to keep busy, but making herself sick won't help anyone.'

'No indeed.'

'Mum, I'm not going to get sick. I'm planning on having fun while I'm here. Adventure, remember?'

But her mother carried on as if she hadn't spoken. 'And if she's looking particularly glum… I don't know, maybe you could find a way to cheer her up a bit.'

Cheer her up? Beau!

She did her best to snort back a laugh. He had myriad talents, but she doubted that was one of them.

'I'll do my best,' he managed.

'That's all I ask of you, pet. It eases my mind knowing she has someone there in Old Blighty who's looking out for her.'

Beau finally allowed Chloe to wrest back control of her laptop. 'You worry too much, Mum. Everything is going to be fine. I'll call you in a few days. I love you.'

'Love you too, sweetheart.'

She closed the lid of her laptop and moved towards the kettle. Finding Beau's proximity strangely disturbing. 'Tea?' Stephanie had told her he usually had a mid-morning tea and biscuit.

'Yes, please.' He was silent for a long moment. 'Why do you need the garden contract so badly?'

'None of your business.'

He huffed out a laugh. 'This isn't going to be a harmonious working relationship, is it?'

'Not shaping up that way,' she agreed, setting the tea to brew in the middle of the table and putting fingers of delicious-looking shortbread onto a blue china plate.

'Why is your mother so worried about you?'

She glanced up and raised an eyebrow.

He stared back and pursed his lips. 'Why do you need to keep so busy?' he tried instead.

She shook her head. 'Nope and nope.' And then gestured at the blue china plate. 'I've never made shortbread. So while Stephanie has left me her recipe, and I'm more than happy to give it a whirl, you might want to savour this while you can.'

'You don't have to do any baking. I'm just as happy with store-bought stuff.'

No way. Her eyes had nearly bugged out of her head when she'd read the figure she'd be receiving for filling in for Stephanie. She had every intention of earning it, which meant keeping both the biscuit and cake tins full while she was here.

'I liked your mum.'

She poured the tea. 'She liked you too.' The thought made her frown. Her mum was normally a good judge of character.

Actually, beside his ghastly suspicions, Beau was probably all right. But she hoped his temper didn't improve too much while she was here, because that meant she wouldn't have to put much of an effort into hers either. It was damn freeing not to have to feign politeness or fake friendliness or any kind of good cheer.

'That surprises you?'

What? Oh, her mum. 'Not really. She likes everyone.'

He rolled his eyes ceilingward. 'And now she's the queen of the backhanded compliment.'

One corner of his mouth hooked up, and she did what she could to ignore the discordant pitter-patter of her heart. Nobody could call Beau Diamond handsome, not any more. But that didn't stop his presence from feeling strangely dynamic. 'I've a whole repertoire of them. *And* I'm still waiting for your apology, by the way.'

'Look, Chloe, I have reasons for being so suspicious.'

She straightened. 'Of me?'

'Not of you.' He waved an impatient hand in the air. 'But I've been burned before.'

She could only imagine how much the press had hounded him after the accident. It was criminal the way some journalists behaved. But… 'That's not my fault.'

He halted with one of those delicious-looking shortbread fingers halfway to his mouth. She gave into temptation and reached for one too, bit into it and nearly groaned as the buttery goodness melted on her tongue.

'I mean, I'm sorry you've had people treat you like you were nothing more than a big news story, but it's not fair I pay the price for other people's sins.'

He set the biscuit down, but didn't say anything. For heaven's sake, she was just here to do a job, but how on earth was she supposed to convince him that was all she wanted?

Except that's not really true, is it, Chlo?

She bit her lip. 'You know, it'd be nice if we could be a bit friendlier to one another. I mean, if we're really going to be working on the garden together, side by side…' she tried to dismiss the images that flooded her mind '…then maybe we could even become friends.'

If they became friends and she told him why it was so important to her, surely he'd let her take a couple of photographs of the finished garden for her portfolio. Just in case she needed to apply for another contract like this one in the future.

His eyes narrowed as if sensing she had a hidden agenda. 'I don't need a friend, Ms Jennings. I just need you to do the job you were asked to do. Do I make myself clear?'

She needed the job so she nodded. 'Absolutely.'

He stalked out of the kitchen without drinking his tea, without eating his shortbread, and without a backward glance. 'So I suppose I can forget all about the apology you owe me,' she growled.

'I heard that!' he shouted down the hallway.

'You were supposed to!'

The exchange left her oddly energised, almost cheerful.

Beau scowled from the desk in his office when he saw Chloe marching across the courtyard towards the gardens a short time later, rugged up as if for an Arctic winter, her hands buried deep in the pockets of her coat, neck swathed in a scarf.

It's not fair I pay the price for other people's sins.

He swore. Her arrival was supposed to herald his resolution to get back to work. He might no longer be able to make the nature documentaries he so loved, but throwing himself into reclaiming the garden would help plug some of the ache in his soul. Her arrival, however, was also bringing home to him that Stephanie was right. He was in danger of becoming bitter and twisted.

To be perfectly honest, he wasn't all that interested in not being bitter and twisted, but Chloe was right—it wasn't fair that she pay the price for others' sins. Maybe she *was* looking for a way to exploit this situation, and he had every intention of keeping an eye on her, but cutting off that call with her mother and bellowing at her without giving her a chance to explain?

That made him a bully.

And he hated bullies.

The image of Chloe's mother rose in his mind, and he found himself fighting a smile. When was the last time someone had called him *love*? Mrs Jennings had a natural warmth he'd found himself drawn to. And it had felt oddly satisfying to pay Chloe back for forcing him to talk to her mother in the first place by refusing to gracefully fade into the background when she'd wanted him to.

Except it had backfired. He rubbed a hand over his face. What on earth had he actually promised?

To keep an eye on Chloe, to make sure she doesn't work too hard and to make sure she eats regular meals.

None of that would be too hard.

To cheer her up if she looks glum.

He glared at the ceiling. What on earth had possessed him to agree to *that*?

He was a fool, but Mrs Jennings's warmth and sincerity had taken him off guard. He'd found himself momentarily mesmerised by the maternal instincts that had driven her to ask for the favour in the first place, mesmerised by her evident love for her daughter.

She was so different from his mother and a part of him had yearned towards the older woman, had wanted to...? He didn't know how to finish that sentence. He had no idea what he'd wanted or what he'd been thinking. Maybe he was losing the plot?

He'd learned at the age of eight—when his parents had all but abandoned him—that the only person he could rely on was himself. It was a lesson he'd forgotten in recent years—to his detriment—when he'd started to trust in his colleagues' respect and the television network's high regard, had believed in his audience's admiration.

His lips twisted. He'd made the rookie mistake of believing his own press, but he'd learned his lesson. When life had gone pear-shaped none of them were to be found. Instead they'd left the gossip-mongers, scandal-hunters and voyeurs circling in their wake. Oh, yes, the message had been received loud and clear. *Rely on nobody* had been burned onto his brain.

None of that, however, meant he had the right to bully a woman like Chloe. And he was beginning to suspect that Chloe wasn't a woman on the make, but someone just searching for a bit of peace and quiet.

Like him.

He blew out a long breath, unanswered questions pecking away at him. Primary among them—why was Chloe *Ivy Belle* Jennings spending Christmas here in England with strangers when she could be enjoying it at home with her family?

Had she needed the garden contract so badly that when he'd suggested she arrive late November, she'd thought that akin to a royal decree?

Swearing, he lumbered to his feet and headed out into the gardens.

He tracked Chloe down to a corner of the walled garden and she turned to him, her face so alive and full of excitement it sucked the air from his lungs. With hair the colour of gingerbread, and eyes a shade darker, she looked like some autumn woodland nymph. An ache started up at the very centre of him.

She gestured. 'This is amazing.'

He glanced around and nodded. This garden was going to be his haven, his sanctuary. Here he'd be able to study the natural world, without interruption. He ground his back molars together. It *would* be enough.

'You are the luckiest man alive, Beau Diamond.'

Oh, really? It took a superhuman effort not to lift a hand to touch the scars on his face.

'Now you said something about wanting to attract wildlife to the garden,' she said, before he could apologise for his earlier behaviour. 'In my original design I suggested planting a mix of both wild and cultivated flowers. Are you still on board with that?'

'I want herbs in here as well.'

She pursed her lips. 'Swiss chard, thyme…sage.'

Perfect. He planned on spending long summer days out here, the flowers and grasses scenting the air as he tracked the different birds, butterflies and insects that the garden attracted.

'But you also want it to look pleasing to the eye. Did you want to keep the current configuration? I know it's desperately overgrown, but it has a pleasing symmetry.'

'I'd like to preserve as much as I can. But I want the addition of a water feature.'

'Any particular sort? Placed anywhere in particular?'

He shrugged.

'How about I sketch a few different designs and you can let me know what you like?'

Sounded good to him.

She turned on the spot, her mobile features alive with an inner fire, and he wished her mother could see her face right now.

'I love that old tree down there.'

He glanced to where she pointed. 'It's an old hornbeam tree—good for shade.' It'd attract birds and insects too.

'This is going to be amazing once we're done. I can hardly wait to get started.'

He recalled Mrs Jennings's warning about Chloe working herself into the ground, and vowed not to let that happen. He adjusted his stance. 'Look, Chloe, you were right earlier. I do owe you an apology. I shouldn't have jumped to the conclusions I did. I shouldn't have ended your video call like that. It was…'

'An overreaction?'

But when he glanced at her, her eyes were dancing and he found his lips almost twitching into an answering smile. 'An overreaction,' he agreed. 'It's just…after you call out the police for the seventh time in three days to remove trespassers bearing cameras with telescopic lenses who've scaled the security fences, it does start to get old pretty quickly. Especially when you factor in the dozens of daily phone calls demanding an interview, and the fact that one's neighbours are also being inundated with opportunistic journalists and—'

She reached out and touched his arm. 'I'm sorry, Beau. I should've been more understanding.'

'No, you're just here to do a job—and I've already railroaded you into taking on additional duties. Understanding the external crap I have to put up with isn't part of your job description.' He was starting to suspect that Chloe had enough crap of her own to deal with.

'Are you still being hounded to that extent?'

'No, thank God.' And he didn't want anything reigniting media interest either. 'But I've learned the hard way to keep a keen eye out for anything suspicious.'

'I can see how you could've misconstrued what I said to my mother.' She started along the path towards the hornbeam tree. 'And, actually, I owe you an apology too because it's not my place to offer to show my family any of your lovely home. I was just…it's amazing and I wanted to share it with her. She's… I—'

He leaned in closer and she shrugged. 'I wanted her to see how much fun I'm having here.' She rolled her shoulders, not meeting his eyes. 'What an adventure it all is.'

She was a terrible liar. 'Chloe, if you want to spend Christmas at home with your family that's okay and—'

'No!'

She looked horrified by his suggestion. *Why?* Her mother was lovely.

So is your grandmother, but that doesn't mean you want her descending on Dawncarden for the holidays.

His grandmother had provided some of the maternal nurturing he'd needed growing up, though her love had been brisk and no-nonsense rather than of the touchy-feely variety. He suspected Chloe's mum was touchy-feely to the core. He loved his grandmother, knew she loved him. But he didn't want her fussing and hounding him this Christmas. All he wanted was to be left in peace.

He glanced at Chloe and a surge of fellow feeling hit him.

Chloe straightened as if aware of his gaze. 'Beau, I want to assure you I won't invade your privacy like that and share photos of your house and grounds with my family. It's not my place and—'

'Look, I understand. No apologies necessary.'

She eyed him for a moment and he couldn't help wondering what she saw. Did she pity him for his scars? Did she find him repulsive?

He jerked away. He knew women no longer found him attractive. It didn't matter. None of it mattered.

'But it does bring me to something I want to raise.'

He turned back.

'When I was staying in the flat in the coach house, I had my own living space.' She twisted her hands together. 'You have a huge house and I just wondered… Would I be able to have a room, apart from my bedroom, that I can work in, and maybe stretch out in to watch the odd film on my computer?'

He should've thought of that. He couldn't give her Stephanie's suite, but… 'How big does it have to be?'

'No bigger than what was in the flat. But it needs to be an area where you wouldn't mind me video-calling with my family.'

He found himself staring at her hair, caught up in its

shine and the richness of its colour. He snapped to, shook himself. 'I have just the space. Follow me.'

They'd reached the hornbeam, and he turned to lead them back the way they'd come, when a pungent odour pulled him up short.

'What on earth…?'

Chloe blinked. 'What on earth…what?'

Not paying her any heed, he ducked under the low branches of the hornbeam and searched the trunk and canopy, and then he caught a hint of movement by the wall. It was the western wall and…

'What are you—?'

He pressed a finger to his lips and, bending down slightly so she could follow the line of his finger, he pointed. 'Can you see?'

For a moment his attention wavered as he caught her scent. She smelled of soap and lavender and for some reason it made his mouth go dry.

'What? I don't see anything— Wait!'

She clutched his arm and her excited whisper made his pulse quicken. She moved further beneath the canopy and then swung to him, her eyes huge and excited. 'It's a bat.'

CHAPTER THREE

'A PIPISTRELLE,' BEAU CORRECTED.

Chloe glanced at him. The volume of his voice hadn't risen above a whisper, but it vibrated with the same enthusiasm as when he'd filmed his documentaries. It hadn't mattered whether those documentaries had been filmed in the depths of a jungle or on some remote island off the coast of Ireland, in the Australian outback or the Serengeti Plains. Beau Diamond had a passion for the natural world in all its variations that his legion of fans had found irresistible.

'There's an entire colony here. I'm going to need to record numbers.'

She wanted to close her eyes and let the butterscotch warmth of that voice wash over her and—

She shook herself. Forced her eyes wide. 'These are rare?'

'Pipistrelle numbers in Britain have been falling. The places where they can safely roost have dwindled, as have their habitats.'

Which she guessed made it doubly important to preserve their current ones. Especially for a man like Beau.

'Chloe, this means things have changed.'

Her gut clenched. If he didn't want this colony disturbed, did that mean she was out of a job? The breath jammed in her throat. She *needed* this job. Not just for the money, even though that was the most pressing concern at the moment, but also for the prestige.

She and Mark had gone into business with his parents, and while the money from this contract meant she'd be able to keep her house, freeing his parents from any sense of obligation they had in relation to that particular debt, if the business should need a quick injection of funds in the future, she needed to pull her weight and find a solution—like attracting high-status design jobs that paid *really* well.

A weight slammed onto her shoulders. If only she'd known about the second mortgage Mark had taken out on the house. If only she'd read the letters his solicitor had sent earlier rather than falling into a bereaved mess and shoving them in a drawer and letting them stack up. If only Mark's parents hadn't shielded her for so long.

If only…

Her lips twisted. Life was full of 'if only', right? But she did know now. And it wasn't too late. She *could* turn things around. She didn't care what she had to do, but she *wasn't* losing the house—the last link to the husband she'd loved more than life itself. And there was no way she was letting the business carry her any longer. She was through with being a dead weight.

'Did you hear me?'

She swallowed the lump in her throat. 'Changes things how?' She glanced away from those piercing blue eyes, not wanting him to see the fear in hers. 'You no longer want to go ahead with the garden makeover?'

'What?'

He reached out as if to touch her arm, and her chest clenched. Instead, holding a finger to his lips, he led her away from the hornbeam tree that sheltered the piece of wall that had become home to a colony of pipistrelles. And while she was happy for them, she couldn't help but feel cursed.

'What the hell are you jabbering on about?' he demanded once they'd made their way into the middle of the garden.

Her head jerked up. This man had no idea how to do polite, did he? She gestured back the way they'd come. 'You don't want the pipistrelles disturbed, you want them to thrive, and I'm guessing that means you don't want any work taking place in the garden now.'

'Then you'd be guessing wrong.'

He stared at her as if she were a first-grade idiot and she found it oddly cheering. 'Oh?'

'We're going to turn this garden into a haven for pipistrelles, Chloe. Not to mention birds and butterflies.'

She tried to not sag too deeply in relief.

'But the design will now need to cater for what's already living here. We won't be disturbing that pocket of the garden and the hornbeam tree stays.'

'Of course the hornbeam is staying,' she said, then winced at how bossy she sounded. Beau was the client. This was *his* garden. If he wanted the hornbeam gone, then that was what would happen. It wasn't her job to judge. 'I just mean...it looks as if it's been here a long time. There's a continuity to keeping it that—'

She broke off, reddening.

He raised an eyebrow. 'Go on.'

The words were uttered as an order rather than an invitation. She shook her head. 'You really need to work on your tone, Beau. No wonder Stephanie calls you *lord and master*. I'm not sure it *is* a joke.'

He blinked. 'You're calling me a bully again.'

It was her turn to blink. 'More like an autocratic grouch,' she hedged.

He stared at her with pursed lips and then shrugged. 'I suppose that's marginally better than being a bully.'

It absolutely was, but she kept her mouth firmly closed.

'Believe it or not, I've never been the most social of men.'

'I'd believe it.'

Her unguarded words, just as direct and rude as his, surprised a bark of laughter from him, and just for a moment she caught a glimpse of a younger, less guarded man.

'Well, believe it or not, even given my lack of sociability I once had a veneer of civility, but since moving back to Dawncarden that veneer has become somewhat rusty. I'm sorry if I sounded autocratic.'

Another apology. Wow.

'And I really would like to know what you were going to say about the hornbeam and continuity and what that signified to you.'

Her heart sped up though she had no idea why.

'Please?'

Pulling her coat around her more securely, she traced a path around the circular garden bed that lay at the heart of the garden, glancing back down towards the hornbeam. 'It just seems right to keep something that has been here so long. Just as your grandmother is the matriarch of your family, that hornbeam tree feels like the matriarch of this garden. It feels ethical to keep it.'

She glanced up to see if he was laughing and thinking her some weird hippy type. Instead he stared at the hornbeam with a light in his eyes that made her breath catch. 'I couldn't agree with you more. I knew you were the right person for this job.'

Her head came up and her shoulders went back. She was going to give him the best damn garden he'd ever seen.

'I want a pond.'

That sounded definite. 'Not a fountain?'

'Still water will attract insects, and bats feed on insects, among other things.'

Ah. She turned a slow circle. 'We could have a sunken pool there.' She pointed to the circular garden bed. 'And if you want we could have a small waterfall beside the wall over there, with a rill leading to the pond…and perhaps another rill leading to a smaller pool here.'

His face lit up. 'That sounds brilliant! Frogs would love it.'

Bats, birds, butterflies…and frogs, huh? She grinned as she saw what Beau wanted to achieve. He wanted to create a wildlife sanctuary here in this lovely hidden garden. A haven for whatever animals found their way. It'd be magical.

A quick glance informed her that his attention had once again returned to the far corner and the pipistrelles. She'd need to do some research on local wildlife. She'd pored over all the resources she'd accrued on English cottage gardens prior to applying for this contract, but that had been mostly plant based. She'd wanted to impress him, and she still did. She wanted to impress him so much he'd relax those crazy strict privacy policies he had and give her permission to take photographs of this finished garden for her portfolio. Behind her back, she crossed her fingers.

'You're itching to get back down there and count them, aren't you?'

'And to take photographs,' he confessed. 'I'm going to document everything I can about them. I want to see if, in the right conditions, that colony can grow. I want to know how many young they have. And in an ideal world I'd like to fit them with trackers. Though fitting trackers to pipistrelles is notoriously difficult, not to mention expensive.'

'You're going back to documentary making?' She only just stopped herself from jumping up and down on the spot and clapping. 'That's brilliant! It's—'

'No!'

The single word rang around the garden, and everything seemed to go suddenly quiet and still. She had to swallow before she could speak. 'But you just said…'

'I'm documenting this for my own edification, nobody else's.'

'But—'

'No buts.'

She slammed her hands to her hips. 'You could do so much *good*.'

His head rocked back.

'You could show people how to protect the country's pipistrelle populations, teach them how to coax pipistrelles into their gardens, and help them thrive and prosper.' How could he turn his back on that?

He gestured to his scars, his eyes chips of ice. 'Apparently this isn't the kind of face television networks want heading up their wildlife documentary series. My network made that very clear when they cancelled my series.'

Her heart froze before giving a giant kick. She leaned in, eyes wide. 'They dumped you because of your *scars*?'

He folded his arms, his face closed up.

But... 'Your fans don't care what you look like!' She gestured wildly. 'What they love is your enthusiasm and your unique take on the natural world, not—'

'Enough!'

She blinked at the savagery of that single word. The unfairness of what the network had done made her want to shred things with her bare hands and yell at someone. 'They're just one TV network, Beau. There are others—'

'No more.' He shoved a finger that shook beneath her nose and she discovered they were both breathing hard. He ought to smell of fire and brimstone, but he didn't. He smelled like a balsam fir, sharp and tangy, clean. She dragged the scent into her lungs.

A strange new energy flooded her and—

She took a hasty step back. *What on earth...?* 'Sorry. I got carried away. It's none of my business.' What on earth was wrong with her? She needed to mind her Ps and Qs. She couldn't afford him cancelling her contract.

She walked across to one of the badly overgrown flower beds and picked a piece of wild rosemary that she lifted to her nose to try and chase the scent of him away. What a sorry pair the two of them were. She moistened her lips and half turned back towards him. 'Because you've been so rude to me, I've taken it for granted that I can be rude back, but clearly that's a juvenile attitude, not to mention unproductive.'

She trailed off, not sure what else to say. 'For various reasons that I won't go into, because...*boring*, I've had to put on a cheerful face back home, and I think the effort has burned me out. We both blamed jet lag for my outburst the other night, but...' Her eyes stung. 'The truth is I'm just too tired to be "nice" at the moment.' She clenched her hands. *You will not cry.* 'But I must try harder.'

'No.'

She turned towards him.

'You don't need to make any such effort for me.'

She had a feeling he meant it, but... 'I don't want to turn into that person, Beau—a bitter and twisted sad sack. I want to be able to like myself.'

A flash of scarlet caught her eye. She tracked it and then stilled. 'Look,' she breathed. 'A robin redbreast. Just like in the movie *The Secret Garden*. I've never seen one in real life.'

'What? *Never?*' He sounded utterly astonished, but then one broad and decidedly attractive shoulder lifted. 'Why would you? They're not native to Australia.'

'We don't get a white Christmas in Australia either, but I've always loved Christmas cards with robin redbreasts in the snow. They seem like such characters.'

'They are.'

She pulled her phone from her pocket to snap a picture,

then remembered the privacy clause and shoved it back. Cool eyes surveyed her and she grimaced. 'Sorry, it's just a natural impulse to want to capture something like that.'

He pressed a thumb and forefinger to the bridge of his nose, looking suddenly old, and she had to fight an odd impulse to walk over and put her arms around him.

'Snap your picture, Chloe,' he said without lifting his head.

Before she could, the little bird flew away, which was probably just as well. She couldn't afford to accidentally contravene that privacy clause.

He let out a long breath. 'I promised to show you the room you could use while you're here.'

They walked back to the house in silence. Considering the words and apologies they'd just exchanged, the silence ought to have been fraught and uncomfortable, but it wasn't. There was something clean and honest about it. She'd discovered that they had a whole lot more in common than she'd realised.

Which wasn't the most comfortable of discoveries, but at least she now knew not to take his grumpiness personally. Hopefully he now knew the same about her.

He led her through that extraordinary baronial grand hall, and down a wide hallway. She knew his study was located at its far end, as Stephanie had showed it to her the previous day. He opened the second door on the right and gestured for her to precede him. 'Will this do?'

She walked in and then slammed to a halt, her jaw dropping. He'd just ushered her into the most magnificent library she'd ever seen outside a movie.

'This room has the big desk you'll probably need, and there's plenty of natural light.'

Light poured in at the three tall windows that overlooked the front oak-lined drive and sadly neglected rose garden that she itched to get her fingers on. The rest of the room was lined with floor-to-ceiling bookshelves. There was an enormous desk with a table lamp that would be the perfect spot for drafting her designs.

'And there are a couple of comfortable sofas for sprawling on when you want to watch a film.' Beau shoved his hands into his pockets. 'Will this do?'

'Do? It's perfect! It's the most wonderful room I've ever seen.' She laughed and clapped her hands. 'We've just changed movies. I thought we were in *The Secret Garden*, but now we're in B—'

She broke off. Oh, God, what was she thinking? She wanted to bite her tongue clean out of her head.

Beau raised a for once civil eyebrow. 'And now we're in…?'

Beau did his best to keep a straight face. He was well versed in traditional children's stories and fairy tales or, at least, Disney's fairy-tale retellings. When he'd been growing up, he and his grandmother had shared regular movie nights. She'd insisted on Disney movies and romantic comedies, while he'd insisted on action movies and nature documentaries. It'd given them both an education.

So he knew exactly which movie Chloe had just cast herself in.

'I…uh…' She floundered, eyes wide, looking everywhere except at him.

'What fairy tale has a library…?' He tapped a finger against his lips. 'Could you possibly be referring to…' he forced his eyes wide, feigning outrage '… *Beauty and the Beast*?' Except his gut had started to churn. Was that how she saw him—as a beast? And even if she did, why did he care?

'I didn't mean it like that!' she burst out. 'I just meant that this is the most amazing library and I used to love to read, and I couldn't imagine a more wonderful room. *That's* all I meant. I certainly wasn't casting myself as Beauty and I wasn't implying that you're—'

He didn't say a word, but it took an effort to not laugh.

'Oh, look here!' She slammed hands on hips, eyes flashing fire. 'The only thing *beastly* about you is your temper!'

'Ditto,' he shot back, unable to hold in a laugh.

Her eyes narrowed. 'You have a warped sense of humour, you know that?'

'And you have a fairy-tale fetish.'

'Nothing wrong with a happy ever after, even if they do so rarely happen in real life.'

Her words had an ache stretching through his chest.

She glanced up at him. 'You're really not offended?'

'I'm not offended.'

She hesitated, and he waited, half fatalistically, for the next indiscreet, foot-in-mouth comment she was invariably about to make. He could stop her, he supposed, but her confession in the garden about having used up all of her reserves of niceness had slid beneath his guard.

He suspected what Chloe really needed at the moment was to snipe and vent. He might have a scarred face, but he also had broad shoulders. 'Out with it,' he ordered.

She wrinkled her nose, and it struck him that she had a cute nose, neat and pert with a sprinkling of freckles that somehow went with the gingerbread of her hair. She might not be considered a classic beauty, but she had the kind of face that made a man like him look twice.

Not that *that* meant anything.

'You don't see yourself as a beast, do you?' she blurted out.

'Of course not.'

Some of the hardness in her spine eased. 'Good. So your scars don't bother you?'

He tried to not take offence, but… 'You think I've shut

myself away because I hate what I look like? You think I'm so vain I can't stand for the world to see me like this?'

She stared back. 'It's one interpretation that could be put on your retreat from the world.'

He went to deny it, but stopped and shot her a glare. 'You know that nothing we discuss here can be shared with anyone because of that privacy clause.'

'I know, I know, or you'll sue me for every penny…blah-blah-blah.' She flopped down on one of the sofas. 'We've established that already. Take it as read.'

'Fine.' He planted himself on the sofa opposite. 'Then perhaps there is an element of vanity to my hiding out here.'

She didn't look at him in sudden disgust, as if he was weak or petty or any of those things, just nodded. 'It makes sense. You've always been handsome in the classic way of Cary Grant, Idris Elba and the Hemsworth brothers—flawless…gorgeous.'

She'd thought him gorgeous? Things inside him stood to attention. Then a bitter laugh rose through him. Thought—*past tense.*

'It was what you were known for, and—'

'I was known for my expertise!' He shot to his feet. 'And the fact I could make my subject accessible and interesting. Damn it, Chloe, I was a whole lot more than a pretty face and—'

'Ha! See?' She pointed a triumphant finger at him. 'I knew other things mattered more to you than your pretty face.'

He fell back down, scowling.

'But even so…' her eyes turned warm with sympathy '…there has to be an adjustment period.' Her gaze moved to his scars and she didn't bother trying to hide her scrutiny. It took an effort to remain in his seat. 'You're not perfect any more.'

'Oh, like that's a state secret!'

'So what? Welcome to the club. Ninety-nine per cent of us aren't perfect.'

He stilled.

'But you're not ugly, Beau, far from it. You're still a very attractive man.'

And then she frowned as if she found the realisation unwelcome.

He shook off the warmth her words created, refused to let them settle over him. 'Vanity isn't the main reason I've retreated to Dawncarden. I just… I hate the way the press treat me now—like I'm not a person, but a thing. I hate the lack of privacy. I really hate the lack of courtesy.' He was quiet for a moment. 'I hate the ugliness I've discovered in other people.'

Her eyes filled with sudden tears and he clenched his hands to fists. 'Don't you damn well cry, Chloe *Ivy Belle* Jennings.' He scowled at her. 'Why would you even do that?'

'It sucks that your network dumped you. I can't believe they did that.'

It had thrown him for a six. He'd needed somewhere private to lick his wounds. Call him naïve, but the fact the networks now saw him as incapable of doing his job because his face was no longer as pretty as it had once been had been a slap in the face he'd not been expecting. That was the real reason he'd retreated to Dawncarden.

All he'd ever wanted was to make nature documentaries. Bringing the natural world into the living rooms of the average person and sharing his wonder with them, making it clear how urgently the planet needed everyone to pull together if they weren't to lose valuable ecosystems and environments—it felt like what he was born to do. Without that direction, he felt rudderless…useless…*ugly*.

It was why he'd been so short with Chloe in the garden when she'd suggested he return to documentary making.

It was what he wanted with every fierce fibre of his being, but that way was closed to him now. And somehow he had to find a way to accept that.

He rose. 'If you're happy with this room, then I'll leave you to it. I need to get to work.'

'Let me guess—pipistrelle research.'

She'd got it in one.

'Thank you, Beau, this is perfect.' She rose too, pressing her hands together. 'I am free to pop into the village whenever I want, yes? I don't have to order everything online. Or is that what you'd prefer?'

'You're not under house arrest. You're free to go wherever you want.'

'Right, well, there are a few things I need, so I might pop down now. Then I'll get to work on drafting my ideas for the water feature.'

'Okay, Dad, it was great to chat! Good luck at golf tomorrow.'

Beau halted outside Chloe's room—which over the last few days was what he'd started to call the library. She'd sounded more cheerful than she had since her arrival.

But when he glanced around the door—she never closed it—she sat with her head resting on the closed lid of her laptop, making low groaning noises. He pursed his lips. Right. So not as cheerful as she'd made out, then.

He tapped on the door and she immediately straightened. 'Beau! Did you need something?'

He'd just wanted to let her know he was there. He just wanted… Rolling his shoulders, he gestured behind her. 'You've started decorating for Christmas.'

She glanced around. 'Oh, yes, well, it's the first of December and… I hope you don't mind?'

But as she turned back, her nose had curled and it made him frown. 'Why should I mind? You haven't got very far, though.' She'd only decorated the bookcases behind her with some holly and ivy, a fake Christmas tree with twinkling lights, and a gaudy plastic Santa. But as of yet the rest of the room was untouched.

She touched a switch and the sparkly lights of the tree immediately disappeared. Did she think he wouldn't like them? That they'd offend him somehow?

Well, where on earth would she get that idea?

The voice sounded suspiciously—and irritatingly—like Stephanie, but it had a point. Not a single Christmas decoration adorned Dawncarden—inside or out.

Chloe's mother's face rose in his mind. 'Would you like some help decorating the rest of the room?' They could make this space ooze with Christmas cheer. In their video calls, Chloe's mother would see this room all cheerful and Christmassy, and surely that would help ease her worry.

'No, thank you, I couldn't think of anything worse.'

She shuddered. She actually *shuddered.* What on earth...?

She shot to her feet. 'Cuppa?'

He'd just finished one, but he nodded anyway. He wanted to find out what was going on.

'So what's going on with the Christmas decorations, then?' he asked when they were seated around the kitchen table eating the last of Stephanie's shortbread. 'If you don't like them, why put them up?'

She blew out a breath. 'Can you keep a secret?'

'I'm a champion keeper of secrets.' He leaned towards her and that clean lavender scent hit him and a pulse came to life deep inside him. He bit back a curse, easing back again. 'But who on earth do you think I'm going to tell?'

'My mother if she ever catches sight of you in the background of one of my video calls home. Or if she ever calls here on the phone,' she added with an ominous lowering of her brows.

Questions started pecking away at him, insistent and impossible to ignore. 'You're right, you know? Sometimes you do have ferocious eyebrows.'

She blinked and lifted a hand to touch them.

'But as I'm never in the room whenever you video-conference with your family, and I *never* answer the home phone, I don't think you need to worry.'

She was quiet for a long moment, staring into her tea. 'I don't want my family worrying about me. I want them to think I'm having a ball this Christmas.'

'Right.' He drew the word out.

'I figured if they saw a few Christmas decorations in the background whenever we video-call it'll make them think I'm full of the spirit of the season, and that will put their minds at rest.'

He didn't know what he'd been expecting, but it sure as hell wasn't that. He set his mug down, his chest drawing tight. 'Why is your family so worried about you?'

He and Chloe hadn't exactly started off on the right foot, but somehow in the last week they'd settled into a comfortable routine. And when it wasn't comfortable, it was enlivening. It'd made him realise how bored he'd become. She had no reason to look on him as a friend, but…

He hadn't spoken so honestly to anyone in the last fourteen months as he had to her. It'd left him feeling lighter somehow…freer. If he could return the favour, he would.

She stared at him, those treacle-dark eyes stormy. She didn't want to discuss it, that much was clear, but she really shouldn't be bottling this stuff up—whatever it was. He chose his words carefully. 'You once told me I ought to consider therapy for my paranoia.'

She winced. 'I didn't really mean it.'

'Should I be finding you a therapist, Chloe? Does your family have a right to be concerned? You're living under my roof. That makes me responsible for you.'

'No, it doesn't!'

But when their gazes clashed, she was the first to look away.

'Fine! But can we walk while we're talking? I need the exercise and I was hoping to go and check out your orchard.'

'The orchard? Why?'

'A girl can dream, can't she?' She rose and wound a woollen scarf around her throat. 'You've a remarkable estate here. In my daily walks I've been exploring what I can and imagining what I'd do if it was mine and money was no object.'

It could be interesting to hear her thoughts. In the long term, he wanted the estate to become more self-sufficient.

They pulled on boots and coats and headed outside. 'You said you loved animals.'

The question made him blink. She gestured at him and then at their surroundings. 'Then where are they? Shouldn't you have a border collie at your heels and a fat contented tabby sitting by the fire inside? And a milking cow…and maybe a horse or two?'

'We've had all of those in the past, but when the last cat died, Stephanie wasn't ready to get a new one. And as for a dog… Well, when I was travelling so much, it didn't seem fair to leave one for other people to look after all the time.'

'But you're not travelling now?'

That was true.

They walked in silence until they reached the orchard. He glanced at her from the corner of his eye. 'So why is your family worried about you?'

She buried her hands deeper into the pockets of her coat. 'Two years ago my husband died and, well…'

His chest grew strangely tight at the sudden thickness in her voice. Chloe was a widow? 'Chloe, I had no idea…'

'There's no reason why you should.'

Except it felt wrong that he hadn't known. He rubbed a hand across his chest. It was clear she'd loved her husband. To have lost him… It didn't bear thinking about. 'I'm sorry, Chloe.'

She shrugged and sent him what he guessed was supposed to be a smile. 'Me too.'

'What happened?'

'A driver had a stroke at the wheel. The car mounted the footpath and Mark was hit—killed instantly.'

He winced.

'At least he didn't suffer, that's what people said to me.' She huddled further into her scarf. 'As if that was somehow a blessing.'

She kicked a tuft of grass. 'Obviously I didn't want him to suffer. But why couldn't the car have mounted the path further down the road where nobody was walking? Or missed him by a hair's breadth? Or even have broken his legs? Being hurt would've been better than being dead.'

She was right, of course. No wonder she had so little sympathy with his self-pity and sense of injury.

His first impression had been the correct one. She'd barely noticed his scars. What she'd seen was a man who'd been involved in a terrible accident, but who had lived to tell the tale. From where she was standing, he was lucky. And for the first time in fourteen months, he had to agree.

CHAPTER FOUR

CHLOE GLANCED AT Beau and tried to not wince. He stared back as if afraid she might break or explode again like a firecracker.

She really had to stop doing that firecracker thing. The disaster that was her life wasn't this man's fault.

His forehead creased. 'So you miss your husband more at Christmas and that's why your family is worried?'

She pulled in a breath. 'Mark's death happened at this time of year.'

She saw rather than heard the breath that he expelled. Noted the way his body became larger as it pulled in another breath and held it. A body that held an undeniable fascination for her and—

She dragged her gaze away and focussed on the wooden fence they were approaching. Then blinked. 'A stile! I've read about them in Enid Blyton books and seen them in Jane Austen movies and things, but…' She shrugged, suddenly self-conscious. 'Sorry, it's just a bit of a novelty.'

'No stiles in Australia?'

She had no idea. 'I think we run more to cattle grids than stiles.'

She took the hand he offered as she negotiated it. Even through her mittens she could feel his heat and strength and it made her ridiculously aware of the breadth of his shoulders and the strength and power of those long legs and lean hips—

Stop it!

'Was the stile an attempt to change the subject?'

She reclaimed her hand. Why was he so interested in talking about Mark? And then she recalled his somewhat silly sense of responsibility towards her and had to smother a sigh. 'It wasn't, but I can't pretend this is my favourite topic of conversation. What do you want to know, Beau?'

That keen gaze raked her face. 'I liked your mum.'

'So you've already said.'

'You and your family are clearly close.'

'And…?'

'It makes me uneasy that you're lying to them.'

He didn't just look uneasy. He looked truly troubled.

The stile had led them into the orchard and she glanced around at the fruit trees, all winter bare and dormant—a lot like her—and huffed out a sigh. 'I just didn't want to ruin another Christmas for them, Beau. Christmas is a big thing for my family and…well, they deserve to celebrate the holiday without anything casting a blight on it.'

He started down an avenue. 'Obviously the Christmas Mark died would've been devastating for everyone.'

She kept easy pace beside him. 'My family adored him. They were all shell-shocked.' While she'd been utterly devastated. 'And then last Christmas, obviously the worst of the shock had passed.' It had been a year, after all. 'But it was the first anniversary and… I don't know, it sent me into a spin.' She glanced up and grimaced. 'I basically spent three days crying.'

'Oh, Chloe.'

He reached out a hand as if to touch her, but she forced herself back into motion, forced her feet to cross to the nearest apple tree to study the suppleness of its branches, too tempted by the warmth and comfort he was offering.

And she didn't want to be tempted by it. She didn't want to notice how virile and attractive Beau was or to begin fantasising about all the ways he could comfort her.

Not that he was offering anything more than a broad shoulder, of course. And she shouldn't be thinking about anything beyond that. But after two years of being on ice, those impulses were starting to thaw. In freezing cold Devon of all places!

She ducked beneath the branches of the apple tree, keeping it between her and Beau. 'The crying jag took me off guard. I didn't expect it to hit me so hard.' But the realisation that Mark was *never* coming back had hit her with such force she'd been helpless to fight it. 'It didn't matter that I told myself I was being self-indulgent and silly, I couldn't stop.'

She'd wrapped one hand around the tree's trunk and Beau wrapped his hand over hers, and while the trunk of the tree remained between them, he drew close and suddenly the tree seemed no barrier against him at all. 'You were entitled to your grief, Chloe. Those sorts of things should never be bottled up.'

She stared at that perfect mouth, bracketed on either side with creases that lent the face strength, and her heart gave a giant kick that knocked the breath from her body.

She reefed her hand from beneath his and took a step back, rubbing her chest. 'Mark's death and then my grief have ruined the last two Christmases.'

'And you were afraid you'd ruin this one as well?'

Actually she'd been doing rather well. Had started to find her feet, had started to look forward to things again—playing with her nephews and nieces, family barbeques, nights out with friends. She'd even started to look forward to Christmas. She'd thought that this year she could turn a corner and set her face firmly towards the future as her mother had been urging her to do.

But then *wham*! She'd received the registered letter from the bank telling her about the second mortgage Mark had taken out on their home and that she was in imminent danger of losing everything the two of them had worked so hard for. And all of her newly hatched optimism had been pulverised to dust.

Mark's family had confessed that he'd taken out the second mortgage to help the business stay afloat. They'd been trying to keep up with the additional payments, but had fallen behind. They'd been doing their best to shield her from it all this time because of her grief. They hadn't wanted her spiralling further into depression.

Dear God, they'd been carrying her financially and she'd been doing nothing to help!

It would've been impossible for her to pretend that everything was okay this Christmas. Her family would know something was wrong if she were there in person. And she wasn't wrecking another Christmas or casting a shadow on their celebrations. Just…*no*.

'I didn't want to risk it,' she finally said. 'This year I want them free from worry. They deserve to have fun. I think they need it. And my argument that I needed a change of scene made sense to them, even if they weren't enthusiastic about it. And I feel I'll be doing my part in making sure they have a good Christmas if I can show them what a great time I'm having here.'

'Even if it's a lie?'

She gave a hard nod. 'Yep.'

They'd started walking down another avenue. She studied the trees growing either side. 'You have apple, plum… cherry.'

'And pear and quince.'

She turned on the spot. 'It's badly neglected, but most of it can be saved, and you really ought to make that a priority, Beau. I suspect you have some heirloom trees here…

and you have a duty of care.' Once trees like that were lost, they were lost for good.

His face had turned grim and she reminded herself she was here as his garden designer, not to lecture him about his orchard. She made herself smile. 'Of course, that all takes money. And money isn't always readily available.' It must cost a fortune to maintain Dawncarden Court.

'The money's available. The estate has one of the largest dairies in Devon. It's just…'

'You don't want workmen invading your privacy.'

He stared up at the sky and then at her. 'You wouldn't want the job of head gardener by any chance, would you?'

To bring this orchard back to life, not to mention the rose gardens, and to see the walled garden flourish would be…

She swallowed and shook her head. She needed to see this contract through, collect the big dollars it would bring in and then return to Sydney to help the business get back on a secure footing. She needed to pay that second mortgage off, and the sooner the better.

If necessary she'd apply for more contracts like this one. But if she was to win them, she was going to need a portfolio that would impress potential clients. She glanced at Beau and bit her lip. A portfolio with before and after photographs of the projects she'd worked on.

He'd stopped and was staring at something in the middle distance. 'You know you could be onto something? My grandmother swears she's spending this Christmas with friends in Florence, but…' He tapped a finger against that perfect mouth. 'I'm not yet convinced that she won't descend on Dawncarden instead.'

'Would it be bad if she was to show up?'

'Don't get me wrong, I love my grandmother.'

'But?'

He raised an eyebrow, those blue eyes piercing. 'Would

it be a bad thing if your family were to show up here this Christmas?'

She forced her legs back into motion. 'Point taken.'

'But if I decked out the hall the way it used to be when I was a boy and sent her a few photographs…'

Those long legs kept easy pace beside her. She ordered herself not to notice his legs.

'Maybe it'd stop her worrying about me so much.'

Ugh, time to come clean. 'I, uh, spoke to your grandmother earlier this morning.'

He nodded. 'She mentioned something about calling you in her last email.'

She let out a breath. Good, that wasn't supposed to be a secret, then.

'But back to decorating the hall, it also has the advantage of you being able to tell your family that you did the decorating and to share the pictures.'

A jolt went through her. 'You'd let me do that?' Maybe it wouldn't be so hard to convince him to let her photograph his garden for her portfolio after all.

'Why not? I think we can help each other out. It's all in a good cause.'

'We just want our families to be happy and have a nice Christmas.'

'Exactly. That's worth going to the trouble of putting up a few decorations, right?'

'Absolutely!' Oh, her mother would be so relieved. For a moment she was tempted to hug him.

Instead she took a step back and tackled the topic of his grandmother. 'Your grandmother made me promise to report in to her.'

His lips twisted. 'She informed me of that too.'

Her shoulders sagged. 'You think I'm a traitor.'

That made him laugh. 'I think nothing of the sort. I *know* my grandmother, Chloe.'

'She said she'd made a deal with you. That she'd let you remain on the estate unmolested by her interference as long as you went into the village twice a month.'

'She'd have let me stay, even if I hadn't made the promise, but I knew she was worried about me and it seemed little enough to ask.'

He might've come across as all grumpy and self-absorbed initially, but she was starting to see that, beneath his gruff exterior, Beau had a kind heart. 'But… What about the press?'

He glanced at her. 'I grew up here. And while I did go away to boarding school, I spent all of my summers here.'

She halted, slapped a mittened hand to her brow. 'The villagers protect you from the press.' She glared. 'And send unsuspecting garden designers on wild goose chases?'

He grimaced. 'Sorry about that. Steph and I got our wires crossed. But, yes, I'm warned if there's anyone suspicious about. And twice a month I spend a quiet hour or two over a pint of bitter in the snug at The Nag's Head—the smaller and less fashionable of the two pubs in the village. And as the hotelier is an old friend…'

'He makes sure no one disturbs you.'

'Exactly.' He suddenly halted. 'Except there hasn't been anyone from the press here in the last three or four months.'

'Clearly you're old news.'

He frowned and it occurred to her then that he didn't find that news as welcome as he'd thought he would.

He shook himself and they started walking again. 'They do a few Christmassy things in the village too. My grandmother has spies in Ballingsmallard who report back to her whenever they see me, so it might be an idea to attend the village tree lighting. There are also Christmas markets.'

Something in her chest lifted. 'Christmas markets?'

'You should go, take a few selfies. Your family would love to see you in an archetypal English Christmas setting.'

She wrinkled her nose. Yeah, like walking around the markets on her own with all of that ghastly Christmas cheer in the air would be fun. *Not.* His grandmother was right, though. Beau needed to get back out into the world again. 'I'm only going if you go too. I'm not mooching around like a Nigel-No-Friends on my own.'

His nose curled, and he rolled his shoulders. 'We can think about it.'

'Deal.'

'And speaking of deals.' Those blue eyes, oddly warm, met hers. 'You will help me decorate the hall, won't you?'

'Absolutely.' She'd do anything to ensure her family didn't worry about her this Christmas. Even if that did mean going to Christmas markets on her own.

'C'mon. You've had ample time to check out the orchard and you're clearly cold. Let's get up into the attic and bring the decorations down. I'll need you to order a tree for delivery too.'

She gave a mock salute, but his sudden sense of purpose lifted something inside her. Beau Diamond might think he wanted to shut himself away in his castle—okay, maybe Dawncarden wasn't exactly a castle, but it was a grand old manor house, which was the next best thing—but the first stirrings of interest in the outside world were making themselves felt and she had no intention of doing anything that would undermine them. In fact, she had every intention of doing what she could to encourage them.

The world needed Beau Diamond.

And Beau Diamond needed the world. She was sure of it.

Beau stood in the corridor and listened to proceedings in the baronial hall and had to smother a grin as Chloe directed the deliverymen to set the Christmas tree into the stand waiting for it beside the stairs. When they'd realised they weren't going to catch a glimpse of the famous recluse, they'd clearly hoped to drop the tree off and make a quick getaway, but she was having none of it.

While her accent was altogether different from Stephanie's, she had obviously decided to channel the older woman's no-nonsense approach with a dash of her own practical flattery. 'Given how much you're charging Mr Diamond for the tree, the least you can do is place it in the stand there. Three burly chaps like you? It'll take you no time at all. And there's fruit mince pies waiting for once you're done.'

From the huffing and puffing that ensued, he guessed she'd convinced them to do as she asked.

'*What* do you think you're doing?'

Her tone of voice had him instantly stiffening, and ready to leap to her aid.

'I…uh…just thought…'

'Put that phone away right now! You do not have permission to take pictures of either the inside or outside of Dawncarden Court. Do I make myself clear? In fact, I'm going to speak to your boss about this and—'

'I'm the boss, miss,' another voice cut in, 'and I can't apologise enough.'

'Have any of you taken pictures while my back was turned?'

She sounded fierce. He'd bet she was using those eyebrows to full effect. The thought made him grin.

'Right, lads, show the lady your phones so she can see there aren't any photos of Dawncarden Court on them. And if I see any of you with your phones out again you'll receive an official warning.'

'Thank you,' Chloe said a moment later, 'and thank you. And now yours.'

'Mine?' the older man spluttered.

But he must've shown her because a few moments later she murmured another, 'Thank you,' and they left.

He emerged from the corridor and she gestured at the

tree. 'It's magnificent! I thought ours at home was big, but this one has to be five times as big.' She checked the branches and the trunk. 'It's nice and healthy too.'

'You did a great job, just then, Chloe.'

She glanced at him over her shoulder and there was something about that gingerbread hair backlit by the green of the tree that had him thinking of woodland groves.

'Oh, so you heard all that?'

She shrugged as if it was no big deal, but it touched him that she'd taken such pains with his privacy.

'I'm the youngest of four. When you have three older siblings, you learn to hold you own.'

He reached out and ran his fingers across the needles of a nearby branch, the scent of lavender and fruit mince pies rising up around him, merging with the scent of pine, and his senses jolted to sudden wakeful life.

'If the truth be known, I just channelled Stephanie.' One shoulder lifted. 'It seemed to work.'

She could say that again. He caught her glancing at him with a question in her eye that was quickly shut off. 'What?'

She shook her head a little too quickly.

'Ask your question, Chloe.' He'd surrendered to the fact that their relationship was going to be far from comfortable, but he found himself trusting her, and that was far more important. Chloe wasn't the kind of person who'd sell him out. She had more important things to worry about.

'If someone did snap a picture of an undecorated tree in Dawncarden Court's baronial hall, would it be worth much?'

'I suspect it wouldn't cause much of a sensation. But now that media interest has waned, I don't want anything reinvigorating it.' Especially not if he was planning on dragging Chloe out to the village in the interest of reviving her Christmas spirit.

Was he really going to do that?

She nodded towards the tree. 'You know, if you snapped a before and after pic of that and put it on your Instagram account, nobody would be able to make any money from it whatsoever.'

He snapped upright. '*Not* going to happen.'

'Fair enough. Just as long as you know it's in your power to beat the tabloids at their own game and normalise your life.'

There was nothing *normal* about his life.

'And give your fans a few scraps.'

He didn't have fans any more.

'So…' She dusted off her hands. 'The sooner we decorate this monster, the sooner it's done.'

He fought the urge then to brace his hands on his knees. The way she said it, as if it were a chore, was a tragedy. This woman had once loved Christmas. Did she really find it so onerous now?

He forced steel to his spine. 'Wait until you see some of these old decorations. They're pretty amazing—even to someone like me who doesn't care one way or the other about Christmas.'

They'd brought all of the boxes down the previous afternoon and had stacked them beside the huge fireplace.

He glanced at her again. Despite her current jaded mood, surely she couldn't help but be impressed by Dawncarden's baronial hall decked out for Christmas, especially with a fire crackling in that venerable hearth.

'Right.' Chloe grabbed the closest box and hauled it over to the tree. 'How are we going to do this? Just chuck whatever decoration comes to hand wherever? Or do you have a system? We used to—*oh*!'

She'd unwrapped the first of the decorations—a coloured glass reindeer—and stared at it in awe. He stifled a smile. 'Pretty, right?'

'This isn't just pretty, Beau. This is *stunning*. A collector's item or…' She suddenly thrust it at him. 'It's probably an antique and worth a fortune! I really shouldn't be handling these. I'd die if I broke one and—'

'Absolutely! It's a capital offence. If you break anything you'll be sent straight to the tower and beheaded in the morning.'

A reluctant smile tugged at her lips and it lightened the heaviness inside him. He wanted her to relax…to have fun.

'Breakages happen. It's called natural attrition.'

These were just things. Things could be replaced. People couldn't. The image of the grief raw on her face when she'd spoken about Mark rose once more in his mind and his gut clenched. She'd clearly loved her husband. No wonder her mother was still so worried about her.

He could do nothing about the loss of her husband, but bit by bit he might be able to bring back some of her Christmas mojo. It seemed the least he could do after all of his ugly suspicions and bad temper.

And getting the great hall decorated was the first item on that agenda. Surely seeing something so grand and festive every day couldn't help but have an impact on her Christmas spirit. 'Don't you think it'd be a shame if these were locked away and never saw the light of day, that nobody had the chance to enjoy them just because someone was afraid of breaking them?'

'I suppose so, but I don't want to be *that* person—the clumsy one that goes down in family lore. "Oh, and the matching pair to this irreplaceable antique glass reindeer was smashed by the lowly gardener of the tenth Baron of Dawncarden, though what on earth he was doing allowing her in the house in the first place is a mystery."'

He couldn't help laughing at her nonsense. 'Would it help if I broke one first?' He made as if to toss a beautiful glass bell towards the fireplace. 'Would that ease your mind?'

'Don't you even think about it!'

Leaping forward, she rescued the bell from his fingers, and for a moment it felt as if he was grasping an armful of warm woman and endless possibilities. But then she stepped away and he thudded back to earth and he told himself to stop being an idiot.

'You channelled Steph perfectly when the deliverymen were here. Channel her again now. I can assure you these don't hold any fear for her whatsoever.'

Her face lightened. 'I so want to be Stephanie when I grow up.'

'Why?'

'She's so…together.'

He laughed and shook his head. 'We'll start with the lights. I'll go up the ladder, and you can pass them up. Then we can get started on the ornaments. I'll do the higher branches and you can do the lower branches. How's that for a plan?'

'Works for me.'

Reaching into his pocket for his phone, he streamed Christmas music through the sound system. She glanced up when it started crooning through the speakers, and rolled her eyes, but didn't say anything.

But when she eventually started humming along, stepping back to survey the tree with her designer's eye, a smile opened up inside him. He didn't completely understand his desire to help her recover her Christmas spirit. It was more than the promise he'd made to her mother, and it was more than an apology or attempt to make up for his earlier bad-tempered suspicions.

He'd been feeling powerless, but Steph's words had left a mark. He wanted to prove that he could still do some good, could make a difference in a positive way. He didn't want to turn into some bitter and twisted shadow of his former self. He just wanted the world to leave him alone to follow his own course.

Besides, Chloe had reminded him that some people really wouldn't care about his scars. He'd become so suspicious of everyone he'd forgotten that. He'd only been able to focus on those who now thought him a freak, or, if not a freak, then damaged goods. If he could surround himself with people who didn't care about his scars…and not even surround, but just have a couple of them in his life, then he could relax his guard and just get on with his research and find a bit of purpose again.

Her audible gasp brought him back to earth.

'Oh, Beau!' She turned with the tree-topper—an angel—held reverently in her hands. 'I've never seen anything more beautiful.'

It occurred to him that angels were always blonde and serene. But what was wrong with a gingerbread-haired angel with a sprinkle of freckles across her nose and a glint of mischief in her treacle-dark eyes? Actually, the more he thought about it, the more he wanted that angel at the top of his tree rather than the one Chloe held in her hands.

He stared at it and then at her. 'Why don't I video you putting the angel in place? You can send it to your family.'

Her entire face lit up. 'Really? You wouldn't mind?'

He liked Mrs Jennings, and he was on board with Chloe's plans to help her family have a Christmas free from worry. 'Pass me your phone.'

She pulled it from her pocket and then paused, consternation flashing across her face. 'I have a few pictures of your garden on my phone. They're just to help me as I draw up my new designs. Not for any other purpose. I'll delete all of them before I leave, and you can watch me do that if you want. I don't want you thinking—'

'Relax, Chloe, I trust you.'

She blinked and then moved closer to peer into his face. 'You do?'

'Yes.'

She didn't say anything so he rolled his shoulders. 'I don't believe you're the kind of person who would sell me out to the tabloids.' Instead she was the kind of woman who was trying to cope with the death of a husband she still desperately missed. She didn't care about his paltry cares and concerns, beyond giving him the garden of his dreams. 'I thought I'd already made myself clear.'

'Well, I know it's what you said, but…'

She hadn't believed him. He suddenly hated how he must appear to her—and this time he wasn't referring to what he looked like physically. Plucking her phone from unresisting fingers, he gestured towards the tree and the ladder. 'I'll hold it steady while you go up.'

Once she was in place, and steady, he videoed her placing the angel on top of the tree. She then climbed down the ladder to gesture at the finished tree with an almighty, 'Ta-da!' Clapping her hands, she grinned madly at the camera. 'Isn't it the best?'

Her excitement couldn't be wholly feigned, could it? His heart thumped as her smile and her lips filled his vision. His blood began to beat out a primitive rhythm, making things inside him draw tight.

She took her phone and watched the piece of video. 'Oh, Beau, this is brilliant! I can't thank you enough. My family—'

She glanced up and her words petered out as their gazes caught and clung. Her eyes widened at whatever she saw in his face, she swallowed…and then her gaze lowered to his mouth and her eyes darkened and her lips parted as if she found it suddenly difficult to breathe.

A fierce primitive joy surged through him, taking him completely off guard. He'd never expected a woman to look at him again with such naked hunger—hadn't dared hope such a thing would be possible. But in that moment he understood that Chloe wanted him every bit as much as he did her. Something in her blood spoke to his.

Their uncomfortable and challenging working relationship hadn't been due to their bad tempers after all, but the physical attraction developing between them. When she was near, his body came alive in a way it hadn't in a long time and he ached to find the kind of release with her that his every instinct told him would be sensational. He wanted to give her that same release.

He reached out to touch her face—gently. She reminded him of some shy woodland creature that would start at any sudden movement. He didn't want to frighten her.

He wanted to give her time to catch up with him, and then he wanted to taste every delicious millimetre of her lips—slowly, thoroughly and without rushing. He wanted to give her the kind of mindless pleasure that would chase all the sadness and worry from her mind for a few short hours.

What would she taste like—honey and ginger? Would she kiss him back gently or fiercely? Would she wrap her arms around his neck and press that sweet body against his?

The sweetest song sang through his veins when she moved a fraction closer and he felt as if he'd stretched out giant wings—not like an angel, but an eagle—and soared on deliriously exhilarating air currents.

CHAPTER FIVE

HAD HER PULSE ever fluttered so wildly? Had her heart ever pounded so hard? As Chloe stared at Beau's bewitching mouth, things inside her thrashed and crashed like a wild horse trying to break free of a lasso. He wanted to kiss her. And she was going to kiss him back. Every instinct she had told her that the experience would be wild and fabulous and freeing.

They stood there, poised between heartbeats, relishing the—

Mark.

His name whispered through her mind. She could almost see the printed letters form in front of her face, which then dissolved to reform into capital letters. MARK! And then they became arrows spearing into her with deadly accuracy.

She flinched.

'No!'

The word sounded unnaturally loud in the silence of the room.

'No!' she shouted again, which was completely unnecessary because it was clear from how quickly Beau had dropped his hand and stepped back that he'd heard her the first time.

She stabbed a finger at him. 'This can't happen. It can *never* happen.'

Wheeling away, she started for the stairs, achingly and

boilingly furious. Not at Beau, but at herself. How could she have even thought about kissing another man? How could anyone ever replace Mark in her heart?

They couldn't!

Sex and love aren't necessarily synonymous.

She batted the traitorous thought away as she stumbled up the stairs. She'd loved Mark with her whole heart and if she couldn't have sex with him then she didn't want to have sex with anyone.

Liar.

'Chloe, wait!'

Something in the urgency of Beau's voice pulled her to a halt.

'Please don't run away as if you're scared of me. Please let me apologise.'

She hauled in a breath. 'I'm not scared of you, Beau. I just need to get away before I hurl ugly awful things at you, things that you don't deserve, things that have more to do with me than you and—' She broke off with a frown. 'Not *thing* things, but words…accusations—'

'I don't mind if you do.'

He had no idea. If he did, he wouldn't be so blasé.

'And maybe I do deserve them.'

He leapt lightly up the stairs, stopping a couple of steps below her, allowing her to maintain the height advantage—not touching her, leaving her free to flee if she wanted to. His pallor and the way the lines around his mouth had deepened made her stomach churn.

'Please allow me to apologise. There's been enough media attention and the whole *#metoo* movement to educate men in positions of power to not put employees in compromising positions.'

Hold on. *What?*

'I apologise unreservedly for putting you in that position and for making you feel uncomfortable. I hate myself for it. And let me assure you that your contract and your position here are in no danger whatsoever of—'

She leaned forward. 'What on earth are you blathering on about?'

'Abusing my position here as your employer and making you feel pressured and—'

She waved both hands in front of her face. 'Look, I don't exactly see you as my boss, okay? I'm my own boss. You're my client. You've simply contracted me to do a job. We signed a contract. If you break it, I can sue you.'

He blinked.

'And if I break it, you can sue me. I don't feel there's a power play happening here. I mean, I know I'm acting as your housekeeper, but that's more as a favour.' She shrugged. 'I know you're paying the housekeeper's wage, but…' Her frown deepened. 'You know, the power in that arrangement feels as if it rests with me.'

He raised an eyebrow.

'*You* want me to be housekeeper more than *I* want to be housekeeper. I could probably behave really badly and take advantage of you, but as long as I don't sell you out to the papers I suspect I'd get away with it.'

His lips twisted as if acknowledging the hit.

'So that—' She waved her hand to the spot beside the tree where they'd—

She shied away from finishing the sentence, from putting into words what they'd almost done. 'It had nothing to do with power plays, so stop already with the self-flagellation.'

His gaze raked her face, and the lines around his mouth eased. 'So I didn't scare you?'

'No.' She'd scared herself. *That* was the problem.

'And you didn't feel pressured by me or in fear that your job and contract were in any danger?'

'No.' The thought hadn't crossed her mind.

Because you were too busy lusting after him.

How could she let herself do that? How could she let herself get so caught up in the moment? It was too soon—

Chlo, it's been two years.

She ignored that too.

Reaching up, he pushed a strand of hair that had worked free from her braid back behind her ear. 'Then, Chloe, what was that about? The expression on your face froze my bone marrow.'

Good! Hopefully it'd mean he'd never try to kiss her again. 'I don't want to talk about it. And you can't make me!'

Dear God, did she have to sound so juvenile and immature?

He eased down a step. 'No, of course not.'

The expression on his face made her feel like a heel.

'I have things to do,' she blurted out and then she turned around and fled.

It was no use! She couldn't sleep.

The Daffodil room was gorgeous—all warm yellow and wood panelling, with a four-poster bed boasting luscious brocade drapes. It was the kind of bed fit for a princess. But she couldn't appreciate it tonight. Tonight her mind was filled with Beau.

When she closed her eyes she saw his face, imagined his hands on her body doing things that made her shift restlessly against the sheets. She wondered what it would be like to run her hands down the intriguing lines of that masculine body—testing the firmness and strength of his flesh—and her fingers flexed.

That moment by the tree… They'd almost kissed. And if they had—

Her eyes flew open and a deep ache gripped her. If she was prepared to throw caution to the wind—

She sat up, dragging her hands through her hair. *Stop it.* Think of Mark. Wanting another man should be a betrayal of the love she'd felt for her husband. Burying her face in her hands, she shook her head. But that wasn't how she felt. And she didn't know what it meant.

Letting out a long breath, she straightened and tried to channel calm. She knew that *technically* lusting after another man, or even sleeping with someone, wasn't betraying Mark. During the course of the last two years she'd been forced to acknowledge that she'd have to go on without him.

And clearly her body was still alive. She was young. This was a normal hormonal reaction. She gritted her teeth. Eventually all of this heated longing, the prickling and throbbing, would go away again. She just needed to wait it out.

Fine. If she couldn't trust her body to behave, then she needed to focus her mind. She might've lost Mark but that didn't mean she was prepared to lose the life they'd worked so hard to build—the house, the business. Thoughts of losing what little she did have left of her husband slowly chased the heat from her body, the fears and worries circling her mind like sharks instead—threatening, ominous… devastating.

Dear God, they weren't going to help her sleep either.

'Enough already.' She threw the covers back with a growl and planted her feet firmly on the floor. She'd make a cup of cocoa, sip it calmly, and then come back and do some relaxation exercises. It was her own fault for having retreated to her bedroom so early. That had been foolish.

But after a far from comfortable dinner with Beau where they'd attempted stilted conversation over the shepherd's pie, it'd been a relief to finally clean the kitchen and retreat to her own little haven. It had seemed like a smart plan. Except thoughts of him had continued to plague her.

Her bedroom was to the right of the stairs. Beau's was to

the left. Six doors separated his bedroom from hers. Unless she slammed her door and shouted at the top of her voice, slipping downstairs at midnight shouldn't disturb him.

Nevertheless, she was careful to open her door quietly and start the descent down the stairs on silent tiptoes. It wasn't until she reached the landing at the turn of the stairs that she realised the man who'd occupied her thoughts for most of the evening sat on the third step from the bottom. He stared at the ridiculously beautiful Christmas tree, lights twinkling and the multitude of decorations sparkling, with hunched shoulders and a bowed head.

She could tiptoe back the way she'd come. He'd be none the wiser…

But something about those hunched shoulders caught at her. She'd been mired in a hell of grief for so long it occurred to her that maybe she'd grown callous towards the griefs and hardships of others. The thought made her frown. She didn't want to become that kind of person.

She forced herself down the stairs to sit beside him, though not too near. 'Can't sleep?'

He glanced around and shook his head.

She bit her lip. 'Are you still beating yourself up about earlier?'

'No.' He straightened. 'Should I be?'

'Absolutely not!'

He glanced back at the tree. 'I'll admit I found it…confronting.'

She winced. 'My temper has a mind of its own at the moment. That's on me, though, not you.'

His smile didn't reach his eyes. 'It wasn't your temper that was confronting, Chloe. Besides, you didn't really lose it, you know?'

Hadn't she? It had felt as if she had. Inside she'd felt as if she'd been hurling things at the wall, totally out of control.

'What I found confronting…'

Perfect lips twisted, and she dragged her gaze away, ignored the pulse that started up deep inside. Broad shoulders lifted. *Nope, not noticing them either.*

'It felt as if I'd come alive again, and that felt wonderful. And then, clearly, it didn't. When you backed off so quickly I worried I'd come on too strong, had misconstrued every signal. And I'm still worried I did—'

She touched his arm to halt his words. 'You didn't misconstrue anything, Beau.' She dragged her hand back into her lap, fingertips tingling. 'It's just… I'm not ready for anything like that yet.'

He stared at her for a moment and she had the oddest feeling he wanted to challenge her. She let out a breath when he let it pass. 'So that's why you're feeling gloomy? Because you thought you'd misread me?'

'I never thought a woman would find me attractive again. And when you retreated, I thought I'd been indulging in a serious case of wishful thinking.'

He was talking now about his scars, thinking most women wouldn't see past them. It took an effort not to yell at him. 'Most people aren't as shallow as you seem to think.'

He stared at his hands. 'I didn't realise I'd be prepared to take the plunge and risk rejection.'

He thought she'd rejected him?

You did reject him.

But not because he was scarred! 'Beau, I don't want you thinking—'

'I don't.'

'You don't know what I was going to say.'

'I know my scars don't bother you.'

Really? One glance into those piercing blue eyes and she found herself nodding. *Good.* 'Then what has you so gloomy?'

He shifted and she realised she didn't want him getting up and walking away. Who had he had to confide in recently? He was so isolated here at Dawncarden, and while she knew it had nothing to do with her, it made all the sore places inside her ache. She wanted to help. If she could.

'I'd like to know,' she added quietly.

He let out a low breath, nodded at the Christmas tree and then lifted a photograph album. 'I was looking through this. It's from the Christmas when I was seven. I wanted to see how the hall was decorated back then. I had some crazy notion that I could recreate it.'

She took the album and turned the pages. '*Oh!* It looks magical.'

'But as I was flicking through, I suddenly realised how much I've been worrying my grandmother.' He pointed. 'That's her there.'

She was a tall, angular-looking woman with piercing eyes just like her grandson's. Everything about her screamed rigid respectability, but her smile was kind. 'I like what she looks like.'

'That's my mother and father.'

He'd received his dark thick hair from his mother and his perfect mouth from his father.

'When my father's business failed he turned to drugs.'

She stared at him, her mouth falling open.

'My mother had a kind of nervous breakdown and has since retreated to some ashram in India where she eschews her old life and goes by a different name.'

'Is your father still alive?'

'He overdosed, but the paramedics eventually managed to revive him. His brain was starved of oxygen for too long, though, and now he's more child than man. He's in a clinic receiving the best of care, but doesn't really recognise anyone any more.'

'Oh, Beau, I'm so sorry! How old were you when this all happened?'

'Eight.' He nodded at the album. 'The year following that Christmas.'

Here she was feeling ridiculously sorry for herself—and angry at him for brooding on his misfortunes—but she'd been blessed with her family. So blessed.

'My grandmother came to the rescue. She provided a roof over my head, sent me to school and made sure I had everything I needed. She was busy with her business interests and charity work, but she made what time she could for me. I'll be grateful to her forever. I love her dearly, but she's the "stiff upper lip and let's get on with it" type, if you know what I mean?'

The poor little boy that he'd been, though, would've craved a mother like hers. One who would smother him in hugs and love, making him feel secure and safe and the centre of the universe.

'But it only struck me this evening, when I was thinking about how you want to give your family a worry-free Christmas, that I've barely given my grandmother a second thought. And she deserves better from me. She must be terrified that I'll follow in the same path as my father and turn to drugs.' He met her gaze. 'Which I'm not, by the way.'

Thank heavens!

'But it's never crossed my mind to reassure her that I'm in no danger of doing any such thing.'

She reached out to squeeze his arm. 'But that's something you can fix. You don't need to sit here in the half-dark beating yourself up about it.'

He straightened. 'I can ring her tomorrow.'

'That's an excellent start. Though, in my experience, actions speak louder than words.'

His brows lowered and he pursed his lips. *Don't look at the lips!*

'You're right. She needs to see me doing things. Decorating the hall is a start. Telling her about my plans for the walled garden and the pipistrelles is another.' His nose curled. 'As would being seen in the village.'

She slapped her hands to her knees. 'Let's call that Plan A, shall we? We can both turn things around. And two heads are always better than one. Together we should be able to find a way forward and get back on track.' She groaned. 'And listen to me descending into cliché like some kind of motivational calendar. Enough with the brooding.' She stood. 'Cocoa?'

'What would you like to drink?'

Chloe glanced at the blackboard by the bar and her delectable lips stretched into a grin. 'Mulled wine, please. It's freezing outside and I want to find out if that stuff really does warm you up.'

He wasn't sure why, but it made him laugh. 'Go grab a seat by the fire and I'll get the drinks.'

She hesitated. 'What?' he demanded, instantly alert.

'Are you okay about being here tonight? There're more people in than I thought there'd be.'

Was she looking for a reason to leave? She hadn't been particularly enthusiastic when he'd suggested the outing. 'It's darts night, that's all. And I'm fine. Everyone here is a local. The tourists all go to The Royal Oak with its refurbished bar, fancy cocktails and even fancier cuisine.'

Without another word, she went to find a table.

'What do you think?' he asked a short while later.

'Of what, the wine or the pub?'

'Both.'

'The wine is…interesting.'

Uh huh. She hated it.

'And I'm in love with The Nag's Head.'

His head came up. She was?

'Oh, and by the way, I've entered us in the darts competition.'

He choked on his bitter. 'You've what?' He came here to be seen. Not to *participate.*

'You said it was darts night, so I figured that's what we were supposed to do. Also there's a Christmas ham up for grabs and I *really* want to win it.'

'You can play?'

'Doh! I have two older brothers. And I'm good.'

'I was *really* good when I was at university,' he shot back.

She raked him up and down with one unimpressed glance. 'How long ago was that? Last century? Come on, buster, we're heading for the practice board to see if we can get your eye in before the comp starts for real.'

He took a generous gulp of beer. 'Game on!'

Chloe was a hit with the other competitors, most of whom had known him since he was a boy. They didn't win the Christmas ham, but they did get third prize of a small Christmas pudding. He also filmed a snatch of video on his phone of Chloe, after her second drink—a pint of bitter—leading the crowd in a round of 'Kookaburra Sits in the Old Gum Tree'. Her mum would love it!

He couldn't remember the last time he'd had so much fun.

He frowned at that thought. Once Chloe's contract was completed, she'd be gone. Just as his parents had gone, and just as his job had gone. Except, in this instance, Chloe didn't owe him anything.

Rely on nothing. Rely on nobody.

He could enjoy it while it lasted, but he couldn't get used to it. He'd help her find her Christmas mojo, she'd help him convince his grandmother he was fine, she'd create the garden of his dreams, and then they'd go their merry ways. Separately.

'So you're happy with all that then?'

Beau glanced around the garden and nodded. In his

mind's eye he could see Chloe's vision for the garden come to life and it was even better than the one he'd imagined. They could turn this garden into a thriving sanctuary.

He should consider establishing some beehives too. Not in the walled garden, but maybe on the other side of the orchard. He'd completed a beekeeping course a few years ago. He suddenly saw that this garden could be the start of something bigger. He *ought* to dream bigger.

'Beau?'

He bumped back to find Chloe staring at him, a frown in the treacle-dark depths of her eyes. 'Sorry, what did you say?'

'You're happy with the proposed water feature? Large pond here, a little rill running either side to a fountain on one side and a pool on the other?'

'Absolutely. That was an inspired idea. I love it.'

She blinked, and he realised how miserly he'd been with his praise.

'You're confident that you, George and I can do all the necessary physical labour?'

'Absolutely.'

She swallowed, her hands twisting together. 'Just so you know, I'll be sourcing what I can locally—stone for the garden beds and paths, all the plants, as well as soil and fertiliser. You might as well generate what goodwill you can in the community.'

Her words warmed him. She'd put a lot of thought into this—was doing all she could to make things easy for him. 'Chloe, you've worked miracles here. I can't tell you how happy I am with everything you've proposed. And how grateful I am for your vision and all of your hard work.'

Her mouth fell open. She hauled it back into place, eyeing him carefully. 'I, um…excellent.' She rubbed a hand across her chest as if to dislodge an ache. 'I'm pleased you're so happy with what we're doing here and I wondered...'

He leaned towards her. 'Yes?'

'Look, Beau, would you consider letting me take before and after photos of the garden for my portfolio?'

Everything inside him snapped tight. 'Absolutely not!' How could she ask him such a thing? His hands clenched and he found himself breathing hard. 'It's out of the question. I thought I'd made that clear.' He'd thought they were on the same page. Realising they weren't cut him to the quick.

Before he could continue to rant, or turn on his heel and stalk off, she raised her hands. 'Okay, okay, keep your hair on. Just thought I'd ask.'

They stared at each other and he did what he could to unclench his jaw.

'So back to what we were talking about before.' She rushed back into speech. 'You're happy? There's nothing you want to add or subtract?'

He tried to get his breathing back under control, and refused to feel guilty for the dimming of the light in her eyes. 'Why? Do you feel there's something missing?'

'Not at all. But it doesn't matter what I think. What matters is making your vision real.'

What she thought *did* matter.

No, it doesn't.

Yes, it does.

Rolling his shoulders, he did what he could to dislodge the weight that wanted to settle over him. Instead he found himself caught in her stare, and those dark compelling eyes—

He dragged his gaze away. Her opinion mattered because she was the designer. That was all. 'I approve of all the suggestions you've made for the garden. You've not just captured what I wanted, but you've built on my original ideas and made them even better.'

'That's good to know.'

The vulnerability he saw in her face, before it was blinked away, caught at him. He wanted to swear and swear. 'I've been so selfishly caught up in myself I hadn't realised how parsimonious I've been with my praise.'

She started. 'Oh, I don't need praise. I just want to be sure I have everything exactly right before we start breaking serious ground.'

He stared at her, things inside him throbbing. 'Ever since I saw the photographs of the garden you won that award for I knew you were the right designer. When that was combined with your knowledge of English country gardens—'

He broke off with a frown. 'Why do you know so much about English country gardens?'

'I took it as an elective in my second year.' She shrugged. 'Blame *Wind in the Willows*, *The Secret Garden* and Beatrix Potter. They were firm favourites when I was growing up, and I was always a bit envious that I couldn't create a garden like that in Sydney.'

He gestured around. 'So why should you feel so anxious now about getting this right?'

Her nose wrinkled in a way that he found enchanting. Except she didn't do it to enchant him, he knew that. But then he was beginning to find a lot of things about Chloe enchanting.

You've been holed up on your own for too long.

He shook the thought off. Once he had the garden to focus on, his life would begin to have a rhythm once more. It would start to feel full. He'd have a purpose.

'I haven't done much design work in the last two years.' She gave a hollow laugh that brought his focus immediately back to the here and now. 'Who am I kidding? I've not done *any* design work in the last two years.'

Not since her husband had died.

It didn't matter if Beau had scars that rendered him unrecognisable or was the most beautiful man in the world. Chloe didn't see him as a man. She'd never see him as a man. Her husband still filled her vision. He thought he'd known grief, but he hadn't known grief like that.

'How have you been making ends meet, then, Chloe?'

For some reason his words made her flinch, and he took an immediate step back. 'Sorry, that's none of my business. It's just…if I were in your shoes I think I'd want to lose myself in my job, try and find some solace in what I was good at.'

'Liar.' But the word carried no sting, and her eyes held no accusation. 'What did you do when your world came tumbling down? You holed up here like a bear with a sore head and bellowed at anyone who came near.'

He rubbed a hand over his face. 'I needed time to grieve before I could find a way forward.'

She glanced up, her eyes sharp. 'And this—' she gestured at the garden '—is your way forward?'

It was.

'Mark and I went into business with his parents—a nursery-cum-garden-centre. After he died, I couldn't face dealing with other people so his parents took over all of the customer service, while I did a lot of the grunt work—the planting, mulching, raising seedlings.' She shrugged. 'I guess I'm just ready now to get back to my real work.'

He had a feeling that process hadn't been as seamless as she'd made it sound. He opened his mouth to probe further.

'You're confident the work we'll be doing won't disturb the pipistrelles?'

Clearly she didn't want to talk about it. He struggled with it for a moment and then let it go. It wasn't his place to probe. 'We're taking every precaution. Once we're done, this is going to be pipistrelle nirvana. I have big plans.'

Her eyes brightened, so he went on to explain how he was purchasing boxes to encourage more pipistrelles to the garden, the research he was doing on tracking devices so he could discover how far afield they went, and how he hoped the garden would—

'Hold on! Hold on!'

He bumped back to earth with a crash, grimaced. 'Sorry, that was probably way more information than you needed.' He'd just wanted to rid her eyes of their quiet desperation.

'No, it's fascinating.' She pulled her phone from her pocket. 'I mean *really* fascinating.'

She meant it, and against his better judgement his chest expanded.

'But you need to record this for your own records. It's gold!'

His head snapped back. 'You want to film me?' The thought had him wanting to yell and thunder, and then punch something.

She looked suddenly and gut-wrenchingly unsure of herself. 'Well, I just thought… I figured when you're writing your research up it'd be a useful record, a kind of diary.' She took a step back. 'Sorry, it was probably a stupid suggestion.'

He felt like a heel.

'Mum, Dad and my nephews loved that piece of video you took of me singing in the pub last night. So I probably just have videoing on my mind.' She sent him an apologetic smile. 'My mum thinks you're the bee's knees.'

He closed his eyes and counted to three. Before he could give himself too much time to think, he opened them again and said, 'Actually, it's a good idea.'

Her jaw dropped.

He winced.

'Sorry.' She dragged it back into place. 'I'm just so used

to saying the wrong thing around you that I thought this was another classic example.'

He shook his head, gritting his teeth. 'I just…it's a stupid thing to get hung up on.'

She opened her mouth and he waited for her to assure him it wasn't stupid at all. She didn't. She just shrugged. 'Then why don't you get un-hung-up about it? Let's do the video. If you hate it, you can always delete it and there'll be no harm done. And if you don't hate it, it'll then become part of your garden diary. And that's interesting in itself, don't you think?'

'Fine.' He refused to think too hard about any of it.

She started filming. 'Tell me what's so exciting about this garden, Beau.'

Without any conscious thought, he slipped immediately into documentary-making mode. He explained how the garden had been in his family for generations, but had been sadly neglected for the past decade. He described how he wanted to create a sanctuary for birds and butterflies and any other wildlife that found its way here.

He strolled down to the hornbeam tree and she followed, her phone trained on him the entire time. He described the unusual smell that had sent him investigating further. Then he took the phone and filmed the tiny bodies of the pipistrelles sleeping in their sheltered corner. He described what they were, how their habitats were being destroyed and how he hoped the garden would become a haven for them.

When he emerged back onto the path, he aimed the camera at Chloe, sitting on the low wall of a garden bed. 'Right, tit for tat. Tell me about the vision you have for this garden.'

Her eyes widened. She shot to her feet and wiped her hands on the seat of her trousers. 'Oh…um…' She made a couple of false starts, insisted they start at the other end of the garden where work was going to start first. And then she walked them through, stage by stage, what they were going to do and how it would all look when it was finished.

She met his gaze and shrugged. 'I think that's all from me.'

He clicked the off button, and they stood staring at each other. He handed the phone back to her, feeling numb. 'I've practically drained your battery.'

She shrugged as if that was no big deal. 'I'll put it on the charger when we go back to the house.'

Batteries could be recharged. She was right. It was no big deal.

'You were amazing.' She stared at him with huge eyes, held up her phone. 'You're a natural. You have such *presence*. You had me mesmerised.' She leaned towards him. 'How did it feel?'

Clearly she thought it'd felt good. Clearly she expected him to feel as elated and exhilarated as she did. She couldn't be more wrong.

A numbness at his very centre had started to thaw, and he didn't want it to—he wanted to put it back to sleep, put it back on ice. But now that it'd started, it seemed there was nothing he could do to stop it. It felt as if his entire chest were caving in from the inside out.

His face twisted. Ugly words clawed at his throat.

She fell back, devastation spreading across her lovely face.

Turning on his heel, he left the garden before he did something, said something, he'd regret.

She didn't call him back, didn't run after him. He told himself he was glad, told himself that he wanted solitude.

He strode into the house and stormed straight to his study, not bothering to take his boots off first. He slammed the door to dispel some of his pent-up aggression, before slumping at his desk, head in hands.

All he could see when he closed his eyes was the expression on Chloe's face when she'd realised how the filming had made him feel.

When he opened them again, all he could feel was loss and pain. That innocuous piece of filming had brought home to him with a vengeance all that he'd lost. He'd thought he'd come to terms with the fact that the career he'd loved was gone forever. His harsh laugh reverberated in the air, mocking him.

His computer pinged to announce an incoming message. He lifted his head to glare at it. He had two messages—one from Chloe's mum and the other from his grandmother. He opened the one from Mrs Jennings first.

Dear Beau,
Thank you so much for taking Chloe out and making sure she enjoyed herself. It was kind of you to film what you did. It did my heart so much good. You're a kind boy.

He dragged a hand down his face. *Not* kind. Making Chloe feel responsible for the fact life hadn't panned out the way he'd wanted it to was the antithesis of kind. Nothing that had happened in the garden this afternoon had been her fault.

He turned to his grandmother's email.

Dear Recalcitrant Grandson of Mine,
I've barely spoken to you in two months. And before you contradict me, I don't consider email an adequate substitute.

The thought of you at Dawncarden alone this Christmas, without even Stephanie to keep you company, is intolerable. You keep assuring me you're fine, but I don't believe that for a moment.

Unless you can convince me otherwise I'm cancelling Christmas in Florence and descending to disturb your solitude.

Damn!

Another ping sounded. An email from Chloe. She sent no message just…

He swallowed. She'd sent him the video file.

He opened it, his heart thumping so hard it hurt. He watched the video all the way through and then turned it off with a savage stab of his finger and leaned back in his chair to glare at the ceiling.

Slamming back to his desk, he watched the video again, and frowned. It was undeniably amateur and yet he couldn't deny that he came across…*well*. Even given his scars. He spoke with assurance, and the video had captured his passion and enthusiasm.

Chloe was right. This would be an invaluable record.

He blinked, electrified for a moment, and then started frantically typing.

Dear Put-Upon-Though-Sainted Grandmother,
Apologies for my lack of communication. Put me in front of a camera and I can talk for hours, but ask me to pick up the phone and I can barely string two sentences together.

Let me assure you I'm well. The reason I've been so quiet is I'm immersed in my latest project—restoring the walled garden. Watch the piece of attached video and I believe you'll find that you can enjoy Florence with your mind at rest.
Your Recalcitrant-But-Ever-Loving-Grandson, Beau

He hit 'send' and leaned back. He even found one corner of his mouth lifting.

CHAPTER SIX

CHLOE BEAT THE shortbread mixture, wielding the wooden spoon like a hoe, putting her whole back into it. She pounded until her arm started to ache, and then she changed arms. She would not cry.

The expression on Beau's face when she'd asked him how he'd felt after that filming…

She flinched as it played through her mind for the hundredth time.

Oh, yes, you thought you had all the answers. Just get him to jump back in the saddle and all would be well, right?

She couldn't have been more wrong if she'd tried.

Dropping into a chair, she wished with everything inside her that she could start the day again, wished she could rethink her impulsive suggestion that he keep a video diary of the garden.

The outline of the table started to blur. It had seemed such a good idea at the time, but it had backfired spectacularly. And she'd do anything she could to spare Beau further pain. He didn't deserve it. He was dealing with enough.

She scrubbed a hand down her face. Somewhere during the last fortnight she'd started to like him. He didn't mind her losing her temper—in fact she was starting to think he encouraged it as if he knew she needed the outlet and was more than happy to be her figurative punching bag. Nobody had ever done that for her before.

Some of the hard knots of anger and ugliness simmering at the centre of her had started to lose their ferocity. That was all down to Beau.

He'd reminded her that there were still things in her life that she ought to be grateful for. Like her family. Not that she'd ever forgotten that, not really. But she could *feel* it again—feel the blessing of it in her heart. It mightn't sound like much, but it made all the difference in the world.

Footsteps sounded in the corridor leading to the kitchen and, as they could only belong to one person, she leapt to her feet and started beating the shortbread dough once again.

Could you pound the dough too much? She shrugged. These were either going to be really good or, um…not.

Her arm halted mid-pound, though, when Beau entered the kitchen. She had no hope of feigning busyness. Not when he looked at her like that. She opened her mouth to say something and then closed it again, lowered her arm. She didn't want to say something inane, but more to the point she didn't want to say anything that would hurt, trouble, perturb or disturb him in any way, shape, form or fashion.

She ached to find words that would comfort and encourage him instead. The thought made her blink. How long had it been since she hoped for something like that for someone else? When had her grief become so selfish?

'I want to apologise for my behaviour earlier.' Beau stared at the dough in the bowl, raked a hand through his hair. 'I was rude, and I expect my actions were baffling, and—'

'No!' The word shot out of her and his gaze speared to hers. Her heart started to pound though she didn't know why. 'No,' she said again, more measured this time. 'I'm the one who should be apologising. I pushed you to do something you didn't want to do. I thought it would be good for you. Ha!' She dumped the contents of the mixing bowl onto the table and started savagely flattening it with hard thumps of her palm.

He frowned and pointed. 'I uh—'

'As if I'm a therapist or something! But what do I know? I shouldn't have—' She broke off, realising he was pointing at the dough. She stared up at him and then down at the lump in front of her. 'What?'

He shook his head. 'It doesn't matter.'

She knew it didn't look like much at the moment, and she no doubt lacked Stephanie's flair, but just wait until she pulled it from the oven later. Mentally, she crossed her fingers.

She pulled her mind back to the conversation. 'I'm sorry, Beau. What I'm trying to say is that I've made enough of a mess of my own life. I've no right to be telling anyone else how they ought to be living.'

'I don't think your life is a mess.'

He didn't?

'I think you're remarkably talented with a bright future ahead of you.'

Her throat thickened. 'Thank you.'

He dropped into a chair. 'And you didn't force me to do that filming. Making a video diary is sensible. But once it was done, once we'd wrapped up…'

She abandoned the shortbread and sat too. It felt as if she ought to give him all of her attention. And she wanted to. She wanted to listen to him as much as he'd listened to her. But her eyes snagged on the breadth of those shoulders and the promise of the strength in that big powerful body and a pulse deep inside her quickened.

She did what she could to ignore it.

He lifted his head. 'It was so seamless, slipping back into character like that.'

He looked completely at a loss. It had clearly taken him

off guard, and the glimpse of his vulnerability made her ache. 'Would you like to know what I think?'

She asked rather than rattling straight into speech and giving her opinion without thought. She had absolutely no intention of giving her opinion where it wasn't needed and making him feel twice as bad. She was through with being that person.

He met her gaze. 'Yes.'

It was just a simple word, but it carried weight. It reminded her that he'd told her he trusted her. And she wanted to be worthy of that trust. 'I don't think you were ever playing a part on your documentaries, so it's not that you slipped back into character, you just started sharing a deeper part of yourself again.'

He frowned.

She leaned towards him and his scent made her suddenly hungry—not for food, but for snow and sun and running and swimming. She eased back, doing what she could to crush her crazy imaginings. *Focus.* 'What I mean is, when you were on the television, you shared your passion for the natural world with your audience. You made us feel it too. You made us care.'

He stared. 'Is that how my documentaries really made you feel?'

She nodded, and then her hands suddenly clenched. 'And now the world is lesser because your stupid TV network dumped you and we no longer get your point of view on the airwaves. It sucks.'

One side of his mouth hooked up. 'You're very good for my ego, you know that?' But then his smile faded. 'That little piece of filming today brought home how much I miss making documentaries. I hate that I can no longer do that, that it's an option that's closed to me now.'

Was it closed to him, though? She had no idea how television worked. Were the networks really so superficial as to rate what a person looked like above their qualifications and expertise?

'I just watched the file you sent me.'

'And?'

'It was good.'

She could've told him that till she was blue in the face, but he wouldn't have believed her. She was glad he could recognise it for himself. 'So you're feeling okay again?'

'I forgot that not everything that hurts is bad for you.'

The words knocked the breath from her body.

'I think that's something you understand. Losing Mark has had a wealth of pain descending on your head.'

Her head, her heart, her life.

'But I don't think you'd give it back, because to not hurt would mean to not have loved him as much as you did.'

She couldn't speak so she simply nodded.

'Losing a job isn't anywhere near as bad as losing someone you love, but...'

With a superhuman effort she swallowed the lump in her throat. 'But you loved your job more than most people love their jobs. It wasn't just a job to you, but a calling.'

They stared at each other for a long time. His eyes had turned dark and his mouth pressed into a hard line as if holding back some strong emotion. 'Thank you,' he finally said. 'I knew you'd understand.'

And in that moment something arced between them and began to burn. He frowned. She frowned. And then he eased back in his seat and she leapt to her feet and started cutting circles of shortbread from the dough.

'It occurred to me that while I might not be able to make documentaries on a large scale any more, I can make them for myself. There's absolutely no reason why I can't keep my own ongoing video diary of the garden. It's going to be fascinating to see how it grows and develops, what it attracts and what comes to live there. I've been focussed on the more exotic picture for so long because it draws an audience, but what happens here in our own backyards is every bit as important.'

But who would get to see those videos? Who would benefit from all of his insight and knowledge? She'd pay good money to watch them and hear his thoughts.

'Can I ask something?'

'Sure?' But a wary light entered his eyes.

'Look, you can tell me to shut up if you want. I won't be offended. It's just I have no idea how TV works.'

'What do you want to know?'

'There's more than one network, right? Just because one network dumped you doesn't mean another one wouldn't want you.' She frowned. 'Or does it?'

He didn't answer immediately, and she spread parchment paper onto a baking tray to appear busy and give him some space, and tried to lift the first of her shortbread circles from the table. It refused to budge. Grabbing a butter knife, she tried to slide it beneath the circle and promptly mashed it.

She glanced up to find Beau trying not to laugh. She spread her hands. She thought she'd followed Stephanie's recipe to the letter. She might've been a little energetic with the beating but…

'Stephanie sprinkles flour on the surface before rolling the dough out.'

She grimaced. 'A rookie mistake.'

'Here, give me a sharp knife and I'll be able to get these up for you.'

She sat while he did it. Each circle left a trace of dough behind. She'd need to scour the table to get it off.

'The networks are all chasing the next big thing.'

She snapped back to attention.

'All that matters in TV land are the ratings. And prior to *the incident* I was ranking number one.'

The incident being his run-in with that leopard. She moistened suddenly dry lips. 'What actually happened, Beau?'

He was silent for a moment, didn't meet her eyes. 'Surely you've read the news reports.'

'They were hard to avoid at the time,' she acknowledged, 'but I never liked the sensationalism. Other than the fact that you were recovering, and I was pleased about that, I can't say I paid a whole lot of attention.' Her lips twisted. She'd been too focussed on her own grief to pay much attention to anyone else.

He set the last circle to the prepared tray and then sat in the chair she'd previously vacated. Instead of the entire length of the table resting between them, they now sat at right angles. She had an insane urge to reach out and trace the muscles in his forearm. She could imagine the living strength of his flesh and sinew and—

'The full story never made it to the papers anyway.'

She snapped back.

'We were filming in Africa, and we'd been following the leopard for a few weeks. We'd been getting some excellent footage, but I wanted to get a close-up.'

'Weren't you afraid? I mean, I know they're absolutely gobsmackingly beautiful, but I'd be afraid to get too close.'

'There's always an element of danger, of course, but we were careful. We knew she'd just eaten, and we hadn't presented any kind of threat to her in the weeks we'd been following her. So we set up and started the filming. I kept my voice low and my body still and unthreatening. All of us were enthralled. The light was perfect, we were getting great shots.'

He broke off and was quiet for a long moment. She swallowed. 'What went wrong?'

He glanced up, his eyes shadowed. 'One of the cameramen…' He turned more fully towards her. 'There's this thing that can happen when you stare at something through a lens. You start to feel removed from it—like you're watching it on your TV set in your living room. He'd become mesmerised. That leopard, she was one of the most beautiful things he'd ever seen and he kept moving closer and closer towards her.'

Her heart lurched into her throat.

'Too close. She felt threatened. We were on her turf and rather than flee, she wanted to protect it. I told him to back off, but it was too late.'

Perspiration broke out on her top lip. 'Beau?'

'It was my fault we were that close in the first place so I did the only thing I could think of. I distracted her.'

Her hands flew to her mouth. She dragged them away, suddenly and irrationally angry. 'You could've been killed! What were you thinking?'

'I didn't want to be responsible for someone else's death. The thought of that was worse than—' he shrugged '—anything.'

'But you could've been killed,' she repeated.

'Is that thought really so bad, Chloe?' he asked gently. 'People die every day.'

'Of course it's that bad! It's an awful thought, Beau. Just...*awful*.'

'You loved my documentary series, that much?'

'No! I mean, of course I loved it but the thought of you not being here...' She shook her head. 'If it'd happened back then before I knew you, well... I'd have been sad in the way people are sad when someone dies before their time. But now that I know you, the thought of you being dead is one of the worst thoughts in the world!'

The mixture of sincerity and horror in Chloe's eyes pierced Beau to his very centre. His heart pounded and his eyes stung. He leaned towards her. 'Why?'

Confusion raced across her features, along with consternation. And anger. Those eyebrows grew suddenly fierce. 'I feel that we understand each other. I feel that we're friends. And maybe you don't feel the same way. And maybe you don't know how rare it is, but—'

'I feel the same way.' The words were out of his mouth before he could help it. But he couldn't let her be the only vulnerable one here. Besides, it was the truth.

Her breath gave a funny little hitch. 'And maybe it isn't rare, this feeling.' She gestured between them. 'Maybe it's just that I haven't found it with anyone else because I've been indulging my grief for too long and since then I've been too busy putting on a happy face for everyone. But I don't have to pretend anything to you, and it feels…'

His heart hovered between heartbeats as if it didn't know whether to crash and burn or set sail. 'It feels?'

She shrugged, her eyes a little wild. 'Like heaven,' she hiccupped.

Which was exactly how he felt knowing she didn't care one jot about his scars.

He stared into those dark compelling eyes, and he felt seen, truly seen. Better still, he knew she did too and it was strangely freeing. Neither one of them wanted to hide.

And then she was in his arms and he didn't know if he'd moved first or if she had, but their lips met with a firm warmth that was neither rushed nor urgent, but irresistible for all that. He shaped his mouth to hers, and something warm brushed across the surface of his skin like a spring breeze, and the scent of lavender rose up all around him. Some hard thing inside him dissolved, replaced with light and warmth.

But when her lips opened beneath his, when her tongue tentatively touched his, that warmth became an all-consuming heat. Her body pressed full length against his and everything inside him raged with the need to possess this woman—to strip her of her clothes and explore every inch of her body, to learn all of its secrets. He wanted to drive her crazy with need until she begged for release.

Her hand snaked beneath his shirt and the skin-on-skin contact had him sucking in a breath. He wanted to feel all of her against all of him. Her head fell back when he pressed a series of kisses along her jawline, her fingers digging into him as if to keep herself anchored, their latent urgency urging him on, until he'd worked his way down to push aside the neckline of her shirt to take the hard bud of one nipple into his mouth through the thin material of her bra.

Her cry rang in his ears, and with a mad growl he pulled her shirt over her head before turning his full attention to her other breast. The sound of his name ripping from her throat, hoarse with desire, nearly undid him. In one fluid movement, he lifted her to the table and moved in between her thighs, pulling her hard up against him.

She flung her head back, her legs encircling his waist as if she had no intention of ever letting him go. Clamping her hands either side of his face, she pulled him down for another drugging kiss, her fingers idly tracing his scars, but it didn't spook him. She touched him the same way he touched her. As if she wanted to learn and memorise everything about him.

He wanted to sweep everything from the table, lay her back and bury himself inside her. Her arms around his neck, urgent, her lips parted with anticipation as if she couldn't get enough, her eyes desire-glazed as they met his…

'I feel that we understand each other. I feel that we're friends.'

Her words replayed through his mind and he dragged in a ragged breath, forced himself to slow down…forced himself to meet those treacle-dark eyes. He wanted to be the friend she needed. He *needed* to be that friend. 'You're beautiful, Chloe.'

She blinked and swallowed, her eyes becoming suspiciously bright.

'And I can't tell you how much I want this—to make love with you. I ache with how much I want you.' With a gentle hand, he pushed the hair that had worked its way free from her braid back from her face. 'But I need to know that you want it too. I don't want you crying with remorse afterwards and I don't want you beating yourself up with regrets.' His chest hollowed out at the thought. 'I don't want to be that man for you.'

He watched, barely able to breathe, as comprehension dawned in her eyes.

'But if you do want this as much as I do—' he couldn't stop his hands from tightening fractionally on her waist '—I can promise you pleasure and release and orgasms that will rock your world.'

'Oh!' She gave a funny little hiccup and he sensed the war raging inside her.

He didn't want to, but he moved back, bringing her with him until they stood once again, both of their feet firmly planted on the floor. Picking up her shirt from where he'd thrown it to the chair behind, he handed it to her.

'You want me to get dressed?' she blurted out.

What are you doing? Kiss her again.

'No.' He clenched his hands to fists. 'I want to do the caveman thing and tear the clothes from your body and ravish you.'

Her eyes grew so wide a man could fall into them.

'But instinct tells me you need some space.' He did what he could to temper the impatience roaring through him, the raging need. 'You said we understood each other. You said we were friends. And I think we are and I think we do.'

She frowned. 'You don't think I want you?'

'No, sweetheart, I know that you do.'

She gulped and reefed her shirt back on over her head,

but her arms got tangled and he had to reach out and help her. Every touch was torture.

He forced himself back a step. 'Would you regret it if we made love?'

She lowered herself to the nearest chair, her lips trembling. 'I don't know.'

He made tea.

'I know I shouldn't feel guilty about making love with someone who isn't Mark.' She blew on her tea. 'In my head, I know there's nothing to feel guilty about.'

'But it's not how you feel here—' he touched a hand to his chest '—where it counts.'

She stared at him with a helplessness that speared into him. 'I'm sorry. I shouldn't have kissed you if I didn't know—'

'Rubbish.' He dismissed that with a single wave of his hand. 'We're adults, Chloe, not teenagers. *Consenting* adults,' he stressed. 'That consent can be withdrawn by either of us at any time.'

She stilled. 'That's true.'

An entirely different thought struck him. 'Have you ever had sex just for fun?'

Her cup halted halfway to her mouth. 'Sort of,' she said carefully.

'What does that mean?'

Her shoulders sagged. 'I've never had sex outside a committed relationship, if that's what you're asking.'

'Do you have a moral stance on it?' Maybe she was the kind of woman who equated sex with love. The thought had him choking. If she did, then he'd just had a lucky escape.

'I've never had a one-night stand or a friends-with-benefits arrangement or…' She set her tea down with a frown. 'Why on earth not? Most women my age have.'

He doubted it was due to a lack of opportunity. There

was something vibrant and compelling about Chloe that even if she hadn't been so attractive would've drawn men to her.

'I guess I never found anyone tempting enough to throw that kind of caution to the wind.'

Her gaze flicked to him and darted away again, and he heard what she didn't say. *Until now.* She found *him* tempting. The thought had everything inside him growing hard and tight.

'How old were you when you met Mark?'

'We met at university. I was doing a Horticulture degree and he was doing Business. We didn't actually meet on campus, but we both worked at a garden centre during the holidays and on weekends.' One slim shoulder lifted. 'I was twenty when we started dating. I mean, we didn't get married until we were twenty-four, but we were committed from the beginning.'

'So you didn't actually have much of an opportunity to explore the sex-for-fun thing.'

'I guess not.'

He leaned close enough to feel the heat radiating off her body. 'Well, just so you know. If you decide you want to explore the sex-for-fun thing now, I'd make the perfect person to do that with.'

Her breath hitched and her pupils dilated, and he moved back, cleared the teapot and rinsed his mug. He wouldn't crowd her, and he wouldn't pressure her.

But he was damned if he wouldn't plant the seed of temptation firmly in her mind before he walked away.

He started for the door. 'Time to get back to work.'

She shot to her feet. 'What? Just like that?'

He closed his eyes and counted to three before turning around. 'Do you have an answer to my earlier question? Can you make love with me without regret or remorse?'

That same helpless indecision flashed through her eyes

and he nodded. 'When you can answer that question with a yes then we have something to talk about. I don't want to be anyone's regret.'

Liar, an inner voice said as he walked away. If she threw herself at him now, threw caution to the wind, he'd be helpless to resist her. Lucky for both of them then that she didn't chase after him and throw caution to the wind.

Except it didn't feel lucky.

He closed his study door and leaned back against it, tried to catch his breath. Perhaps what had happened in the kitchen shouldn't have taken him off guard, but it had. The intensity and the need had shaken him to his foundations.

Maybe it was the sheer honesty between them—the initial snarling at one another that had given way to understanding that was now turning into friendship. Whatever was between them, though, it was only temporary. He knew that in his bones. Their lives were on very different trajectories, and, while he might have started to see that he didn't necessarily need to live like a monk, he wasn't giving up his solitude for anyone.

But it didn't mean they couldn't help each other in the meantime. Or find release in one another. Mark had been dead for two years. For two years it was clear that her grief had overshadowed everything else. But some instinct told him she was finally starting to come out the other side, and that she was ready to explore a physical relationship with a man again.

His heart pounded at the thought, and then he stilled as the suspicion that had been niggling at him for days finally crystallised. Why now, *in particular*, was it important for Chloe to put a front on for her family? Didn't the fact that she was designing gardens again prove that she was finally moving on with her life? Was she really worried she'd fall apart again this Christmas, or was there something more?

He moved across to his desk and tapped his fingers against the wood, and then he picked up his mobile and rang the house number.

'Dawncarden Court.'

'It's the tree-lighting ceremony in the village tonight,' he said without preamble. 'Interested? It'll provide us with another photo opportunity for your family. Also, my grandmother emailed earlier. She's worried about me and is threatening to change her plans and spend Christmas here after all, and I don't want her doing that. I sent her the piece of video you took of me earlier to explain why I've been so busy. But if I'm seen out and about in the village, hopefully one of her spies will report back.'

'You rang to tell me this rather than walked the length of the hall like an ordinary person?'

'Yep.' He didn't bother telling her he'd thought it wise for the two of them to cool down before they clapped eyes on each other again. 'You have a problem with that?'

'Seriously?'

Her outrage made his lips twitch. 'There's a reason Stephanie calls me lord and master.'

'Clearly!' she huffed, but he could tell from her voice that she was trying not to laugh.

'So do you want to go?'

She was quiet for several long moments. 'Okay,' she finally said. 'I've never been to a tree lighting. It'll be something fun to tell my folks about.'

'Don't bother with dinner, we'll grab something in the village.' And then he replaced the receiver before he said something he'd regret. Like, *Let's make love.*

A moment later he heard stomping at the far end of the corridor. 'It's polite to say goodbye before hanging up!' she hollered down the hallway. 'Oh, and by the way, I burned the shortbread. So bad luck if you were hoping for a piece of it.'

And then she stomped away again and he found himself grinning like an idiot.

CHAPTER SEVEN

CHLOE HUDDLED INTO the extra warm scarf Beau had loaned her. She'd wound it around her neck twice and it still covered her from chin to chest, the tails of the scarf angling beneath her coat to cover her breasts. The thought of chests and breasts, though, had her recalling the broad, lean strength of Beau's chest under her hands earlier. And when he'd touched her breasts…

Her lungs cramped and it was hard to breathe. Closing her eyes, she did what she could to unclench herself.

Thank God he'd given her time to think.

Thank God he'd kept his wits about him.

If he hadn't they'd have made love and… She swallowed. It would've been a mistake.

Are you sure about that?

Of course she was! It—

She bit back a groan. She ached with need. She wanted Beau so badly it had become a physical pain and she couldn't think of anything else. Didn't want to think of anything else.

She ought to be thinking about Mark!

Why? some inner demon demanded.

She choked on her glühwein. He'd been her *husband*. She'd loved him!

Had been. Had loved. Past tense, Chlo.

For the first time, rather than tear her apart, that realisation simply made her sad.

'Too strong?' Beau asked, nodding towards her environmentally friendly cardboard cup.

The stall vendor had told her that once he'd watched Beau's first documentary about the impact of plastics and global warming on the natural world, he'd immediately moved to more environmentally friendly products. In fact, the whole village had. They were so proud of him. She didn't think he realised just how much.

'Would you like me to get you something else instead? Hot chocolate?'

Her head lifted. 'Hot chocolate?'

'Made with the finest Dutch chocolate on real milk.'

Oh, my God, that sounded delicious—perfect, sweet… comforting.

He laughed at whatever he saw in her face. Moving to a nearby stall, he returned moments later with a steaming mug of hot chocolate.

She buried her nose in the fragrant steam, glancing everywhere but at him. Coloured lights hung from the shops that surrounded the village green and the scent of cinnamon and gingerbread filled the air. She pulled the fragrance into her lungs. 'The village looks pretty.'

'It really does.'

His frown had her eyebrows lifting. 'Why the surprise?'

'I don't know. I just…forgot.' He shook his head, his frown deepening. 'I'm coming to the sobering realisation that maybe I've been focussing too much on the ugliness of life rather than its beauty.'

The admission speared into her.

'Once upon a time I always noticed the beauty. I could see beneath any surface ugliness to what was hidden below. Deserts and mudflats aren't necessarily beautiful, but the life they contain…'

'The fact that life can exist in such harsh or strange places, there's beauty in that.'

'Exactly.' He gestured around. 'But one doesn't need to dig deep to find the beauty here in Ballingsmallard. The stone houses, the pretty lights. And nearby Exmoor is stunning.'

She'd read about Exmoor National Park and had every intention of visiting. 'When was the last time you had a ramble there?'

He didn't answer and she knew he hadn't been to Exmoor since his accident, even though it was practically on his doorstep.

He gestured. 'Looks like the ceremony is about to start.'

Three dignitaries mounted a temporary stage in front of the giant tree at the centre of the green. She sipped her hot chocolate and tried to focus on the festive message that the mayoress gave, but she was too aware of Beau—of his heat and latent power and how her body responded to every minute movement he made.

She straightened, though, when the tree lit up in a riot of colour. It was so pretty! Then the church choir sang 'Silent Night' and a lump lodged in her throat. She found herself leaning into Beau, needing the comfort of a friend in the same way she'd needed the comfort of the hot chocolate.

She was grateful when he didn't say anything, just put his arm around her shoulders and drew her against the warmth of his side. There was nothing suggestive or sexualised about the act. It was comfort and friendship. Nothing more.

But you want it to be more.

She ignored that. When the choir broke into a joyful rendition of 'Hark! The Herald Angels Sing' something inside her felt suddenly lighter.

'Okay, quick,' she ordered, moving out of his arms. 'You have to capture this on video.'

He snapped immediately into action and she could've hugged him.

He recorded a short video of her telling her family all about the tree lighting, extolling the virtues of hot chocolate, and then she pointed towards one of the nearby food vendors. 'I have no idea what that vendor is cooking, but it looks intriguing. As long as it's not something disgusting like snails or puppy dogs' tails, I'm going to try it.'

'Roasted chestnuts,' Beau said.

'Roasted chestnuts? Sounds delicious! I'll let you all know what I think in my next email. Love to everyone! I miss you all.' She blew a kiss to the camera and Beau sent her a thumbs up.

'That was great. You're a natural.'

He was the natural. She was just chatting to her family, and that was a piece of cake. There was no way she could speak to a camera knowing thousands of strangers were watching. Beau was the one with real talent, and a part of her wept that all of that talent and passion was going to waste.

'You're doing a great job, you know, Chloe.'

She snapped back.

'This is going to assure your family that all is well.'

Actually, the smiling and acting happy hadn't been as hard as she'd thought it would be. The thought made her frown, but she shook it off and followed Beau to the roasted chestnut stall.

'Can I ask you something?' he asked a little while later when they were munching on roasted chestnuts.

Which, by the way, were *truly* delicious. She glanced up. 'Sure.'

'It's personal,' he warned.

She spluttered a laugh, even as things inside her tightened. 'Of course it is. I'm not sure we know any other way to be with each other.'

That utterly divine and perfect mouth firmed…gentled… and then smiled. 'You could be right.'

She dragged her gaze from his mouth. 'Your question?'

He popped a chestnut in his mouth and chewed thoughtfully. 'I understand why your first Christmas without Mark was devastating. And I understand why the second one was too, marking as it did the anniversary of his death and knocking you for six again.'

She waited for the bone-crushing tension and weight of her grief to crush her, as it always did whenever she spoke about how lost she'd been without Mark during those first two Christmases, and kept waiting. Oh, there was the weight of sadness, but it wasn't crippling. Not as it had once been.

An awful thought struck her. Had her anger extinguished it? Anger that he'd taken out the second mortgage without telling her? That anger had been directed at herself just as much as it had been at him, though. She didn't want anger to be the lasting legacy left between them.

She halted and forced herself to bring his face to mind. It didn't make her flinch. It didn't make her want to cry… or to rail and rage. Was that a loss or a blessing?

'Chloe?'

She glanced up into summer-sea eyes. 'I don't miss him the way I used to. I feel bad about that.'

'It's to be expected,' he said gently. 'It's been two years. You've been forced to live without him, been forced to move on whether you liked it or not. It doesn't make you a bad person.'

'We promised each other forever.'

He took both bags of chestnuts and pushed them into the pockets of his coat before seizing her hands. 'Chloe, the two of you were hoping for forever, but you promised *till death do us part.*'

His words should've made her flinch, but they didn't.

'Would he want you to grieve him forever?'

'Of course not.' Nobody wanted that for the people they loved. They'd want them to move on and be happy.

'I feel like somewhere along the line I moved on and said goodbye without even realising it,' she blurted out. 'It feels wrong. Surely it should've been marked by some grand event or...'

She couldn't continue as tears clogged her throat and she found herself engulfed in Beau's cool, rich scent as strong arms went around her and pulled her to his chest. After a moment's hesitation she wrapped her arms around his waist and held on and tried to focus on her breathing. Holding onto Beau made her feel anchored as the panic and confusion pounded at her. For as long as she held onto him, it felt as though the badness couldn't overwhelm her. And like a storm blowing itself out, the guilt and regret slowly bled away.

She bumped back to earth, aware of people milling nearby and casting curious glances in their direction. Heavens, she was drawing attention to them and that was the one thing Beau hated.

She eased away and sent him a shaky smile. 'Sorry.'

He shook his head, those eyes searching her face. 'Nothing to apologise for. You okay?'

'Strangely enough, I am.' She laughed and pushed her hair back behind her ear, tried to appear perfectly normal.

Except being so close to him had ignited that latent demon inside her—the one that wanted her to drag Beau back home to his grand manor house, tear his clothes off and make wild, uninhibited love with him *just for fun*. And as soon as the notion lodged in her brain, a part of her demanded to know why that couldn't happen.

Because she'd be filled with regret and remorse afterwards.

No, you won't.

The denial rang through her, making her blink…making her stand taller.

'Hungry?' Beau asked. 'Did you want to go across to the pub for something more substantial than chestnuts?' He glanced down and stilled at whatever it was he saw in her eyes.

'I'm hungry, but not for food.' She kept her voice low. She didn't want anyone overhearing their conversation. 'Can I ask you a question?'

'I haven't asked mine yet.'

That made her blink. 'Okay, well, ask it.'

'I think I'd rather hear yours.'

Desire had flared to life in his eyes and it made her knees weak. Nobody had made her knees weak before. She'd had butterflies, happy shivers, and that sense of free-fall floating before, but not weak knees. All of them assailed her now.

She gripped the tails of her scarf in an effort to stop from throwing herself into his arms and making a spectacle of them both. She moved into the deeper shadows, away from the enormous lighted Christmas tree and food vendors, and he followed.

'You said that if I wanted to have sex just for fun that you would be the perfect person to do that with.' His quick intake of breath sounded loud in the quiet and shadows and an ache started up at the centre of her. 'What does that mean? That you've a lot of experience with that kind of thing?'

'I've had some experience,' he said carefully, 'but that's not what I meant. Your life isn't here in England, but mine is. If you and I are the proverbial ships passing in the night then Dawncarden is merely the harbour you've docked in for the next couple of months. If we were to become lovers, Chloe, there'd be no expectations. We both know you're leaving at the end of your contract, and whatever happens between us is temporary. There's something freeing about that, don't you think?'

She nodded slowly. 'It makes me feel…uninhibited.' She shivered, but not from the cold. Beneath her layers of clothes her nipples beaded.

'You can explore a part of yourself you never have before.'

'And what about you? What do you get?'

He moved in so close she could feel his breath on her cheek. 'I get to make love with a woman who has bewitched me from the moment she introduced herself as Chloe Ivy Belle Jennings. I get to feel alive again in a way I never thought I would. I get to…not hide.'

That last admission punched the breath from her body. He didn't need to hide. Not from her.

'Beau?'

'Yes?'

'Can we go back to Dawncarden *now*?'

He didn't answer. He just grabbed her hand and started for the car.

The moment they burst through the back door and into the warmth of the kitchen, Chloe seized Beau's face in her hands and kissed him, open-mouthed and hungry. He answered her hunger with his own. Thrusting a hand in her hair, he cradled her skull, angling her head until he could ravish her mouth, raking her need until his name was dragged from her throat.

She needed him now!

He glanced at the kitchen table. 'I've had dreams about stretching you out on that table and doing things to your body until you're screaming for a release, but tonight at least I need to pretend to be a gentleman rather than a caveman and—'

'To hell with that!' She was tugging off her boots and

socks and leaving them where they fell and dropping her coat to the floor. 'I don't want a gentleman. I want you, Beau.'

She hauled her jumper over her head, taking the long-sleeved T-shirt with it. Her hands went to the waistband of her jeans, but he moved in close, his hands clamping over hers, and that weak-kneed, tummy-fluttering thing swamped her.

'Are you sure about this?'

She nodded. 'I'm sure, Beau. Very sure. I want you *now*.'

It was a cry from her soul and he answered it with a deep drugging kiss. All she could do was wrap her arms around his shoulders and hold on tight.

He divested her of her jeans and panties, her bra, and she'd managed to drag his jumper over his head, but then his hands were on her nakedness, doing things to her that made her breath catch and gasp and sending her mindless with desire and need.

Lifting her, he laid her on the table with a gentleness that had a lump forming in her throat. His eyes glittered as he stared down at her. She had a feeling she ought to feel self-conscious, but she didn't. The approval and fire in his eyes were all that she needed. She wanted to be wanton for him, to prove that he was virile and beautiful despite his scars.

'You are beautiful,' he said, his voice hoarse.

'And you're wearing too many clothes,' she said, her voice just as husky.

That glorious mouth hooked up. 'You have no idea the kind of lustful thoughts I've had about you and this table.'

'Then let's put them into action,' she said, feeling bold as the demands of her body for release overcame any veneer of either politeness or composure.

'Oh, I'm planning to, sweetheart, don't have any doubt about that.'

Seizing her legs beneath her thighs, he pulled her down

the table until she was flush against the hardness in his jeans. Stars burst behind her eyelids.

'You need to be naked,' she started to croak, but he leaned down instead and took one beaded nipple into his mouth and grazed it gently with his teeth, his hands resting firmly on her shoulders to keep her in place, and nothing had ever felt hotter in her life.

Beau explored every inch of Chloe's body and revelled in the scent, feel and taste of her. Her gasps and moans urging him on. This moment, now, marked a new beginning for her, and he wanted to help her mark that milestone with fireworks and fun. And no regrets. It was that knowledge that helped him keep his rampaging desires in check and to focus wholly on her.

Settling between her thighs, he loved her with his mouth and tongue, his hands firm on her hips to keep her still as he concentrated on bringing her to the brink of orgasm and holding her there in the throes of imminent pleasure before hurtling her over the edge. Her cries rang in his ears, making something in him lift and dance. He rested his cheek lightly on her stomach as he waited for her to descend back to earth.

He didn't move until he felt her hands flutter, and then he glanced up to find her eyes had filled with tears.

'Oh, sweetheart.' His gut clenched and for some absurd reason his throat thickened, his eyes stinging too in sympathy. 'You promised me you wouldn't cry.'

Before he could pull her into the shelter of his arms, where he wished he could wipe away all her pain, she sat up, her hands going either side of his face, and she shook her head. 'Not sad, not regretful—happy tears.' And then she pulled him in for a kiss so full of warmth and joy he felt as if he were wrapped in a blanket in front of a roaring fire with a myriad woodland animals cavorting around him.

Oh, for God's sake, get a grip.

She rested her forehead against his. 'Thank you, Beau. Just…thank you.'

She made him feel like a superhero, as if he were capable of anything and everything; that he was the best lover that had ever lived. 'Any time,' he said with a grin, and he meant it.

'So…' She eased back and moistened her lips, her eyes going so dark they were almost black. 'You've played out your fantasy. Does that mean I can play out mine now?'

She could have whatever she damn well pleased 'What's your fantasy?'

'Getting you naked and straddling you in that chair.' She nodded at the nearest kitchen chair. His groin, his throat, his very skin tightened until he thought he'd burst. 'Condoms are in my bedside drawer,' was all he could manage to croak.

'My fantasy just changed to straddling you in your bed.'

Her breath had grown shallow and uneven and if he could've, he'd have laughed at the speed of her reply. Instead he lifted her in his arms and strode through the baronial hall, up the staircase, and down the corridor to his bedroom.

They shucked his clothes with more speed than grace and then she pushed him back onto the bed and he submitted. She clearly wanted to be in charge and he wanted her to have everything she wanted.

'I don't want to wait,' she whispered.

He nodded to tell her that was fine by him, unable to get words out through clenched teeth as she sheathed him with a condom. Her hands on his body set off electric charges. Then she lowered herself onto him with an impatience that he found edifying but it pushed him immediately to the edges of his limits.

Dear God! She felt warm and soft and perfect and the

way her body gripped him had him throwing his head back with a low growl.

She stilled. His eyes flew to hers and he found her staring at him, eyes as huge as an owl's. He took her hands, lifted them to his mouth. 'Is everything okay? If you want to stop, Chloe, that *is* okay.' He gritted his teeth and it took all of his strength to not move. It would be okay. It was her prerogative. He would behave like a gentleman, not a caveman.

'I don't want to stop.'

He gazed heavenward. 'Thank you, God,' he whispered.

'It's just…you feel perfect.'

She moved up and down tentatively, making him grip the sheets in his hands. 'So do you,' he ground out.

'*Really* perfect.'

He realised she was right. Had he ever felt so in tune with someone so immediately? He started to frown, but then she moved with a calculated intent and a growing passion that he was powerless to resist. He didn't want to resist. It flung him out of himself and had him hurtling towards the stars. When her body clenched around his as she climaxed, he followed with a loud cry that felt wrenched from the very depths of his soul. A cry that left him feeling clean and whole…and happy.

He pulled her close into his side, and they lay there with closed eyes, relishing the warm hum of their bodies. And it was a long time before either one of them returned back to earth and reason.

They made love again later that night, and then again in the morning when they showered together. As they lay in his king-size bed, her fingers lightly playing across his chest as his brushed up and down her spine in light lazy strokes, he wanted the moment to last forever.

'So…' She rested her chin on his chest and glanced up

at him, her lips curving into a smile that had him itching to kiss her again. 'What was the question you were going to ask me last night? The *personal* question?'

Ah...

She frowned and eased away. 'Is it something awful?'

He smoothed out her brow with his finger. 'I don't think so. If it is, then just say so and we'll forget about it.'

'Okay, spill.'

'I just wondered why, when you haven't put on a front for your family for the last two Christmases, why you're doing so this Christmas.'

Her lips immediately drooped and he mentally kicked himself for asking. He should've saved it for another time. Or not asked about it at all. She rested her head on his shoulder and he could no longer see her face. 'We don't have to talk about it, Chloe. Not if you don't want to.'

'It's okay. I feel as if I could tell you anything and you wouldn't tell another soul.'

Her words shorted his breath. He had to swallow before he could speak. 'I know what it's like to feel exposed. I'd never reveal your secrets, even if I didn't agree with them.'

'Ditto,' she murmured, her breath a soft brush of warmth on his chest.

She was quiet for a long moment, before pulling in a deep breath. 'I told you how devastated I was after Mark died and how I lost interest in everything. I did the physical work required of me at the garden centre, but I was moving through a thick fog and mentally not present most of the time.'

His arm tightened about her. He wished she'd been spared such pain.

'Earlier this year, I started to come out of that fog, much to everyone's relief.'

'You'd started to turn your face to the future. You shouldn't feel guilty about that, Chloe.'

She nodded, but it was more an absent acknowledgement than a heartfelt acceptance. 'It meant that Mark's parents finally felt able to tell me the dire straits the business had been in.'

He stiffened.

She eased away and they both sat up against the pillows. 'They'd been trying to protect me but could no longer keep the truth from me. Without my knowledge, Mark had taken out a second mortgage on our house to help keep the business afloat. And the bank was threatening to foreclose.'

Hell!

'And then I got so damn angry—at Mark for doing that without discussing it with me first, with my in-laws for keeping me in the dark for so long, though I know they were only trying to protect me, but mostly with myself for taking so long to care about anything else beyond my own grief when I could've been doing something to help turn things around.'

'I'm sorry, Chloe.' Would she accept a loan from him? Whether the answer was a yes or a no, instinct told him now wouldn't be the right time to make the offer.

'But, Beau, I've put *my* family through enough. They loved Mark. I didn't want to burden them with any further woes.'

His heart burned. She'd been dealing with this all alone?

'But I knew I'd never be able to get through Christmas convincingly enough for them, and my mother...' She blew out a breath, looking deliciously rumpled and sexy. 'Well, you've met her. She can be like a dog with a bone once she senses something is wrong. Besides, I want to fix the problem on my own, and I don't want them offering to go into debt to bail me out. I'm not letting them do that.' She met his gaze. 'They deserve to enjoy this Christmas unmarred by my dramas.'

He didn't know if he agreed with that or not, but he

couldn't deny that her actions were pure. She loved her family. She wanted only good things for them. And she wanted to protect their memory of Mark. But… He dragged in a breath. 'Are you, though?'

'Am I what?'

'Fixing the problem.'

She gnawed on her bottom lip. 'The commission you've paid me so far has giving me breathing space as far as the house goes.'

But she probably needed another contract like this one, maybe two, to get back on her feet properly. She probably needed to keep the money rolling in and—

Beau slapped a hand to his brow. 'That's why you asked if you could take photos of my garden for your portfolio!'

'But I totally see your point,' she said, neither confirming nor denying the claim. 'The garden is going to be your haven. I understand why you don't want to share it with anyone.'

She made him sound like some kind of selfish recluse!

'I respect that, Beau.'

He went back over all the things she'd said and all that he knew about her and frowned.

She sat up straighter. 'What?'

'We need coffee and toast and bacon.'

'You want to build me up before slugging me with more reality?'

He ignored that. 'Would a testimonial from me help?' She could add that to her portfolio and it would help provide the kudos she needed.

Her face lit up as she pulled his robe around her. 'Yes!'

'Consider it done.'

'Oh, Beau, thank you and—'

He waved her thanks away. 'Meet me in the kitchen in five.'

He cooked because, despite evidence to the contrary, he

did know his way about a kitchen and he wanted to cook for her, wanted to care for her. Last night—and this morning—had been special. He wanted her to feel special too.

They dug into their food with gusto. Once the worst of their hunger had been sated, he eased back in his chair. 'Chloe, tell me, what's the worst thing that would happen if you couldn't pay the bank back?'

Her knife and fork clattered to her plate. 'I'd lose the home Mark and I made together.'

'Do you the love the house?'

'Of course I do! It's where we planned to have a family and *everything*.'

She might've felt that she'd said goodbye to Mark in some significant way, but clearly she wasn't ready to let him go completely. 'You want to keep living there although he's gone?'

Her eyebrows grew fierce. 'I don't see why not. It's not like I'm ever going to have another long-term relationship.'

Everything inside him stilled. 'Why not?'

She leaned towards him. 'Because losing someone you love is too hard. I feel as if I lost the last two years of my life, Beau. I'm not going through that again.'

But she had such a big heart. She deserved someone who'd love her and cherish her and look after her.

'Besides, the house is close to the garden centre, and once I've made enough money to get out of debt, I'll throw all of my energies into building up the design side of things there.'

His heart began to pound. 'Is that really the life you want? It seems to me that working in a garden centre would stifle your talents, rather than making the most of them.' And working with Mark's family would certainly stifle her love life. 'You think you'd be content designing suburban backyards instead of making over the gardens of grand estates or parks?' Which was clearly where her talents lay.

She opened her mouth but he pushed on. 'Think about it. You were forced to take drastic measures—like pitch for a high-status job like the one you landed here—but can you deny your enthusiasm for it? You can try telling yourself it's because circumstances demanded you needed to do something big to bring in a decent amount of money fast, but I've seen the way your whole being lights up when you're in the garden out there. Your vision is *big*. Would working at the garden centre bring you the same sense of satisfaction?'

She stared at him as if she didn't know what to say.

He pointed at her. 'You could sell up and strike out on your own. For heaven's sake, you should be designing amazing gardens—both public and private—not talking customers through the pros and cons of x mulch versus y mulch or how to deadhead azaleas.'

'Mark and I planned—'

'Mark isn't here any more.' He said the words as gently as he could. 'Why do you feel honour-bound to lead the life you planned together without him?'

'You want me to reimagine my whole life?'

'Why not? Your whole life was turned upside down after Mark's accident. Why not decide what *your* passion is and chase that instead?'

CHAPTER EIGHT

THE WORDS HELD a temptation Chloe didn't want to acknowledge. They made her feel as if she were betraying Mark in a more fundamental way than making love with Beau had.

Making love with Beau hadn't felt like a betrayal, but a step forward. This though…?

She leapt up to pace, flinging out her arms. 'You're a fine one to talk about chasing one's passion. Look at you, hiding away here like some tragic Victorian madam. It's laughable! And a damn shame too, if you ask me.'

'Nobody did ask you.'

His lips had turned white and he'd become as icy as she was heated. 'Oh, I see.' She slapped a hand to her head as if in sudden enlightenment 'I ought to follow my passion and the things that bring me joy, while you get to hide yourself away from all the things that remind you of your former life.'

He shot to his feet. 'I'm building a new life!'

'No, you're not! You're just trying to hide from your old one, trying to hide from all that you've lost and desperately want back. And the walled garden is a sticking plaster that isn't going to cut it, not in the long term.' He deserved better. Couldn't he see that? 'And what's the real reason you continue hiding out here? Because you're scared people are going to stare at your face and point. *Get over it!*'

'Easy for you say!'

'I'd rather be coming to terms with scars than coming to terms with my husband's death.'

Her words echoed in the sudden silence. Had it been unworthy of her to hurl them at him?

She dragged in a breath, tried to moderate her breathing. 'You love making documentaries. You came alive when you spoke to camera about the pipistrelles. It was amazing. And you want to know why it matters so much to me?' She ploughed on before he could tell her he couldn't care less. 'The world needs people like you, Beau. People who can show the rest of us the small changes we can make in our lives that will have a big impact on our forests and oceans, people who teach us to value all living things and can convince us to make the sacrifices necessary to ensure those living things get a chance to survive…people who make us care.'

He stared at her as if he had no idea what to say.

'You made us care about things that really matter, Beau.' Tears burned her eyes. 'It'll be a tragedy if you don't keep doing that.'

'I was dumped.' His hands clenched. 'My network dumped me.'

'So maybe you can't keep doing it in the same way. Maybe you need to find another way, even if it is on a smaller scale. Start your own YouTube channel and do all the filming yourself or hook up with a community channel or something. Or think bigger.'

One eyebrow rose.

'You have a lot of money, right?' She hitched up her chin. 'So buy a TV network of your own. Nobody could sack you then.'

He leaned towards her, brow furrowed. 'Damn it, Chloe, you have no idea how these things work and—'

'But you do!'

He stilled. Blinked. She didn't know if her words had struck a chord. Or hit a sore spot.

What she became increasingly sure of was that the heat that had engulfed her was now less about temper and more about desire. She couldn't stop her gaze from travelling over the powerful lines of his body, or stop remembering all the ways they'd given each other pleasure.

She wasn't sure if he recognised the new direction her thoughts had taken or not, but his shoulders lost their tension and while he still scowled at her, it had lost its heat. 'Clearly, just because we've become lovers, doesn't mean we've learned to be more polite to each other or less inclined to speak our minds.'

'I don't see why that should change. You think I'm being an idiot and weren't shy about telling me so. I don't see why I shouldn't tell you that you're being an idiot too.'

'I didn't call you an idiot!'

'It's what you meant.' She glared at him. 'It doesn't mean I don't still trust you. Or like you.'

'Ditto.' His nose curled, but she could've sworn there was a hint of a smile in his eyes.

He raked her up and down with that hot gaze and everything inside her clamoured for him and the release she knew he could bring her. 'I can't get enough of you at the moment,' she blurted out, unsure if that was a good thing or a bad thing. 'You are so *hot*.'

'And you are temptation personified.'

She glanced at the kitchen chair she'd pointed to last night and then raised an eyebrow. 'Yes?'

'Yes,' he growled back.

She pushed him into the chair and followed him down, straddling his lap, and he started laughing. Things inside her suddenly soared free and she found herself laughing too. And then her mouth met his in a hot hungry dance and blotted everything else from her mind.

Later that afternoon, lying naked on a thick rug in the baronial hall, a fire crackling in the hearth and the lights of the tree twinkling, and with Beau's broad chest beneath her cheek, Chloe couldn't remember feeling so replete or when she'd last felt such peace.

Obviously she must've done in the past with Mark. They'd been so in love. But peace had eluded her since his death, and she welcomed it now. Maybe that was why she allowed her mind to go over all that Beau had said over breakfast about finding a new direction for her life.

'Do you really think I could make a go of it if I went out on my own as a garden designer?'

The hand tracing intriguing patterns on her back stilled before beginning its idle tracing again. 'I do. You're wonderfully talented. You can look at a space and see what it can become. When I first saw the initial plans and the sketches you'd made for the walled garden, they blew me away.'

Really?

'You'd captured everything I said was non-negotiable, but you put them together in a way I hadn't envisaged, and then you added elements I hadn't considered. I found myself wanting those elements more than my original vision. It was both familiar and not. You made it better than I could imagine.'

She lifted her head. 'What a lovely thing to say.'

He glanced down at her. 'It's the truth.' And she could tell he meant it. 'That's why the contract went to you, even though you didn't have the same level of experience as some of the other bidders. You have a vision that's unique. It's a gift. And I think once the right people realise it, you're going to be in serious demand.'

She rested her cheek against his chest again, pulled the blanket up a few extra inches to keep him warm.

'Tell me about the garden centre. Why did you and Mark decide to go into business with his family?'

She nestled into him, relishing his warmth and vitality, along with his clean scent and the very *maleness* of him. He was right. Sex for fun could be a *very* enjoyable experience.

'I think I mentioned before that Mark was doing a Business degree when we met.'

'You did.'

'His parents owned a little local hardware store in the south-west of Sydney and the nursery next door came up for sale just as we were finishing up our degrees.' She shrugged. It'd felt like a no-brainer at the time. 'We took it as a sign that we should combine the two businesses. I could take care of the nursery side of things with a view to moving into garden design once we were in the black, Mark was to take care of the business side of things, while his mum and dad headed up the hardware side of the business.'

He shifted slightly and then pulled her even closer. If he did too much of that, there wouldn't be conversation again for a very long time. How could she still be so hungry for this man?

'But you'd won an award. You could've found a position with a big-name firm doing large-scale design work. Didn't you resent not being able to follow that path?'

'I won that award while I was still at uni, Beau—for one of my assignments. One of my tutors entered it without my knowledge. Don't get me wrong, I was over the moon to have won, but I hadn't figured out what career direction I wanted to take at that stage.' She'd been too in love. 'And the thought of Mark and I being able to work together, well…we both thought that was wonderful.'

'I see.'

She heard the frown in his voice and sat up, keeping the blanket clasped to her chest in the interests of modesty. Not that modesty had been all that important to her an hour ago. 'What?'

He eased into a sitting position and then picked her up and moved them to the sofa, the two of them propped up on opposite ends facing each other, their legs entangled. The blanket was big enough to cover them—from her chest to his waist. If she tugged it just a little, though, it'd slide down and—

'Behave,' he said with a low laugh, and she found herself grinning. 'Before we get sidetracked, I want you to know that my *I see* wasn't about you. It was about me.'

'How so?'

'I'm clearly a selfish sod, but I'm glad I didn't meet anyone while I was studying, that I felt free to follow my own dreams.'

He'd started to massage her foot and it took all of her strength not to start purring. 'That's not being selfish. It's just being focussed. You always knew you wanted to make documentaries?'

'I always knew I wanted to be a natural historian, and the moment I took a documentary elective, the moment I started talking to a camera…' He shrugged. 'You're right, it felt as if something inside me had come alive.'

Did that mean he was considering what she'd said to him earlier? She bit the question back. She'd said more than enough on the subject for one day.

'I'm glad I had nothing distracting me from following the path I'd started to see for myself.'

She'd fallen in love with a person. He'd fallen in love with a career. But what if she hadn't fallen in love with Mark? What if they'd never met?

The thought made her blink. Maybe she'd have gone on

and made a name for herself, just as Beau had said. Maybe she'd have been gloriously happy and successful.

The thought shook her to her foundations. She'd always thought fate had thrown her and Mark together, but maybe there wasn't just one path a person was meant to follow, one path that would make them happy. Maybe there were multiple paths that led to all different kinds of fulfilment and happiness.

So what if she lost the house? Maybe she could get a trendy apartment in the inner city. Maybe she could travel the world designing amazing gardens and working with designers she revered.

A strange new energy stirred inside her.

'Did you enjoy working at the garden centre?'

She pulled her mind back. 'In the early days it was exciting. It was great to have free rein to do what I wanted. And we developed a great team. The staff became like family. I was proud of what we were achieving.'

He nodded. 'Good.'

'Of course, that all changed when Mark died.'

He held her foot to his chest, just above his heart, and she could feel the strong beat through her sole. 'I'm sorry that happened, Chloe.'

'I know.' But would she have eventually become bored with the garden centre? Would she have wanted the bigger dreams Beau had held up to her? 'If I sold the house I'd be able to pay the bank back and help the garden centre get back in the black. I'd be able to repay Mark's family for carrying me as a deadweight for the last two years.'

'I bet deadweight isn't how they see you.'

'They wouldn't. They're lovely people. But it's the truth. They've been carrying me for far too long and that has to stop.'

'Good for you.'

'You might have a point, Beau. Maybe I do need to rethink my direction and start dreaming different dreams.'

His fingers stilled on her foot. 'You mean that?'

'I don't know.' It scared her senseless, but beneath it lay a thread of something that felt right too. At the very least it deserved consideration. 'But I'm prepared to make a deal with you.'

His eyes narrowed. 'What kind of deal?'

'That I'll think very carefully about all you said to me earlier, if you'll do the same about what I said to you.'

He tensed, and she sensed his immediate antipathy. Before he could reject it outright, she added, 'All I'm asking you to do is *think* about it. To not dismiss it out of hand until you've considered it from all angles. Maybe it's not the right way forward. But maybe it is. And if it is then you need to work out a way to make it happen.'

His nostrils flared and his hands tightened about her foot, but eventually he let out a breath and his grip eased. 'All I'm promising is to think about it? And in return you will too?'

She nodded. 'But this is a real promise, not just something either one of us is paying lip service to. If you make the promise, I'm trusting you to keep your word.'

His gaze darkened. 'If I make you any promise, Chloe, I *will* keep it.' He settled back against the arm of the sofa. 'If I agree, will you let me see your breasts?'

She choked back a laugh. 'Yes.'

'Then we have a deal.'

She immediately lowered the blanket, laughter bubbling up through her, and when his laughter joined hers it made her feel invincible.

Beau only made the promise because every instinct he had told him Chloe would be happier following a new direction—one she forged for herself. She shouldn't be shackling herself to an old dream that would prove empty and unsatisfying without Mark. She deserved something more than a life throbbing with loss.

Besides, he'd only promised to think about it. That was all. How hard could it be?

He rolled his shoulders. Considering how much he'd avoided thinking about it for the last fourteen months, he suspected it'd be awful. But…

Maybe it was necessary. Maybe it'd help him move into the future with a lighter heart.

'There's something else I want to ask of you.'

The tone of Chloe's voice had all the fine hairs on his arms lifting, though he kept his voice deliberately light. 'What's that?'

'You said you want to ease your grandmother's worry?'

The deeper reason for his grandmother's concern, the reason she'd enlisted Stephanie and George's help to ensure he didn't descend into the extremes of despair that had led his father into addiction, all while doing her best not to stifle him, made him sick to the stomach. He should've realised it sooner. She deserved better from him.

'Beau, you study the natural world.'

She leaned towards him and the blanket shifted slightly, hinting at the shadows between her breasts, and his mouth went dry. For a moment all he could think about was making love with her again.

'You have Exmoor practically on your doorstep. You should be taking advantage of it and losing yourself there.'

Things inside him shied away in protest. At the same time, though, the natural historian in him raised its head. The temptation had been rattling around inside him ever since she'd mentioned Exmoor the other night.

But he would inevitably come across other ramblers, maybe even other researchers. And what if the press got wind of it and came hunting him again? He couldn't stand a repeat of that media circus.

She leaned forward even further. He did what he could to keep his gaze on her face rather than her chest. 'Before I go back to Australia, I want you to take me on an excursion to Exmoor and show me something amazing.'

What on earth would she consider amazing?

He scowled, but he suspected it lacked its normal heat because she merely eased back and raised an eyebrow, not looking the slightest bit intimidated. 'And what do I get in return?'

'You get to show your grandmother a piece of video footage that you take there and the satisfaction of knowing you're easing her mind.'

She made a strong argument. Knowing he was spending time in the national park would ease his grandmother's mind as nothing else could. It ought to have occurred to him sooner.

'And I'll cook you turkey with all the trimmings on Christmas Day,' she added, as if she could get around him via his stomach.

He stared at her. Her mother would love the photos of a Christmas dinner with all the trimmings. 'You'd do that for me, even though you're not all that interested in celebrating the season?'

'Absolutely.'

He held out his hand and they shook on it.

'I've thought of something else your families would love, Chloe.'

That bright gaze swung back.

'What if we were to video-call with them on Christmas morning, and show them how much we're enjoying all the trappings and outline our plans for the day—including that roast turkey dinner?'

She hesitated. 'Are you sure you wouldn't mind appearing on screen with me?'

Not if it meant easing her mother's mind. 'Like I said, I liked your mum. It'd be nice to see her again.' And he was curious about the rest of her family—her dad and brothers and sister. It'd be nice to put faces to names.

'You're an absolute sweetheart, you know that, Beau Diamond?'

If she kept looking at him like that he was going to have to kiss her.

'There is a catch, though.' He bit back a grin. 'It means buying each other Christmas presents.'

She blinked and a slow smile transformed her face, and it made his heart bump and bounce in his chest. 'You're talking about making up silly Christmas stockings for each other, aren't you?'

He nodded.

'*That* is inspired.'

He wished her mother could see her face now. Because it was clear to him that Chloe's Christmas spirit was beginning to return. The thought that he'd had a hand in that lifted him as nothing else had in the past fourteen months.

'Right.' He clapped his hands. 'Sounds like we'll be visiting the Christmas markets in the village tonight.'

While the markets weren't huge, they were a long-established tradition and Ballingsmallard was picture-postcard-pretty, which meant they did draw people from further afield. Beau was careful to keep his beanie drawn low down on his forehead and his scarf wrapped up high to shield his face.

'The presents need to be surprises.' Chloe pointed one mittened finger at him. 'That's part of the fun.'

He'd do anything to keep that smile on her face. 'Let's split up, then, and meet back here in an hour.'

He hadn't realised before that Christmas shopping could be so much fun. In the past he'd always considered it a bit of a chore, but trying to figure out what to put in Chloe's Christmas stocking—what would make her smile and laugh—had him glued to the task. While he was at it, he found a beautiful silk scarf he knew his grandmother would love. He'd send it express post to Florence, so she had it in time for Christmas.

He was back at the designated spot with plenty of time to spare, but he didn't mind waiting. It was a cold night, but he'd rugged up warm. A glance at the sky informed him they were in no danger of rain…or snow. The stars twinkled brightly and—

He stilled…and clapped a hand to his brow. Chloe had said she wanted to see *something amazing*. He knew exactly what he'd show her. And it'd blow her socks off.

A few minutes later she came running up, her breath misting the air and a smile on her lips. 'I love the Christmas markets!'

He pointed at all her bags. 'I bet the vendors loved you too. Did you leave anything for anyone else to buy or did you clear the stalls out?'

'I had to buy gifts for everyone at home and…oh, it was just irresistible. I forgot how much fun it was to buy presents.'

'What did you get?'

He pretended to crane his neck to peek at her bags. Laughing, she hid them behind her back. 'Never you mind, Mr Stickybeak.'

'Dinner at the pub?'

'Sounds perfect.'

Much, much later, when she was wrapped up in his arm and he was drifting off to sleep, Beau couldn't help but think the entire day had been perfect.

All the fine hairs on his arms suddenly lifted and his

eyes snapped open. He'd been here before, feeling on top of the world and thinking everything was perfect. It had been a *good* day, but this was all temporary. He'd been a fool to forget it.

Letting out a breath, he relaxed back against the pillows. He knew the score. He could enjoy this while it lasted without thinking it meant anything. It was simply all of those feel-good endorphins their lovemaking had released. He closed his eyes. He wasn't a fool. He had no intention of mistaking them for anything else.

'We're going out?'

'Rug up warm,' he ordered, tossing her one of his warmest woollen jumpers. 'Put that on over your own jumper, wear two pairs of socks under your boots, plus you'll need your gloves *and* mittens, and your coat.'

Bending down, she glanced out of the window. 'But it's going to be dark soon.'

'Hence the reason you need to rug up warm.'

'We're going out *again*? But that'll be two nights in a row.' She stared at him, hands on hips. 'Careful, Beau, you're in danger of turning into a social butterfly.'

Her words made him throw his head back and laugh. In a little while she was going to retract that accusation roundly. She stared, her lips parting as if she'd found it suddenly hard to get air into her lungs. As if the sight of him laughing did something to her. Their gazes caught and clung. Maybe going out could wait till tomorrow night and—

With an effort he dragged his mind back to the task at hand. The weather was changing tomorrow, and he'd promised to show her something amazing. Besides, he was eager to see her reaction. He wanted to see if she'd love it as much as he did. 'C'mon, chop-chop. Time's a wasting.'

Without further ado, she did as he said.

She jumped in the Land Rover a short time later when

he held the door open for her, but when they set off in the opposite direction to the village she began to pepper him with questions. 'It will all become apparent soon,' he promised, holding a finger to his lips.

She subsided with the faintest of frowns, and a short while later he pulled the car off the side of the road. 'We're here.'

'Where's here?'

'Exmoor.'

Her gaze sharpened.

'You said you wanted to see something amazing.'

'I do.'

'Then follow me.'

He shrugged on the backpack before adjusting her scarf so the cold air couldn't touch her neck and throat and then took her hand and started along a trail.

'How far are we walking?'

'A mile in and a mile out.'

'But that means it's going to be dark by the time we come back.'

'It's a popular trail, well maintained, and I brought a torch.'

'What are we going to see?'

She was practically jumping up and down with excitement and it made him grin. 'Do you trust me?'

She stilled, suddenly serious. 'With my life.'

Her words speared into him, making him feel about twenty feet high, and invincible. He had to clear his throat before he could speak. 'Then wait and see. Just enjoy the walk.'

With a nod, she did as he said. And as they walked side by side in the twilight a peace he had never known—not even prior to his accident—stole over him. He didn't know what it meant, but he sensed a part of himself that had been badly damaged was starting to heal, and probably not before time. Maybe it was a gift of the season, but mostly he suspected it was due to the woman beside him.

He'd try and work out what it all meant another day. For the moment, all he wanted to focus on was showing her something amazing.

When they reached their destination, he pulled a blanket from the pack and spread it on the ground and seated her on it, before laying a second blanket over her lap. Pouring them both mugs of hot chocolate, he had her hold them as he dropped three marshmallows in each.

She gave a delighted laugh. 'You came well prepared.'

'And the *pièce de résistance…*' With a flourish he pulled out fat slices of fruitcake.

'If my hands weren't full, I'd clap!'

He snapped a picture of her to send to her folks, before settling beside her and taking one of the mugs. They sat there, shoulders and knees brushing, sipping their steaming chocolate and munching cake as the darkness gathered around them.

'So,' she eventually whispered, 'what are we waiting for? Badgers?'

'They're not very active at this time of year.'

'Red deer?'

'We should be so lucky.'

Her brow creased as she turned to him. 'Owls?' Her face suddenly lit up. 'Bats?'

He could've hugged her for that. 'Look up, Chloe,' he said gently.

She did as he bid, blinked as if to clear her vision, and then the breath left her on a whoosh. 'Oh, Beau,' she breathed in a reverent whisper.

He nodded. It was almost impossible to describe. 'You said you wanted to see something amazing.'

'I'd have never dreamed this in a million years.'

'In 2011 Exmoor National Park was designated an International Dark Sky Reserve. It's one of the darkest places in England, and one of the best places to stargaze.'

She rose to her feet, her eyes not leaving the sky. 'I've never seen anything more spectacular in my entire life.'

The sky was an explosion of stars—black velvet dotted with sparkling diamonds—the Milky Way spreading in an arc above them so dense with individual stars it made the mind boggle. Staring at it made him aware of the vastness of the universe, made him aware of the smallness of his own troubles. He couldn't say why, but staring up at all of that beauty gave him hope.

She swung back. 'I know next to nothing about astronomy.'

He gestured her back to the blanket, pulled her down to sit between his legs, her back resting against his chest as he pulled the blanket around them both.

He pointed out Venus and Mars, traced out the constellations of Ursa Major and Cassiopeia for her, relishing her warmth and wonder.

She pointed. 'How far away is that star?'

Light years didn't mean much to the average person. 'If you were to jump in the fastest rocket humankind has ever built, it would take seventy thousand years to reach that star.'

'No way,' she breathed, nestling back against him. 'That's awesome.'

Chuckling, he pressed a kiss to her hair. They sat like that for a long time, just drinking in the wonder and the beauty, but he knew he'd have to rouse her soon. It was cold and he didn't want her getting a chill.

As if reading the direction of his thoughts, she turned in his arms and kissed him with a deep heartfelt gratitude that made his heart beat hard. 'Thank you, Beau. Thank you for bringing me to this wonderful place. I'll never forget it.'

'I was worried you'd think I was cheating bringing you here at night time.'

She shook her head. 'That—' she waved at the sky '—is amazing.'

He shrugged, trying not to get too caught up in her praise.

It was such a small thing that he'd done. 'I can bring you back to Exmoor during the day if there's anything in particular you want to see too,' he surprised himself by adding.

'I want to see really old forest,' she confessed.

'Too easy.'

What on earth…?

Ignore it. Go with the flow.

She beamed at him, and it was the only reward he needed.

The following week passed in an energising routine of gardening and lovemaking, and long conversations beside a warm fire. In between times Chloe cooked up a storm, though she couldn't seem to master shortbread, while Beau continued his pipistrelle research.

His mobile phone pinged, but he finished reading the latest research paper he'd found online before glancing at it. It was probably just his grandmother letting him know she'd received the parcel he'd sent.

He turned the screen towards him and blinked. What on earth…? It was from his agent. He hadn't heard from Bryce in months.

He opened the message and everything inside him turned to ice. Following the enclosed link, he watched the footage of himself in his own garden talking about pipistrelles and it was all he could do not to throw his head back and howl.

Swinging to his computer, he checked all of the social media sites—Facebook, Twitter, TikTok—he was trending on all of them. And the full effect of his scars on the bigger screen had his hands clenching to fists.

There was only one person who could be responsible for this, and the sense of betrayal sent pain ripping through his chest. How could Chloe have done this?

He'd trusted her.

Seizing his phone, he started for the kitchen, the storm raging in his heart black, ugly and demanding an outlet.

CHAPTER NINE

AT THE SOUND of Beau bowling into the kitchen, Chloe turned with the oven trays in her hands. She'd been making spiced cookies and the kitchen smelled like cinnamon and spice and every good thing. 'Which ones look better? The snowmen or the stars?' She frowned. 'Or maybe I should've just stuck with circles.'

She glanced up and dropped the trays to the table, the cookies immediately forgotten. Beau looked as if the sky had fallen in! 'What is it?' Had something happened to his grandmother? She moved across to take his hand, but he pulled away.

'What were you thinking?'

She flinched at the fury in his voice—fury reflected in the flashing blue of his eyes and the tight set of his mouth. She took a step back, searching her mind for what she could have done to make him so mad.

He thrust his phone towards her. She took it, glancing at the screen and her jaw dropped. The video she'd taken of him in the garden was playing on the screen. Her heart pounded up into her throat. It already had over eight hundred thousand views on social media and it'd only been uploaded four hours ago.

'How did this…?'

He plucked the phone from her fingers, his face growing stony and grim. 'You're going to play the innocent and deny you've any knowledge of this?'

He thought *she'd* uploaded it?

She clenched her hands, waiting for her temper to fire to life, waiting for ugly words to claw at her throat, words she had no intention of holding back. She waited for it to overtake her so she could tell him what a paranoid piece of work he was and ask who did he think he was to accuse her of such a thing. But the anger remained inconveniently absent. In its place was an overwhelming urge to burst into tears—not just tears, but ugly, snotty, entire-body sobbing.

The kind of sobbing that you couldn't help because your heart had been broken.

What the hell? She clenched her hands harder. Her heart *wasn't* broken.

And yet that searing anger still didn't come to her rescue.

His lip curled. 'Nothing to say?'

She nodded at his phone. 'I had nothing to do with that.'

He bent down to glare into her face, his eyes flashing, and deep in their depths she recognised the betrayal he felt, but that did nothing to ease the screaming ache in her chest or the nausea churning in her gut.

'I don't believe you.'

She swallowed the lump in her throat, holding his gaze. 'All of your proclamations of friendship, all your assurances that you trusted me, were lies? Why? To get me into bed with you?'

His head rocked back as if she'd slapped him. 'Don't try and put this onto me.' His lips thinned. 'Why did you do it?'

'I will repeat it again, I had nothing to do with that.'

'There *is* no one else. You, me and my grandmother are the only people who had that footage, and my grandmother would never do something like that to me.' He stared at her, his eyes throbbing. 'Is it because you really can't face the thought of losing the house you bought with Mark? And selling that piece of video means you won't have to?'

She shook her head. He was in deadly earnest and it took all her strength not to fall into the nearest chair and drop her head to her hands. 'I thought we were friends,' she choked out.

A spasm passed across his face. 'Or did you think you were helping me? Did you think this would somehow reinvigorate my career?' His brow pleated as if he was searching for a less ugly reason for her supposed betrayal. 'Damn it, Chloe, you don't have the right to force my hand like that! You—'

His phone rang. 'Grandmother,' he said, pressing it to his ear. 'Yes, I've seen it.' His face tightened. 'It's everywhere. I expect the whole world has seen it.' He listened and then he froze. '*You* uploaded the video.'

And so the mystery was solved.

He swung to face her, but she was already turning away. Very quietly she let herself out of the back door, winding a scarf around her throat as she went and shrugging into her coat.

Grabbing tools from the garden shed, she headed straight for the walled garden. She didn't even consider which from the array of tools to use. Shrugging off her coat and scarf, she grabbed the sledgehammer and immediately set to work dismantling the wall of the second of the garden beds that needed to be completely rebuilt. George had already demolished the first.

She pounded at it with the same savagery that Beau's accusation had pounded at her, the shocks reverberating up her arms and through her entire body. She kept it up until her whole body ached, until her mind and heart finally—*thankfully*—went numb.

So what? So what if Beau hadn't trusted her after all? So what if they weren't, in fact, friends? So what if it had all been a lie? The fact their budding friendship was destroyed was disappointing, but she'd get over it.

Inside her something shrivelled and withered, but she ignored it.

Halting to wipe sweat from her eyes, she half turned to find Beau sitting on the low wall of the neighbouring garden bed.

He immediately stood. 'Chloe, I don't know what to say.'

'I believe sorry is the traditional approach.'

'I am sorry. More sorry than you can know.'

'I expect you are,' she agreed, abandoning the sledgehammer for a hoe, and setting to work at extracting a stubborn clump of agapanthus. She loved agapanthus, but they had no place in this particular garden bed. Her lips twisted in the briefest, and probably bitterest of smiles. Now there was an apt metaphor.

'Chloe, I'm sorry I jumped to conclusions. I saw that piece of video and...'

'And I was the obvious culprit.'

'When I saw the number of views I panicked.'

He'd turned grey, and a part of her did feel sorry for him, sympathised. Even understood.

'I suddenly saw my life turning back into the circus it was fourteen months ago and I—' He broke off, shaking his head, looking haggard...exhausted...haunted. 'You copped the brunt of that, which was spectacularly unfair.'

Yep.

'I know it's asking a lot, but can you find it in that rather lovely heart of yours to forgive me?'

She broke off to lean on her hoe and raise an eyebrow. 'Was that an attempt at flattery?'

He met her gaze. 'You do have a big heart. I should've taken better care of it.'

She had to grudgingly admit that he could do a halfway decent apology when the occasion demanded it.

'Why did your grandmother do it?'

He dragged a hand down his face and seemed to brace himself, before meeting her eyes again. 'She's of the same opinion as you—that I should be focussing on reinvigorating my career, not hiding from it. She decided to force my hand. She thinks it'll prove to me that I still have an audience.'

'Have you forgiven her?' She didn't mean to ask the question but it slipped out. He nodded, but it was a heavy movement that couldn't hide his confusion or his sense of betrayal. It took everything she had not to walk over and put her arms around him.

He straightened. 'It's after lunchtime. And I promised your mother I wouldn't let you work too hard.'

She glanced at her watch. She'd been pounding away out here for a lot longer than she'd realised. She and Beau might no longer be friends, but she was still his temporary housekeeper.

'Can we continue this conversation back at the house over a bite to eat?'

As far as she was concerned, the conversation was over, but with a curt nod, she collected up the tools—at least the ones he didn't grab first—and they stowed them away before returning to the house.

She made thick ham and cheese sandwiches while he brewed a large pot of tea.

Sitting across from him at the table, she focussed on eating at least half a sandwich, even though it sat like a lump of lead in her stomach. Given all the calories she'd just burned she ought to have worked up an appetite.

He remained silent, sipped his tea but didn't touch his sandwich. She opened her mouth to tell him to eat, but shut it again. He shook himself with a sudden start, and she concentrated on eating her sandwich again.

'Chloe, when I returned to Dawncarden after I was released from hospital, I was in…hell.'

She could see that.

'Not only were my dreams dust, but the people who'd once supported me were nowhere to be found. That's when I realised they hadn't supported me so much as supported my success. When I was no longer a success, they wanted nothing to do with me.'

Her stomach twisted.

'I'd released myself from hospital early as I couldn't stand the media circus, and my doctor only agreed on the proviso that I hire a nurse.'

She frowned. What was he trying to tell her?

'Unbeknown to me, she took photos and tried to sell them.'

What?

'Luckily I was alerted by a contact in the media and my lawyer was able to take action and prevent the photos from seeing the light of day.'

She closed her eyes. As if he hadn't had enough to deal with.

'You once accused me of being paranoid about my privacy. But it's incidents like those that have made it hard for me to trust anyone.' His shoulders sagged as if a weight had dropped onto them. 'It's not an excuse. I should never have accused you like I did. But I thought knowing some of what I've had to deal with might help explain why I reacted like I did.'

It did help. A little. But it didn't change either the significance or the outcome of what had happened. She and Beau were over.

His eyes burned into hers. 'Can you forgive me?'

She shrugged. 'Yes.'

His entire face lit up, but then his gaze raked her face

and that light died. 'But it doesn't change the fact that I messed up or that I hurt you.'

'I thought we were friends.'

'We are friends! Once you cool off, you'll see that.'

'*No!* We're employer and employee.'

'Client and contractor,' he corrected, something flashing in his eyes. 'I swear, Chloe, I can make amends. I'll do everything I can to make this up to you and prove that you can trust me.' He shot to his feet, hands clenched. 'I know I messed up but—'

'The sex isn't just fun any more, Beau.'

He opened his mouth, frowned. 'I'm not talking about sex. I'm talking about friendship.'

'I want to talk about sex.'

He sat. 'Okay.'

'We were all about the good time and having fun, yes?'

He nodded.

'You just said that when I cool down, I'll see that we're still friends, but the thing is there's nothing to cool down from. I didn't get angry in the first place.'

He frowned.

She gestured between them. 'You and I do anger and snarling at each other really well, but my reactions have changed…evolved…become something different.'

'Different how?'

'Instead of flying off the handle at you I was just…' She moistened parched lips. 'I was gutted you'd think I'd do that to you.'

He paled.

'Anger wasn't my main emotion, hurt was.' She spoke words that *really* frightened her. 'And that made me realise that I'm in danger of feeling more for you than I'd planned to. I'm certainly in danger of feeling more for you than I'm ready to feel for anyone. I never wanted anything permanent. And neither did you. So the sex thing was great while it lasted, but it stops now.'

He stared at her and something in the backs of his eyes made her squirm but she kept her chin high. 'It's not *just* fun any more. It's threatening to become something deeper. I don't *want* deeper. And neither do you.'

His eyes flashed. 'So if you can't have sex you're not interested in friendship either?'

'Don't you dare!' She shot to her feet. 'I'm not the one who broke faith.'

'No, but you're sure as hell grasping for a reason to retreat now. And it's easier to blame me than to acknowledge your own fear.'

'What do you know? *Nothing!* As today has proved.'

His lip curled. 'Looks like you found your snarl again.'

'And you have no idea how happy I am about that.'

'Yeah, you look over the moon.'

God, what were they—children?

Closing her eyes, she dragged in a breath. 'Let's get one thing straight. I came here to do a job. I'm going to do that job—you'll get your fabulous garden while I'll get the satisfaction of a job well done. And then I leave. End of story.'

'End of story,' he agreed, slamming out of the kitchen.

She glared after him. 'I'm glad we got that sorted out,' she yelled at the top of her voice, but she couldn't help feeling she'd just lost something infinitely precious.

Beau slammed the door to his study and it reverberated with a satisfying crash, echoing throughout the house. He hoped it reached the kitchen. He hoped Chloe heard it and—

Who was he kidding? He wasn't angry with Chloe. He was furious with himself!

He paced the room like some restless caged beast. How could he have messed up so badly? What had he been thinking?

He hadn't been thinking, that was the problem. He hadn't stopped to question the suspicion that had overtaken him. He'd simply gone in half cocked, all guns blazing. So damn sure that another person had let him down.

His phone pinged with an incoming message. Bryce. He shoved the phone back in his pocket.

She'd told him repeatedly that she wasn't responsible, but he hadn't even given her the respect of listening. He'd refused to let go of his self-righteous anger, he'd refused to let himself feel vulnerable because…

His hands clenched and unclenched. Because he'd felt so damn gutted that she could betray him. He'd been so damn afraid that sense of betrayal would overwhelm him he'd fed his anger in an effort to protect himself.

Instead he'd hurt a woman he'd come to respect above all others, and had lost a friendship that meant more to him than he'd realised. Chloe had forced him out of himself. She'd made him laugh. She'd let him snipe at her guilt-free—and he had because he'd needed it and so had she. She'd reminded him there were people in the world who didn't care about his scars.

She'd made him consider the possibility that he still had a career ahead of him. It might look different from the one he'd had previously, but so what? She'd made him focus on the good rather than the bad—the good in himself, but more importantly the good in other people. He had to find a way to win her friendship back.

He had to.

He'd miss the sex. With an ache that was physical. But the thought of losing Chloe's friendship was a thousand times worse. To know that when she left here in a month's time he'd never see her again…

He couldn't let that happen. Slamming to a halt, he ordered himself to think. His phone rang again. Bryce.

He turned it off and planted himself in his seat and did

an Internet search on how to win a friend back. He was desperate. And he'd try anything.

Apologise. Hear the other side. Give them space.

Make an effort.

Strengthen the bond by making them feel important by sharing things with them.

He'd written each of those items down, and he tried over the course of the following three days. He'd apologised again, but she'd told him there was no need, he'd already apologised and she knew he was sorry.

He was careful to keep his temper and impatience in check at the distance she deliberately created between them, at her aloofness. She clearly needed space. He'd give it to her if it killed him.

He invited her to play darts again on Thursday night. She declined. She didn't offer an excuse, and he didn't press her for one. He didn't fly off the handle. He kept his temper.

Actually, he didn't feel like yelling or losing his temper. He just ached that he couldn't bridge the gap. He ached at how much he'd hurt her. Chloe was the last person on earth who deserved to be hurt. She'd been through enough. She'd trusted him and he'd let her down.

He counselled patience. One article he'd read had said persistence was key. If there was one thing he could be, it was persistent. But he didn't want to be annoying.

So he went out alone, hoping his absence from Dawncarden would help her relax and feel not hounded or pressured by him. When he returned, empty-handed as he'd won nothing, he was careful to pass along the messages the other players had sent her. Those at least made her laugh.

He worked alongside her in the garden. They didn't chat as they previously had, but the physical exercise was good for the soul. And there at least they fell into a rhythm that was comfortable. That was when he felt most at ease. That was when his heart stopped burning for a few short hours.

He nearly swallowed his tongue when she glanced up from pressing rich brown earth around the roots of a freshly planted azalea and fixed him with a frown. 'I take it the constant pinging from your phone is your agent, Bryce?'

Bryce had called the house the previous day. Chloe had passed on the message, but he'd ignored it. He didn't have time for Bryce. He needed all of his focus to mend things with Chloe.

He pulled out his phone and glanced at it. 'Yep.'

'And I bet he's sent you multiple emails too.'

What did that have to do with anything? 'Probably. I haven't been checking my emails.'

'Why not?'

He shrugged.

'Have you checked your social media accounts?'

'God no.' He hadn't wanted to see the commiserations, the pity…the voyeuristic hunger of his so-called fans.

She thrust her trowel into the earth and rose. 'You promised you'd think about the possibility of returning to documentary-making in some way, shape or form. Was that a hollow promise?'

'No!'

But she was right. Since he'd screwed up so spectacularly, he hadn't given it any thought whatsoever. Make an effort. Strengthen the bond by making her feel important by sharing things with her.

He swallowed. 'I guess I've been avoiding thinking about it.'

She folded her arms when his phone pinged again. 'Surely step one in that process would be to talk to your agent about your options.'

His nose curled, even though he tried to stop it.

'What are you afraid of?'

She looked genuinely flummoxed. He didn't want to talk about it, didn't want to give voice to those fears. *Make an effort. Strengthen the bond by making her feel important by sharing things with her.*

He kicked at a weed. 'What if I don't like the options Bryce offers? Or, worse still, what if there aren't any options?'

Those treacle-dark eyes softened. A man could lose himself in eyes like those. She glanced away. 'He wouldn't be so persistent if you had no options.'

He stared and then squared his shoulders. If it made her feel important, talking to Bryce would be a small price to pay. 'If I don't like what he has to say or I'm not interested in whatever he has to offer...'

She glanced back. 'Then you can politely decline and carry on as usual.'

He moistened dry lips. 'You want to come and read my email with me?'

Her eyes widened, but then she took a step away. 'It has nothing to do with me.'

'It has everything to do with you. If you hadn't extracted that promise from me, I'd—'

He dragged a hand down his face. *Be honest.* 'I wouldn't be opening myself up to this kind of disappointment.'

Her jaw dropped as if she hadn't even considered disappointment a possibility, and a part of him loved her for it—loved that she had so much faith in him.

He pressed his momentary advantage. 'I might need a friend nearby, as I read them.'

Her eyes flew to his.

'And in the absence of Stephanie, you'll have to do.'

He smiled and she rolled her eyes, but he suspected she was biting back a smile too.

'I'll make a deal with you. You come and eat spiced cookies and drink tea with me, while I check my emails, and I'll take you to see really old forest in Exmoor before you leave.'

'Deal!' She blinked as if startled at how quickly the word had left her.

He didn't give her time to rethink it, but collected up their tools. 'Okay, let's go do this.'

An hour later they stared at each other across the expanse of his desk.

She leaned towards him. 'Let me get this straight. Bryce is saying the TV network is offering you a contract to create, shoot and present your own nature series?'

He nodded, still trying to take it in. 'It's a rival network to the one I was with before.'

'And yet the old network is interested in reopening negotiations with you too.'

'In their dreams.' He wasn't going back to a network that had treated him so shabbily.

That didn't change the fact that another bona fide, legitimate network wanted him. *Him.* He grinned at her. He couldn't help it. She blinked before pointing at his computer. 'Why haven't you rung Bryce already, telling him that you want that deal?'

Because winning back her friendship was more important than anything else at the moment. He didn't just want to be the best documentary presenter the country had. He wanted to be a good person. And making things right with Chloe felt like the first step in reclaiming his humanity.

'Are you worried about people seeing your face and your scars?'

He rubbed a hand over his face. 'A little. The thought of being at the centre of another media circus doesn't fill me with a shred of enthusiasm.'

'You'll only be the centre of attention for a little while though. Until people get used to seeing you again.'

That was true. 'Maybe I can speed up that process by taking your advice and posting to my social media accounts again.'

Her face lit up. 'Exactly!'

'God, Chloe, you're making me think this could all be possible.'

She reached across and clasped his hand. 'It *is* possible, Beau. Ring Bryce.'

He did. Ending the call ten minutes later, he stared at her. 'Apparently I'm spending the next three nights in London.'

She clapped and did a happy dance. 'And when you get back you can show me those really old trees in Exmoor.'

'It's a deal.'

He hadn't left yet and already he wanted to be back.

The discussions he and Bryce had with the network went even better than Beau could have hoped. That piece of video that had gone viral on social media had revealed that there was an audience out there hungry for all Beau had to offer.

As a result, the network weren't only offering him a lucrative contract, but more importantly they were promising him full control over the direction the series would take. The thought that he would once again be filming and sharing his passion with a hungry audience should've filled his soul with fire.

He signed the contract on the second day of negotiations. The network treated him and his new team to the finest French champagne and a ridiculously expensive dinner in the private dining room of one of London's poshest hotels. His new co-workers were good-natured and full of enthusiasm. And yet, when he returned to his hotel room, something still felt as if it was missing.

What was wrong with him? He now had everything he'd said he ever wanted.

Chloe isn't here to share it.

And none of this would've been possible without her.

He rang, even though it was late. She answered on the second ring. Did he dare hope she'd been waiting to hear from him or was that wishful thinking? Shaking the thought off, he told her about the contract, about the team…about the ridiculously over-the-top menu at dinner.

She congratulated him, he knew she was happy for him, and he even felt that he'd made some ground in winning back her friendship. But as they rang off, he found himself prowling restlessly around his room.

And just like that, it all fell into place—like a key turning in a lock and revealing the secret behind the door. He should've realised it sooner. Much, *much* sooner.

He'd fallen in love with Chloe.

I'm never falling in love again. The words she'd spoken to him weeks ago rang in his mind now and he swore.

Squaring his shoulders, he thrust out his jaw. He wasn't letting the woman he loved walk out of his life without a fight. He'd prove to Chloe that he could make her happy. He'd do everything he could to make it as hard as possible for her to leave.

CHAPTER TEN

CHLOE MOOCHED AROUND the kitchen, not sure what was wrong with her. She'd tried making another batch of shortbread, but something had gone wrong with it. It had been so crumbly the only way to eat it had been with a spoon straight from the baking tray.

She made a fresh batch of spiced cookies instead. Beau gobbled those up as if they were going out of style. Except he wasn't here to gobble up anything. And now she had over three dozen of the darn things just sitting there, and *she* didn't want them.

She made a mental note to give a dozen to George.

She'd spent a long morning in the garden, making excellent progress until torrential rain had driven her indoors. She'd put a luscious beef and vegetable casserole into a slow oven and the kitchen was starting to smell delicious. She'd had a full day.

She shouldn't feel so restless.

Opening the refrigerator door, she glared at the bottle of champagne she'd made a special trip into the village for. Clearly they'd need to celebrate Beau's new contract when he got back tonight. Because, hello…*good news*. So why wasn't she jumping up and down and excited?

She dropped down to the table, chin in hands. She *was* happy for him. This new contract was his dream come true. He deserved it. It was what she'd wished for him.

But that didn't stop her feeling flat. When she'd been working in the garden this morning she couldn't help wondering if he'd now spend any time there at all. She was working so hard to create the garden of his dreams, but…

But what? She'd still be paid for it and that was all that mattered.

She made tea. When she turned with teapot in hand she found Beau standing in the doorway. She blinked, but he didn't disappear. She gripped the handle of the teapot so hard her fingers started to ache, fighting an insane impulse to throw herself into his arms. 'I didn't hear you come in. You're early. Tea?'

'Yes, please.' His gaze raked her face and his eyes narrowed. 'You haven't been working yourself into the ground, have you, and doing stupid things like twelve-hour shifts in the garden?'

She bustled about getting him a mug and pouring the tea. 'Of course not. Even if I wanted to the weather made sure I couldn't.'

He grimaced. 'It was a bit wild and woolly on the roads, but I'd had enough of London and just wanted to get home.'

His words made something inside her lighten. She motioned him to a chair. 'Cookie?'

He grabbed several, and that strange restlessness dissolved. They settled back sipping tea and munching cookies. The house no longer felt strange and hollow. It felt exactly as it ought to.

The garden started to take shape and Chloe could see exactly what it would look like in a few years' time once it became established. She wondered if Beau would let her visit then.

Ha! He'd have forgotten who she was in another couple of years. She abandoned her trowel to press fingers into the small of her back. Besides, he'd be too busy shooting his marvellous documentaries in far-flung corners of the world and probably wouldn't have the time to appreciate the garden or—

'You're looking glum.'

She glanced up to find Beau watching her. He was supposed to be in his study, working.

She smoothed out her face. 'It's starting to look fabulous out here.' The garden beds had all been mended, and she'd started on the pruning, trimming and weeding. They'd even started some new planting.

'And that's a reason for looking glum?'

'Of course not.' For no reason at all, her heart started thump-thumping. 'Beau, I'm glad that you won't be burying yourself here in the garden. It's wonderful that you have a new contract.'

She gritted her teeth. It was. It really, *really* was.

'But?'

Those clear blue eyes focussed fully on her and things inside her pulled tight. Perspiration prickled her nape and the valley between her breasts, an ache started up low in her abdomen. How could she still want him so much? How could she remember so clearly the way he'd trail his fingers down her naked body and—?

She dragged her gaze away. Now that they were back on a *friendly* footing, she had no intention of threatening that by reinstating their friends-with-benefits arrangement. But the temptation hovered on the edges of her consciousness and it was an effort to remember all of the reasons why it would be a bad idea.

Besides, he clearly wasn't having the same difficulty. Her hands clenched. She had no right to resent that when *she'd* been the one to call a halt to things.

Gritting her teeth, she dug fingernails into her palms. She'd do the job she came here to do, get a sterling testimonial from Beau, before returning home and throwing herself into building up the design side of things at the garden centre.

Or you could sell the house, settle your debts, and begin a new life.

'Chloe?'

She shook herself. 'I was going to suggest you consider employing a gardener so the garden doesn't get so wild again.' Her voice came out husky and low. As if she was propositioning him.

He frowned.

Oh, Lord. Could he tell how much she still wanted him? She rushed into speech. 'Did you come looking for me for a reason? Is there something you needed?'

He straightened. 'There's something I wanted you to see.'

'Oh, but…' She gestured to the garden bed. She hadn't finished weeding this one yet.

He tapped a finger to his watch. 'You've been out here for four hours.'

She stared. 'Oh, my God! Lunch—'

'Can wait. I've been working on something all morning and I want you to see it. Besides, it's Christmas Eve and you deserve a holiday.'

He'd collected up her tools as he spoke, leaving her no choice but to trail after him. She stared at his back, her nose wrinkling. Did he want to show her the premise for some wonderful episode of his new series? Her shoulders drooped with every step she took. She wondered where it'd be filmed—the Amazon… Africa… Antarctica?

She shook herself. What on earth was wrong with her? *You will be enthusiastic.*

You bet your sweet patootie she would be. She'd hounded the poor man until he'd realised his options weren't as limited as he'd feared. She'd challenged him to be brave and the least she could do now was be supportive.

'Are you sure you don't want me to make you a sandwich or—?'

He grabbed her hand and towed her through the house. 'I'll make ham and cheese toasties once we're done with this.'

'But I'm supposed to be housekeeper and—'

'My house. My rules.'

With a shake of her head, she submitted. Besides, ham and cheese toasties sounded delicious.

He planted her in his seat at the vast desk in his study. He clicked a button on the keyboard, a video appeared on the screen—a video of Beau in the garden. She leaned forward. This was part of the video diary she'd urged him to keep. And then the voice-over started.

There were three short videos in total, and she watched each of them transfixed.

When they were finished, she turned to him, opened her mouth but couldn't force a single word out.

He gestured at the screen. 'You wanted before and after shots of the garden for your portfolio, but I think these are a hundred times better. What do you think?'

He'd outlined in detail the plans she'd drawn up, had revealed what each section of the garden would become, and he'd actually referred to her by name. He'd referred to her as a talented designer, had praised her to the skies, and said how lucky he'd been to find someone with her vision.

'The garden is your haven,' she blurted out. 'This—' she gestured wildly at the computer '—it's too much, Beau.' He might now have his brand-new documentary series to make, but she also knew how much his privacy still mattered to him.

'It's nowhere near enough,' he answered.

For a moment she imagined heat in his eyes, but then he blinked and it disappeared. 'You owe me nothing,' she whispered. He was still trying to make amends for losing her trust and it made her want to weep. 'You don't need to do this.'

'I know I don't need to, but I want to. You made me realise something, Chloe. In sharing my wonderful garden—the garden of my heart that *you're* creating—I won't be losing anything.' His hand closed over hers, squeezing it, before releasing it once again. 'It's still my garden. I can retreat here whenever I want, lose myself in its beauty and peace, and the abundance of life it holds. But in sharing it, I might inspire someone else to do something similar with their garden.'

'I…'

'You made me realise I needed to share my passion, not keep it locked up behind big stone walls.'

Her eyes stung and her throat thickened.

'I'll do more videos as work progresses, and I might even do an annual update. I'll send all of the video files to you to use in any way you see fit. I also plan to upload them to my social media channels.'

She could hardly get her head around the enormity of it all. 'That's the kind of promotion that makes careers, Beau.' Once his fans heard about her, she'd be inundated with offers of work.

'It only seems fair. You made me realise I still have a lot to offer the world. I want you to realise that you have a valuable gift of your own to share.'

If she dared.

'Hungry? C'mon, I'm starved.'

He was at the door before she could speak. 'Beau?'

He halted and turned.

Walking across to him, she stood on tiptoe and kissed his cheek. 'Thank you.'

CHAPTER ELEVEN

CHLOE LEAPT OUT of bed on Christmas morning and rushed to the window. Last night Beau had told her that there was every chance there'd be snow today. She didn't know why it felt so important that she get her white Christmas, only that something inside her hungered for it.

The moment she reached the window, a ray of sunshine emerged from the wall of cloud to sparkle on the dew, the grass and trees, but it didn't sparkle on snow. There wasn't a trace of that to be seen.

Her shoulders slumped.

In the next moment, she shook herself upright. It was Christmas morning and she was going to talk to her family in a little while and she had a lot to be grateful for. Yesterday, with Beau's gift of those videos, it had consolidated a bond of friendship she could no longer deny. After breakfast they'd exchange their silly Christmas gifts—she couldn't wait to see his face when he opened his—and her family would be delighted.

She hugged herself. The day was going to be perfect. Yesterday she'd been forced to acknowledge Beau's big-heartedness. It had made things right between them again and she was more grateful for that than she could say. She now knew that, no matter how much time passed, they would always be friends. With an excited wriggle, she rushed to get ready.

She and Beau met on the landing and they grinned stupidly at each other, before wishing each other a merry Christmas. He leaned down to kiss her, but somehow, rather than touching his lips to her cheek, their lips met. Had she turned her head to meet his lips? Or had he deliberately kissed her?

It was warm. It was brief.

It was irritatingly chaste.

He eased back to stare into her eyes, but then blinked and smiled, and she kicked herself for trying to read anything at all into it. 'Bacon and eggs?' she said with determined cheerfulness.

'Yes, please. I'll set the laptop up in the hall with the tree, and I mean to get a good blaze going.'

The house wasn't cold, the central heating saw to that, but the fire looked amazing when lit.

An hour later they were exchanging greetings with her family with the fire crackling in the background and that marvellous tree behind them. The time difference meant it was evening in Sydney, and her family sat around the dining table, which was set with leftovers. She had a sudden and piercing homesickness. 'Oh, I miss you all so much,' she blurted out.

'We miss you too, Chloe, honey! But you're looking rosy-cheeked and well. Did you wake up to snow like you hoped?'

'No, despite Beau assuring me that there'd be snow today. But there's a big frost and it looks so pretty out.'

'Hey.' He feigned offence. 'The day has only just begun. There's plenty of time for snow yet.'

'She has her sights set on the sled stowed in the barn, Beau,' her mother said with a smile. 'Merry Christmas, pet, it's nice to see you again.'

'Merry Christmas, Mrs Jennings. And I haven't given up on the chance of sledding yet either.'

His grin pierced Chloe's heart. He looked so happy to chat to her mum again and meet the rest of her family, and the effort he was going to for her warmed her all the way through.

'Is that a stocking I see beneath the tree?' her father piped in.

Beau waggled his eyebrows. 'It appears that we both have Santa sacks under the tree.'

A chorus of 'Open them!' sounded from her family and with laughs they exchanged sacks. Like her, he'd wrapped the presents, and they couldn't help laughing as they tore off the wrapping.

He'd given her a bright red Christmas jumper with a reindeer on the front that she promptly put on, a new trowel, and a recipe book for shortbread that made her laugh—and everyone else when she told them about her so far disastrous attempts at baking shortbread. Her final present was a set of darts that had her grinning madly.

She'd bought him a pair of pyjamas splashed in a Christmas print of bright red and white candy canes. He stared at her, one eyebrow raised. 'It's a tradition in our family,' she told him. 'We all get Christmas-themed PJs.' Her family held theirs up for him to see and he grinned with so much delight her heart started to ache.

Next came a book on the art of insults, which had him laughing, and last of all he unwrapped the dartboard. With a grin, he held it up for her family to see. 'Guess what we'll be doing this afternoon?'

It was all simply *perfect*.

Beau glanced at Chloe after they ended the call with her family. She stared into the fire, rubbing a hand across her chest. He reached out and gripped her hand, imagining how much she must miss them.

'Okay?'

Her fingers tightened about his. 'Yes. Sorry! I just… we did it.' She drummed her heels on the floor as if she couldn't contain her delight. She reached across to grip his other hand. 'We did it! They're not worried or fretting or anxious about me. I didn't spoil their Christmas and…oh, I can't tell you how happy I am.'

She didn't have to. Her delight was evident.

'You didn't ruin their Christmas, Chloe. Not one jot. I mean, they clearly miss you, but they enjoyed our present opening every bit as much as we did.'

She eased away, a slight frown creasing her brow as if it hadn't occurred to her that she'd had fun too, as if her own happiness hadn't been part of the equation.

Oh, Chloe, sweetheart.

'Anyone who loved you, Chloe, would be happy and relieved to see you having fun and embracing the spirit of the season.' Including Mark, though he didn't say that out loud.

If Mark had truly loved Chloe, and he suspected he had, then he wouldn't want Chloe to close herself off from all the good things life had to offer. He didn't say that out loud either. Chloe already knew it. It was no longer Mark's memory that held her back but her own fear.

'I've never had a Christmas morning that was so much fun.'

That immediately pulled her out of her reverie. 'Truly?'

He shrugged. 'Maybe when I was very small, but the memories are hazy like they belong to someone else. Usually my grandmother and I spend Christmas together and it's a quiet affair. I mean, we exchange gifts and it's nice. I'm not complaining. It's just—' he gestured at the laptop '—that was a revelation.'

'And fun,' she said, nodding.

He made himself grin and ooze Christmas spirit. 'I can't help feeling it's the right way to do it. And I've no intention of stopping now.' He seized the dartboard. 'You ready for a Christmas darts tournament?'

'You bet.' But then her phone pinged with an incoming text. She read it and grinned.

His hands clenched. *Who* had made her grin like that?

She stowed her phone and glanced up, eyes bright. 'I did get you one more present.'

She had? His heart started to thump. Had that smile been for *him*?

He did what he could to school his face. *Be cool, Diamond. Don't jump to conclusions.* But in that moment it occurred to him that Chloe had feelings for him. Deeper feelings than either of them realised and it gave him hope. 'I got you something else too.'

She blinked. 'But…you shouldn't have!'

He shrugged. 'Pot? Kettle? Which one do you want to be?'

Which made her laugh. 'Well, let me get your present first.' She pointed. 'Stay right where you are and don't move. Promise?'

He crossed his heart. She disappeared in the direction of the kitchen. Had she baked him something amazing? Or maybe she'd bought him some wonderful plant for his garden? Or the house! If she had, he'd treasure it forever and—

'Close your eyes and hold out your hands,' she called out. He did as she bid.

'Now keep them closed.' He could smell her as she drew closer, the scent of lavender merging with the scent of pine. He pulled it into his lungs, glorying in it. 'Careful now,' she murmured as she placed something soft in his hands, her hands curling around his and moving his arms so he cradled whatever it was against his chest.

Something soft that…wriggled.

'Open your eyes,' she whispered.

He glanced down to find he was holding a sleepy puppy

that was starting to wake. Puppy eyes met Beau's as Beau lifted him until they were face to face, and the puppy promptly licked his nose before yawning.

Beau fell in love on the spot.

'He's a beagle cross, and is going to be a whole truckload of mischief. I organised him before you signed your new contract, but I did speak to Stephanie first, and she's more than happy to be a surrogate puppy parent when you're not here.'

Chloe hadn't wanted him all alone in this vast house. He couldn't speak for the lump that lodged in his throat.

'He's from a litter of puppies from one of the local farms,' she babbled, 'and they were desperately looking for homes and—'

He reached out and pressed a finger to her lips. 'I love him. He's perfect.'

Her lips were perfect too, especially when they curved in a smile. He wanted to lean across and press his lips to hers and—

She shot back as if she read that thought in his face. His heart thumped and protested, but he did what he could to keep the smile on his face.

Rome wasn't built in a day.

'How on earth did you manage to hide him from me?'

'George collected him for me from the farm this morning, on his way to his daughter's for the day.'

He stroked a finger across the puppy's head. 'He's the most perfect gift I've ever received. You couldn't have given me anything I'd have loved more.'

Except your heart.

The words whispered through him and he glanced at the twinkling lights on the tree. Christmas was supposed to be a time of miracles, wasn't it? Maybe he'd get his very own Christmas miracle this year.

'His basket and food bowl and all the things he needs are in the kitchen. What are you going to call him?'

'Rudolph,' he decided, and she clapped her hands, pronouncing it perfect for the little puppy. 'Rudy for short.'

Rudy had clearly had a busy morning because he yawned and curled up on Beau's knee and promptly fell asleep. Only then did Beau reach into his pocket and pull out the present he had for her. 'I saw this when I was in London and it made me think of you.'

She glanced at him uncertainly, but took it. 'You didn't have to get me anything else.'

'You didn't have to get me a puppy either, but that doesn't mean I'm not glad you did.'

She turned the present over in her hands. 'It won't bite,' he promised.

That made her smile and without any further ado she tore away the paper and then sent him a startled glance when she discovered the velvet box beneath. But when she opened the lid her lips parted on a silent exhalation. 'Oh, Beau, it's beautiful.'

She pulled the necklace from the box, and the diamonds glittered in the light.

'Please tell me these are crystals or cubic zirconia.'

'They're crystals or cubic zirconia,' he promptly replied. 'Actually, it doesn't matter what they are. What matters is, do you like it?'

'Yes.' The single word was fervent.

She'd taken her jumper off when she'd returned with the puppy and she swept her hair to the side, to catch the latch behind her neck, before straightening, her fingers dancing across it lightly. 'How does it look?'

From a thin bar of platinum, five white gold flowers rose—all different heights and shapes, their petals sparkling with diamonds. She'd probably have a pink fit if he told her how much it had cost. 'Perfect.'

She raced across the room to a low-hanging mirror and surveyed her reflection. 'Oh, Beau, it's the most beautiful thing I've ever seen.'

'The garden you're creating for me is more beautiful.' And she was more beautiful than all of the gardens of the world. 'But it suits you. I thought it'd be a memento of your time here.'

She turned. 'Thank you, Beau. I love it. It's perfect. But I don't need a memento of my time here. I'm never going to forget it.'

Her brow suddenly wrinkled as if the fact she'd never forget Dawncarden—and him? he crossed his fingers—perturbed her. He wasn't letting anything bother her today. 'Right, let's find Rudy's basket, and then you and I are having a darts tournament to end all darts tournaments. The winner gets to eat all the spiced cookies they want.'

They ate their huge dinner in the grand dining room at two p.m. because that was the tradition at Dawncarden, and they stuffed themselves so silly they could barely move. The roast turkey and baked potatoes, the Brussels sprouts and gravy, not to mention the plum pudding with brandy custard, were utter perfection.

Chloe glanced around and couldn't help but be secretly delighted by the sumptuousness of it all. 'There're enough leftovers to last a week,' she groaned.

Beau rubbed a hand across his stomach. 'That's one of the best things about Christmas. Besides, doorstop-sized turkey sandwiches are the best.'

Which sounded perfect for lunch tomorrow.

They played with Rudy, who was full of puppy playfulness and fun, but he fell asleep with the same kind of prompt solidness of a toddler. The way Beau looked at him—as if he were a miracle—made everything inside her ache and burn and want to hug him.

Oh, who was she trying to kid? She wanted to tear the clothes from his body and ravish him. Over and over. The burning attraction should've eased by now, but it hadn't. It had grown into a roiling, bubbling roar of blistering need. And try as she might, she couldn't seem to move beyond it.

'Look out the window, Chloe.'

Glad for the distraction, she leapt up and moved to the front window. She swung back, clapping her hands. 'Snow!'

'Told you.'

'Oh, my God!' She raced for the front door and launched herself outside.

Glancing upwards, she held her arms out and turned on the spot. Huge white flakes drifted down from the sky and settled over everything, utterly transforming the lawn, the trees, the fences. *Oh, this was glorious.* Opening her mouth, she caught a cold flake on her tongue. Spinning on the spot again, she found Beau watching her from the doorway, the hugest grin on his face.

Six weeks ago the man hadn't known how to smile, let alone grin.

'Merry Christmas, Chloe.' He ambled towards her with a lean-hipped grace that made her mouth go dry. He gestured heavenward, but his eyes didn't leave her face. 'You got your Christmas wish.'

She had. 'I—' She swallowed, but she couldn't look away. 'I so wanted a white Christmas. I can't believe it's happened.' But all she could see was him.

'Oh, ye of little faith.'

But his breath quickened and hers did too.

His gaze darkened. 'You look like an angel standing in the snow.'

The naked desire in his eyes stole her breath. She didn't know who moved first, her or him, but she found herself wrapped in his arms, and his mouth moving over hers with a reverence that had tears prickling her eyes.

He eased away, his throat bobbing as he swallowed. 'Sorry, I probably shouldn't have done that.'

'I wanted you to.' Her pulse jumped and jerked and her lips tingled. 'If we're being honest, I want to do a whole lot more than just kiss, Beau.' She tried to steady her breathing. 'I know I called a halt to that side of things, but maybe I was hasty and—'

'I want more.'

His eyes burned into hers, but his words pulled her to a halt. She frowned. 'But wasn't that what I was just saying…offering?'

He dragged a hand down his face and then braced his hands on his knees before straightening. 'You're offering me your body, Chloe, and while I'm burning for that too, I want more.'

Her breath hissed from her lungs as his meaning became clear. She took a step back.

'I want your heart, Chloe.'

CHAPTER TWELVE

No.

'I didn't mean to fall in love with you.'

Chloe wanted to block her ears against Beau's words. *No!*

'But I have. I know the thought of love scares you and so does the thought of turning your face to the future, but I love you. There's nothing I can do about it. But for what it's worth, I think love is worth risking everything for.'

He was wrong. So, *so* wrong. Losing love made you lose your very soul. It made you hurt so badly in ways you didn't know you could hurt. Losing love was brutal and pitiless and barbaric in its totality. 'No.' She took another step away from him, shaking her head. 'It's *not* worth it.'

He paled.

Her heart pounded so hard she thought it would leave bruises. 'I'm sorry, Beau. I didn't want you to fall in love with me. I thought I'd made that clear.'

He didn't answer.

She forced the words from an aching throat. 'My heart isn't on offer. I can offer you friendship and sex. But not love.' Never that.

The lines around his mouth deepened and his eyes dulled. She wanted to drop to her knees and sob. He kept his chin high, though. 'I think you need to look inside your heart, Chloe. I think the feelings you have for me are stronger than you want to admit. It's why, when I let you down, it hurt you so badly. It's why you tried to protect yourself so fiercely afterwards.' His gaze held hers. 'It's why you forgave me.'

'You're wrong,' she snapped, suddenly incensed. 'I forgave you because you're human and we all make mistakes and…' she waved her arms wildly about '…because we're friends and that's what friends do.'

'I think it's why you gave me a puppy. You didn't want me to be alone.'

'That's just… I mean… *You like animals!*'

'Chloe—'

'I'm not listening to any of this. It's nonsense!' She waved her hands in front of her face. 'I need some air. I'm going for a walk.'

His hand closed about hers, pulling her to a halt. She tried to tug free.

'Chloe!'

His voice, its volume, pulled her from her fog.

'I won't stop you going for a walk, but you need to put on a jumper, a scarf, your coat and boots.'

He was right. Without another word, she marched straight into the house and did exactly that.

'I know you don't want my company, but I ought to follow behind at a distance—'

'Don't you dare!'

'I won't as long as you make me a promise.'

She hitched up her chin and glared at him.

'There's not going to be enough snow for sledding until tomorrow, so it's safe enough for you to go walking now, but snow changes the landscape and can make it hard to get your bearings. Promise me you'll stay on the grounds and not go wandering further afield.'

The suggestion was sensible. It shouldn't make her want to rage and rail at him. She gave a single nod.

He pushed her phone at her. 'And ring me if you find yourself bamboozled or lost. Promise me.'

She pulled in a breath. 'I promise.'

She didn't know for how long she wandered. One thing became clear, though. She sure as heck wasn't enjoying the beauty of the landscape as it turned into the kind of winter wonderland she'd only read about in fairy tales.

And it deserved to be enjoyed!

She jumped up and down on the spot in sudden fury, grateful no one was nearby to witness her temper tantrum, but she needed to rid her body of the panic and anger that gripped it. She succeeded eventually by trudging so hard and so fast repeatedly around the orchard that instead of wanting to hit something, she wanted to cry.

Why did Beau have to go and ruin everything?

Fashioning snow into a ball, she hurled it at the trunk of a tree. And missed.

It had been such a perfect day until he'd gone and ruined it. She thought back to their present opening beside the Christmas tree, her family's high spirits, the fire in the hearth… Brushing snow from the stile, she planted herself on it, chin in hands, wishing she could scrub the memory from her mind as easily.

The presents he'd given her… The jumper had been Christmas fun, pure and simple, but the darts and the recipe book were perfect. *So perfect.* Because of the memories they'd made since she'd arrived here, the in jokes they'd developed. They'd *meant* something.

Her shoulders slumped. She didn't want to lose Beau's friendship. It was the last thing she wanted to do.

Her fingers stole to the fine chain at her throat. The necklace he'd given her was the most beautiful thing she'd ever seen. She was creating a garden for him and he'd given her one to take with her wherever she went. It was beautiful, filled with meaning and—she swallowed—romantic.

But she didn't want romance.

Look inside your own heart.

She shot to her feet. Damn it, Beau Diamond had no idea what was in her heart.

She set to pacing again. The urge to weep and wail, to throw things and yell at the top of her voice, gripped her in waves.

Eventually she slammed to a halt.

Oh, for heaven's sake, get over it. So what if the man loves you? You were upfront. You didn't lie. He'll get over it.

Except… She swallowed. It wasn't fair. Beau didn't deserve a broken heart. He'd been so kind to her—grumpy and blustery when she'd needed him to be, but generous too. And he'd challenged her in ways that no one else had. In ways that had made her start to see the future in a very different light. She owed him so much.

And now that he had finally reclaimed the dreams he'd thought were dust, he deserved to go into that future with a heart full of hope.

Her lip curled. 'While we're on the subject, Chlo, why haven't you been over the moon about his new contract when it's what he wanted and what you urged him to fight for?' Because that *did* deserve some serious soul-searching.

Because he'll forget all about his secret garden.

'No way,' she breathed. 'I am not that petty and small-minded.'

Because he'll forget all about you.

Her hands clenched. 'But that's what I want!'

Somewhere inside her, her secret hidden self raised a fierce eyebrow. *Really?*

Her mind whirled. Beau's presents might've been perfect, but her presents to him had been equally perfect. *Per-*

fect. It occurred to her then how often she'd used that word today and her mouth dried.

This Christmas had been perfect, not because they'd managed to put on a damn fine show for her family, but because she'd spent the day with him. She and Beau had created all the trappings of a perfect Christmas and thrown themselves into it wholeheartedly.

She just hadn't wanted to acknowledge how wholeheartedly.

Because the feelings she'd developed for Beau were deep and strong and lasting, and that terrified her. It had sent her running like a champion sprinter.

As if she could outrun a broken heart!

Her heart thumped and she had to brace herself against an apple tree. If she walked away from Beau now she wouldn't just be breaking his heart, she'd be breaking her own too.

She loved him. She loved his sense of humour, she loved the way he laughed, and she loved his passion for the natural world. She loved his kindness, his wisdom and the way he touched her. She loved his courage. She loved *him.*

But if he should die in two years' time, leaving her alone and the life they'd built together shattered… She covered her face with a groan. Oh, God, that would be harder than walking away now. So much harder.

If you had your time again, would you walk away from Mark to spare yourself the heartbreak?

The breath jammed in her chest. Would she?

Very slowly she shook her head. *No.*

So was she going to live a half-life now, protecting her heart and keeping it safe? Or was she going to find the courage to choose perfection with no guarantees?

Their life together might only last a year or two.

But it might last a lifetime.

She was barely aware of turning, but she found herself

running towards the house as fast as she could, shouting Beau's name at the top of her voice.

He burst from the house and pelted towards her. 'What's wrong?' He grabbed her by the upper arms and scanned the surroundings. 'What spooked you?'

'Me,' she wheezed, gripping his forearms and bending to try and get air into burning lungs. 'So unfit,' she wheezed, straightening.

'It's the cold, makes it hard to catch your breath.' He frowned. 'And what do you mean you spooked yourself?'

'Love.' She released him to press her hands into the small of her back and drag in as measured a breath as she could, tried to slow the crazy racing of her heart. 'Love spooked me.'

One eyebrow lifted. 'Like that's news.'

She folded her arms and glared back. 'You snuck up on me. You weren't supposed to be so damn perfect. You sure as hell weren't supposed to be so hot! I didn't want to feel things again, but you made me feel things anyway.'

'So? You made me feel things too. While calling me an idiot, I might add. Only seems fair to me.'

'Oh, really?' She poked a finger to the delicious hardness of his chest. 'You think love's fair, do you?'

He stilled.

'I didn't want to fall in love with you, Beau Diamond!' Was she yelling?

He stilled.

'I've been trying to hide from that truth, using every means at my disposal, and then you just oh-so-casually tell me you love me and want more, and—' she hitched up her chin '—you have to know that's going to spook a girl like me. I mean, how are we even going to work? We live on different sides of the globe, and you're going to be flitting here and there all over the world filming your new series. When would we even see each other?'

His face gentled. 'Chloe—'

'Don't you dare interrupt me!' She pointed a finger at him, but her vision had blurred, and she had to blink hard to bring him back into focus. 'I love you, Beau.'

He smiled down at her, those blue eyes so true and knowing. 'I love you too, Chloe.'

She had to fight the answering smile building through her too. She shrugged, aiming for casual. 'I know, you already said.' That delicious grin of his widened and it took an effort not to get all caught up in it, to just kiss him now and save the hard questions for later.

She sobered and straightened. *Be brave.*

'You said you wanted more. How much more do you want? Because I have to warn you I want it all—lifetime commitment, children…the works.'

'Then we're on the same page.' He swept her up in his arms and kissed her so soundly and thoroughly that if any doubts had remained they'd have dissolved beneath the fierceness of his lips. Lifting his head, he stared down at her, and the possessiveness in his eyes made her soul sing. This man was hers. And she was his.

'Right, then.' She hiccupped, and tried to get her rampaging pulse under control. 'You're going to have to promise to be really careful around big cats, and alligators and hippos and any other dangerous animals you're going to be filming from now on.' She couldn't ask him to walk away from his job—it was his passion and he was brilliant at it—but minimising risk wasn't too much to ask.

He smiled down at her, his eyes gentle. 'I've no intention of putting myself at risk, sweetheart.'

The endearment turned her insides to mush.

'And there's something I haven't told you yet about my new series. I've no intention of traipsing to the far-flung corners of the world any more.'

She blinked.

'Being back here at Dawncarden, discussing the garden and the pipistrelles with you, has given me a brand-new direction. I want to show people—*real people*—what we have here right on our doorstep. I want to show them how they can nurture wildlife in their own gardens. I want to inspire them to at least try.'

She had every confidence he would too. 'That sounds wonderful.'

'I've been given the go-ahead by the powers that be, and we're going to start filming in three months.'

Hope stirred. And excitement. 'Are you saying you're going to be based here at Dawncarden?'

'That's exactly what I'm saying.' He grinned. 'And I was thinking that if you happened to find yourself offered contracts to makeover gardens on grand estates here in the UK, maybe I could convince you to make Dawncarden your base too.'

That sounded *perfect*.

A short time later she found herself sitting in his lap on the sofa in front of the roaring fire, Rudy curled up in his basket nearby making cute little puppy noises as he dreamed. 'I was an idiot for blurting out that I loved you the way that I did, Chloe. I'm sorry, I knew you needed more time.'

'Well, if I hadn't tried to get you into bed, you wouldn't have needed to tell me you wanted more than just sex.'

'You have no idea how tempted I was to take you up on the offer and to hell with the consequences.'

She rested a hand against his cheek. 'No, you deserved more, and you were right to demand it. You should never short-change yourself, Beau. *Never*.'

His finger trailed a path down her cheek to her collarbone, those perfect lips lifting. 'It was you who taught me not to settle for something less.'

Her?

'You made me realise that in shutting myself away all I was doing was hurting myself. Some people aren't worth my trust, but they're also not worth me burying myself for either. You made me see there are people in the world who can see behind the scars and gossip. You taught me to fight for what I want. If you hadn't come to Dawncarden, I'd have still been here in fifty years' time, a bitter and angry recluse.'

She shook her head. 'You'd have found your feet again. I'm sure of it. You were ready for a push, that's all. And we both know I'm the pushy sort so clearly it was a match made in heaven.'

He kissed her, and she kissed him back with everything she had—all her joy and gratitude and love.

He lifted his head, breathing hard. 'What made you decide to take the risk on us?'

She glanced down at her hands. 'Losing Mark was… It was awful.'

A finger beneath her chin lifted her gaze back to his. 'I know you loved Mark. There's no need to feel awkward about that. I'm not jealous. I'm sorry he died, and I'm sorry you had to go through so much grief and heartache.'

The warmth in his smile eased the burn at the centre of her, and she nestled against him more firmly. 'Clearly—' she rolled her eyes '—I never expected to find another man who could be so perfect for me, but I think I fell in love with you from the very first moment you snarled at me. Crazy, right? But I just felt so free to be me again. It was such a relief, Beau. I just didn't recognise then what it was or what it meant.' They'd both been on such a journey during the last six weeks.

'When I was stomping around your orchard in the snow just then I realised that, even given all the pain losing Mark caused, I would never give up the time we'd had together.'

She placed her hand over his heart. 'And then I realised

that I'd be a fool to walk away from you and the life we could have, just because one day I might lose it. Nothing else in this world could make me happier than you, Beau. *Nothing.* So, in the end, although it took me far too long to work it out, it was a no-brainer.'

His fingers trailed across her cheek. 'You are the most amazing woman I've ever met—beautiful, brave, smart. I'm going to cherish your heart, and I'm going to make you feel blessed every single day.'

'And will you promise to still snarl at me when you feel snarly?'

'I will if you will.'

She crossed her heart. 'And will you promise to keep kissing me every single day as if it's your favourite thing to do?'

He grinned. 'That's easy to promise. It *is* my favourite thing to do.'

'And will you promise to keep sampling my attempts at shortbread?'

He threw his head back and laughed. 'Now that's going above and beyond, but I promise.'

And then he kissed her, and they didn't speak again for a very long time.

EPILOGUE

Two and a half years later

'TA-DA!'

Chloe blinked when Beau whipped off the scarf he'd used to cover her eyes. She stared at the scene in front of them and her heart expanded until she thought she might float right up into the sky.

Beau had set a table with the same French champagne and selection of delicacies that they'd had for their wedding twelve months ago. Not only that, he'd decorated their secret garden with ribbons and bunting and fairy lights, just as it had been on their wedding day.

She clasped her hands beneath her chin. 'Oh, Beau, how did you manage to do all of this without me knowing?'

He shrugged, and his mouth hooked up in one of *those* grins, making her pulse flutter. He must've been up with the larks. Speaking of which, they had a nesting pair in the near corner and every day she expected to hear the sound of baby birds cheeping.

He popped the champagne. 'Happy anniversary, Chloe.' He raised his glass. 'To the most wonderful woman I've ever met. The last two and a half years have been the happiest I've ever known.'

She touched her glass to his. 'To the most wonderful husband a woman could ever have.' She took the tiniest of sips, glancing around again, remembering the scene here a year ago.

Beau had flown all of her family and friends to the UK. Beau's grandmother and Chloe's immediate family had stayed at Dawncarden, while extended family members and friends had been put up at The Nag's Head and various bed and breakfasts in Ballingsmallard. Mark's family included. They'd been so happy for her. The whole village had been buzzing and, of course, had turned out for the wedding too.

They'd had a simple service here in the walled garden, with a festive buffet lunch afterwards, overseen by Stephanie, in the orchard. Long tables that had been set beneath the fruit trees, and a local band had played. It had been a meal filled with love and laughter and more joy than Chloe had ever thought possible. The day had been *perfect*.

'Happy?' he murmured, entwining his fingers with hers and strolling along one of the paths, the garden lush and green and gorgeous all around them.

She squeezed his hand. 'More than I ever thought possible.'

He pressed a kiss to her knuckles. 'In a small way, I wanted to recreate our wedding day. Marrying you, Chloe, was the happiest day of my life.'

'Better than getting the news that your new series had topped the ratings?' she teased.

'Even better than that,' he said, but his shoulders went back. 'That was a pretty good day too, though.'

She'd been thrilled for him. He'd worked so hard to make the series not just interesting and informative but enthralling. She didn't know how he did it. And she wasn't the only one impressed. The fan mail he received blew her away. He was having such an influence on what people now wanted to achieve with their gardens and the wild places in their neighbourhoods.

'I'm not the only one who's gone from strength to

strength.' His hand tightened about hers. 'Have you decided which contract you're going to accept next?'

In the last two years, she'd transformed not one, but three gardens on grand estates—one in Dorset, another in Cheshire and the last in Norfolk—as well as working on a public park in Birmingham. Though she and Beau did their best to align their schedules, there were the inevitable absences. It was the only shadow in an otherwise sunny existence, and as they both loved their work it was hard to begrudge it.

As all of the gardens she'd worked on had been high profile, receiving a lot of publicity, she was now in high demand in her own right. She'd recently been asked to create a knot garden at a royal estate, to transform the grand gardens of a Kensington mansion, while the Australian Botanical Society had asked her to provide a series of online guest lectures for their members. It all seemed to have happened so quickly. Never in her wildest dreams had she expected such success.

She smiled to herself. She was going to have to slow down a little soon, though. She glanced at Beau. She was waiting to find the perfect moment to share her news with him.

She slipped an arm around his waist. 'I was waiting to find out what your schedule was before making a decision.' It'd be wonderful if they could at least work in the same county for part of the coming months.

They stopped by the hornbeam tree. It was the untidiest corner of the garden, and still their favourite. 'I want to run something past you, Chloe.'

'That sounds ominous.'

'Not ominous. An opportunity. The TV network wants to know if you'd consider filming a segment on each of my shows, giving viewers gardening tips. It'd work brilliantly if we could somehow tie it into the theme of each episode.'

She pulled away, her nerves twanging. 'No way! People don't want to see me. They want to see you.'

'They want to see you too.'

'Not a chance! I—'

'You're chicken, that's what you are.'

Her mouth opened and closed, but she couldn't spit out a single word.

'You're scared of appearing on camera.'

'Happy anniversary, Chloe!' She glared and folded her arms. 'Being on camera is your dream, not mine, and I think one diva in the family is enough, thank you very much.'

'Helping people create wonderful gardens *is* your passion. The series is going from strength to strength. The general public have such a hunger to create their own mini wildlife paradises. *You* can help them do that. Imagine the reach you'd have if you appeared on my show *every week*.'

'Yes but—'

'No buts. This is a great opportunity and you know it.'

Be that as it may, the thought of appearing on TV scared the bejeebies out of her. She'd be tongue-tied and stupid. She'd fumble and mutter and be stupid and—

Gah! She was dying a thousand deaths even thinking about it.

He crossed his arms, his eyes full of challenge. 'Working together means we wouldn't have to spend long periods apart. We'd see each other more, get to spend more time together.'

Which would be perfect, but…

Tongue-tied, fumbling...stupid.

She shuddered.

He bent down to peer into her eyes. 'What are you really afraid of?'

She hitched up her chin and glared. 'I don't know how to talk to camera.'

'You wouldn't be thrown in at the deep end. You'd get training from some of the best in the industry.'

She would? She rolled her shoulders as temptation coiled around her. It would mean spending more time with Beau. She shook herself. 'I'd make mistakes and look stupid on camera, and that'd make me sound like I've no idea what I'm doing or what I'm talking about. I'd lose all credibility.'

'Do I look stupid when I make mistakes?'

She waved that away. 'You don't make mistakes.'

He laughed as if she genuinely amused him and she could feel her eyes narrow. He held up his hands. 'You would have a final say in what went to air. If you don't like something, we cut it.'

She stilled. Her heart started to pound. 'Do you mean that?'

He crossed his heart.

She pointed a finger at him. 'You've pulled strings to make this happen.' Because even through her fear of appearing in public, she could see how perfect this could be.

'I swear I haven't. It was the network head's idea. He's friends with Abercrombie.'

The owner of the garden she'd made over in Norfolk?

'He's done his research, been to have a look at each of the gardens you've worked on. It's why he invited himself to Dawncarden for the weekend last month. He wanted to see how you sounded, how you moved, and if he thought you'd be able to do it.'

Which probably explained the man's somewhat puzzling interest in her plans for Dawncarden's orchard.

'If I'd known what he was up to, I'd have warned you.'

She believed him. They might not always see eye to eye, but they always had each other's back.

He pulled her in for a heated and very thorough kiss. When he eased away she had to brace a hand against his chest and fight the urge to pull his head back down to hers.

'Will you at least think about it?' he asked.

When he looked at her like that she couldn't deny him anything. She pulled in a breath, faced her fear. If there was one thing she'd learned since meeting Beau, it was to not let fear govern her. 'Beau, there's nothing to think about.'

His eyes dimmed, but he reached out and touched her face and found a smile anyway, before taking her hand and starting back along the path. 'Okay.'

'No.' She shook his hand. 'What you're suggesting is *perfect*. I'd be an idiot to turn such an opportunity down.'

He swung back, his face lighting up.

'But you have to promise you won't let me look stupid on camera.'

'I promise.'

His eyes burned into hers with such warmth, she told herself she could deal with a few nerves if it made him happy.

Speaking of happy…

Her heart started to thump. 'It's perfect, not just because it means we'll see more of each other, but I want to start slowing down a little. I need to.' She took his hand and held it against her stomach. 'Beau, we're going to have a baby.'

He stared at her as if he couldn't comprehend what she was telling him. 'A baby?' he parroted, and she found herself suddenly laughing for the sheer joy of it.

'The doctor confirmed it through the week. Both me and baby are doing fine. So that means you need to get to work redecorating the nursery.'

With a whoop, he lifted her up and swung her around. Setting her back on her feet, he smoothed her hair from her face, his eyes shining. 'That's the best news ever.'

Lifting her into his arms, he strode the length of the garden to set her on a chair at the table, his gentleness bringing tears to her eyes. 'You need to rest.'

'Nonsense!' But she let him fuss because it was lovely,

and the light in his eyes made her melt…and because she loved him so much.

'You're happy?' he checked, kneeling by her side.

'Over the moon,' she assured him. 'You?'

'So happy.' He cupped her face. 'It's perfect. I feel…' he shook his head, his eyes shining 'blessed.'

She nodded.

'I was blessed the day you came into my life, Chloe *Ivy Belle* Jennings. You made me realise my life could still be full and worthwhile and good.'

She leaned forward and pressed her lips to his. 'You gave me back to myself, Beau, helped me be whole again. And together we're going to create a family that will love and laugh and be strong for each other.'

He kissed both her hands. 'I am going to do everything I can to look after you and the baby, Chloe, and anybody else who comes along. I don't want any of you wanting for anything.'

'Beau, all we want is you.'

Her breath caught at the look in his eyes and her pulse fluttered. She pulled him up to sit in a chair and planted herself in his lap. 'Did you bring a blanket?'

'Of course.'

'And did you lock the garden door behind us?'

He nodded, his eyes dancing. 'The key is in my pocket.'

'Then I think it's time you kissed me again.'

'I couldn't think of anything I'd rather do.'

And then he kissed her, as if kissing her was his very favourite thing to do.

* * * * *

WHIRLWIND FLING TO BABY BOMBSHELL

ALLY BLAKE

MILLS & BOON

To libraries and the librarians within them.

For the books recommended, the hot desks away from home, the heart-warming support of my writing, and the ever-constant sanctuary.

Thank you from the bottom of my adoring heart.

CHAPTER ONE

A Cole Porter playlist crooning through her earbuds, hand shielding her face from the brilliance of Melbourne's sharp autumnal sun, Adelaid Adams took in the sublime façade of the Big Think Corp building, a sense of inevitability quickening inside of her.

For once she stopped faffing about outside and walked through those doors, she would be taking a genuine step towards her dream career.

And yet, her feet did not move.

Adelaid tugged on the cuff of her houndstooth jacket, the chafe of vintage wool over her fingertips helping her stay inside her own skin. With its sharp shoulder pads and wide-legged pants, the moment she'd seen the op shop suit she'd thought, *Katharine Hepburn!* Woman of the Year!

"Dress for the life you want, not the life you have," Adelaid's mother used to say, while swanning around the kitchen wearing a feather-lined satin robe, martini in hand at eight in the morning on a school day. As if the life *she'd* wanted was one of a once-lauded nineteen-forties movie star on the downhill slide.

Adelaid had definitely inherited the grandiosity of her mother's dreams, among other things, though hers were hopefully more achievable. Along the lines of "highly respected, sartorially envied writer of warm, witty, winning profiles that stun readers with their erudite observations, empathy and heart."

But a girl had to eat, so she'd kept the cushy digital media job she'd taken on right out of uni. Writing lists such as *Top Ten Mafia Reverse Harem Christmas Novels* and creating cutesy "click-happy" headlines for a wonderful editor who trusted her to do her thing and penning stories of quiet heroism for community publications, for little money, on the side.

Till last week, that was. When she'd given it all away. For the chance to walk through the gigantic rotating glass doors, and interview one Ted Fincher.

Ted Fincher one of the trio of hotshot, wunderkind, zillionaire founders behind the inventive, innovative, future-focussed juggernaut that was Big Think Corp.

World-renowned scientist lousy with international prizes, scientific breakthroughs galore and more qualifications than she had shoes was rather a step up from telling tales of retired nurses, or dogs that saved their owners' lives.

But people were people. And she was ready. Itching to draw on connection to build empathy and write something truly special.

The itch might have been the vintage wool, tickling at her wrists. Still, channelling Katharine Hepburn couldn't hurt.

Over the big band now blasting in her ears, she heard a clock tower bell boom nearby. Aware that her attention was skipping like a needle over a broken record, Adelaid hitched her bags higher on her shoulder, gathered every lick of moxie she had at her disposal and strode purposefully through those doors.

Only to rock to a halt the moment she spilled out the other side. For if the exterior of the Big Think Corp was an architectural wonder, the inside was simply dazzling.

From the wall of smoky glass showcasing the view over the Paris end of Collins Street, to the acre of inlaid marble covering the lobby floor, to the sumptuous leather couches and elegant tables and potted white flowers dotting the extravagant three-storey atrium, it had an Art Deco sensibility that she adored. If Big Think Corp headquarters had been designed to inspire shock and awe, it worked.

Adelaid's phone buzzed through her earbuds, jerking her into the present. A quick glance at the screen showed a new message on the Adams family chat.

Jake: Sunday lunch canned. Joey brought gastro home from kinder.

Avatars belonging to all four of her brothers immediately popped up with responses.

Brad: Inconsiderate of him.

Bill: Better you than me.

Sid: Gross.

"Ms Adams?"

Adelaid looked up to find Audrey Hepburn—if Audrey Hepburn was taller, curvier, in her late twenties and had a penchant for tiny wrist tattoos—standing before her.

"Hi! Yes! Adelaid. That's me!" she said, sliding her phone, messages unanswered, and her earbuds into her handbag.

Then she rummaged through her work tote to find the printout of her official invitation. As provided by Big Think's flashy new PR firm, who happened to employ Adelaid's best friend, Georgette, who'd wangled Adelaid the fantasy opportunity, for which she would be forever grateful.

"Don't mind all that," said Audrey II. "No one gets in without us knowing exactly who they are. My name is Hadley. Welcome to Big Think."

Hadley passed Adelaid a lanyard hooked to a visitor pass sporting a recent photo and her name, spelled correctly, which only elevated Adelaid's impression of the place.

"So, you're interviewing our Ted," said Hadley, beckoning over her shoulder as she sashayed away at a fast clip.

"I am." Curling the lanyard around her neck, Adelaid followed.

"Most journos have their sights set on the other two."

Adelaid had no doubt, for "the other two" were none other than Ronan Gerard—the brains of the operation, of the richer-than-Midas Gerards—and ex-football star and one time Australian of the Year, Sawyer Mahoney—the brawn of the group, though it was, as yet, a little unclear to her what he brought to the endeavour bar a sexy smile and celebrity.

"That's partly why I'm so keen to profile Mr Fincher," said Adelaid.

There wasn't all that much out there about the guy, apart from his incredible success in the field of medical research. Basically, a science nerd with the benefit of more funding at his disposal than the GDP of most small countries, he'd also seemed the least intimidating of the three. Win-win!

"Clever choice," said Hadley. "I wonder what you'll make of his lair."

"Lair?"

Hadley shot Adelaid a smile over her shoulder as she made a beeline for the opposite corner of the ocean of marble. Which, under foot, did not sound or feel like marble at all.

"The Batcave," said Hadley, waggling her fingers. Then,

noticing Adelaid's vintage brogues testing the floor as she walked, said, "Did you know the building is carbon negative? The flooring, for instance, is recycled. Throughout the entire building. Impressive, no?"

"No. I mean, yes. It's…" Adelaid's gaze grazed the vertigo-inducing balconies looking down from the first two floors of office space above. "Fantastical. I feel as if I've stepped thirty years into the future."

That earned Adelaid a Mona Lisa smile.

"Before I send you up," said Hadley, "would you care for a self-guided tour of the building? We provide disposable degradable headphones and an app, as well as an upgrade to your visitor card to allow you access to the relevant areas."

Adelaid's Spidey-senses tingled. A tour would be the physical version of a press release. And pretty much everything she'd read about the company had been cannibalised, repurposed from elegantly curated tales of origin and purpose that could be found on the company website.

She was after something richer. Deeper. Something honest and real.

Connections and empathy. That was her intention.

Someone else could look after carbon.

Fingers stimming over the corner of her visitor pass, Adelaid said, "Another time. I want to be ready for Mr Fincher when he's ready for me."

A quick flick of Hadley's gaze seemed to take in the whole of her, from the fluff of her curly braid to her op shop suit, before she said, "But will he be ready for the likes of you?"

Before Adelaid could make heads or tails of that, they reached the lifts.

Clicking her hand towards Adelaid's visitor pass, Hadley mimed for Adelaid to swipe it over a small square panel in the wall after which the lift doors opened on a quiet swish.

Adelaid stepped inside. "Where to?"

"Your pass has been set to two stops, the Batcave, and the lobby." Then, as the lift doors closed, Hadley added, "Good luck."

The doors closed and the lift was off and away before Adelaid could say thank you.

As the lift hurtled her skyward, she tapped into sensory techniques she'd learned in her teens, to help snag her attention before it strayed too far too fast. She noted a subtle scent of orange blossom, and the whir of electricity through her feet. Found herself wondering what Ted Fincher's quirk might be, maybe a daffy number of lab coats?

Her phone buzzed again, yanking her out of her exercise. She couldn't deal with her brothers right now.

They were not yet privy to the fact she'd quit her job to "follow her dream," and she planned to keep it that way till the profile had found a home. The last thing she needed was their united disappointment, or concerns it was something their mum would have done.

In some deep, unspoiled place inside of her, she hoped they might see the risk as ballsy and brave. Proof that after all her challenges, she'd turned out okay. More than okay. That she was flourishing.

Connections and empathy, she reminded herself as the tone of the lift changed.

Adelaid looked to the display to see which floor she'd reached to find not a number, but the initials *TF.* Suddenly her hopes for a daffy number of lab coats didn't seem likely.

When the doors slid open on a satisfying whoosh, the first thing she noticed was the quiet. No voices, no tapping keyboards, no music, no people bustling by. As someone who needed white noise in order to function, the stillness made her twitch.

The next thing she noticed was the space. For as far as she could tell, Ted Fincher had the entire floor.

Outside the lift doors sat a couple of caramel leather

couches, like those downstairs, more plants, a table with notepads and a neat grouping of sharpened pencils and a coat rack. A black freestanding wall had been propped behind them, in the centre a massive framed Carl Sagan quote.

Somewhere, something incredible is waiting to be known.

"Hello?" she called out, her voice barely carrying. Then, "Mr Fincher? Ted?"

No answer.

Curiosity piqued, she poked her head around the wall to find herself in a cross between Leonardo da Vinci's workshop, Dr Strange's mansion and, yep, the Batcave.

The deeper she went, the more dedicated spaces she found. A library with a cosy reading nook. A row of meeting rooms in green glass and blond wood. Arrays of supertech that would blow her brothers' minds, including VR set-ups with requisite floor space. By the windows at the far end of the floor, three beautiful telescopes of varying sizes stood regally, pointed towards the sky, and in what felt like the centre of the space, a massive bronze globe hung like a chandelier.

The kookiness spoke to her own eclectic sensibilities, but it also had a hermetic, dust-free kind of symmetry. Every notebook lined up with every pencil, every chair was tucked in, as if everything had been placed exactly where the owner wanted it to be. Which was definitely not her.

A sound scraped along the edge of her wildly overstimulated mind, and she flinched.

"Hello?" she called. Then again, after her voice cracked the first time, "Mr Fincher?"

There was a shift of paper, the shuffle of fabric. Then a deep, gravelly voice called out, "Come on through. I'll be with you in a second."

Adelaid hitched the straps of her multiple bags and moved carefully around a maze of cabinets containing awesome collectibles. Geological wonders and old medical equipment and a life-sized replica of Han Solo trapped in carbonite—at least she assumed it was a replica—

"Oh," she gasped when she found herself facing a real live man, sitting at a drafting table.

Maybe it was the simplicity of the man jotting notes using a cheap pencil and dime a dozen notebook, the slightly crooked glasses, the analogue watch sitting low on his wrist.

Maybe it was the way light bounced perfectly off the globe above, creating a cascading golden glow over his outline, making the man appear as if he possessed some magical inner warmth.

Or maybe it was the sheer size of him—huge shoulders, thick neck, legs like tree trunks, scruffy stubble. Like Beauty's Beast might have looked in suit pants and a pale blue button-down.

Add overlong dark auburn hair, aquiline nose, a dark, long-sleeved T-shirt doing its best to contain more muscles than Adelaid knew by name and roping veins jerking in his forearms as he sketched, the man was Marvel-level gorgeous.

Aquiline? some voice queried in the back of her head. She didn't even know what *aquiline* meant, only that it had sprung, unbidden, from some ancient place inside of her that spoke to classic hotness. As if even her ancestors were impressed.

Then he placed the pencil on the table. Neatly. Lining it up with the edge of his notebook. Before his big, squared-off fingers pushed his sleeves higher at his elbows. And he turned to face her, a welcoming smile already in place.

Only when his gaze met hers, he stilled. His muscles

jerking, his jaw clenching. His eyes a rich warm molten brown behind the glints of his lenses.

Adelaid's mouth dried up at the sight of him. Completely and utterly. To the point she had to prise her tongue from the roof of her mouth in order to breathe.

Then he blinked, as if coming out of a daydream.

And Adelaid's lungs whimpered in gratitude when she'd remembered to fill them again.

The man pushed his glasses higher on his nose, pressed back his chair and stood, showing off the kind of tall that came with breadth. And heft. And all of it seemed to be in Vitruvian proportion.

"Ted Fincher?" she asked. For she had to be sure before she started wasting so many good words on the man.

He nodded. Then in a voice so deep that she felt it in the backs of her knees, the man said, "Hi."

Adelaid reminded herself that this was a moment that required a surplus of attention rather than her usual deficit. Her only chance to make a good first impression on the man who held all her eggs in his basket. So to speak. She took the final few steps the man's way, smiled and held out a hand—straight arm, strong thrust.

"Mr Fincher," she said. "I'm so happy to meet you."

Katharine Hepburn would have been proud.

One second Ted's heart was doing as it ought: beating a neat fifty-six beats a minute, pushing oxygen-rich blood to his body's tissues, before drawing the oxygen-poor blood back again, ready for nourishment.

The next it forgot its very purpose. Seeming to hover inside his chest cavity, like a lump of wobbly gristle, before finally going back to keeping him alive.

The only possible justification for the aberration was the apparition before him. A wild-haired, pink-cheeked, bright-eyed, fidgety woman, who seemed to crackle with energy even while standing still.

Though, at second glance, she wasn't standing still. She rocked from foot to foot, her hand outstretched, as if waiting…

Waiting for him to shake it.

Ted nudged his glasses higher on his nose, took a step her way and took her by the hand.

He tracked the musculature, the bones, the ridges of knuckle and skin. Everything was where, and as, it should be. And yet…that spark; as if some kind of electrical impulse had leapt from her hand to his, or vice versa. That was new.

He felt the relaxing of her grip, a sign that she was ready to end the holding. Not that they were *holding hands*. A handshake was not at all the same thing. Yet when Ted pulled his hand back into his personal space, he cupped it, the flat tip of his thumb pressing against the sensations playing havoc with his nerves.

"I'm sorry," he said, his voice rough from underuse. How long had it been since he'd spoken aloud to another human being? Hours? Days? "Who did you say you were?"

He was ready this time, when her gaze met his. Braced. Her eyes were wide, lovely and a pale alchemical green. A colour that eyes should not be. Not if someone wanted to be able to look at a person without staring.

"I didn't say, did I?" she said. That *voice*. Breathy and full. Then hand to heart she said, "I'm Adelaid Adams, one 'e,' and I am so excited we get to do this together."

"One 'e'?"

Do what, exactly?

"The 'e' is in the middle," she said, writing her name in the air between them, "not the end." Then, remembering the lanyard around her neck, she took another step closer and lifted it so he could see.

Close enough he noted a mass of tiny curls twisting away from her head, a smattering of freckles on the bridge of her fine nose, the sharp bow of her top lip.

Who was she? He didn't remember her name attached to any of his rigorously guarded slate of projects. Not that he was concerned, as such. She'd never have made it to this floor without getting past Hadley. He was curious. So he let himself off the leash, just a smidge.

And asked, "What exactly are we doing together?"

Her eyes flickered, long tangled lashes sweeping shadows over her cheekbones. "A series of interviews? Me writing a profile on you? You—" She paused to swallow. "You didn't know I was coming."

Ted ran hand up the back of his neck. "Are you sure you weren't after Sawyer? Or Ronan?"

"Nope," she said. "I'd much prefer you."

"If only they were here to hear you say that my year would be made," he said. Only to hear his own words bounce back at him on delay. It sounded like flirting. Was he flirting? It had been a while since he'd partaken in the practice. And never while working.

Working.

He glanced over his shoulder at the desk, at the work he'd been focussed on for the past several hours. Work that had fled from his head the moment he'd seen Adelaid Adams standing before him. He noted the papers he'd mussed up by sitting on them and pulled himself back to standing so that he might tuck them back into a neat pile.

"Hadley," Adelaid said, "gave me this pass. In case you're worried I'm some kind of burglar intent on stealing any of your fancy stuff. Or…mussing up your pencils."

His gaze shot back to hers. Was she flirting now? Or just funny? Her expression seemed…friendly. Curious.

The resultant whoosh had him wondering when he'd last eaten. Or had any water.

He said, "I'm not sure pencil mussing comes under the purview of the burglar."

A glint of mischief lit those mercurial eyes. "And yet, once they get a load of those neat lines and sharp points, the urge might overcome them."

The word *urge* backed up inside his head. Along with *flirt. Staring. Lips. Spark.*

And he wondered, honestly, how long it had been since he'd had an interaction with a human person that did not involve statistics, or study results, or funding.

Long enough he'd let her stand there, carrying what looked to be an inordinate number of heavy bags, for too long.

"Forgive me." Ted looked about, found a stool and carried it to her. Placing it by her. Close enough to catch a waft of berries, of something light and sweet, like icing sugar.

He backed up, giving her space, inviting her to sit. To stay.

Which she did, with a quick smile, wincing as her bags slid from her shoulder and slumped to the floor at her feet. As she pulled her phone free, a flutter of flyaway blond hair wafted over her face before she shot a gust of air from the corner of her mouth to blow it back into place. He was fairly sure she'd had no idea she'd done so.

And when those huge wild green eyes of hers once again found his, heat rushed to his face, while goosebumps rushed down his arms. It was a temperature-controlled space, meaning his reaction had to be due to adrenaline. Fight or flight. Not that he had any intention of doing either.

Attempting to exhibit some measure of self-control, Ted settled back into his own seat, and asked, "What will this involve? If you don't mind me asking."

Snapping the button, rhythmically, on her phone case, she said, "Ask anything you'd like. I don't want this to feel like an interrogation. More like…a conversation."

As she spoke, her right leg started bouncing up and down. Making him wonder if regular movement, for her, was the norm rather than an exception.

"A conversation," he encouraged.

"Exactly! My aim is to give readers a glimpse into other people's lives. To showcase what makes the subject unique but also what makes them the same. So, in your case, I'd love to know more about your work, as well as the man behind the glasses."

Her focus shifted, intensifying, travelling over his face, down his neck, pausing on his chest a moment, before lifting quickly back to his eyes. Her hair fluttering slightly as if she'd sucked in too quick a breath.

"For what purpose?" he asked.

"The profile? The pursuit of connection. And empathy." A shrug. "To get there, as per the rather vociferous contract negotiated with your rabidly intense lawyers, we will catch up several times over the next weeks. There will likely be phone calls, emails, for clarification as we go. And you look dubious."

He felt it. All over. Which was why such appointments usually went Sawyer's way, or Ronan's. He'd much rather do the work than talk about it.

As if she sensed it, she picked at her thumbnail, before seeming to come to a decision. "I'm not here to write an exposé, or delve into anything you decide is too personal. My jam is the weird and the wonderful, their whys and wherefores—as I believe it encourages open minds. Understanding. Acceptance. And I think… I've *seen* how so much of that has been lost of late. Paths of information are narrowing when they ought to be opening up."

A smile, a shrug. Then another long moment in which she simply looked at him, before she shook her head and said, "And I get that people might find your compatriots easier to write about. The magnate and the football star.

Please," she scoffed, though there was a glimmer of humour in her eyes. "Do they have multiple PhDs? Are they out there curing diseases? Or making names for themselves regards the Glasgow accords? All that wrapped up in—"

Her words stopped, but her hand kept going—flapping at him, all of him, as if intimating he was as impressive as his résumé.

Then, when she seemed to realise what she had implied, she pulled back her hand, before lifting a bottom cheek and sitting on her fingers.

It was enough to make Ted's head swim. In fact, it *was* swimming. And his belly—it was rumbling. Hollow. How long *had* it been since he'd eaten? Seriously? This lightheadedness was not normal.

"Now I've said enough, and this is not meant to be about me, so how about we pick a time for our first proper chat. One day this week?" She turned her phone, finger flicking over the screen to find her calendar, then looked to him in anticipation.

"Thursday," he said, picking a day at random that was long enough away to find out what was actually going on.

"Perfect. First thing?"

He nodded. Knowing he just had to say the word and Ronan would make it go away. For the work came first. Their mission far too important to brook distractions. Though the thought of Adelaid Adams walking out of here and never seeing her again—

"Great!" she said, hopping off the stool and grabbing her gear, then slipping her phone into one of her plethora of bags. When she stood, wisps of hair floated around her like a halo.

Ted pressed finger and thumb into his eye sockets, before running a hand over his chin, feeling the rasp of whiskers against his palm. How long had it been since he'd *shaved*?

Adelaid wavered. “Do you have any questions for me, before I go?”

Are you single?

What’s your favourite colour?

How do you take your coffee?

Where do you store all that excess energy and can I have some?

Are you happy?

Would you like to have dinner with me sometime?

Ted shook his head. “Let’s save it for Thursday.”

Once he’d shaved, and eaten, and guzzled a gallon of water. And seen sunlight. And tidied his desk. And no longer had the scent of her every time he breathed in. Like berries and sugar. Like cake. No, like *muffin*. Heaven help him, Adelaid Adams smelled like a blueberry muffin.

“Okey-doke,” she said, then turned to leave. Stopping when she realised she wasn’t sure which way she’d come in.

“I’ll walk you to the lift.”

“Still afraid I might steal something?” She looked back over her shoulder as if checking he was still following. Which he was. Tugged by a thread in his chest yanking him forward.

“Afraid you might get lost. I’ve been told my plan for the place makes little sense to anyone else.”

“I like it,” she said. “It’s like Disneyland—a new world around every corner.” She turned and, walking backwards, held out her phone. “Do you mind if I grab your details? For some reason, your lawyers wouldn’t blithely hand over your phone number, home address, mother’s maiden name…”

He reached out, his fingers almost brushing hers as he slid the phone from her hand. *Almost*. And still he felt that spark, like an echo of her life force, a tingle in his fingertips as he tapped in his mobile number, his private email and a couple of other ways of getting hold of him. Just in case.

She smiled her thanks when he handed back her phone.

After which she tapped in a message, his phone in his back pocket buzzing. "Now you have mine. If you need to get in touch. About anything. Any time."

A flush of pink rose to her cheeks. Blushing being the physiological response to an emotional stimulus.

Their gazes held a mite longer than polite, before she blinked and looked away.

They walked the rest of the way in silence.

At the lift, he leaned past her, waving his card over the sensor pad. Notes of berries making his head spin.

She glanced up. "I'm really looking forward to getting to know you, Ted. You're going to be so glad you did this. Hand to heart, I will not mess it up."

He saw the moment she wished she could take those final words back. A widening of her eyes, a twisting of her full mouth, before she breathed deep and tipped her chin; as if daring him to contradict her.

Which was when all that crackling, compelling nervous energy began to make sense.

Bravado had brought her here. *Gumption*, as Ronan would say. Ronan would like her, Ted thought. Then the thought of Ronan *liking* Adelaid Adams made him feel as if he had heartburn.

As hunger and friction and exhaustion and attraction and the tightening of the rubber band that kept him tied to his desk coalesced into a tight knot inside of his hollowed-out belly, Ted held out a hand. "Till Thursday."

Adelaid hitched her bags before taking his hand in hers. Holding it for a beat. Then a few more.

The lift doors opened and she sprang back, as if caught doing something untoward. But then, before stepping inside the lift, Adelaid reached out, and nudged the notebooks and pencils on the table by the Carl Sagan wall till they sat askew.

"There," she said, grinning, "that's better."

Then she bounded into the lift, and lifted her hand in a wave as the doors closed.

Ted saw his own hand lifted in response in the reflection of the closed doors. He let it drop. While the very room seemed to settle with a sigh now that she was gone.

"What the hell was that?" he said, his voice rough.

Now that he was alone, now that he could think, all evidence pointed to mitigating circumstances. A man of his size had specific fuel requirements. He'd been known to hallucinate entire conversations when he lost track of time, when the work was going well.

Once he'd called Sawyer to ask his advice on where they might set up a lab in Sydney, only to find it was three in the morning, and Sawyer was in Bolivia. And then there was the time he was sure he'd seen Ronan and Hadley making out in a broom closet at a party in their pre–Big Think days, which they'd assured him, vociferously, he had not.

Turning, Ted lumbered back to his desk—but not before quickly tidying the notebooks and pencils—and finished off the notes he'd been making before he'd been interrupted.

He took out his phone to put in a call to their executive chef—one of the better additions Ronan had insisted upon when they'd built the place—he found a new message. From a new number.

Ted, this is Adelaid. One "e", see! Looking forward to Thursday. And don't worry, if anyone can ferret out the weird and the wonderful, it's me. All you have to do is show up.

He slid the message away, put in an order for a lot of steamed chicken and vegetables, then dropped to the floor and did as many push-ups as his body would allow, in the hopes of returning to some level of normal.

CHAPTER TWO

"ARE WE READY?" asked Ronan as he strode into the Big Think founders' private meeting room—less fancy board-room, more like the university lounge in which Ted, Ronan and Sawyer had first met.

Ronan headed straight to his corner of the room, the chair he'd brought in rather reminiscent of a throne.

"Ready," Ted concurred, grabbing sushi bites from the tray Hadley had asked the chef to whip up, and dropping into his battered blue lounger in the corner.

The chair had been his dad's. After his dad's sudden passing, he'd dragged the thing back to uni, and it had come with him ever since. A touchstone. A reminder as to what he was doing with his life and why.

"Ready," Hadley agreed, leaning in the doorway like some kind of upmarket bouncer, an edge to her voice, as if having to sound off to Ronan was beneath her.

If Sawyer was in town, he'd be pulling up a random chair, turning it backwards, straddling the thing and tossing something from hand to hand.

"Talk," said Ronan, waving a hand like a Jedi.

"Ted had a girl in his lair." That was Hadley.

Ted flinched so hard he pulled a muscle in his neck.

"What girl?" Ronan barked.

"Not a girl," said Ted. "A woman."

A lanky blonde with pink cheeks and a habit of nibbling

her bottom lip. He'd thought about that bottom lip, the way she'd messed up his pencils, her sweet scent, far too often in the days since. It had been distracting. Enough he planned to fix it, in this meeting. One hundred percent.

"Her name was Adelaid Adams," Ted added when the others continued staring at him. "One 'e.' She's a journalist." Then, seeing where he'd actually gone wrong, added, "If that was to whom you were referring."

"You let a journalist get to Ted?" That, from Ronan.

Hadley bristled in Ronan's direction. "You're the one who insisted upon some outside PR after lamenting that our press was beginning to stagnate. 'We need to be humanised,' you said, right here in this room. 'Given the warm and fuzzy treatment.'"

"That last part does not sound at all like me."

A shrug. "Either way, the PR mob have been proficient, if overzealous. I sifted through the hundreds of requests to interview *you* and winnowed them down to a couple of dozen."

A slight bow of thanks.

"Nearly as many are ready for Sawyer, when he's able. But Ms Adams requested Ted. So, I looked into her. Melbourne uni. Earned her master's part-time while also working for a light online ezine with big numbers. But it's her side hustle I like—writing longer form features for community papers. Open-minded, insightful, clever with a lovely edge of dry humour. Nice fit for our Ted."

Hadley shot Ted a smile, reminding him of a Venus flytrap.

If was enough to have Ted shifting in his seat. He wondered if Adelaid's fidgets were due to sugar levels, or sudden strange feelings and needing somewhere to put them.

Not that he'd get the chance to find out, for there was an eighty-five percent chance he was putting a stop to the whole thing. If Ronan didn't put a stop to it first.

Then Ronan said, "Things are chilly out there. Purses are tight. A new angle might help. Ted?"

Leaving Ted seventy-three percent sure they'd not blink if he asked not to do the interview.

But Ronan was right. For all that their start-up capital had been immense, their turnover eye-watering, the kinds of projects Ted was determined to see through—curing every damn kind of cancer on the planet, and that was just the start—needed more. And more. And more.

"Whatever you need," he found himself saying. "I'll make sure it doesn't interfere with the work."

Hadley reached over and patted his knee. "Let her interfere, Ted. Might do you some good."

Ronan coughed out a laugh, then covered it with a stately clearing of the throat. "Hard to imagine, but our Ted had game, once upon a time. Girls on campus would flock towards him, in droves, cartoon love hearts beating out of their eyes."

Hadley looked to Ted, a newfound glint in her eye. "Ted was a playa?"

Ted shrugged it off. Not a player—tall, clean-cut and a good listener adept at balancing work, study, family, girls. Till he'd taken a gap year, mid-degree, and his whole world had flipped on its head. His priorities shifting so drastically "game" had been the last thing on his mind.

"Come to think of it," said Hadley, "I am often hit up by women making wildly inappropriate offers in order to be seated at Ted's table at Big Think fundraisers. If I knew you were up for it, Ted, I could be filthy rich by now."

Ted held up a hand. "Thanks all the same."

Hands raised in submission, Hadley glanced at Ronan, smirking when Ronan's eye twitched with the effort not to ask how many women had asked the same about him.

Then Ronan waved a hand, done with the conversation. And he moved onto the minutiae of running their company.

Leaving Ted to figure out how to manage the Adelaid situation, now that it wasn't going away.

Chemistry could explain the flush of hormones that led to an unnatural feeling of euphoria, biology the inclination to ensure the propagation of the species, and physics the attraction of materials, specifically unpaired electrons spinning in the same direction.

He was currently unpaired. Had been for some time. His relationships fizzling out rather quickly due to a lack of time. One ex claiming she'd have had better luck if he'd found her at the bottom of a Petrie dish.

Adelaid's "pairing" status was unknown. Perhaps *trusting* that she was paired would negate the physics. Tipping a portion of control back in his favour. Though, like his initial conclusions, it was untested or peer reviewed.

"That it, then?" Hadley asked.

"Somewhere better to be?" Ronan asked.

"Always," she said, shooting him a saccharine smile before shooting out the door.

Ted hauled himself from his dad's lounger, gave the arm a quick pat, saluted Ronan and left.

On his way to their private lift, Ted pulled out his phone, and opened a secure, well-sourced search engine the three of them had invested in during their university days, the huge success helping them make their first million as a team.

He typed *The science of attraction.*

Before meeting Adelaid again, Ted intended to arm himself. It was time to hit the books.

Adelaid strode up Collins Street, drinking in the gothic architecture glistening with the wash of recent rain, Gene Kelly skiting about his excellent rhythm via her earbuds.

She adored this part of Melbourne. *Grace* Kelly would have fit right in, swanning past the glamorous designer shops. In fact, she'd had Grace in mind when pinning a black velvet flower to her French twist and donning a collarless shirt with capped sleeves and ruching across the torso, tucked into a black crepe poodle skirt that swished as she walked.

She'd sent her revised pitch—complete with Ted's shiny new release form—to her top editors, publications and websites. Now all she had to do was wait for the bidding war to ensue, and the whole thing to go down in folklore. Oh, and interview Ted Fincher several times and write the thing, and keep hustling for extra work on the side so she could pay her rent.

At the very least she could be grateful not to be sitting at her old hot desk, mainlining dodgy drip coffee and trying to find a new angle from which to talk about period cups and K-pop.

Her phone buzzed in her ears. She checked in case it was Ted; alas it was the Adams family group chat.

Jake: Sunday lunch back on. False alarm.

Sid: Can't, working, booked in a big new job.

Brad: Go get 'em.

Jake: Great work, mate. Addy, bring chicken wings.

Nose scrunched at her phone, Adelaid considered copying and pasting Sid's message.

Can't, working, booked in a big new job.

It would be the truth, after all. But whereas for Sid it was all pats on the back, for her it would only bring down an avalanche of questions. A broken record of big brotherly worry.

She would wait till she had real news. Irrefutably fabulous news. Till then it was full steam ahead, following her dreams!

When Adelaid reached the café, she quickly checked to see if Ted had beaten her there. While she'd learned to manage most other symptoms of her condition relatively well, her relationship with time remained tense. When there was no sign of him, she tipped her earbuds from her ears and slipped them into their case, the white noise of the café lifting around her.

Only to leap from her shoes when she heard a familiar deep voice right behind her say: "Adelaid Adams."

She spun, the soul of her ballet flat catching on a tile, knocking her off balance. She grabbed for the only thing within reach to stop herself from falling on her backside. She grabbed Ted.

Ted's shirt to be exact, her fingers gripping, slipping and ripping, an opalescent button flying past her nose.

The world took a moment to stop spinning. A moment in which Adelaid realised Ted had caught her, his big strong arms holding her in something akin to a Hollywood dip. While her fingers gripped his torn shirt and his meaty shoulder respectively with all she had.

He'd shaved, she noticed, now she was up close and personal. Gone was the scruff from the day they'd met, and in its place, granite jaw, and cheekbones, and wide kissable lips.

Kissable? They were just lips. There, ready to do whatever other things lips did.

Moving away from his lips, she noticed his glasses were different from last time too, though still slightly crooked. No, not his glasses, his nose. There was a bend, as if it had been broken at some point. Though, instead of marring what was an otherwise impossibly beautiful collection of features, right up there with the likes of Paul Newman, and Montgomery Clift, that nose gave him an edge. Grit. The kind that planted a seed in a woman's belly, and before she knew it there were vines twirling about her inside, every which way.

Ted's hand at her waist gripped a smidge tighter, his fingers digging into her side in a way that made all kinds of warm sparkly feelings tumble through her.

She realised, belatedly, he was only readying to pull her upright. Her body lifted to land flush against his. Putting her eyes level with the second buttonhole which was now devoid of a button, the shirt pulling open a smidge so that she was looking at a patch of warm male skin.

"Oops," she managed, her fingers sliding to the offending spot and attempting to tug the fabric together.

"It's fine," he rumbled in a cavernous voice that vibrated through her. "Are you okay?"

She looked up, and up, and up. "I'm fine. Mortified, but fine. You?"

He lifted a hand to cover hers, which was when she realised she hadn't stopped playing with the gap in his shirt. Fiddling was par for the course for her, fiddling with other people something to be avoided, at least without prior permission.

Mortification deepening, she stepped back, arching away from his embrace, and he let her go.

The moment might have been salvageable, if not for the flower in her hair choosing that moment to pop free till it dangled over her ear. She quickly plucked the thing off and shoved it into a bag.

Ted hadn't missed a moment of her circus act. And yet, there was no judgement in his gaze. None of her brother Sid's eye rolls. Or Brad's sigh of disappointment at seeing her make a klutz of herself. No flicker of wariness that came over most new people of her acquaintance during such moments. Just warm, polite interest. In fact, he looked so clean cut, so neat and tidy, so big and unimpeachable, butter wouldn't melt. And yet instinct had her feeling something warm and new and dangerous arcing between them.

"Shall we sit?" she asked, her voice a little reedy.

He nodded and held out a hand so that she might lead him inside.

His gaze burning a hole into her back, she led him to a semi-private booth that—along with the cookie dough and fresh coffee scent—would help them both relax.

Adelaid slid into a seat. Only to find Ted staring at the tight space, as if trying to work out, mathematically, how he could curl his gargantuan body into the right pretzel shape so that he might fit.

"Oh," she said, holding out a hand. "Hang on, we can move!"

He shook his head, and somehow managed to curl himself between the table and bench. Till he tried to find space for his long legs, only for his ankles to slide along hers.

Adelaid covered it with a quick, apologetic smile, and tucked her feet as far beneath her as they would go, and hoped her pulse would calm the heck down. Not easy when the feel of Ted's arms, and chest, and now leg, had left lasting imprints on her skin.

"What can I get you?"

Adelaid could have kissed the friendly face of the waitress who had popped up beside them. She ordered strong coffee and a piece of the apple rhubarb pie; Ted ordered a fresh squeezed juice and an egg white omelette.

"You sure?" Adelaid asked. "The cakes here are amazing."

"I'd last five minutes before needing to eat again," he said. "The bane of being this big."

The waitress sighed and left. Then it was just the two of

them. Sitting across the table from one another, the scent of sugar on the air.

"Let's get this show on the road!"

Adelaid found her phone deep inside the wrong bag, made sure Ted agreed before turning on the recorder app. Then she reached into her work tote, grabbed a couple of pencils, chose the one that didn't need sharpening and the notebook in which she'd been jotting research and question ideas. A few random sticky notes fluttered to the table, and she shoved them in the back of the notebook.

Once she had everything within reach, she looked up to find Ted leaning his chin on his upturned palm as he took in her mobile office.

He picked up a pencil shaving that must have been stuck to…something, and his eyes met hers. Warm behind his dark-rimmed glasses. She may have swayed a little from the impact.

Adelaid shrugged. "It's…organised chaos."

"It's *pure* chaos."

He laughed as he said it, as if there was wonder behind his comment, not sanction, yet something ugly shifted in Adelaid's chest. Echoes of the multiple times she'd had similar words tossed her way.

"You're late, again."

"Can't you just sit still?"

"Anyone ever told you how tactless you can be? It's frustrating as hell."

But his gaze was curious, kind. Reminding her there was no way he could know he'd poked at a sore spot. And the fact she'd borne witness to the anal—in her opinion—neatness of his workspace, to her mind indicative of its own kind of pathology, helped her settle.

And say, "Yet, for me, it works. Which is what matters, correct?"

A little thinking time, then a nod. "Correct."

"Great. First question. Any subject you'd prefer *not* to touch on?"

"No."

Though a muscle in his jaw ticked, and Adelaid made a mental note to tread carefully till she found *his* sore spot. "What if I'm…an industrial spy? Like Ingrid Bergman in *Notorious*."

"She was a political spy, if I'm not mistaken."

Adelaid blinked. "I can't believe you just corrected me on an old-timey movie. That would be like me correcting you on the chemical formula for…butane."

"C4H10," he said with a smile in his eyes.

Pencil waggling at the ends of her fingers she said, "How about you tell me your safe word, just in case."

"My *safe word*?" he repeated, gaze glinting, voice dropping.

"*A* safe word," she adjusted, her cheeks warming. "A word you can use that tells me I've pushed too far. We can come up with a new one, you know, in case you have one you use in…other parts of your life."

If only he'd look away, then she might stop babbling. But those eyes of his—all that deep, soft, warm, inviting, molten, chocolatey brown—made her ears ring and her pulse throb. Made it hard to concentrate. And when that was already an issue for her, she had to work extra hard to stay on task.

"Adelaid?"

"Mmm?" She came to, to find that she was now leaning forward too, her pencil tapping madly on the table. "Look, I'm nice but I'm pushy. Chances are I will, at some point, wander into a paddock you think is clearly out of bounds, but unless there's a great big 'keep off the grass' sign, I'll stomp all over the place."

He breathed in, slow and deep, the light now reflecting

off his glasses so she could no longer quite see his eyes. Then he said, "Muffin."

"You'd like a muffin?"

He shook his head, and blinked a couple of times, as if coming out of a daze.

"Our *safe word* is 'muffin'?" Adelaid's mouth quirked as she wrote the word on her notebook. Drawing a cloud around the edges, with little rays of sunshine bursting out in all directions. "Any particular kind of muffin?"

She looked up in time to see a muscle ticking at the edge of his jaw. Then his gaze dropped to her mouth as he rumbled, "Blueberry."

Oh, my. "Blueberry muffin, it is. Now, let's start with an easy one. How did you, Sawyer and Ronan meet?"

Ted finally leaned back, arms moving to cross over his impressive chest. Meaning his legs stretched out further under the table too; a shift of air told her how close his foot was to hers. Unfortunately, she couldn't tuck her legs any deeper under her seat or she'd end up under there herself.

"University."

Adelaid nodded, encouraging him to go on. But he was done. Flicking to a fresh page in her notebook, she wrote down, slowly, in big bold letters, *MET AT UNIVERSITY*, and doodled as she asked, "Were you in the same class?"

"No."

"Same…dorm?"

"No."

She stopped doodling. "Ted. Your origin story is no secret. In fact, it gets an airing in pretty much every Big Think story out there. Sawyer Mahoney, Ronan Gerard and Ted Fincher were best friends at uni. Young Ted—that would be you—"

Ted's eyebrows rose a smidge.

"Became friends with Ronan—a risk taker with an eye for talent. Sawyer one day wandered into a meeting they were having when he thought he smelled cookies. How am I doing?"

"Close." He ran a hand over his chin, and she could all but hear the rasp of fresh stubble against his strong hand. As if the clean-cut look took work. As if the bit of rough she'd seen the other day lived just beneath the surface. "Except the food."

"What was it, then? If you say *blueberry muffin* I might cry."

"Well, we wouldn't want that, now, would we? Not on day one."

She barked out an unexpected laugh. Once again, that unexpected flash of grit getting under her skin. Twirling her pencil, she tried a new angle.

"What did you study at uni?"

"Everything."

Putting aside the buzz of concern that Ted Fincher might actually turn out to be a dud interview, Adelaid reminded herself that *she* was the experienced one in this situation. That it was on her to take control.

"Ted. It might sound contrary, but this will all be over faster if you avoid one-word answers."

He breathed in, his chest rising and falling. And his foot rubbed against hers. The slide of it making her breath hitch. Which he did not miss, as his gaze was locked onto hers.

"Here we go!" said the waitress, leaning between them as she passed out their food. As she turned to leave, she shot Adelaid a look that said, *You go, girl.*

Ted missed it all, as he was already ploughing through his huge omelette. "How about you?" he asked, taking a breath between bites.

"Me?"

"Where did you go to uni?"

"This isn't about me," said Adelaid. First rule of journalism—don't put yourself into the story. "How about insight into some projects you're overseeing?"

"Which?"

She tilted her head. Gave him a look.

He grinned. A flash of big white teeth. And eye crinkles. And mouth brackets. And so many lovely, charming things she found herself a little starstruck.

"Pick one," she said. "I beg you."

This time he laughed, a rich chuckle that rocketed down her spine.

He rearranged his large body again. "I'm not in the habit of talking about myself, Adelaid. Theory, progress, budgets, logistics, with those who are working alongside me, yes. Sawyer is the salesman. Ronan the negotiator. I just—"

"You just…?"

"Do the work."

"So, tell me about that. The work. Tell me something you'd like the world to know about what it is that you do. Help me help you."

He stared at the table for a bit. Then, with a nod, he said, "Okay. When you found me the other day, I was working on something we've dubbed the Noah Project."

Even while her fingers itched to get around a pencil—to scratch out arrows, bubbles, squiggles all over the page, for doodling helped her remake connections when she looked back at her notes, Adelaid didn't move lest she spook him. For once he got started talking about the clean water project they had been working on for the better part of a decade, he was wonderful. Not a dud, not even a tiny little bit.

"I choose projects," Ted said, winding down, "which have meaning to me. It may sound selfish, and it is, to a point, but there also has to be some structure, some finite parameters, or we would be stretched too thin. Success is imperative. Not merely progress but results. I leave the red tape to others to sort out, because the work—whether it be vaccines, or clean water, or disease eradication—is what matters. It's all that matters. And your eyes are glazing over."

Adelaid blinked, realising she'd cradled her coffee at her chest the entire time she'd listened to that rough rumbling voice. Watched his big, elegant hands swish through the air as he became increasingly animated the more he talked about his work. And gazed into those lovely, warm, crinkling, chocolatey eyes.

"No! That was great. Honestly."

Ted's hand moved to the back of his neck. "It was esoteric."

"It was impassioned." Adelaid sat forward, knocking a pencil with her elbow, the thing rolling to the floor. "What's your mission statement?"

His eyebrow kicked north.

"Come on, I know you have one. Written on a napkin or printed on a T-shirt."

His gaze caught on hers, his expression serious as he said, simply, "To save the world."

And there was not a drop of irony attached.

"See," she said, still trying to shake off the dreamy feeling that had come over her. "You're a natural at this. You just needed a little nudge."

He looked at her then, as if trying to figure out if she was making fun.

"Do you know what my favourite part of my job is?" Adelaid asked.

"Stationery," he said, eyes roving over the spread now covering half the table. Eyes still gentle and kind.

"A teeny tiny smidge above stationery," she said, picking up a pencil and writing words and underlining them on the page. "It's the people. People with tall tales, and big dreams, and unique stories. People who surprise me. Who will surprise readers into realising that every single person on the planet has something to offer. A story to tell. A lesson to teach. And enough in common with everyone else that they are worth caring about. Even if that person seems so very different from them. Especially if they seem…"

How to put this?

"More weird than wonderful," said Ted.

Adelaid looked up from her frantic underlining, surprised he'd remembered her exact words. What was not a surprise was the buzz that came with landing on something real—interview one, day one. The logistics, science, tech and political manoeuvring—all that would elevate the piece. Create hooks on which to sell it.

Ted Fincher wasn't some run of the mill, big, handsome cinnamon roll, genius billionaire. He had edges, reasons, passion. He was the real deal.

"Okay," she said, snapping her notebook closed.

"We're done?"

"For today. Don't want to wear you out."

"Do I look worn out?" His arms once again folded across his insanely broad chest, long blunt fingers curling around meaty forearms. Only this time it wasn't in self-protection.

For the man was smiling, his gaze lit with interest. Curiosity. As if, now that he was fed, he was…switched on.

"I'd booked you in for an hour. It's been closer to two."

Ted jerked, then checked his watch—which meant twisting his arm, the face of the chunky analogue piece having settled over his inner wrist.

"Shall we go?"

He nodded, tidying up his side of the table, which meant lining up knife and fork in perfect parallel.

The waitress was back, flirting with Ted, giving Adelaid time to gather up her accoutrements only to remember the dropped pencil.

She reached out with her shoe. Finding no luck, she shuffled her backside as low as it would go beneath the table, sweeping her foot over the floor, only to feel her skirt bunch in a loud crinkling mass all the way to her hip when her inner thigh brushed right along Ted's.

She froze, balanced precariously on the edge of the seat, her arms straining to hold her in that strange off-kilter position, eyes so wide they began to burn for lack of blinking.

Ted looked cool as a cucumber. As if he sat entangled in women's legs, a knee positioned danger-close, day in day out. He didn't even break eye contact with the waitress, who was now leaning her backside against their table as she told a story about her adorable new niece.

Then he had to go and breathe.

His chest rising, filling deeply, his leg shifted, infinitesimally, towards her. His knee now millimetres from where a man's knee ought not to be. Not till the second date, at least.

Not that this was a date. It was an *interview*, a chance to get to know the man beneath the suit. Not that she was thinking about him that way. *Suit-less.*

Before this went downhill completely, she held her breath, quickly spread her legs wide enough to disengage and then dragged herself back to sitting. Then, feeling itchy, and pink, and hot, and breathless, she made a big to-do of gathering her things.

Enough that the waitress leapt up from the table.

Giving Ted leave to finally look Adelaid's way. His eyes were dark, the edge of his mouth hooked into a smile. "You all right over there?"

"I was trying to find the pencil I dropped earlier. Not…" *Feel you up with my thigh.*

Ted carefully eased himself out from behind the table, bent and came up with her pencil. "Yours?"

"Yep! Thanks." She snagged it from his hand, hooked her bag straps over her shoulder, ran a quick had over her messy hair and slid out of the booth.

"Have a good day now," the waitress singsonged, and Adelaid jumped, having forgotten she was still there.

Nerves snappy, Adelaid kept up her pace as she led Ted through the café. He reached past her to hold open the door, standing back to wave her through.

Out front, beneath the awning, the day having warmed, the earlier rain giving the air weight, Adelaid clasped her bags against her front. Like a shield.

"You that way?" He glanced down Collins in the direction of her pointing thumb, away from Big Think. "I'll walk you to your car—"

"No car. I don't drive. Tram. Then train. And I've kept you from saving the world long enough."

A muscle flickered under Ted's eye, too quick for her to guess why. But he nodded.

"I'll message you so that we can set a date for our next chat. Okay?" She was already backing down the street.

He nodded again. All talked out apparently, his one-word answers now down to no-word answers.

"Fair warning," she called, lifting a hand to her mouth, for some reason loath to turn and leave him behind. "I'll not be quite so easy on you next time."

Ted lifted a hand, holding it over his heart, as if shot, then lifted the hand in a wave, that big hand of his half blocking out the sun.

And there he stayed, beneath the twee red gingham awning. She'd have bet quite a bit that if she glanced over her shoulder he'd still be there.

It took every ounce of willpower she had not to look back to check.

"Dammit," he growled, still in the shade of the café awning for a few long moments after Adelaid walked away, even when the sun shining through the squares above began to play hazard with his eyeballs.

The excessive amount of time he'd given over to learning about the science of attraction prior to today's interview had clearly not helped when it came to navigating it in the field.

Take *muffin*. He'd actually said the word out loud. The scent of it, of her, when he'd held her in his arms in that wildly unexpected moment in the doorway of the café. Berries. And sugar. It made his head go foggy. *She* made his head go foggy.

When his head could not *be* foggy. Ever.

His constancy, his focus, his unimpeachable dedication to the cause, were his greatest assets. It gave him an edge over every other clever scientist out there trying to scrounge for the same fundraising, the same lab time, the same journal space.

He wanted it more.

He lifted his hand to his late father's watch, tugged it till it sat flat against his wrist, reminding himself why that was.

He knew he wasn't the only person out there trying to cure cancer. Or autoimmune diseases. Or Alzheimer's. Or give marginalised communities access to better healthcare. But if he didn't use the assets at his disposal, to his utmost ability, and someone he knew fell ill, and he couldn't help them, then that was on him.

For the rest of his life.

And still he watched Adelaid: the heel-toe walk, the brave set of her shoulders and wild flutter of her hair. The constant adjusting of the strange assortment of bags she seemed to insist on taking with her wherever she went. Finding her endlessly fascinating.

"Enough," he said, then turned to leave right as Adelaid glanced back.

Finding him there, watching her still, she stumbled. Instinct had him reaching for her, though she was a good fifty metres away. He turned it into a wave.

Adelaid shot him a jaunty salute, which brought a smile

to his face. And he could only be thankful it wasn't happening anywhere near Sawyer, or Ronan, or gods forbid Hadley, or he'd never hear the end of it.

With that he spun on his heel and headed up the hill, filling his lungs with the scent of wet roads and diesel. Anything but sugar and berries, which, it turned out, were his own particular brand of kryptonite.

Understanding the science hadn't worked. So, what next?

Compartmentalisation. He was *good* at compartmentalising. It was how he was able to juggle as many disparate projects as he did.

Where to put Adelaid?

They weren't colleagues, though they were connected through his work.

They weren't friends, though they were engaging in social interactions, with the main goal to get to know one another. At least hers was to get to know him. While his, apparently, was to gaze at her in wonder while keeping track of her stray stationery.

He could, of course, forget about trying to put her anywhere, grow a backbone and keep these messy damn feelings in check.

Maybe he should just pull the pin. If he needed to get out of a contract, Ronan would make it happen. Ronan would lock down the entire building if that's what Ted needed in order to do the work.

Save the World. Their lofty mission statement promised on a three-way handshake when Ronan, Sawyer and Ted were barely into adulthood, now written out in life-sized letters on the floor of the foyer, for those who worked in their building to see every time they came down in the glass-walled lift.

But he couldn't do it. Couldn't do it to Adelaid. This interview was clearly important to her. Cutting her off would hurt her. And, it turned out, hurting her was simply not an option.

Compartmentalisation, it was.

Decision made, he waited for a break in the traffic and jogged across the road towards the gleaming tower his work had built.

CHAPTER THREE

ADELAID WAS LATE.

Ted rubbed his eyes behind his glasses so that he didn't have to watch the emails leaping into his inbox like lemmings following one another over a cliff.

Somehow, in the past five minutes—minutes during which he ought to have been meeting with Adelaid—a small fire had broken out in the Nice lab, which would now be closed till insurance signed off on repairs, and there had been a staff walkout in the Phoenix lab due to a love triangle between the project manager, a lab assistant and a delivery driver.

It was rare for Ted to wish he'd spent his early years concentrating on cloning, or time travel, so that he could be in all places at all times, but sometimes it felt as if no one else took the work seriously.

Took *his time* seriously.

Fixing his glasses back into his nose, Ted twisted his father's watch, giving the face a quick swipe with the flat of his thumb, before checking the time again.

When another email popped up with the subject heading Black lace panties found in office desk drawer. He forwarded it to Hadley to sort out, knowing she'd relish it.

She responded in seconds.

Brilliant. And she's here. Sending her up now.

Ted pushed his chair back so fast it tipped onto two legs before settling back to earth with a bump. It was time. Time to switch from work Ted to interview Ted.

Compartmentalisation time.

Leaving the email lemmings behind, he jogged to the lift, swiped his ID card and pressed the button for the fifth floor.

As part of the compartmentalisation tactic, he'd suggested Big Think as the location for their next interview. Then called on Hadley to source a spare room in the building. Something large and utilitarian. Blank walls. A large table so there was no chance of accidental footsies. A water cooler, a coffee machine and snacks—he wasn't a barbarian—and excellent ventilation so the space didn't instantly fill with the scent of berries and sugar.

Once in the lift he rolled his neck, stretched out his shoulders, bounced up and down so as to increase the oxygen flow to his brain. Like a prize-fighter going into battle. Only the battle here was with himself.

When the lift door opened, he even had the words *You're late* on the tip of his tongue, but they dried up the moment he saw her, waiting for him in the hall.

Today's getup consisted of woollen pants that swept the floor and sat high on her waist and a sleeveless frilly shirt that showed off lean muscled arms, probably from constantly carrying so many bags, her dark blond waves twirled into some fancy knot at her neck.

"Hi," he said, a smile tugging at his mouth before he even felt it coming.

She spun to face him. And if he pretended not to notice that she too was a little breathless, her cheeks a smidge pink, her green eyes sparking the moment she saw him, then it was all in the name of the cause.

"You look—" Ted stopped himself, realising it would not help to tell her he thought her spectacular.

"Frazzled?" Adelaid ran a hand over her hair, which instantly sprang back into soft fluttery waves. "Sorry I'm late. I was called in last minute to watch my twin nephews for my sister-in-law Betty, so she could go to a doctor's appointment. I adore them, but…wow. You have any?"

"Doctor's appointments?"

She grinned and he felt it like a flaming arrow to the chest.

"Nephews."

He shook his head, marvelling at her energy. She was bottled lightning.

"I have a dozen. Nieces and nephews. Needless to say, I am quite the in-demand babysitter."

"I was going to say you look ready and raring."

"I am that too," she said with another blinding smile. Then looked up and down the empty hall. "Are we in the right place?"

Ted ushered her down the hall, sensor lights brightening their way. "This is, currently, unused space. We designed the building with a view to the future. To expansion. To giving back. We have several floors dedicated to free space for use by innovative young entrepreneurs, so that they might spend all their time, energy, money on the work."

"Look at you go, selling the place."

Ted shot her a look. "This looks like the spot," he said when they reached an open door. Inside he found coffee, snacks, water, as requested. Along with his favourite notebooks and pencils, lined up in neat rows.

Adelaid noticed, and gave him a sly smile, before heading in and choosing a chair.

Ted chose another at minimum safe distance, took out his phone, put it on silent, facedown.

Adelaid, on the other hand, emptied her tote bag, spread out her things, made piles of seemingly random scraps of paper, and coloured things, and joining bits. To him it looked like everything had been tossed about willy-nilly. Yet Adelaid sighed in satisfaction. The sound curling about his insides like smoke.

Then her gaze found his. "I know it looks a mess," she said, "as if there is no rhyme or reason, but it's—"

"Colour-coded, right?"

A blink, then, "Right."

"Ronan works the same way. Sawyer bought him a set of pastel highlighters for his last birthday. He acted as if he could not think of anything more ridiculous, but those things get a lot of use."

Adelaid grinned. Frowned. Then grinned again. Her energy fluctuating with such rapidity, such animation, Ted felt as if he had a sudden case of vertigo.

Then she breathed out hard and said, "Let's go. Are you a Theodore?"

Ted said, "Blueberry muffin."

Adelaid burst into laughter. A bark, husky and dry. Then she leaned forward, her hand reaching towards him. "Hang on, are you serious? That's the hill you choose to die on?"

He shook his head. "I am a Theodore. Full name Theodore Grosvenor Fincher. All family names."

"I'd hope so," she shot back, grinning now as she wrote his name in big bold strokes in the middle of a half-used page, drawing a big starburst around the lot. Adding shading. And little fireworks.

"Can I call you Teddy?" she asked, pencil tapping against her bottom lip.

"Not if you expect me to answer." When he found himself staring at her mouth, Ted shot from the chair and moved to the coffee station. Maybe the compartments ought to have been physical. The both of them seated easier either side of a wall.

He lifted a coffee cup in question. She answered with a nod.

"How about you?" he asked. "You ever get Addy?"

"Often," she said, pencil now rolling between her lips. "I have had *many* nicknames in my lifetime. Four older brothers made sure of that."

"I'm sorry, did you say four?"

"Yup. So whatever you might come up with, it's been done."

"You tell me yours and I'll tell you mine."

Her eyes narrowed as she considered. Then, curiosity getting the better of her, she said, "Shortcake. Blondie. Devil Incarnate. I was pretty wild as a kid. Knock-Knock, as in Who's There? Complete with tap on the forehead. You?"

"Chrysler," he said, "as in the building. I was six feet tall by the time I was twelve. Six-four by the time I was fourteen, which led to Optimus, as in Prime. When the glasses came on board, Kent."

"As in… Clark?"

"That's the one."

Her gaze roved over him then, unimpeded. As if deciding whether or not it fit. When her teeth tugged on her bottom lip and she let go a soft sigh he figured her a Superman fan.

Then she frowned, and grabbed her pencil, and began drawing random squiggles on her notebook. "Mine were *all* obnoxious, while yours were positive assertions as to your—"

"My…?"

She waved a hand at him, up and down, as if it was obvious.

A voice in the back of his head told him to press, but he had asked Hadley to put them in this dull white room for a reason.

He finished making their coffees, passed hers to her, then sat back down.

"So," she said, her gaze now serious. "I'm thinking we go warm and fuzzy today. Save deep and meaningful for when we know one another better."

Ted winced. "What's behind door number three?"

"You'll do fine. Imagine, if you will, the kinds of stories they always put at the end of the news."

"Such as?"

"Ah, ever rescued a dog lost at sea?"

"Not that I recall."

"Pity. How about a little old lady from a house fire? No? A cat up a tree?"

"Don't be fooled by the glasses, I'm usually locked up in the lair rather than out in the world, ears cocked for cries of distress."

"Mmm. I don't know about that. If half of what I've read about you is true the glasses are no disguise at all." She shuffled on her chair and a hank of hair that had fallen from the twist fell over one shoulder, giving off serious Lana Turner vibes. "Ted, your work is nothing short of heroic. It's my job to balance that out with a little everyday down-to-earth stuff. Or readers might swoon themselves into a stupor."

"Swoon. Into a stupor."

She waved a hand at him, once again as if that was simply obvious. If he wasn't careful, she was going to give him a complex.

"Help me out here!" she begged. "Something funny from the lab? Have you accidentally torn a hole in the space-time continuum? Or genetically crossed a chicken and a goat?"

He lifted a hand. "Now we are treading close to proprietary information."

She laughed again. The sound husky, and raw. Scraping against his insides like fingernails down his chest. Like her fingernails, when she'd played with the hole in his shirt. The hole *she'd* torn.

"Chick-goats hidden in some secret lab?" she asked.

Jaw tight, Ted shook his head. "No goat-kens, either."

"Disappointing," she said. "So, no rescues. No lab accidents. How about—? No." She stopped, her voice catching on a husky note. Her gaze darkening. Her fingers running up and down her pencil. Before she blinked madly and looked to her notebook where she was suddenly taken with doodling little waves.

"How about?" he encouraged, even while he heard the sirens warming up inside his head.

She took a breath and looked up. Looked him dead in the eye. "I was going to ask, for the warm and fuzzy angle, if you were, perhaps, seeing anyone."

Her eyes were overbright as they held his. As if she was trying desperately to hide how much she wanted to know the answer. And if he'd still been unsure if she felt any of what he felt, he got his answer.

And there went any chance of compartmentalisation.

"I'm not," he said, holding her gaze. "Currently. Seeing anyone. You?"

Her throat worked. "This isn't about me."

Ted leaned forward, his forearms on the table. "Adelaid."

Hot pink flushes rising in her cheeks, she still held his gaze as she said, "I'm not. Seeing anyone. Currently."

"Good," he said. Then, belatedly, added, "That wasn't so hard, was it?"

The pencil went back to tapping against the table—*tap-tap, tappity-tap*—before she said, "Don't think you're off the hook. We've still not found your warm and fuzzies. What did you want to be when you grew up?"

"A scientist. Not the kind that crosses chickens and goats, just a regular, run of the mill scientist."

"Well, that's nice," she said. "As family folklore goes, I wanted to be a tractor."

"Writing came later?"

"Writing came later." She laughed. "Thankfully. For I'm far better at writing than tractoring. I bet you're feeling really glad about that right now."

Infinitely, Ted admitted to himself. Turns out he was infinitely glad.

It was just on dusk when Adelaid left her day shift at the bar.

Her weekly alarm went off, reminding her to drizzle some water on her pet cactus—Spikesaurus Rex. She shot off a quick text to her housemate and best friend, Georgette, reminding her to water her own cactus—Rick the Prick—as well, for he never looked quite as juicy and loved as Rex.

Glancing up as she walked to the tram, so as not to walk into traffic, Adelaid checked her emails, to find her very first response to her on-spec pitch.

Her heart rocketed when she saw it was from her old employer, who had fingers in all kinds of publishing pies, only it was not from her wonderful editor, Deborah. Some assistant responded and it was a polite, but firm, "Thank you for submitting but it is not what we are currently publishing."

Adelaid's heart blew a gasket and sputtered slowly back to earth.

Disappointing, yes. But not entirely unexpected. There were plenty more fish in the sea.

Her phone rang right as she slipped it back into her backpack.

Ted! Realising her enthusiasm at seeing his name had less to do with the piece, and more to do with the man himself, she frowned.

Yes, he was lovely and polite and kind, yes, he was so gorgeous she felt like her bones were made of butter any time he was near, and yes, she liked the way he looked at her, as if everything she did was pure delight, but it would be very silly to take any of it personally.

So, she cleared her throat and found her professional voice, before answering.

"Ted, hi." Was she late? She sniffed at the argyle vest she wore over a men's button-down. Only a slight scent of beer. "I'm on my way. Promise."

When he spoke the sound broke up, but she thought she heard, "…have to postpone."

"Where are you?" she asked, pressing her earbud to her ear as she tried to pick out the background sounds.

"Helipad atop Big Think."

"Right." She had a money tin in which she saved all her coins to pay her electricity bills. Ted had a helipad.

"Last minute trip," he said, his voice thin but sounding as if he as shouting, "in the hopes of buying a business that makes medical supplies. Ronan seems to think if I flap my cape and jiggle my glasses, the stockholders will…how did you put it?"

"Swoon themselves into a stupor?"

"That's the one. Anyway, I'm sorry we have to postpone."

"It's okay," she said, and was surprised to find she actually meant it. She'd been given the brush-off enough times to know this wasn't that.

If she'd been in any doubt at all, it fled when Ted shouted, "Don't hang up. I have a minute."

"How about you call me when you get back?"

"Talk to me now," he said, his voice clearer, as if he'd tucked himself out of the way of the whipping wind.

She looked around, found a bench to sit on. Then reached into her tote for a random pencil and notebook. "Okay. We'll make it a quickie."

"If that's your preference," he said, in that deep husky Ted voice that slid through her like a hot knife through butter.

"Not usually, but needs must." Adelaid bit her lip. They

skirted the edges of flirtation every time they met. Apparently, all they needed were phones in hand and the walls came tumbling down.

"Okay, Mr Interviewee, lightning round. Here goes. Ah, what are you reading?"

"Audiobook, *Rivers of London* series. Kindle, *Lincoln in the Bardo*. I don't have as much time to read as I wish. You?"

"Biographies." Adelaid grimaced when she remembered she was meant to remind him that this was her, Adelaid, getting to know him, Ted. Not the other way around. "Religion. Into it?"

"Organised, no. Curiosity as to the why and wherefore? Lifetime hobby. You?"

"Not about me. Sport?"

"Total pro, at watching."

She thought of the way his clothes clung to him, the peaks and valleys of what appeared to be a very well looked after specimen of manhood. A vision of him dripping sweat, in baggy shorts, boxing gloves and nothing else leapt unbidden into her head. A chunk of his dark auburn hair falling over his eyes. Jaw tight. Skin gleaming…

"Adelaid?"

"Sorry. Pets?"

"No."

"Not even a goldfish?"

"Not home enough to take care of one. You?"

She didn't even bother reminding him that time. "What about a plant?"

"You'll find plants are not pets."

"Agree to disagree. So, no plants? Not even a cactus? They're famously low maintenance." A little prickly on the outside, but flourished with the slightest amount of care. Cacti were her people.

"No," said Ted. "Wouldn't be fair."

Fair. To a cactus. Adelaid bit back her sigh.

Then, in case he heard it, she said, "Now this might be several years spent working for a female-centric online social media site talking, but are you by any chance a commitment-phobe?"

He laughed. Then paused. Long enough some deep, soft, shadowy part of herself began to ache.

"No," he said. "In fact, I'm extremely committed. To my work."

"Work schmerk. Haven't you ever come close to…cactus ownership?" She'd nearly said, *Falling in love, settling down, having a half-dozen beautiful, clever, polite babies.*

Something in the way he said, "I have not," had her thinking he'd understood the metaphor just fine.

"But why?" She knew that if he were sitting across a table from her there was no way she'd be so bold. Yet, with the afternoon sun creating great swathes of golden light between the city buildings, and the soft sensuous waft of the evening breeze tickling at her ankles, she felt a little brave, and maybe a little rash. "Have you been unlucky in love?"

A beat, then, "I wouldn't say that."

"Burnt by love?"

"No burns. No scars. My time is simply too precious to have made unjustified choices when it has come to…cacti."

Yeah, he got the metaphor just fine.

"Right, right. So, reading between the lines, it's your fault."

"Excuse me?"

"You have some terrible secret flaw."

"Such as?" he asked, a touch of laughter giving his voice that edge that cut through all her defences every time. Leaving her feeling awfully vulnerable. As if all her cactussy prickles had been plucked away leaving her completely exposed.

"Do you snore, really badly? Or listen to hard-core rap? Or have…a raging case of herpes?"

Definite laughter that time. She could even picture him running a hand up the back of his neck. A thing he did when abashed. It was rather adorable. He was rather adorable, for a huge, hulking, genius billionaire who was the subject of the most important interview of her life so far, and nothing more.

Adelaid prepared to put their phone chat to bed, when Ted said, "My life goals simply do not run in that direction."

"Herpes?"

"Family."

"I have…no idea how to respond to that."

How could a person's life goals not run to family? She'd adored her mum, despite her mum's best efforts to not always be so adorable. And for all that her brothers drove her bonkers with their overprotection, they'd been the one constant in her life. The ones who loved her, always, despite her nuances.

If her career goal was to be a "highly respected, sartorially envied writer of warm, witty, winning profiles that stun readers with their erudite observations, empathy and heart," her life goals were far more basic.

Security, shelter, family.

"Oh, I doubt that," said Ted.

To which Adelaid blurted, "You can't mean that. Just because you're focussed on work now doesn't mean it has to be your sole focus. And if any genetic material needs to continue on, it's yours. You are doing my entire sex a disservice taking yourself off the market that way!"

Adelaid bit her lip. Clearly, she was the one in need of a safe word.

"Actually," she said, "strike that."

"Which part?" he asked, his voice so deep she felt it

rather than heard it. "The bit about my genetic material or the bit about your sex?"

Adelaid scrunched her eyes shut tight. "I think we've covered that subject to my satisfaction." Not even close, but it was too damn bad. "Let's move on. Favourite colour?"

She felt his pause, felt how far things had suddenly shifted. If her first rule of journalism was to keep herself out of the story, the second was to stay in charge.

"Favourite colour?" she repeated, her voice clipped. No nonsense.

"Green," he said.

"Favourite song?"

"Adelaid," he crooned.

At the tone of his voice, the intimacy, her tenuous hold on tact snapped and she said, "Well, it's either that or I ask *why* you don't imagine yourself having a family. Don't you want kids?"

"No."

"Back to the one-word answers, I see." And not even a second's hesitation.

There was now no stopping the thread of disappointment tying itself in knots in her belly. No denying the fact that while she'd tried to pretend her shock was on behalf of the entire human race, it felt awfully, terribly, dangerously *personal*.

Which was crazy! There was nothing going on between them. Nothing to warrant such a feeling. And yet the ache… it felt all too real.

"Do you not *like* kids?" she asked, a dog with a bone.

"Sawyer's sisters have a bunch. Noisy, sticky, hilarious. Ratbags, but good fun. Harking back to previous points, my commitment is to my work. So, it wouldn't be—"

"Fair," said Adelaid.

"Hmm," he said. Then, "My ride's here. I have to go."

Yes, she thought, *go*. "Thanks for squeezing in a lightning round. I'll use the extra time to really hone my next questions. Sharpen them till they're super-pointy."

"That wasn't pointy?" he asked, his voice rising, the wind once again whipping from his phone to her ears, so that she had to hold the phone away from her ear.

"Ha. Yeah. Maybe a little."

Then the sound became too much, his voice too broken, and as she tried to pick out his words, somewhere in the back of her head she thought he said, "—miss you!"

Which was how Adelaid found herself shouting, "I'll miss you too!"

Before she yanked the phone away from her ear, and jabbed at the red button to hang up the call.

She'd miss him? What on earth was that?

Looking around, reminding herself where she was, she found an old man sitting at the other end of the bench watching as their tram pulled up before them.

He gave her a smile. "Ah, young love."

She opened her mouth to tell the stranger that he had it wrong. That it was nothing like that. Except, the truth of it was, the lines felt a little fuzzy.

Not good. Not good at all. Considering how much she had riding on this.

In the end she gave the stranger a smile. Before hefting her bags higher on her shoulder, jumping on the next tram and heading home.

Ted sat in the bland white room on the fifth floor of Big Think, staring at the empty space where the coffee machine had been.

After the last interview, he'd asked Hadley to strip back even further. Even so far as making the room uncomfortable. And she hadn't disappointed. The blinds had been drawn, the chairs had been swapped out for recycled plastic and the temperature had been turned down to a wintry chill.

Only now—after little more than power-napping for three days straight, needing to liaise constantly via video with the team in Lisbon, who'd had a major breakthrough in a malaria tablet they'd been working on for several years—he could have done with a coffee.

He was so damned spent he hadn't even bothered to come up with a new plan as to how to cope with seeing Adelaid. Maybe that was the answer. Mental and physical exhaustion. When the hairs on the back of his neck tickled, he glanced over his shoulder to see why.

Adelaid Adams stood in the doorway, her hand lifted ready to knock.

Swathed in rich, touchable black velvet that slashed across her decolletage, pinched at her waist and hugged her all the way to her knees, along with a pair of sharp black heels, she looked like she'd stepped straight out of *Mad Men*.

Five days. It had been five days since he'd seen her. Five days spent reliving the moment he'd thought he'd heard her call, "I'll miss you!"

After a week of inhuman hours and intense pressure, that face, those eyes, the frenetic electric energy she carried with her wherever she went, made him feel punch-drunk.

"You okay?" Adelaid asked, not quite meeting his eye as she entered the room and set herself up, tipping her papers and pens and earbuds and phone into the table till the bland room instantly filled with colour and life. "You look a little rough."

Ted could only laugh, considering he'd just been thinking how delectably fresh she looked. "Big week."

Adelaid smoothed her skirt beneath her and sat, before her eyes swung to his. She frowned. Then she reached into her array of bags and pulled out a bag of lollies for herself, and a larger plastic container which she popped open and slid to him.

"Eat," she commanded.

He looked inside and saw a muffin. An actual muffin. Huge, sprinkled in sugar, filled with juicy blueberries. It smelled like warmth, and comfort, and home, the mix creating an unexpected ache deep in his belly that he knew had nothing to do with hunger.

Misreading his silence Adelaid said, "It's homemade."

"By you?"

"Yes," she said, shuffling her papers officiously.

"For me?"

She shot him a look. But didn't deny it. Then fussed with getting her phone recorder set up as she said, "I've seen how much more relaxed you are when fed. When you are relaxed you are more verbal. I've been warming you up till now. This is where we start to get sharp and pointy, remember?"

He remembered. Remembered talking about cacti and goldfish. About partners and children. He also remembered how verbal she'd been when he'd intimated such things were so low on his list of life's priorities they'd fallen off. How inordinately disappointed.

He reminded himself not to let his mother within ten feet of her, as they'd have plenty to talk about.

Ted tore a chunk from the top of the muffin. When it hit his tongue his brain all but whimpered in relief at the hit of sugar, and fruit and warmth.

Burning the midnight oil and eating when it occurred to him might have suited when he was nineteen, but he truly needed to look after himself better. If he collapsed, he'd be no use to anyone. And yet while his life was dedicated to taking care of others, this was the first time in as long as he could remember that someone other than his inner circle had gone out of their way to take care of him.

"Shall we?" she said.

"Hit me."

"Tell me about your family."

Ted coughed on the muffin. Adelaid noticed. But she did not back down. In fact, there was a newfound determination in her today. Back straight, fidgets minimal. He wondered why.

She didn't give him the chance to ponder, saying, "Let's start with your mum."

Leaving Ted to remind himself that this was their relationship. She the interviewer, he the interviewee. His mission to help create a new narrative for the company, to build trust with new investors, to show them why Big Think deserved their benefaction above all other options.

So he began. "My mother, Celia. Imagine a small, neat, red-headed whirling dervish always off volunteering or taking classes. Stubborn, adoring, brilliant, wise. I—"

"You?"

"Ought to give her a call."

At that, she softened, just a smidge. "Yes, you ought. And your dad?"

Ted had been waiting for this one. His origin story was branded into Big Think legend: his father's sudden illness, how it had sparked his determination to turn his talents to curing the world's great ills. He had a stock answer to such a question that he had been using for years—three lines total, ready and prepared.

Only this time he had the taste of berries and sugar on his tongue. And a woman in the pursuit of…how had she put it? Connection and empathy.

He looked to his father's watch, ran his thumb over the face and said, "I was nineteen when my father died. It was unexpected. Devastating, in fact."

The stern comportment flickered. Her voice, when it came, gentle, yet unyielding. "How?"

"Cancer."

"What kind?"

He lifted his eyes to hers. "Pancreatic."

She nodded, her eyes clear. No pity, no sorrow. Her expression measured. As if she understood trauma. As if she'd been honed by it herself.

"I was away," said Ted, "when he fell ill. On a gap year part way through uni. Three days after his diagnosis, he was gone."

"Do you mean… Did you get home in time? To see him before he passed?"

Ted shook his head. "I tried. But we didn't know it would be that fast. There were no signs, you see. No warning. Or I'd have never…"

Ted shifted in the small hard plastic seat, cursing himself for thinking it would make a lick of difference. "Looking back there was weight loss, lack of appetite. Ironically, they were on a health kick. Turned out he was suffering terrible pain for some time but did not want to worry Mum, as they were due to meet me overseas for her fiftieth birthday."

"You said it was devastating. What did that look like?"

He glanced to her. Her eyes were huge, brimming with empathy. But still she didn't back down.

"I was angry, for a long time. Guilt-ridden, of course. But also filled with a river of rage. Towards him. Towards my dad, for not letting on." Ted ran a hand over his mouth, elbows now braced against the table. "Once home, I stayed. Moved from straight science into medicine. Hurtled through a five-year degree in three. Wangled my way into concurrent doctorates. As if it might somehow contract time and undo what had happened. Needless to say, I wasn't in my right mind for some time. It was only due to Sawyer, and Ronan, that I stayed out of any real trouble, as I was looking for it all the same."

Movement dragged Ted from his memories, and he looked up to find Adelaid had her elbows on the table now too. Her chin on her palm, her expression gripped. He'd surprised her, proving himself not quite the good guy she'd built him up to be. And yet, she wasn't fazed. Quite the opposite. Something in her eyes willed him on. Green fire that shone from within.

"Does that make me sound cold?" he asked her, voicing something he'd long since wondered but never said out loud, not to Ronan, or Sawyer, or even to himself. "Does it make me a cold-hearted bastard wishing he'd lived longer, not for himself, but for me?"

She shook her head. "It makes you human."

At which point she put down her pencil and went to switch off the recorder on her phone.

Till Ted held out a hand. His reach bringing his fingers near hers. "Don't stop." Ted pulled his hand back to his side of the table and licked a stray crumb from the end of his thumb. "Perhaps there is magic in your muffins, after all."

"No perhaps about it," she said, her gaze caught on his mouth, darkening when his tongue swiped over his bottom lip.

When she drew in a long deep breath, her composure slipping, the energy she'd been containing, on his behalf, now rushing through the room, all but lifting his hair, Ted had to shift again, but for other reasons.

"Was he much like you?" she asked. "You described your mother as small, so I imagine your father must have been quite the opposite."

"In looks, yes. He was a big guy, upright, imposing. In temperament he was more studious. A professor of history. A lot of my childhood was spent reading in our library. My mother, smarter than us both by half, prefers romance novels. Truer than any tale told by old men with a legacy to protect, she likes to say."

Adelaid laughed, the sound intimate, husky. "I like the sound of her, very much."

Ted leant forward, his forearms resting the table as he

picked up one of Adelaid's pencils and twirled it back and forth. "She'd like you too, I think."

"You *think*?"

He lifted his eyes to hers. "I know it. In fact, she might like you more than me."

Adelaid blinked. Several times in quick succession. Her cheeks pinking, her mouth kicking up at one corner. "I doubt that."

"Ah, but I'm busy. And don't make time. While I feel as if you would be the opposite. That you dote on your family."

"Don't be so sure." Then, noting her relapse, she sat up tall. Notched her shoulders back and asked, "Siblings?"

He shook his head.

"So you're an only child. Do you think *that's* part of your reason for not imagining yourself with a family?" she asked, her eyes suddenly intense. "Because I'm from a big family and can't imagine anything else."

"I'm not sure I understand..."

Her mouth popped open before she snapped it shut. Then she shook her head and said, "Sorry, um, I mean... Your parents—was it their dream to have a small tight family, such as it was?"

"Ah, no," he said. "I think my mother would have loved a big family, but there were complications, after I was born. My mother jokes about it, says I broke the mould. But my dad always..." He paused. "My father used to look so stricken whenever it came up, so I imagine it must have been fraught. He adored her, you see. They adored one another. Very much."

Watching his mother grieve had been untenable. His own guilt and rage and sorrow nothing compared to hers. He knew then that he could never put himself in such a position. Especially since using his gifts to stop others from feeling such pain was a more noble pursuit.

A scraping sound reached Ted's ears, before the small

container of snake lollies appeared under his nose. "In my experience, sugar always helps."

Ted laughed. And took a few.

"You should know how nice it is, hearing you talk about your parents that way. Fondly. With such acceptance." Adelaid's hand stayed near the container, fingers curled towards her palm. "And in case I didn't make it clear, you can call blueberry muffin at any time. Even retroactively."

"It's okay," he said, feeling light-headed, and not from the sugar. As if he'd loosened his grip on things he'd been holding too tight for too long. "Do with it what you will."

"Thank you." With that she pulled her hand back, collected her phone and pressed the button to end the recording.

Only she didn't make to leave.

And neither did he. "You mentioned brothers. Are you close with your family?"

"Ah. Too close, one might say." A shrug. "They are all a fair bit older than me, and a long time ago took it upon themselves to keep a close eye."

"Did you need a close eye?"

Her mouth twisted. "At one time. My childhood was a little less stable than yours. No reading in the library, that's for sure. My mum had my oldest brother Brad when she was really young, and was never quite able to make a go of things from there. We each had different fathers. Not a one of them stuck around."

Unlike Ted's dad, who he'd loved so much he was still trying to save him more than a decade after his death.

"And my mum… She died when I was really young."

"Sorry to hear that."

A quick smile. A learned response. "I don't remember as much as I would like. Flashes I'm not even sure are even real. Are they based on photos? Or stories my brothers have told? I wish I could be sure."

"It terrified me," Ted admitted, "how soon I began to forget my dad. The sound of his voice, the timbre of his laugh. After the blur of the early days of his loss, I took the time to talk to his students, his colleagues, his friends. I researched memory tricks. I started wearing his watch, all so I could feel close to him again."

Ted slipped the watch off his wrist and looked at the face.

"May I?" Adelaid asked.

He handed it to her, watched as she felt the weight of it in her hand.

When she ran the pad of her thumb over the face of the watch, the exact way he himself did a dozen times a day, something yanked hard in Ted's belly. And he felt himself unspool, completely. Such that he might never be put back together quite the same way again.

She passed the watch back, and he slid it straight back onto his wrist, looking to tap into some place solid, and familiar.

"I do what I do because of him. Big Think exists because of him. We do what we do here so that less and less families will suffer as mine did."

If I stop, Ted thought, *stop working, stop pushing, stop focussing, stop working through the night if that's what it takes, then who am I?*

"Thank goodness for you," Adelaid said with a sigh. "Because suffering sucks."

"Did cancer take your mum too?"

"Ah, no. She fell. Slipped on the driveway. Hit her head. I was home from school that day. Home from school a lot of days actually as time management was not her strong suit. I was the one who found her."

Ted ran his hand over his face, before he let it drop to the table, near hers. A small gesture of solidarity.

"She drank, you see. A lot. Looking back there was likely some underlying factor, bipolar, perhaps? But she was never diagnosed. Would never have occurred to her to try. Despite that, or maybe because of it, she was really special, my mum. My brothers, being older, remember things a little differently, but to me she was this funny, bright, shiny, wonderful creature. And she adored us. So so much."

She lifted her hand in a shrug before letting it drop to the table, face up, now mere millimetres from his own.

Before he could think about it, Ted tipped his thumb so that it stroked along the side of her hand. Her fingers curled towards her palm, as if the nerves had been switched on by his touch, and his insides responded in kind. Tightening. Tensing. Readying.

Then slowly, slowly, she turned her hand, tipping it into his. An exploration. Then a tangling as their fingers moved over one another, hooking and touching and—

Adelaid withdrew her hand with an indrawn breath, tucking it under the table, out of sight.

But it was too late. The moment had happened. Attraction, magnetism, compulsion, chemistry, biology, physics. All were at play here—within her as they were within him.

Her energy crackling now, spilling out of her till it filled the room, Adelaid's eyes were wide and bright as they connected with his.

"It might not have been bipolar," she said. "Might have been ADHD. It tends to run in families. And I have it. I have ADHD."

Her face came over a little pale as she dropped the news. Her body braced, for…what? For him to wince, or scoff, or gasp in shock?

It wasn't shocking to him in the slightest. He'd had some idea that might be the case. The circles he ran in, neurodiversity was essential. Imperative to finding new angles from which to attack the kinds of problems he was determined to solve.

His only concern was the way she'd told him, like she

was dropping a little bomb. And why she'd chosen that moment to do so. Right on the back of a level of intimacy that still had him reeling.

Adelaid was testing him. To what end?

His mind sifted briskly through research he'd read, and conversations broached over the years with colleagues with ADHD—both impulsive and inattentive, figuring Adelaid likely the latter.

"Day dreamer?" he said, keeping his face neutral.

She jerked, gaze wary, but at least colour crept back into her cheeks. "For sure."

He motioned to the now empty muffin container. "You prefer baking to standing over a stove?"

"I do. I get too distracted. It's not safe. I set fire to the microwave once, defrosting a piece of bread." Her eyes glinted as she tossed more and more grenades. "Typed in twenty minutes rather than twenty seconds, drifted into the room next door and forgot about it. My housemate, Georgette, who was in the shower, alerted me to the fact the house smelled funny."

Ted nodded. Avoiding looking at her scattered notes, the pages covered in question marks and balloons, and remembered when he'd called it *pure chaos*.

The flash in her eyes that day hadn't been fighting spirit. It had been hurt. Because to her it wasn't chaos; it was the opposite. It was determined organisation of scattered thought. It was a pathway through.

And, it seemed, he was not the first to call attention to it in a way that made her feel bad.

Wishing he could go back, and handle himself better, show her that he didn't find her ways confronting, that he thought her an absolute delight, he instead smiled into her eyes.

"I had to learn ways," he said, "to manage my rage. To

manage my grief. To not give in to it, but to *harness* it. I expect you've learned to do the same."

Her eyes flicked to his. As if she couldn't quite believe how this conversation had gone. Should she keep fighting him or talk to him? Give him some insight into her life for a time.

"Calendars," she said, stopping to lick her lips, "timers. Music helps, the white noise in my ears helps me concentrate. As does pen on paper, doodling. Change of scene if I can't stay on task. And being around people who get it, who roll with it rather than finding it frustrating. That helps. Though it's been by far the hardest part."

He understood that. All too well. Knew how lucky he was to have had Sawyer and Ronan.

"And where do you fall down?" he asked.

She laughed, though there was no humour in it. "You say that as if it's totally okay to fail."

"Isn't it? I fail all the time. Constantly. Science is ninety-nine percent failure. But without knowing what's not true, how will we ever find out what is?"

He watched her as she took that on. As she let it slide into her psyche. As she let it change her. This open-hearted, open-minded, gladly evolving creature of light and wonder and—

"I can be a little tactless. At times. And I internalise," she said, her gaze no longer avoiding his. In fact, she seemed more than happy to keep her eyes on him. "A lot. I'm not very good at asking for help. Probably because my brothers have been determined to give it to me whether I need it or not."

Then, after nibbling at the inside of her cheek, she said, "I'm pretty good at impulse control except when it comes to vintage clothes. I'm hypersensitive to certain fabrics, but I can't resist anything that looks like it might once have been on a fifties movie set. My mum and I loved watching those old movies together. The women were so beautiful. And so bad-ass."

Ted laughed. And earned himself the sweetest smile, pure sunshine.

Then she asked, "How about you? Where do you fall down? Personally, I mean, not with the science. Or is that a silly question? You're so successful, and have more money than any one person ought. Your best friends are your work partners, and you sound more like brothers than colleagues. Despite needing to call your mother, I'm certain she's beyond chuffed to have you as her son."

Ted could see how she thought all of that, but every brick she laid on the pedestal she built wobbled at least a little.

When had he last had a drink with his friends? When had he last celebrated a breakthrough, rather than swiftly moving onto the next? When had he last made actual dedicated time for a woman? When had he last slept? He wondered how well he'd been coping, after all.

He ran a hand up the back of his neck. "I fear you've built far too generous a picture of me; your readers will hardly believe it's true. Give it time and I'm sure you'll uncover enough flaws to balance it out." Then, "How about we call time on today?"

"Yes!" she said, sitting up tall. "Of course."

Then she swept her gear into her bags, heaved them over her shoulder and followed Ted out of the room. Where they walked down the empty hall, side by side.

When they reached the lifts, Ted asked, "When can I see you again?"

Her eyes sparked, then dimmed. "For the next interview. Um, I'll text you?"

"Okay."

Her lift opened first and she stepped inside. "Till then."

"Till then," said Ted, watching her till the doors closed.

And when they did, he breathed out hard. Alone in the

darkening hallways as the sensor lights dimmed, as if she'd taken the light with her.

He swiped his card over the sensor, readying to head back to his lair. Back to the email lemmings, and the malaria tablets.

Only something stopped him. Some new flicker of sense. The knowledge it might actually serve him better to ease off the accelerator on occasion. To sleep, to eat, to call his mother.

Inside the lift he pressed the button for the lobby.

And once outside he breathed in fresh air. Smiled at strangers. And if he checked each tree he passed, just in case a kitten might need a little hand from a tall guy with a little unexpected time on hands, then so be it.

CHAPTER FOUR

ADELAID SHUFFLED UNSEEINGLY through the rack of vintage dresses.

She usually found the op shop scent of camphor and the scratchy feel of old wool a comfort. But her mind was all over the place.

Except it wasn't all over the place. It was in one place. Replaying the joy on Ted's face when she gave him the muffin. The ache in his kind brown eyes when he'd spoken about his dad. The absolute ease with which he took the news of her ADHD. The way he'd held her hand.

Or had she held his? In the end it had been mutual, that much she did know. Fingers slipping over one another, slowly, intimately, searchingly. It had been one of the single most sensual moments of her entire life.

She'd never played footsies or handsies with an interview subject before. In fact, the very thought was utterly laughable! No, not laughable. Wrong. Very, *very* wrong.

So why had it felt so utterly, so absolutely, so heartachingly, right?

"Addy!"

Adelaid flinched, before turning to find Georgette hustling into the op shop. "Hey."

"Find anything good?" Georgette grabbed a felt fedora with musketeer feather off a mannequin's head before putting it on her own and heading to a table covered in concert T-shirts.

Adelaid checked the price tag on a silk shirt before putting it straight back on the rack. Working three part-time jobs—writing small pieces for community papers, working the occasional shift as a bartender in a city dive bar and a little dog-walking—while taking her shot, rather than one time-sucking job that paid rather a lot more, meant she had to be careful with her money right now.

"Plenty. But my cupboards are full."

She headed over to help Georgette look through the stacks for a Guns N' Roses shirt she'd been searching for for months, then they were heading to a local café. They had a shared home office in their rental around the corner, but a change of view was one of the best ways Adelaid had learned to stay on task.

Unlike work colleagues she knew who could only write with quiet and a shut door, she could work from home, in cafés, in parks, on trains, at a rock concert. A true benefit of her condition. And it *did* have benefits. Ted was right about that.

And there she was, thinking about Ted again.

Yes, she was easily distracted. Yes, she never remembered where she'd left her keys. Yes, she struggled with time management. Yes, she could be quick-tempered. But she loved that she was a dreamer. It was one of her favourite things about herself. She lived for the great bursts of creativity, the endless energy, the wells of enthusiasm. If she found something engaging, if she spent time doing the things that brought her joy, her hyper-focus made her unstoppable.

When he'd asked how she'd learned to "harness" her condition, as if that was a perfectly normal question, she could have kissed him. Literally climbed over the desk, taken his beautiful face in hand and kissed his beautiful mouth.

Again, *wrong*. Which was how she'd managed to contain herself. Just.

Except no one, not a GP, not a counsellor, not anyone in any online groups she dipped in an out of, had ever put it that way.

As for her brothers? Sheesh! They *still* couldn't commend her for how she managed her condition. They only saw the times she lost time, or was a little tactless, or zoned out mid-conversation as proof that she wasn't "getting better."

When it was normal to slip.

Getting back up again was the important part.

"Your brothers called," said Georgette, right on cue.

Of course they did. "Which ones?"

"Sid. Brad. Invite to a kindy music event for some nephew or another. Asking if you need money. Checking to see if you're alive. The usual."

Adelaid shoved her hands into the pockets of her second-hand overalls, and managed not to roll her eyes so far they hurt. For something else that had come out of her conversation with Ted was some new insight into why her brothers acted the way they did.

Being so much older, they'd no doubt seen far more of their mum's erratic behaviour. That must have been pretty frightening at times. Surely it had impacted them in ways she'd not been privy to. That, then losing their mum, and taking on responsibility for an eight-year-old girl, it couldn't have been easy.

She so desperately wanted them to give her some grace, but there might be room for her to do the same for them.

"I'll call them back later. Shall we?" Adelaid asked.

Georgette put the hat back on the mannequin and followed her out of the op shop and up the road to the café.

Where they plonked themselves at the tall bench by the window and set themselves up for the morning.

"How's your thing going?" Georgette asked as she perused the menu.

"It goes…fine." Adelaid opened the so-far-blank Word file on her computer.

"Just fine?" Georgette nudged, for she had skin in the game, having given Adelaid an in with the PR firm she worked for.

"I meant amazing," said Adelaid, wafting a hand over her notebooks. "So amazing you will bathe in the reflected glory of my glowing words, for the story will be amazing. Because Ted is amazing. And, as you well know, I am—"

"Amazing?"

"Exactly." Adelaid batted her lashes at her friend before looking back at the blank screen. Then she blurted, "I told him I have ADHD."

"Oh, wow." Georgette had been around long enough to know how that usually went down. "Were you okay? Were you having an episode?"

"I was fine! I am fine. I just…told him." To be true, she'd kind of thrown it at him in a fit of panic. Not one of her proudest moments.

"And how did he react?"

"With aplomb. Did I mention he's kind of amazing?"

"Huh. I saw him the other day, when I was given a magical golden ticket into the Big Think building to pitch some social media stuff. Two of them—your Ted and Ronan Gerard—walked through the lobby and you could feel the oestrogen levels rising. All loping alpha strides, full-on Disney prince hair and those shoulders. Why didn't you tell me how gorgeous he was when you pitched the story?"

"I didn't know how gorgeous he was then."

"Fair enough. Just tell me this—what does he look like without the glasses? Has he spilled some scientific experiment on himself mid-interview and had to change, in front of you, from one hot button-down shirt into another?"

Adelaid gave Georgette a look. "You know I can't talk about what I'm writing while I'm writing it."

Georgette sighed. "Your muse is so bloody precious."

He really was. But that wasn't why she'd yet to write an actual word about Ted Fincher in an actual Word file.

In her old job she'd been trained to write succinctly, to write with a clear intention and to write fast. She worked like a machine.

But there was also a healthy kind of disconnect. A sense of hovering above, writing from a bird's-eye view, that kept her focus entirely on the subject. She took care not to impose any of herself on her writing, other than natural empathy that it was her mission to impart.

Ted asked her about her life all the time. About her family, her foibles, her vulnerabilities, her hopes, the things that made her happy. While she, for some reason, couldn't seem to get past the fact that he didn't imagine himself having a family of his own.

Disconnect wasn't possible when Ted held open doors for her, and made her coffee, and ate the food she'd baked for him. When he looked at her the way he did, and listened to her the way he did, and saw her the way he did, and touched her the way he did.

It was hard. And getting harder to keep things…separate.

But what choice did she have?

She set up a pomodoro timer on her phone, popped her earbuds in her ears and placed her fingers over the keys.

She had plenty to work with now—his college days with Ronan and Sawyer, stories of his good works. And now she had the puzzle piece that always brought a story together, that gave it gravitas, that would spark empathy in the reader.

She had the why. His father. He'd done all that he'd

done, built an empire, in fact, because he hadn't been able to save his dad.

Feelings swelling inside of her as she remembered the way he'd looked at her when she'd held his father's watch, she placed her fingers over the keys and—

Her phone pinged.

Ted. Was he thinking of her, thinking of when their hands had touched? Thinking of what it might have felt like if they hadn't stopped there?

She reached for her phone so fast she nearly knocked it to the floor. Only to find the Adams family chat.

Brad: Sunday dinner. My place. Be there.

She put her phone down, only for it to ping again.

Brad: Addy? Knock-knock?

Adelaid: Can't. Working.

Brad: Take a break.

Adelaid: Don't want to.

Brad: Don't want to, or boss won't let you. Need me to have a word?

Just like that all the love and understanding she'd been feeling for her brothers went up in smoke.

Adelaid: As I have told you, on many occasions, I am a grown-up person who is fully able to fight my own battles. Make my own decisions. I'll come see you all soon. When I can. Promise.

She turned her phone to silent.

The sooner she had her interview done, and written, and in the marketplace, the sooner she had a fancy by-line and a nice cheque and her next big story lined up, the better.

When her phone buzzed again, she ignored it.

Let her mind go to Ted, to his warm eyes, and his deep voice, and his kindness, then made herself focus on his conviction. To big traumas, that led to big dreams.

To the story she could tell.

And she began to type.

Ted's phone rang as he was pounding the indoor running track built into the private gym a couple of floors below his lair.

He tapped the button on his earbuds to take the call, his voice hoarse as he said, "Fincher."

"Darling!"

"Mum?" Ted slowed to a jog.

"Of course it's me. Unless someone else in your life calls you darling. Though I wouldn't put it past Sawyer. Such a cheeky boy."

Her ears must have been burning. His last chat with Adelaid had forced him to admit he'd been slack when it came to checking in of late. They had a weekly call every Friday at five, but apart from that he'd not found the time to call more for a while now.

About the time she'd started nudging him about his quality of life. Which, she'd begun to intimate, meant more to her than his work ever would.

But she was his only family, and he hers. He needed to do better.

On that, it was neither five nor a Friday, meaning she was the one calling out of time.

"What's wrong?" he asked, breaths coming harder as he paced to grab a towel from the bench by the double-glazed windows looking out over the Melbourne CBD. Even without his glasses he could see the rain pelting down outside, coating the glass in tracks of steely grey.

"Wrong? Why does something have to be wrong?"

When he heard the clatter of cutlery and laughter in the background, the sounds of a busy café rather than a busy hospital, his heart ceased to rattle inside his chest.

His mother's voice softened, as if it had occurred to her that, belatedly, considering their history, his question had weight. "I'm fine, darling. I just miss the sound of your voice. Hang on a second."

The phone muffled as if his mother had pressed a hand over the microphone, though he could still hear her shout, "Proper milk, cream on top and chocolate powder. No sugar!" before she came back with, "Now, where were we?"

Ted wrapped his towel around his neck and stretched out his shoulders. "You missed the sound of my voice."

"Right. So tell me, what's new with you?"

"Promising outcomes in the treatment of throat cancers from the Singapore lab."

"That's nice." A pause, then, "Though I was hoping you might have been up to something on a more…personal front."

And this was usually where things started to get tense. Celia pressing forward, Ted retreating. Only this time, before he had the chance to duck and weave, Adelaid Adams slipped into his mind. Her smile, her bright eyes, her chin resting on her palm when she forgot she was meant to be taking notes, and simply listened as he spoke.

Then there was that husky intake of breath when he'd stroked her hand with his thumb. That had played out on repeat in his mind for days.

"Nothing to speak of," he croaked, then cleared his throat.

"Hmm. And yet a little bird told me you have been spending time with a lovely young woman."

Ted dropped the towel onto his head. "What little bird might that be?"

Ronan? Surely not. Hadley, then. For she enjoyed nothing more than watching Ted, Sawyer and Ronan squirm.

"Someone who adores you," his mother chastised. "And like me believes you need to be thinking of yourself more. You're not getting any younger, my love. And I'd hate for you to wake up one day and realise how much time you've wasted—"

"Mum. I am not wasting my time." Quite the opposite. He had used every second he had.

"Of course not, darling. Now tell me about her. Is she kind? Funny? Smart? Of course she is. Or she'd not have caught your attention. Is she pretty? Not that it matters. What's her name?"

As Celia kept chattering on, asking all sorts of questions, from the ridiculous to the sublime, Ted grabbed his father's watch from the bench and placed it over his wrist. Swiping his thumb over the face. Checking in.

Only this time he didn't simply see his father's kindly face. He saw him rolling his eyes at his mother's chatter. Before those same eyes swam with adoration for the woman he'd married. As if he couldn't believe his luck that a quiet, studious nerd such as himself had landed such a woman. Had been gifted such a family.

Ted sucked in a breath. His fist pressing against his ribs.

That might have been his father's dream, but it wasn't his.

Maybe, a voice popped up in the back of his head, *maybe it might have been. It would have been likely, in fact, if circumstance hadn't ripped your family apart.*

But it had been ripped apart. Broken. Missing a piece so that it could never be whole again. There was no getting around that. No getting over it. No way would he put himself in a position to go through that again.

When his mum started asking after his "new lady friend" and her medical history, including potential allergies, in case a time came that they ate together, and it was Celia's turn to choose the restaurant, no doubt picturing the two-storey house they could move into, bay windows, big backyard, oak tree with a swing, a library she could help fill, Ted cut her off.

"Mum, Adelaid is a journalist. Writing a story about Big Think. That's why we have been spending time together. That's all."

"Oh. There's really nothing more?"

"Mum."

"Adelaid, you say?"

"With one 'e,'" Ted added, then shook his head.

"That's different. Lovely but different."

A frisson of warmth wavered down his spine, hearing his mother describe Adelaid to a T, without having met her. As if knowing that's exactly the kind of woman he'd spend time with, if it was up to him.

"Well then," she said, "I guess the little bird was wrong. I look forward to reading her article."

"Great." Ted rubbed a hand over his eyes before putting his glasses back on.

"Talk soon. And be good!"

"You too," he said. Then rang off.

Too cool to keep running, despite the energy now coursing through him, energy in need of release, he stretched out his legs to stave off lactic acid itch.

And uncooperative thoughts. Meaning Adelaid Adams.

The time came in any series of experiments when a scientist had to admit defeat. Einstein himself was meant to have said that insanity was doing the same thing over and over again and expecting different results.

Adelaid was under his skin. Rather than expelling so much time and energy into pushing her away, perhaps the time had come to make room for her instead, lest she barrel right through him.

His intention, when committing himself to Big Think for life, had never been all work and no play. Meaning he needed to be elastic enough to allow for a little levity, for some pleasure. So long as it fell within a predetermined margin of error. So long as he remained in control.

He employed thousands, across continents. He was in charge of billions of dollars of funding. He made decisions that meant life-changing research was funded, while others were not. The level of control, of discipline, of focus, that required was astronomical. And he did so without breaking a sweat.

Surely, he could let himself adore Adelaid Adams, if that's what it took to survive her?

Juggling her bags, and a coffee, and the funny little thing she'd picked up for Ted, Adelaid trekked across the Big Think forecourt.

Her head was tight from staying up too late writing. But it had been exactly what she needed. A fire lit under her, reminding her that while she seemed to have developed a little crush on her subject, the purpose of their meetings was for her, Adelaid, to get to know him, Ted. And that was all.

"Adelaid?"

She looked up to find a woman walking her way. Late sixties, neat auburn bob, pleasant. A stranger yet somehow familiar.

"Hi?" Adelaid said.

Hand to heart the woman said, "I'm Celia Fincher. Ted's mum. I adore your outfit. Reminds me of Rosalind Russell in—" Celia clicked her fingers.

"His Girl Friday?"

"That's the one!"

Adelaid couldn't help her smile. The shoulder pads were a bit tricky to navigate especially with her work tote, laptop bag and handbag, but the "newspaper woman" suit was a favourite. And she needed all the help she could get.

She hitched the bags slipping off her shoulder. "Are you here to see Ted? Did I get the time wrong? It happens."

"Not at all. Ted took me out for breakfast, and when he mentioned he was meeting you, well… I may have stretched out our catch-up a little longer." A crafty smile, then, "And what's that you've got there?"

Adelaid followed Celia's line of sight to find the cute little cactus with its tufty pink flower on top sitting high in its bright yellow pot. "It's for Ted."

Celia's eyebrows rose. "It's not his birthday till September."

"It's a bit of an in-joke."

Was it? Or was it that she couldn't let go of the fact that he thought himself not cut out for a family? If she proved that he could keep a cactus alive he might change his mind. Best not share all that with his mother.

"You're itching to ask me about him, aren't you?" Celia said.

"What? No. Of course not." Except… Ted Fincher's mother. Right before her. Clearly keen as mustard to talk about her son.

"What would you like to know?" Celia asked.

Everything. Every moment, every heartache, every joy, every success, every misstep, that made him the man he was today.

Adelaid waved a hand in the air between them. When it dropped to her bag strap she began to fiddle with the stitching. "I'm fine. Really."

"Are you sure? Ted's never been much of a sharer. Holds it all in. Strong silent type, like his father."

Not with me, Adelaid thought, then bit her lip.

Right then, Ted burst through the rotating glass doors in the distance, glancing at his watch, then running a hand through his thick hair. Clearly not happy that, for once, he was the one who was late.

Then he began to jog. All long loping strides, his hair lifting and falling. Sunlight glinting off his dark-rimmed glasses. Clark Kent through and through.

When he spotted her, a smile broke out across his face. And Adelaid could only hope it wasn't obvious, *to his mother*, that her heart had begun to thump against her ribs at the sight of him. Her *little crush* feeling mighty heavy against her chest.

"Mum?" said Ted, slowing as he neared, his hand landing on his mother's back as he pulled up beside her.

"Ted, darling. Look who I just banged into."

"Right. So you've introduced yourselves, then."

"We've had a lovely chat."

He sent Adelaid a look of deep apology, even going so far as to mouth the word *Sorry!* behind his mother's back.

Adelaid shook her head, infinitesimally, intimating it was just fine. Even while she gripped the cactus pot a little tighter.

"And now we say goodbye, Mum."

"Goodbye, darling," said Celia. She lifted her cheek and he kissed it. "Lovely to meet you, Adelaid. Make sure you show the world how special this one is. He broke the mould."

"So he told me."

"He did? Well, fancy that."

Ted gave his mother a look, then a gentle turn and a gentle shove, which made her laugh, before she waved and left.

Once it was just the two of them, Ted moved closer to Adelaid, hands delving into the pockets of his suit pants as together they watched his mother totter towards a nice-looking town car with a driver ready to whisk her away.

"So that's your mother," said Adelaid.

"Mmm. Any chance you're going to tell me what you were talking about?"

"Toilet training, your favourite cuddle toy, your Superman onesies."

When she looked his way, he was watching her. Watching her with an intensity she'd not seen in him before now. "I never had Superman onesies."

"Really?" She swallowed. "My mistake."

When he kept watching her, his mouth lifting into a smile that said things, meant things, asked for things, she felt her bones start to go all noodly. For, when he chose it, that smile of his was a freaking weapon.

"Here," she said, shoving her gift at him. "This is for you. It's a powder puff."

Ted took the cactus, the pot engulfed by his large hand. "It's a cactus."

"A *pet* cactus," Adelaid corrected.

She saw the moment he got the joke, his eyes crinkling, his cheeks lifting before he burst into laughter, the sound as deep and rich and wonderful as she'd imagined it might be.

"Thank you. I'll take good care of it."

She nodded. "I know you will."

Then, because all the swirly undercurrents of unsaid things began to feel a little heavy, Adelaid started walking towards Big Think, hoping the ground might shore up sometime before she got there.

Till Ted tilted his chin in the opposite direction. "Let's walk a little. I've started having nightmares about that office and its freaky white walls."

"I didn't want to say, but it's not really the most inspiring space."

"That was the point, I'm afraid. I thought it might help us both...stick to the brief."

Adelaid went to ask why he thought they'd needed help, till it hit her. That would be opening up a can of worms they'd not be able to put back.

"Somewhere new this time?"

"Sounds good." His smile was warm, easy, his comportment looser than usual as he fell into step beside her, cactus balanced on the palm of his hand.

When his eyes found hers again his smile deepened. Made her feel all hot and melty inside.

"So, that was your mother?"

Ted winced. "That was my mother. I blame you for all that back there. After our conversation the other day I felt guilted into taking her out for breakfast."

"Ah. No wonder she was so keen to meet me."

"Oh, I'm certain that's not the half of it," he said, but left it at that.

Adelaid breathed out. Hard. While she'd been busy reminding herself that they were interview subject and interviewer, something quite other had come over Ted. And for the first time since they'd met, she wasn't sure who was in control.

"Either way," Adelaid said, "she raised you well. She must be chuffed to have such a polite son."

He shot her a look, but the watery sunlight glinted off his glasses and she couldn't see his eyes. "Polite."

"You are polite! It's a good thing. I promise. Lovely, really. A lost art. I've met plenty of people who are not nearly as kind, or understanding, or patient, as you."

"What people?"

"It doesn't matter."

"Give me their names."

"I'm not giving you any names." Adelaid laughed up at him, then took his arm as they squeezed up against a building when a widespread tour group went by. When she went to take her hand away, his closed over hers, keeping it there.

Using it to tug her to a halt in the middle of the footpath, turning so he faced her. “I can be grumpy.”

“Sure, you can.”

“Surly too.”

“If you say so.”

“If frustrated, tired, hungry, ignored, I can be downright grim.”

His touch was light, and yet she felt as if her arm was on fire. So much so she let her bags slide down her arm, and used it as an excuse to move out of range, as she went to loop her bags over the other shoulder.

At least that was her plan, till Ted’s long blunt fingers hooked under the straps, and easy as you please he tossed them over his own beefy shoulder.

“I can carry my own bags,” she said, feeling flustered now. By the change in him. And meeting his mother. And the fact that he was helping her when she did not need his help. The way her brothers did all the time.

“I’m well aware,” he said. “Probably why you walk with a tilt.”

She was building up a nice head of steam but that stopped when she rolled her shoulders, wriggling her hips to see if he might be right.

“Coming,” he said, her bags still in place, for they wouldn’t dare slip off his shoulder. Oh, no. His gaze determined. Not to be messed with. As if he’d come to some decision, and enough was enough. Add mussed dark hair with those glints of auburn, and crooked glasses, and superhero jaw walking by him, up close and personal, near enough to feel the heat emanating from him, it was quite the thing.

So, she joined him. She’d take her bags back in a bit. Once feeling came back to her arm. “I might do things differently to the way you do them but that does not make me helpless."

"I know."

The thing was, she believed him. While the very last thing she needed in her life was another man thinking she needed looking after, she was tired and he was there, and even while acting all alpha and in charge, he never made her feel dependant.

He made her feel seen.

Unprepared for that revelation, she felt it like a shock of adrenaline to the heart. As if her crush had been given growth hormones, it swelled till she could no longer grapple the thing. No longer keep it under wraps. All she could hope to do was keep Ted distracted so that he had no clue.

"What was your mum's name?" Ted asked.

"Aren't I the one who's meant to be asking the questions?"

"Change of plan," said Ted, his jaw hard, his gaze intent.

"Just like that?"

"Just like that."

Well, if he was asking questions, maybe he wouldn't notice the fact that her pulse was throbbing in her throat, or that her cheeks felt as if they were on fire, or that every time his arm brushed hers, she shivered. Adelaid began to feel hollow inside. As if she could sense the thing that would fill her, only was too afraid to ask.

"Fine!" she said, throwing out her hands. "My mum's name was Vivian."

"Tell me a memory you think is true."

Not sure where he was going with this, she answered, "I think I mentioned she wasn't much into clocks, rules, school. She was a little wild. Made choices that made it harder for herself." A shrug, then, "I think it was easier to sit me down with an old Danny Kaye movie than deal with my behaviour."

Ted hummed, taking the words in. No judgement. Just encouragement. And kept on walking, at her pace. And without her bags weighing her down, the words bubbled up inside her and had nowhere to go but out.

"I adored her though. With the wild came such energy, such joy. Mentally… I don't know. My brothers remember the days in bed, the stints in care, which they shielded me from as much as they could. I'm mad at them for that, actually. For thinking I couldn't handle it."

"Mmm. Seems you are the lucky one for remembering her well."

"Ironic, that." A quick smile before she added, "I think that's why I love writing about people. Why I lean into their eccentricities. Why I want others to see those differences as marvellous, rather than something to shy away from. Because my mum was amazing. And difficult. And unrepentant. And she loved us so fiercely. If people can see past the hard stuff, to the hearts of other people, it can only make us more forgiving. More compassionate. I don't know. Does that sound like too much?"

"Adelaid, if you could hear yourself. It's not too much. You're not too much. You're marvellous yourself. Now, in what ways do you see *me* as marvellous?"

She looked to him then, really looked. "Are you okay?"

"Do I not seem okay?"

"You seem…high."

He grinned, and it was a miracle she didn't trip over her own tongue.

"I'm great. Fantastic even. Slept a treat last night. Am lighter for having seen my mother. Someone else is currently dealing with my emails. And I'm strolling down this beautiful street on this lovely Melbourne day with you at my side."

He bumped her with a shoulder, and forgetting how big he was as compared with her, he knocked her sideways. Then reached out and caught her, hauling her back to his side.

And they walked that way, his arm around her shoulders, for several steps, before Adelaid had to extricate herself before she began to whimper with the pleasure.

"You might have all the time in the world for a stroll, but I have people to see, places to go. So, if you pass over my bags, we can find somewhere to sit and get cracking on our next interview."

But he wasn't having any of it. His gaze was sharp, his voice determined. "Not today. Today is me, Ted, getting to know you, Adelaid. I'm thinking we can start with the day you were born. What you were like when you were six. Any broken bones. Your first crush. Your favourite teacher. But as to the sitting and the eating, yes."

Handing her the cactus, he then took her by the other hand and dragged her down the street and into a restaurant.

Shocked into silence by the sparks travelling from his hands to hers, and settling around her heart, Adelaid could do nothing but follow.

Adelaid's legs jiggled madly as she watched Ted take off his glasses and toss them gently to the bar in which they'd found themselves. His cactus—as yet unnamed—sitting, protected, in the cradle between his elbows.

The place was dark and moody, all shiny wood and golden chandeliers. And somehow, once again, they'd picked a spot where her leg kept knocking against his, no matter how she sat.

Ted's thumb and forefinger rubbed over his eyes, as he groaned, "Now you're just pulling my leg."

"Nope. My brothers are all named after male leads in Doris Day movies." Adelaid lifted a hand to count on her fingers. "There's Brad, *Pillow Talk*. He's a plumber. Jake, *With Six You Get Eggroll*, he's an electrician. Wild Bill, *Ca-*

lamity Jane, he's a first responder. And Sid, *The Pajama Game*, is a cage fighter."

Ted looked up at that.

And it was the first time Adelaid had seen him without his glasses.

Unimpeded, the man's eyes were stunning. Beyond beautiful. He was beyond beautiful. The dim yellowy light rolled over his cheekbones like liquid gold, playing off the ends of his tangled lashes. The dips beneath his eyes were smudged—late nights, heavy burdens—and boasted a few creases at the corners. Making him seem less Clark Kent and more like a real live, flesh and blood man.

"A cage fighter," Ted intoned.

"He's a builder. I was just checking if you were still with me."

"I'm with you," he said, those eyes now hooked onto hers. His voice deep, and a little rough. "I've been with you since the very beginning."

Feeling light-headed, Adelaid asked, "What was the name of my fifth-grade teacher?"

"Mrs Hennessy. You were kidding about Wild Bill too, right?"

"Actual name on his actual birth certificate. Adelaid, one 'e,' is also from *Calamity Jane*. Have you seen it?"

He shook his head.

"Oh, you must! It's so wonderful. One of the best. Adelaid Adams is a glamorous showgirl. Secondary character though, which the boys never let me forget."

Deliberate too, Adelaid had long since thought. Her mum's funny way of conditioning her to never stop fighting to be seen, and heard.

Ted shook his head. Still without his glasses. Looking right at her. Nostrils flaring slightly, as he breathed out, hard. As if he just realised this was the first time they were seeing one another without anything getting in the way.

Needing to cut the tension, before it ate her alive, Adelaid waved a hand in front of his eyes. "Can you even see me without those things?"

He squinted. "You're a little blurry around the edges."

Ted leaned in, resting his forearm on the bar, his hand precariously close to her chest. "There," he said. "Now you're in focus again. I've never in my life seen anyone with eyes quite like yours, Adelaid Adams. I look into them and it's like I can see your whole life looking back at me."

Feeling restless, and overheated, and out of her depth, Adelaid started to lean back.

"Stop," he said, his voice gentle. But firm.

She stopped. But said, "I'm not a fan of being told what to do. Four older brothers, remember."

Ted lifted his hand and rubbed it over the corner of his mouth. "Were you aware that you have a habit of dropping truth bombs, trying to scare me off, any time you feel I might be getting too close?"

Adelaid swallowed. Then asked, "Whatever do you mean?"

"First your ADHD. Then the veiled threat of four older brothers. Just so you know, I'll call you on it, every time."

Adelaid blinked. So used to having to assert her right to take up space in the world was she, when her back was against the wall, she'd learned to push people away, before they could do the same to her. And it had been heartbreakingly easy.

Ted was the first person to ever look her in the eye and say, *I see what you are doing. I see why. And I'm not going anywhere.*

"Is this because of the politeness thing?" she rallied. "Is this you proving you can be sullen?"

He refused to bite. He waited till her eyes were once more locked onto his before saying, "This is me telling you that you're wonderful. And I like you. And I wanted you to know it."

"Ted."

"Why do you get to tell me, constantly, that I am polite, and clever, and cute, if I can't say that I think that you are lovely, and interesting, and driven, and bright, and lovely?"

She opened her mouth to tell him he'd called *her* lovely, twice, before she realised he was well aware. "When have I *ever* called you cute?"

Ted's mouth kicked up at one corner. Then he waved a hand over her, the way she had done to him more than once, making it all too clear she believed him empirically gorgeous.

"Whatever," she said.

"Not *whatever*," he said, his voice now deep enough to scare small children. "You own every opinion you ever have. You like me, Adelaid. You might even be nursing a little crush. Own that."

Heart now beating in her neck, her toes, the backs of her eyes, she scoffed, "Pfft. You, Ted Fincher, are not cute. You're…" She waved her hand again, taking in the swishy hair, the granite jaw, the warm eyes, the muscles, the height, the heft.

But it was the smirk that did it. The smirk that turned up the flame that had been burning inside of her from the moment she'd laid eyes on him.

One second she was mooning into his eyes, the next she was overcome by the urge to wipe that smirk off his face. As if a pair of hands landed on her back and pressed her off her stool, Adelaid tipped forward, until her lips landed on his.

Eyes wide open she saw that his were open too. Open and lit with surprise.

Only by the time any of that made its way into the red fog inside her brain, Ted's eyes slowly closed, his hand had moved to cup her jaw, holding her with both tenderness, and intent. Holding her in place, he tipped his head ever so slightly to one side and kissed her back.

Only barely. A rush of air, a brush of lips. Like butterfly kisses. Till she found herself leaning deeper into his space, following the kiss, chasing it.

While around her, time itself seemed to slacken. To stretch. The world beyond Ted's hold, Ted's kisses, a blur of grey noise and smudged shadow and light.

Till Ted's fingers slid along her jaw, around the back of her neck, diving into her hair as he opened his mouth to play hers.

Drowning. Drowning in his heat and taste and skill, a small voice in the back of her head piped up asking what the hell she thought she was doing.

And she pulled back on a gasp. Breathless, trembling, her fingers lifting to her mouth to find it damp, swollen and aching.

What the heck was she thinking? So reckless. So impulsive. So much worse than footsies.

While she braved up enough to make eye contact, she found Ted smiling at her.

"Well, that's one way to own a crush," he said.

"Oh, shut up."

He held up both hands, in surrender. But the light in his eyes told her he planned to do anything but. There was an edge to him now. It wasn't just the lack of glasses. It was as if he'd been bitten by something that was making him bite back.

"Who are you, and what have you done with Ted Fincher?" she asked, still feeling a little feverish. What had got into him? What had got into her? "Did you cure something overnight? Did I make you walk too far? Are you hungry?"

"So hungry," he admitted, blinking and looking around

for the first time since they'd sat down. "They serve food here, right? Not just beer nuts? Breakfast for my mother means nursing an espresso without drinking it."

Oh no. She knew how he was when he was hungry. Was it possible that all that just now wasn't about him burning with desire for her? He simply needed food.

Cheeks burning all the more with the realisation, Adelaid fussed about, sourcing a menu, put in an order, then watched him scoff down two large pub meals, while she sipped on a glass of iced water and stole his chips when he wasn't looking. Because she was a girl on a budget these days.

After a few minutes, his edge had been tamed, lost within a food fugue. "Is this the part where I get to say how grateful I am that you chose to do a profile on me? Not the other two monkeys, but me."

"No."

"When?"

"Never," she said, pushing his elbow so he'd keep eating. She needed that last little bit of glint in his eyes to disappear. In case it called to some other feverish part of her that had her straddling him at the bar.

"Why is that?" he said, a smile tugging at the corner of his mouth even as his gaze roved over her face, shamelessly, now that she'd kissed him.

"Because it's not...proper."

"Proper she says. And when did we land in a Jane Austen novel?"

When you kissed me the way Darcy might have kissed Elizabeth. With just enough reserve so as not to scare her off, yet such a rich slow burn that left her unsure as to how she'd ever truly lived before that moment.

"What we are doing here, together, with this profile,"

Adelaid somehow managed, “transcends gratitude. So stop flirting with me and eat.”

And with one last smile that made Adelaid’s toes curl, he finally did as he was told.

CHAPTER FIVE

THREE DOGS TUGGING hard enough on their leads to trip up someone less prepared, Adelaid wiped sweat from her eyes as they hauled her up the footpath. Didn't help that her mind wasn't exactly on the job. Hadn't been for the past few days, not when every waking moment had her reliving that kiss.

Not only her part in it—so reckless—but *Ted's*.

Yes, she'd kissed him, but he'd sure as heck kissed her back. And it had been good. Dreamy-good. Keep a girl up at night, tangled in her bedsheets good.

Only while she'd felt as if she was burning up, he'd come out of it cool as a cucumber. As if her kiss had merely proven his crush theory, and nothing more.

Which, she supposed, was a good thing. For it wasn't as if the kiss could *go* anywhere. It wasn't as if the two of them could *be* anything.

There was their working relationship for one thing. While she was beholden to no one, and this was no "investigative" piece, and the entire point of her writing was to be affected and affecting, kissing her subject was still, probably, frowned upon.

Beyond that, Ted was wildly different from her. He was organised, on time, neat as a pin, while her work tote contained broken pencils, used lolly wrappers and sticky notes from three jobs ago.

She was also at a very different point in her life: hustling like crazy to get the slightest foothold on her dreams. While he was so successful, so well off, so far ahead in his field, dreamers only dreamed to be him.

Sensing Adelaid's lack of attention, the lead dog—a Shih tzu named Voltaire—darted left, towards the road and the park across from it. Instinct had her loosening the leads rather than tugging. The trio, losing tension on their leads, all but tripped over one another before straightening back onto the path.

Leaving her mind to trip straight back to Ted. And the small, hard ache inside, the knowledge that there was no point in starting anything as one day it would have to end. Not, for once, because the guy found her impossible to be with. But because they wanted very different futures.

She wanted a family, he did not.

Not that she saw every guy she met and thought—will he have babies with me one day? But Ted was different. He was spectacular. A good, strong, thoughtful, beautiful, weird and wonderful human being who looked at her as if she was pure delight.

That was possibly the worst of it. She'd finally found a man she liked, who clearly liked her back, who saw her ADHD as one small, *interesting* part of her rather than a huge red flag. And if things progressed past kissing, she was in danger of feeling way more than a crush. And fast. How could she not?

Making a mental note to write all of that down when she'd finished walking her neighbour's dogs, a bullet list, a big one, she looked both ways, then jogged the dogs across the road to the dog park, where she let them off leash to run to their hearts' content.

While she found a patch of shade and leant against the fence, working out how she might next get in touch with Ted. To line up their next interview.

For the time had come to wind it down. To get the story done.

Because, so far, no one was biting. She'd expected resistance. Her by-lines were suburban, rejection was par for the course. She wouldn't start worrying till she'd finished the piece and was on to her final pitch.

Her watch buzzed on her wrist, announcing a phone call.

Maybe, just maybe, this was the editor of her dreams offering to buy her story, right now! She pressed her ear-buds to answer the call, her voice hopeful as she said, "Adelaid Adams!"

"Adelaid." Ted's deep voice rumbled over the phone, and Adelaid's knees gave out.

"I was just thinking about you."

"Were you now?"

Dammit. "About calling you to set up our next interview. In fact, having looked over my notes…" *and considering what happened last time we met* "…it might just be our last."

Ted's pause was telling. Or maybe she was projecting like crazy. Imagining his fist pressing into his chest, right over his heart, aching at the thought that soon they would have no reason to meet.

"When are you free?" she asked.

"Actually, I was calling to let you know I'm heading to the Gold Coast for a couple of days."

"Oh," she said, the single world dripping with disappointment.

"I've asked Hadley to keep an eye on Fuzz Lightyear, if that's your concern."

It wasn't. "Fuzz—?"

"My pet cactus."

Adelaid's heart lifted and fell with such suddenness it actually hurt when it landed. "You do know you only need to drip a little water on it, like once a week. Less is better. It takes very little work to make it happy. As for us, I mean, our next interview, do you want to get in touch when you're back?"

"That's the thing. There's room on the jet if you'd care to join me."

Adelaid blinked. "I'm sorry, did you say room on the *jet*? As in *private* jet?"

"I did." Into her silence he said, "I have a meeting with the lab I told you about, the one we are looking to acquire. I thought you might like to come along, see me in action. Two birds one stone." A pause, a clearing of the throat, then, "It'll be an overnight stay. Separate rooms, of course. If that's overstepping—"

"No. Not at all! I've never been on a private jet before. Or to the Gold Coast for that matter. We weren't exactly a 'going on a holiday' family growing up. Or 'plane people' for that matter." She stopped to take a breath. "You still there?"

"I'm not going anywhere."

As lines went, that one was like an arrow to the heart. Dead centre. Hitting the great push and pull of her life—craving her independence while dreaming of one day finding someone with stickability. Not that he meant it in that way. He was simply a good guy. Possibly even the best of the lot. Alas.

"Well, you are, actually," she said, keeping her voice bright. "To the Gold Coast. On a private jet. With me. I won't get in your way, I promise. I'll use our time wisely. In fact, I plan to use this opportunity to interview the heck out of you, Ted Fincher!"

"I look forward to it. Where are you now?" he asked in a voice that might have asked, *What are you wearing?*

"Dog park," she blurted, before it occurred to her to say something more elegant and aspirational. "I walk them sometimes. Dogs, not parks. For extra money. It's something people do when they're not, you know, billionaires."

"Dog walker and writer," said Ted.

"And occasional bartender, barista, babysitter, tutor and writer for hire. There's good money being the subject of university experiments."

"Please tell me you're joking. About the last one. The rest sound like fun. Great ways to find fodder for your stories, I expect."

Adelaid looked to the sky for help. Her brothers saw her hustle as continued proof she needed minding. Ted saw it as integral to her career. It was really, truly, not fair.

He said, "I'll have a car pick you up in three hours."

"Great. And in case I forget to tell you later, thank you for inviting me along."

A chuckle. The kind that sent shivers through her limbs, the tingles settling right in her middle. "You're most welcome."

With that Ted rang off. Adelaid held her phone to her chest, let herself indulge in a few moments of ridiculous excitement. Then set to rounding up three small excitable dogs.

Bags over her shoulder, vintage trolley suitcase bouncing behind her on the tarmac, with the roar of the engine, the rush of wind and the aroma of jet fuel filling her senses, Adelaid might have been Katharine Hepburn striding to meet Howard Hughes.

Till she spotted Ted, grey suit doing its very best to contain his beastly size, one foot on the staircase leading up into the gorgeous Big Think jet, and everything else became white noise.

Yes, this was a working trip. And yes, she was fully prepared to pretend their kiss was an aberration. A mental hiccup on her part, hunger on his. But come on—a private jet, to the beach, with a gorgeous billionaire? She was allowed to lean into the frivolity, just a smidge.

When she reached Ted, his hand landed on her waist as he leaned in to kiss her cheek. Instinct took over, her eyes fluttering closed as his lips brushed the edge of her mouth.

A beat slunk by before either of them pulled back. Then their eyes met.

"Hey," he said, his voice a deep growl.

"Hi."

Then, before she could stop him, Ted relieved her of the handle of her suitcase—no request, it was just happening.

Only this time, she reached out, and grabbed it back. "Thanks," she said, "but I can look after myself."

His hand resting beside hers on the handle, he searched her eyes. And whatever he saw there had him nodding. "Of course."

Of course. Of course his little finger brushed hers as he let the bag go, and of course she felt that small touch all over her body.

"After you," he said, meaning she could feel him behind her as she dragged the heavy bag—*clunk-clunk-clunk*—up the stairs.

At the top, Adelaid peeked around the corner into the cabin and her mouth dropped open. Literally. For it was pure Tony Stark. All cream leather and dark wood trim, with lounge-looking chairs, TVs and fancy-looking gadgetry imbedded into the walls and, at the far end, a very well-stocked bar.

Ted eased around her, strode up the aisle and called out to the captain, Donna, and flight attendant, Stacey, so as to make introductions.

"Stacey, remind me to send you the link for Ms Adams's story about the twelve-year-old who collected enough aluminium cans to fund a soup kitchen for a year."

"You read that?" Adelaid asked.

"Of course. Research is what I do. Had to know what I was up against."

"I—" *Don't know what to say.*

"Champagne?" asked Stacey, holding the backs of the seats as she walked down the aisle.

Adelaid shook her head. "Water would be great."

Stacey smiled a knowing smile. "Get settled and I'll bring you both some lemon water, and a nice light meal, and with Mr Fincher as company you'll be golden."

Ted filled the aisle as he strolled back to meet her, his big hands holding the backs of the chairs nearest. "Don't hold back on my account. The booze on board is top notch."

"I'm working," Adelaid blurted. "This is a work trip. So best not."

"Rightio. Now, may I pop your suitcase in the overhead?"

Adelaid thought about it. About the way he'd paid attention to her desire to manage her own affairs. And how, considering his height and strength relative to hers, she'd be a fool to reject his offer.

"You may," she said, letting go of the handle well before he reached for it.

Once he'd double-checked the luggage hatch was secure he turned back to her. Then he huffed out a breath as he took her in. "In case I forget to tell you later," he said, his voice low and sexy, "I'm glad you came."

Adelaid did her all to control her faculties, but it really was all a bit much. The jet, the tension, the man. She could feel her chest rising and falling. Feel the heat creeping into her cheeks. Feel her fingers aching to fiddle with something. Anything. So that she didn't spontaneously combust.

"This is crazy posh, Ted!" she blurted, giving herself the chance to break eye contact.

"It is a bit much," said Ted, his hand running up the back of his neck. "And I'm not in love with the footprint. But I assuage my guilt in knowing the convenience means the work is served."

A timely reminder that his commitment was to his work. And only his work.

"I'd imagine," she said. "Not sure why I didn't think of it sooner."

"Mmm. Now go pick a seat," he said, moving to give her space. "Anywhere you like."

Adelaid tugged back the tension roiling through her and nodded. "Okay."

She went to move past Ted, only the man was so big there was no passing without feeling the heat of him all over, getting a lungful of his clean masculine scent. A slight panic overcoming her, she tried to turn back, but her shoulder bags twisted, leaving her stuck. Stuck up against Ted.

A glutton for punishment, she lifted her eyes to his to find they were about as close as two humans could be without it being entirely deliberate.

Her imagination went a little whackadoo at that point. Wondering what he might do if she grabbed a hunk of his shirt and dragged his mouth to hers. Or if she scraped her teeth along his stubbled jaw. Or sucked that bottom lip into her mouth and gave it a tug.

Then his gaze, all heat and intent, dropped to her mouth. And damn it if the man didn't lick his lips.

"Here's your lemon— Oh! Excuse me."

Adelaid turned to find Stacey hotfooting it back up the aisle and behind the privacy screen. It was enough for her to yank her bags free and follow.

Dumping her shoulder bags on a random seat, she dumped her wobbly body beside them. Belted herself in. And wished she could bend at the waist and hold her head in the brace position for the entire flight.

"Look!"

Ted blinked and glanced up, the world beyond the edge of his computer, the neatly stacked reports he'd been rereading about the lab he was due to tour, coming into focus.

Adelaid—who'd moved about four times in the thirty

minutes since they'd taken off—now sat in the seat facing his, a table between them.

"Look!" she said again, hands braced either side of the window.

He was looking. At Adelaid. Which had become one of his very favourite things to do. There was always so much going on. The flicks of hair that found a way to escape. The flush of adventure riding high on her cheeks. The heady attraction swimming in her liquid green eyes which made him feel like there was a fist permanently gripped around his lower spine.

She flicked him a glance, a crease popping in and out of existence above her nose. "Not at me. Out there."

"Right." Ted looked. *Out there.* They were cruising above a carpet of cumulus cloud, the kind that usually meant relatively smooth flying. "What am I looking at exactly?"

"The insane blue of that sky. The perfect puffs of cloud. All of it," she said, her voice awash with awe. "I'm not religious, but damn. That's some miraculous stuff right there."

Ted looked harder, opening up a sliver of space in his brain to see the view as she did. Not the topography. Or the science of convection, pressure systems and refraction of light.

Looking at the view from her angle, through her eyes, it was indeed quite beautiful. It was meaningful due to nothing more than how it made a person feel.

It was something worth pausing for.

When he heard a sigh come from Adelaid's direction, his gaze moved back to her just as she faced him. Her eyes lit by that deep underground river of kinetic energy, right there for anyone who cared to look.

"Sorry," she said, wincing, "you were working. And I promised I wouldn't get in your way."

"It's fine. But you can interview the heck out of me *after* the lab visit. It's even in the schedule."

"Really?" she said on a laugh.

Ted pulled up the schedule on his phone and showed her. When she leaned in, he was suddenly back in that moment in the aisle when she'd tangled herself up in her bags. Her gaze warm and unfocussed. Her teeth worrying her bottom lip. She'd smelled like sunshine and sugar. Made his synapses misfire and his nerves tangle. To the point that he'd had to pinch himself in the side so as not to lean down and claim that bottom lip. Soothe it. Own it.

She smiled at seeing her name in his calendar, newly colour-coded and all, before her eyes lifted and tangled with his. Then she crossed her legs beneath the table, bumping them against his.

"Jeez, Ted," she said, pulling her leg away and wriggling to sit higher in her seat. "How do you cope?"

"With?"

"All those legs!" She reached out with a foot deliberately that time. The rounded toe of her shoe tapping at his shin. *Tap-tap-tap. Spark-spark-spark.* Like flint on steel.

"Last time I checked I had the regulation two."

"True. They're just so long, and big. Don't they get in the way?"

"Rarely." He shifted his legs under the table till he found hers.

"That was deliberate."

He smiled his answer. And for his efforts earned a slight bob of her throat, her pupils swarming into the soft green till there was nothing left.

"Pot calling the kettle black," he said.

"Are you accusing me of playing footsies with you? I'm…a wriggler. ADHD, remember? All that nervous energy has to go somewhere."

Ted kept his foot next to hers, watching her decide if

she ought to move it, or leave it there. In the end she left it where it was.

Good decision.

Then she reached into one of her many bags and pulled out a container, before pushing it across the table towards him. "So your blood sugar is all good for your important meeting."

"Please tell me that's a muffin."

"Raspberry and white chocolate."

He opened the lid, pulled it out and took a bite. It tasted like heaven. "For a guy who's never had much of a sweet tooth I'm getting used to this."

She grinned. "You're evolving. Good for you."

He laughed, then went back to his reports. And if their legs happened to brush past one another several more times during the flight, neither of them said a thing.

Adelaid should have known the bubble would pop. It was the story of life with ADHD. Ups and downs, yin and yang, intense periods of productivity followed by complete psychic depletion.

After freshening up at their hotel, her room even more posh than the jet, they headed straight to the lab.

Shucking a lab coat over her vintage wool pants and high-collared button-down shirt made her look like an Oompa Loompa. Then she was off, sporting goggles, gloves, booties, and clutching a non-disclosure agreement she'd signed while on a video call with Hadley who had talked her through it; Adelaid tagged along behind the dozen others on the tour.

The lab was out of this world. All shiny surfaces and insane technology, and more big pointy things with "scope" at the end of the name than she could hope to remember, not that she was allowed to write about them.

And then there was Ted. The shiniest thing of all.

Yes, she'd spent time with Ted in his Dr Strange lair. She'd watched him work with his fancy computers and his neat rows of pencils, while wearing his serious face. She'd heard him on the phone, using his boss man phone voice, and it was hot as hell.

But here, in the wild, prowling through his natural environment, surrounded by groupies drooling over his every word, the man was king.

People came out of their offices to meet him, swarmed him like he'd just kicked the thousandth goal of his career and they were there to witness it. He asked cutting questions, drilled down hard into the answers he was given, with no compunction at all. He led the lab owners around their own space as if he owned it already. And they loved him for it.

Somehow, over the past weeks, she'd forgotten that *that* was the reason why she'd wanted to interview him in the first place. Not merely because he was a cute billionaire, and that kind of things sells, or so that she might get to know the man behind the name, but because he was a man of import.

His work was groundbreaking. His time infinitely precious.

He was Ted Freaking Fincher, literally saving the world one discovery at a time.

Her small suburban dreams were nothing compared to his. Yes, they were valid. And important. To her. She'd fought for them, worked for them, earned them.

But just because he kept a cactus alive, or enjoyed her muffins, didn't mean he was changing. Or able to change. His path was well-carved, from hardest stone. Believing he might change his mind, so that he could squish himself into the small box she'd carved out for herself, was only going to end in heartbreak.

Feeling like an overfull balloon that had suffered a tiny

prick and was slowly deflating, Adelaid slipped quietly away from the group and made her way back outside into the bright beachy sunshine.

Finding a bench by a fountain in a small private garden in which to wait out the tour, she slipped off her mask, and gloves, and checked her phone.

There was a R-rated message from Georgette in response to the news she wouldn't be home that night.

And another from her oldest brother, Brad.

Called you at work. They said you don't work there anymore. What the ever-loving hell, kid?

CHAPTER SIX

LATER THAT NIGHT, Adelaid stood on the balcony of her suite—not room, *suite*—looking out over the unimpeded ocean view: a half-moon casting silvery light over the cresting waves, and an eerie blue tinge on the curving horizon. And she felt more emotionally spent than she had let herself be in quite some time.

Her phone call with her brother had gone down pretty much as she'd have expected. Lots of sighing. A lack of understanding that she was working towards something more than simply being gainfully employed. Insistence she come to Sunday lunch.

Trying to convince Ted, when he'd found her in the garden, that she was just a little over-stimulated, that the lab was fabulous and that he was a rock star, hadn't gone down much better.

He'd looked at her with concern. Which she hated. She much preferred when he looked at her like she was magic.

She'd put on quite a show in order to get him to take her to dinner. So that she could finish off their final interview. He'd picked a burger and beer joint with warm, gentle lighting and a constant low hum of white noise, as if he'd known that was all she could handle. And it had taken everything she had not to fall in love with him then and there.

And there, sauce dripping from their fingers, she'd interviewed the heck out of the guy, as promised. No flirting, no distractions, no hunger issues, no segues, no footsies, no hand touching accidental or otherwise, no mistimed move that ended up with her in his arms.

And yet, now, standing on the balcony of her amazing suite in the most glamorous hotel, a gentle wisp of salty evening breeze playing over her warm skin, she felt hollow. Even a little morose. As if that overblown balloon had finally lost all of its air and was now just a blob of limp rubber.

Because after this her time with Ted was done.

"Hey."

As if she'd conjured him out of thin air, Adelaid looked sideways to find Ted standing several metres away. "You're on my balcony."

"It's a shared balcony, actually," he said, pointing a thumb towards the room behind him. "The company has permanent access to both suites, and they can be opened or closed as we see fit. I hope that's okay." He made to move, to move away.

"Stay," she said, her voice slightly breathless.

And he stayed. His pose was relaxed. The gentle breeze playing with his auburn hair.

He really was the most beautiful man she'd ever met. Way out of her league. Wanted none of the things she wanted most in her life. So utterly wrong for her.

All this she knew with every fibre of her being, and yet, in shortie pyjamas with a cactus motif, instead of her usual sartorial armour, she was completely unprotected. As such, she cocked her head, beckoning him to her side.

Ted's movements were unhurried as he walked across the wide expanse, past a big outdoor lounge and a huge private spa. He'd changed into old jeans that hung low and soft off his hips, an olive-coloured tee, and his feet were bare. His glasses were clear in the low light.

While Adelaid's heart began to beat like it had never beat before.

"Done for the night?" she asked.

He rubbed a hand over his face. "For now. Unfortunately, night and day are mere constructs when you run an international concern."

"Can I quote you on that?"

He looked to her, his face scrunching in chagrin. "Please don't. If not the most pretentious sentence to ever come out of my mouth I don't know what is."

"It's all good. You're just lucky you were a pro tonight. I have more than enough to finish out my piece," she said, taking her chance to drink in his profile. She'd looked up *aquiline*, only to find his nose didn't fit the description at all. Too straight, too fine, but her ancestors would have approved all the same.

His brow twitched, before he turned to face her. "So are we really done?"

"Mmm-hmm. Any last fact checks I can follow up with Hadley. I've taken up more than enough of your time."

He didn't say a thing. Just watched her. With the late-night stubble shading his granite jaw, his eyes dark in the half-light, it was a sensory barrage. *He* was a sensory barrage. But not the kind that sent her looking for a quiet dark place in which to recharge. The kind that made her feel like her blood was lit with static, the kind that left her wanting more.

Which accounted for her next words.

"This is the part where I say how grateful I am that I, Adelaid, got to know you, Ted." Her hand, which had at some point moved to cover her heart, lifted from her chest and moved to touch his. She stopped herself just in time, her fingers curling into her palm.

Till Ted reached out and caught her hand, his long blunt fingers wrapping around hers, before placing them gently over his heart. Her fingers splayed out, as if desperate to cover as much of him as they could.

"Can you feel that?" he asked, his voice rough. And so gentle she could hear the swish of the distant waves.

Though that could have been the sound of blood rushing by her ears as her heart worked overtime.

"If you mean your left pec," she said, "then sure. It's impressive."

"Adelaid."

"Where do you even find the time to work out? Because from what I am feeling right now, you work out."

"*Addy*," he said, in reproof. "I can see you are attempting the truth bomb thing again. Though you're either losing your touch, or you're just not trying as hard."

Her chest rose and fell, her lungs needing more air than they'd ever needed before, as panic swept over her. Panic and lust and feelings and more panic. "I don't know how you expect me to respond to that—"

"Muffin," he said.

"Muffin? As in you're hungry and want a muffin? Please don't tell me you're looking at me like that because you're hungry. Again!"

Ted's confusion was clear. "Muffin," he said, his voice a rough burr, "as in stop telling me what's what, and listen."

His fingers curled around hers, while still keeping them near his heart. And yes, she could feel it beating. Solid, strong, *whump-whump-whump*. His very life force. And soon it matched hers. Her pulse leaping at her temples, at her throat, in her belly and lower.

"My heart," he said, "hasn't been beating quite the same ever since you walked through my door."

Oh boy.

"I tried to explain it away at first, via the science. My decrease in appetite, raging insomnia, wandering mind—all of which point to higher than normal levels of dopamine and norepinephrine. Turns out they belong to the catecholamine family of hormones, which play a big part in the chemistry of attraction."

Adelaid was trying to keep up, she really was. But when his spare hand lifted to cup her cheek, his thumb caressing the curl of her ear, dislodging her loose scrunchie, which plopped to the floor, every sense bar touch was out of luck.

"They can make a person feel giddy," he said, moving in closer. "Energetic. Even euphoric. Any chance you've been feeling any of that of late?"

"I have ADHD," she blurted. "I feel those things all the time."

He sniffed out a laugh, then levelled her with a hot dark stare. Reminding her that he was not to be deterred. That he was way too smart for her usual tricks. That she didn't need to assert her right to take up space in his world, for he was more than willing to share.

Which made her feel brave enough, safe enough, to ask, "Are you, in your own inimitable Ted language, saying that you are attracted to me, and asking me if I might be attracted to you? Because I think the fact that I kissed you the other day pretty much gave me way."

The hand on her face delved deeper into her hair. His thumb playing gently over the edge of her mouth.

"Tell me what you are feeling," he said, close enough now his breath wafted over her ear.

Her mind tumbled. Her limbs trembled. Her eyes fluttered, but she forced them open. "I feel…everything."

He smiled, his killer smile, and she splintered into a thousand hot pulsing shards.

"May I kiss you, Adelaid Adams?"

"Are you always so bloody polite?" she managed, even as she curled her fingers into his shirt, dragging herself up his body.

"Not always," he growled, before he leaned down and traced his tongue over the seam of her lips.

Her bones lost all structure, yet her body tensed as if she'd been hit with an electric shock. When her mouth dropped open on a lush sigh, that was all he needed to claim her mouth with his.

While their first kiss had been sweet, gentle, tender, this kiss went from zero to wild in two point three seconds.

Adelaid gripped Ted's shirt hard as his tongue swept over hers. As his lips took her to heights she'd never known existed before, he also dragged her under with a litany of sweet, deep, drugging kisses.

She ran her hands over his big meaty shoulders, into his hair, down his arms, around his hips. Yanking his shirt free her hands swept up his back, digging into the smooth hot muscle, savouring his hardness, the shape of him, that'd had her feeling feverish for so long.

With a beastly groan, he cupped her backside and lifted her so that she might wrap her legs around him.

Which she did.

Her centre pressing up against the hard, long length of him, giving every indication the man's proportions continued under his clothes.

And when his arms embraced her, held her, protected her, Adelaid fell into Ted's kisses, heart first.

It was then that a tiny spark of sense flared to life. The reminder that she wasn't meant to be doing this. Wasn't meant to be kissing him, holding him, and she certainly wasn't meant to be feeling so many feelings for him.

"Wait," she managed, coming up for breath.

Rearing back, she nearly tipped out of his arms, but his hand ran up her back, scrunching up her T-shirt as he caught her, his palm finding bare skin. And she saw the moment he realised she was braless. His eyes dark as midnight, his jaw like rock, tendons strained in his neck.

But still he waited. Her word gold.

Then he hitched her a smidge higher and… *Holy moly.*

Adelaid gripped Ted's biceps, pressed into what little give they would allow. Tried to stop her eyes from rolling back in her head from the feel of him. The heat of him through her thin pyjamas. Only to curl like a cat against his hand. Her body rocking into his out of pure instinct. And yearning. And need.

She wanted this. She wanted him.

What if this was not so much reckless as inevitable? And who said she had to be blameless all the damn time? Who said she wasn't allowed to make mistakes? Especially the kind she went into with eyes wide open.

She began to slip and Ted hitched her again, his hand dragging her shirt higher still, his eyes hot and apologetic.

So she rocked into him again, leaned forward to rain kisses along his jawline. "You taste so nice," she whispered.

"Nice?" he managed.

"Like the sugar I've been plying you with is dusted over your skin."

"Please tell me this means you've let me off the leash?" he said.

She leaned back just enough to whip her T-shirt over her head, and tossed it over her shoulder, in the direction of the sea, wondering, for a half a second, if it might have gone over the balcony and right now be fluttering down the side of the building.

Then she slid her hand into his glossy auburn hair and demanded, "Kiss me, Ted."

And he did. He kissed her till she couldn't remember why waiting had ever been a consideration.

As he walked her into her suite, he murmured against

her ear, "By the time I'm through with you, Adelaid Adams, the word *nice* will be so far down the list of words you decide to use to describe me, it may even fall off."

And he spent the night showing her how not nice he could be.

Adelaid sighed as her eyes tried to open. But the light was too bright. The mattress too soft. The arm pinning her to the bed Ted's.

Her eyes flung open. Her brain cataloguing the crash of surf, the murmur of traffic far below, balcony doors flung wide open, gauzy white curtains fluttering in the warm breeze. Warm even breaths tickling the back of her neck as Ted spooned her for all he was worth.

So, that had happened.

After circling one another for weeks, living with a slow burn that had felt sweeter and lovelier than any actual relationship she'd endured, *whoomph*! It had blown like a pressure cooker that had popped its lid. At least, she was the pressure cooker. His mouth on her, big blunt hands holding her wide, his tongue having its merry way, she'd blown for sure.

Biting her lip to stop from moaning at the memory, she lifted her head in the hopes of spying her clothes. Then dropped back to the bed when she remembered she'd flung her pyjama top goodness knew where. Leaving her topless when he'd tossed her to the bed. A gorgeous grin on his face as he'd whipped her pyjama bottoms from her legs in one go, the undies with them, proving his skill sets went way beyond human, and into wizard territory.

Everything from there was a blur. Kisses, caresses, the slide of hands, the sweep of tongues. All heat and sweat and bliss.

Thank goodness for Ted, who'd had provisions, for Adelaid wasn't on the pill. It exacerbated her symptoms. Badly.

Ted had made sure they were safe, every time. And made sure *she* was aware that he was making sure of it.

The last thing *he* wanted was an accidental pregnancy.

Adelaid grimaced. *Nobody* wanted that. Including her. Even while she and her brothers were all the result of such folly, or so her mum had told her. And there was a memory Adelaid preferred had been lost to time.

Feeling abashed, and achy, and a little muddled in the cold hard light of day, Adelaid tried to extricate herself. A shower, some clothes and a few robust mantras tossed her way in the mirror would set her up better for facing him.

Facing whatever came next.

Moving, it turned out, was no small feat. For Ted was a cuddler. Every bit of skin he could manage to press up against her he did. And there was a lot of skin. Smooth, tanned, tight, toned skin. Some of it covered in a smattering of coarse dark hair. Then, as if she'd been thinking hard enough to rouse him, Ted moved. Stretching, his bicep brushing the edge of her breast, creating skitters in its wake, before his hand came searching till it found what it was looking for.

And while, admittedly, she could happily have stayed wrapped in his arms, his hand over her breast, his breath wafting over her ear playing havoc with her nerves, it had been a night out of time.

It was not real life. Neither could it be.

Focussed on the pair of freckles that lived either side of his old-fashioned watchband, she wrapped her fingers around his wrist, lifted the dead weight, then wriggled free.

Sitting on the edge of the huge hotel bed, the blankets on the floor, pillows askew, she looked back, half expecting to find those warm brown eyes looking back at her.

But on he slept. A hank of hair had fallen over half his face. His cheeks were flushed from the warmth of their bodies. The twist of the sheet revealed acres of hard muscular torso but draped just so over his groin.

He looked like a felled giant—all potential energy and brute strength. But his jaw was unclenched, his mouth soft. As if the night before had given him a break from how hard he worked all the time. The man with self-confessed raging insomnia had slept. Because she was in his arms.

When her heart began to beat anew, and her belly tumbled over on itself in an effort to chase the feelings swelling inside of her, Adelaid pressed herself up and off the bed, hurried over to her suitcase, picked an outfit from the clothes spilling out of the thing and hustled into the bathroom, breathing again only once she was on the other side of the door.

Maybe it had been reckless, thinking she could have him and walk away unharmed. Maybe it would still somehow bite her on the backside down the track. The thought of which reminded her Ted had done the same: flipping her over to nip her flesh, kneading away the pain, before lifting her hips and making it all better.

But she knew, right deep down inside, that she would never regret her night with Ted Fincher. Not for a moment. Not for the rest of her life.

Turned out, she needn't have worried about facing Ted.

For by the time she was out of the bathroom, Ted was gone, having left a note to say he'd had to take an emergency call about the lab, and could she be ready to leave by eight as their flight had been moved up, and had he mentioned two of the directors of the lab were joining them on the flight back?

Now in the car, on the way to her house, Ted continued to work. Having charmed the directors and sent them off in another car heading to Big Think, feeling well fed and deep in work mode, he was clearly in his happy place.

While Adelaid—itchy with sunburn from her quick beach walk after breakfast, and gritty from a lack of sleep, her nerves feeling more and more high-strung the longer they went without mention of the fact they'd been naked in one another's arms not all that many hours before—pretended to be intrigued by the suburbs dashing by past the car window.

She told herself that if he was cool about it, so was she. Or if not cool, then wishing she was. Which felt like nearly the same thing.

Adelaid's phone buzzed and she was happy to check her phone.

She found a slew of Call me! messages from Georgette.

Adelaid: In the car. On the way from airport.

Georgette: Was there one bed? Please tell me there was one bed.

Adelaid laughed, though it felt like a half-sob.

Adelaid: My room had one bed, not sure about his.

Georgette: :(

Adelaid glanced up to find they had turned into her street. She leaned forward, said to the driver, "It's just up there on the right. Jacaranda out front, pale green picket fence."

"Are we near?"

Adelaid spun to find Ted watching her, his big body at rest, reminding her how relaxed he'd been wrapped around her as she woke.

"Yep!" she squeaked. "Super close."

As the driver pulled a deft turn into her driveway Ted

leaned to look out her window. His voice low, intimate, as he murmured, "Sorry we've not had a moment to ourselves this morning. I'd hoped we'd have more time."

"It's all good!" she said, whipping open the door, her foot already on the sidewalk before the car had rocked to a full stop. "It was a work trip. And you have a lot of people wanting a piece of you. You wouldn't have the position you have at Big Think if you weren't the guy."

When she glanced back it was to find he'd already hopped out of his side of the car. Where he pressed his fingers under his glasses, rubbing at his eyes, the first sign that he wasn't feeling quite as cool as she'd imagined. "I'm not the guy, Addy. Sawyer is the guy. Ronan is the guy."

Her fingers curled into a ball on the roof of the car. "Sorry to tell you, Ted, but while Sawyer can kick a ball and charm a room, and Ronan terrifies everyone into giving him what he wants, it's you out there saving the world."

"Addy," he said, his voice thick.

But she was already at the back of the car, waiting for the driver to pass her her case. Her toes scrunched, her fingers played with a belt loop, till she had her bags in hand.

And when the boot lid slammed shut, Ted was waiting for her. Hands loosely in the pockets of his suit pants, a gentle smile on his beautiful face.

When she tried to hitch her shoulder bags into a more comfortable position, while struggling with the handle of her suitcase, Ted held out a hand.

Letting go of a frustrated sigh, she stepped back, waited for Ted to slide the handle of her suitcase free, before walking it up onto the footpath. Sun glinted through the jacaranda leaves above, dappling his hair, his glasses. Creating a golden halo around his big body.

When he passed the handle to her, he moved in closer and used his now free hands to tidy the straps of her tote, her laptop bag and her handbag till they sat neatly on her shoulder.

"Thank you," she said.

"My pleasure" his gaze hot.

"Not for last night!" she said, her cheeks heating with the force of a thousand suns. "And not for this either." She motioned to the suitcase. The bags. "I could handle that on my own."

"I know you could," he said easily, a smile stretching across his face.

A breath in, a breath out, a sudden need to hold back tears. "I mean, thank you for allowing me the chance to get to know you, to have some insight into your work, your life. It's been a privilege."

His eyes narrowed before he offered a tight nod.

When he said nothing more, she looked away. Over her shoulder towards the house, expecting to see the curtains flicker.

Yes, he was mostly a man of few words, but she kind of wished he found some then. Which words, she couldn't say. She didn't dare try to fashion any inside of her head, lest they haunt her as soon as she walked away.

When she glanced back, readying to say goodbye, Ted took a step her way. That was all it took with those long legs of his. A single step.

Then his hand was behind her neck, and he was kissing her. A hard, hot, deep, sensuous kiss. In broad daylight. For all the world to see.

Adelaid felt her bags slump to the concrete as she let them go. Tipping up onto her toes she dragged her hands through his hair and kissed him as if she might never get the chance again.

An eon later, a millennia, Ted broke the kiss, pulling back to nuzzle her nose with his.

And Adelaid heard the buzz of his phone, growing

louder and louder in his pocket. His world intruding. His work beckoning him back.

"You'd better go," she said, letting her fingers curl over his shirt before she forced some air between them. She could have sworn he placed a soft kiss atop her head before he moved away too.

"Adelaid," he said, his voice holding a note that felt far too bittersweet for her liking.

So she cut him off. "Now, Ted, this is the part where I go deep into my cave to get my story finished. Deep. It's the process, you understand? *I'll* call if I need any fact checks, otherwise I'll be deep. In the cave."

He nodded. Then with one last smile, the kind that made her heart catch, he stalked around the car, gave her a long look from the other side, slid into the back seat and was gone.

Leaving Adelaid standing on the footpath outside her house, a finger to her lips, feeling as if she had walked through some mirror into Wonderland where everything looked much the same, but was—quite simply—not.

And might never be again.

CHAPTER SEVEN

WHILE HADLEY AND Ronan snapped back and forth regards budgets, travel, staff benefits and the massive biyearly fundraising dinner Hadley was in charge of planning, Ted slumped in his dad's battered blue lounger in the Big Think founder meeting space, twisting his dad's watch around his wrist.

Life had snapped quickly back to normal after the Gold Coast trip. Normal meaning seventeen different projects suddenly requiring his rapt twenty-four-hour attention. Meaning reports to be read, funding approved, visits to labs in need of commendation or a shakedown.

He was swamped with fascinating, cutting-edge, eminently satisfying work, and yet the days had plodded slowly by. For "normal" also meant life without Adelaid Adams.

Adelaid had made it clear that she needed space to finish writing. That *she* would contact him if she needed him. Which she hadn't. Called, or needed him. And he *missed* her. Missed her smile, her mess, her electric energy. Missed her to distraction. More than distraction. To the point of physical discomfort.

He knew why. He'd done the research.

Oxytocin and vasopressin were now running rife throughout his system. The latter helped maintain blood volume and internal temperature, leaving him hot and cold, exhausted but wide awake, and as if his skin no longer fit quite right. It also played a role in regulating his circadian rhythm, his very sleep.

This, he'd read, was the attachment phase.

He sat forward and let his face fall into his hands. Rubbing life back into his face.

So what now? Following the science hadn't worked, so there was no point trying that again. Compartmentalisation hadn't worked. Exhausting himself hadn't worked.

The only thing that had given him any relief had been letting her in. Looking at the world through her eyes. Talking about whatever she wanted to talk about over burgers and beer. Holding her, having her, and having the best night's sleep he could ever remember. As if his psyche had been clenched for weeks and had been finally allowed to breathe out.

Only now it was somehow worse. Because he'd let her in and then blithely let her go.

But what was the alternative?

What if… What if he didn't let her in, but *invited* her in? Made real space for her? What if he allowed himself the grace of actually *being* with her?

Adelaid had walked into his world and shaken it from the roots. There was no point looking at her with the same rules as he did for anyone else, for she lived by her own rules. She was independent, pragmatic and self-aware. She was also stubborn, and tough, and fierce. She was determined to assert her independence, and had passions of her own.

And she *knew him.* Knew his goals, knew his motivation. His ambition. And his limits. Knowing all that, she had opened her arms and let him in too.

A chair scraped and Ted flinched.

"So the profile," Ronan barked. "It's done?"

Ted lifted his head, looked at Ronan through bleary eyes. Tipped his glasses back onto his nose, and he sat up and said, "My part in it, yes."

"So it's back to business. Good."

Ted bristled, even though he was well used to Ronan's blunt focus. "I think you'll find I did manage to spend time with a woman and do business at the same time."

Ronan's pause was telling. "It's doable. I know. I plough through several—interviews, that is—a week. This one took you, what, a couple of months?"

"That's because Ted's not a 'wham bam thank you ma'am' kind of guy," said Hadley. "And while you shoot sound bites at people, Ted was part of a profile requiring finesse, percolation. And wooing."

"Wooing." Ronan glanced at Hadley, then at Ted, as if suddenly noticing something was different about him. "Is that what's been happening here? Has there been wooing, between you and the writer?"

"Adelaid," Ted gritted out. "Her name is Adelaid. One 'e.'"

"Well, what do you know?" said Hadley, her eyes soft, her smile kind. Before she seemed to realise it and went back to lounging insouciantly in the doorway.

Ronan tapped a finger against his lips, his eyes hard. "Anything I need to know?"

Ted faced his friend. "Why? You looking for pointers?"

Hadley snorted, then rolled her eyes with enough elegance to make up for it. "Seriously. You," she said, pointing at Ted, "be nice. And you," she said, pointing at Ronan, "have no right to ask any of us what we do in our own private time. In fact, what the heck are we even doing here on a Saturday? Just because without Ted there is no Big Think does not mean he is married to his work. Day in, day out, like some automaton. Call me when you're done with the alpha crap. Till then I'll go back to running your company for you."

And then she left.

Leaving Ted and Ronan facing off.

"So," said Ronan, face unreadable bar the lift of a single eyebrow. "What now?"

Now Ted had to decide if he was going to be nice and polite and thoughtful and do what Adelaid had asked of him, and wait, or call her out for finding an excuse to push him away. Again.

Ronan said, "See if you can't get something in the piece about the wind energy start up in Tasmania. Help grease some government wheels for us!"

But Ted was already out the door.

Adelaid lifted out of her office chair to rotate Spikesarus Rex a half-turn on the windowsill, so that his thorny backside might get a little sun.

Then she plonked back down in the bouncy chair in the home office she shared with Georgette, and went back to staring through her laptop screen The Sinatra crooning through her earbuds was usually a winner at keeping her on task, but her muse just wasn't playing ball.

In fact, he hadn't been playing ball for the past couple of weeks while she'd been trying, desperately, to wrestle Ted's damn profile into shape.

Didn't help that her brothers were constantly beeping at her from the Adams family chat. Or that she'd taken on a bunch of extra busywork so as to fill the time she'd usually been spending researching Ted, or talking to Ted, or hanging out with Ted. Or that she'd been feeling off-colour. Bone tired. Foggy in the head.

The skeleton of the piece was there, the structure, the information. But what it was missing was the heart. The soul.

The Ted.

Because she was missing the Ted too.

She *knew* herself enough to know that giving in to her crush was not going to serve her.

It wasn't his fault. He'd been a total doll. He'd actually

listened when she'd told him not to call, unlike others in her life who ran roughshod over any personal request she ever made. And he'd promised her nothing.

It was all her. Her and her tender, searching, hopeful, dreamy damn heart.

"Adelaid!"

Adelaid plucked the earbuds from her ears and looked over her shoulder. "Hmm?"

Georgette was balancing a pencil between top lip and nose, the Big Think Instagram page open on her mega monitor. "You're tapping your pencil against your mouth so hard you'll chip a tooth."

Adelaid stopped the tapping.

"What are you working on?" Georgette shuffled her wheelie chair over to Adelaid and squinted at the search page she had open.

Studies suggest oxytocin is the chemical messenger associated with trust, empathy, relationships. It's also used in sperm production...

"Adelaid?"

Oxytocin was also known as the love hormone. Not that she was about to tell Georgette.

Adelaid's head fell into her hands. "I'm stuck. Like, really stuck. I've tried all kinds of ways to find a way into the piece, but nothing is working!"

"Not even the R-rated stuff?"

Adelaid looked through her fingers and felt a blush rising up her neck. "I'm hardly going to tell the world he has a triptych of freckles along his hip bone."

Georgette grinned. "Pity. You'd make a packet!"

"This should be the easiest thing I've ever done. He's so easy to like and respect and his story is heartbreaking and heartwarming and he's so deeply real. I just need to get it all down in a vaguely readable way and it will sell. I know it."

"So, what's the problem?"

The problem? "I asked him to give me room so that I might finish writing. Without distraction. Two weeks ago. And he's actually done as I asked."

"The bastard."

Adelaid laughed, despite herself. "I know, right?"

"Can I help? We can brainstorm?"

The thing was, the person she'd become used to talking to about, well, everything was Ted. She'd become used to calling him up any time she thought of him. Sending him articles she thought he might find of interest. Knowing that, like her, he was up at odd hours. Like her, he was always happy to chat.

"I think I know what my problem is. I can't write about him because I miss him."

"Oh," said Georgette. Then. "Oh, my."

Indeed.

"So call him. Ask him out. Take the guy to a movie. How about that Hitchcock retrospective at the Avalon?"

Could she? Adelaid grabbed a printout of a particularly heart-stopping picture of him holding his glasses frames and looking just off camera, lab coat on, that hank of hair threatening to fall into his eyes. "He's Ted Freaking Fincher!"

Georgette shrugged. "And you're Adelaid Freaking Adams. I know you, darling heart. You're quick to retreat if you sense ambivalence. Meaning this guy must be as amazing as you've made out. And someone's gotta date him, so why can't it be you?"

Why couldn't it be her?

Because…because she liked him far too much. Enough that she was researching love hormones. Enough that she was having dreams about a future with a man whose vision of the future did not come close to matching her own.

The very thought had her stomach turning over on itself. Then it did so again. Imagining it must be anxiety, she closed her eyes and breathed through it till it settled.

Right then, a knock rattled the front door.

"I'll get it!" said Georgette, leaping from her chair. "Waiting on my book subscription. I'll leave you to your sperm 'research.' And romantic thoughts of Ted and—"

A creak of the front door was followed by Georgette saying, "You're not books."

A murmur in response. A deep, smooth, husky murmur that sent sparkly shivers down Adelaid's arms.

She rolled her chair to the doorway of office and poked out her head, to find Ted standing on her front porch in a white T-shirt, navy sports jacket, jeans riding low on his hips, the sheer size of him blocking out the watery sunlight.

It had been thirteen days since he'd dropped her home and driven away. Thirteen days since they'd spoken. Since they'd kissed. She'd had longer bouts between catch-ups with the man, yet this time, the yearning that filled her at the sight of him made her head swim.

Movement must have caught his eye as Ted looked over Georgette's head, his gaze clashing with hers. Heat and grit chasing one another through the warm brown depths.

"Addy," he said, his voice catching on her name. "May I come in?"

He fiddled with his dad's watch, as if riding a surfeit of energy. Currently picking at a tear in her old jeans, Adelaid felt a rush of endearment.

"Of course," she said, pressing out of the chair, "come on in."

Only then did her mind leap from the dishes piled in her sink, to the stretched-out Taylor Swift T-shirt a brother had given her for Christmas a zillion years ago, to the hair scrunched atop her head in a messy knotty bun.

Had she even brushed her teeth that morning? A quick swipe of tongue over teeth told her she had. Phew.

Georgette cleared her throat.

"Ted," said Adelaid, shaking her head in an effort clear a way through the fog, "this is my best friend, Georgette Gallagher. Georgette, this is Ted."

"Pleasure," said Ted, holding out a hand.

"Georgette works for Big Think's new PR firm and was the one who helped land me your interview."

"How so?"

"Funny story," said Georgette. "In her old job Addy had to write these top ten lists and was struggling to fulfil a brief entitled *Top Ten Sexy Single Billionaire Bachelors Under Forty*. I mean, have you seen the state of the world's billionaires these days? It's rather dire. So she called me!"

Ted looked to Adelaid, who shrugged. There was no stopping Georgette at this point.

"'What about the Big Think guys?' I suggested, for the firm I work for had just been hired by you guys to do some freelance PR. 'Not sure if they're billionaires or merely millionaires, but according to the literature we've been commanded to learn off by heart they're right up there.'"

Georgette looked to Adelaid, encouraging her to take it from there.

"I looked you up," Adelaid said, her cheeks warming. "Found the source material highly curated. Controlled. And kind of dry. I thought you were crying out for my special touch."

Ted's cheek twitched. "Why me?"

"Two cocky alphas and a cinnamon roll. Which would you pick?"

At that he laughed.

"When she told me what she was thinking," said

Georgette. "I dragged her into my boss, and she was given the green light within the day."

"And here we are," said Adelaid.

"Here we are," said Ted, his gaze stuck on Adelaid, his barrel chest rising and falling.

Georgette looked from one to the other before disappearing into the office, then coming out with her laptop. "So, I was just leaving. Nice to meet you, Ted. Keep up the good work. At work, I mean. Not when it comes to—"

She flapped a hand at Adelaid, then realised what she was intimating. Mouthing "sorry" a half-dozen times, Georgette finally slipped out the door, shutting it behind her.

Leaving Adelaid and Ted in a cloud of heavy silence.

"Would you like a tour?" Adelaid asked.

When he ran his hand up the back of his neck, she was nearly undone. "Sure."

"Not quite carbon negative," she said, motioning to the ancient light fixtures and the peeling wallpaper. "I bet you live in some fancy mansion, or penthouse, or Bat Tower." She glanced over her shoulder as they reached the sweet little kitchen that had made her fall in love with the place.

Though the pale yellow cabinets, gingham curtains and harlequin floor didn't seem to grab his interest quite so much as her face.

"I have a place in the city," he said. "Not far from Big Think. I'm rarely there. This," he said, eyes finally grazing over the second-hand kitchen stools and pictures of apples and oranges one of her nieces had painted now framed on her wall, "is much nicer. This is a home."

Something flashed over his face then. Some memory. Or some pain. And she remembered the way he'd spoken about his parents. About his cosy suburban upbringing. The kind she'd one day want for her own family.

Only the thought of kids, and Ted, brought with it a

sharp jab of pain right through her middle. Shaking it off, she scooted past him, back into the hall.

Only, as she passed, his fingers curled warm and tight around hers and tugged her back.

"Why are you here, Ted?" she asked, needing to know. Needing to hear him say the words. "Was there something I forgot to ask? Some important hobby, or childhood memory?"

His thumb running over her wrist, his dark gaze roving over her face, he said, "Ronan would like a mention of our wind energy startup in Tasmania."

"Well," she said, her breaths now harder to come by, "we can't forget Tasmania."

With that Ted spun her against the wall, his big hot body trapping her there. "You asked me to wait," he said, his jaw tight, his voice subterranean. "So I waited. I waited long enough."

His hand hit the wall beside her head, as if he needed it to keep himself from touching her.

"If you want me to go," he said, his eyes on her mouth, "you're going to have to say the words."

His words were strong, but he looked ruffled. Unkempt. As if he hadn't shaved since—shock-horror—the day before. Considering all the crazy mental gymnastics that had been messing with her head, it was heady to think Ted might be feeling as out of his depth as she.

It was enough for her to admit, "I'm glad you came."

He breathed out, took off his glasses and put them on the small hall table that was perfectly within reach. Because he was a planner, her Ted.

Up close, his eyes were so clear. The whites a perfect white. She could fall into those eyes and never want to climb out. Maybe she already had.

She reached up, her thumb grazing the edge of his nose where his glasses had left a red mark. "What do you want from me, Ted? What are you hoping might happen between us? All evidence to the contrary, I'm not usually the kind of girl who sleeps with a guy, then doesn't call for two weeks."

His jaw twitched, his eyes roving over every inch of her face as if committing her to memory. "I was in the middle of a meeting, and then suddenly I was on my way here. That's not something that usually happens to me. *You're* not something that usually happens to me."

She made a noise. A soft sigh of yearning. Her hand reaching between them to give herself one last chance to stop this. To stop him. To protect herself. Only to cover his heart, while Ted sought out any last remnants of space between them and he filled it. Leaning in, infinitesimally. Overwhelmingly her completely.

Then his knee brushed the inside of hers, pressing them apart.

"How does it make you feel," he said, his voice like gravel. "Knowing I can't get through a day, an hour, without imagining what I'd like to do when I see you again."

"Tell me," she whispered. Turned out she was a masochist, after all. "Show me."

As if that was all he was waiting for, Ted leaned down to cover her mouth in a hot, open-mouthed kiss.

And the past two weeks of yearning, of missing, of reminding herself why going back to normal was the smart thing to do, turned to dust. Adelaid was lost. To touch. To feeling. To warmth. Sensation. Breath.

And after that first searing moment, as anticipation spun out into reality, the whole world gentled. Became more of a meeting, a testing, a tasting. Every slide of a hand considered. Every sip from one another's lips deliberate. Every moment so lovely, and sweet, it made her heart hurt.

So lost, was she, in Ted's hold, in his tenderness, when he pulled away, she whimpered, her mouth following his.

He made a rough noise in the back of his throat, before

his hand swept over her cheek, his fingers delving into her hair, and he kissed her once more. The kind of kiss that could keep a girl going for days. Weeks. Months.

Then suddenly Ted was on the other side of the hall. His hair was a mess, his clothes askew. Most adorably, he squinted, just a little, as his glasses were out of reach. It took every bit of self-control not to rush him, jump him. Screw the consequences.

"I came here with a plan."

She rolled against her wall, and Ted pressed so hard against it the house groaned.

"I came to ask if you would like to go out with me. On a date. A proper date. Dinner? Drinks? A movie? All of the above? There is a Hitchcock retrospective not far from here—"

"Yes," she said, her voice lit with laughter.

"Yes?"

She nodded. Then laughed, the sound a burst of joy spilling from her. "Did you mean right now?"

"Absolutely." He swallowed. "If that's what you want."

The answer rang in her head. Crystal clear.

She wanted Ted.

She wanted to have him and hold him, and kiss him, and wake up in his arms. Only this time she wouldn't slip out from under his arm. This time she'd turn to him and kiss him awake and do it all over again.

She didn't want to be good, and sensible. She didn't want to think about the future. Not now. Not today.

Adelaid pushed away from the wall, held out her hand, waited for Ted to place his palm in hers and led him to her bed.

Ted woke to find himself facedown, spread-eagled, in a too-small bed, his feet hanging over the end.

He opened an eye and came face to face with a pink

fringed lamp, and a dog-eared biography of Judy Holliday. Squinting he made out shapes of floral wallpaper, a spring-green wicker chair covered in clothes, a small freestanding canary yellow wardrobe, doors wide open, boasting suits and dresses and hats and fancy shoes.

Adelaid.

Smiling, he rolled onto his back, stretched, then pulled the sheet with him, found his glasses on a chest of drawers and ventured out into the hall.

A quick search found Adelaid in her kitchen, music playing softly from another room. The morning sun pouring through the window glinted off wild wavy hair which spilled over her shoulders. A hand was wrapped around a huge mug, the other gripped her phone, a frown tugged at her nose, creating a pair of vertical lines between her brows.

His heart hurt just looking at her. But while at any other point in his life the very thought would have had him running for the hills, he breathed through it. Letting it simply be.

"Hey," he said, his voice rough.

She flinched, water leaping out of her mug and onto the floor. She mopped it with a small brown mat that was already on the floor, her gaze scooting from his face to his chest, to the sheet he had gripped low at his hip.

"Coffee?" she squeaked. "I didn't feel like it this morning, which is super weird. But I can make you some."

He went to her, leaned down, kissed her on the forehead. Then tipped her chin to kiss her on the mouth. "Good morning to you too. Sleep well?"

She levelled him with a look. For the neither of them had slept much at all. "Can you put some clothes on?"

"Why?" he asked. "Is Georgette about?"

"Well, no. She stayed at a friend's place last night. It's just obscene how cut you are, and I don't have the energy this early on a Sunday to suck in my stomach."

He slid his spare hand around her back. "I love your stomach. And your neck," he said, moving her hair aside so he could breathe her in, before scraping his teeth over that spot, just above her shoulder, that made her body roll. "And I'm quite partial to many of your other bits too. So, if you want to strip down, I'd have no complaints."

She leaned back, looked him in the eye and shook her head. He saw wonder in her gaze, disbelief, but also a spark, a sizzle. An undercurrent of heat and…something else. Something weighty and deep and rich. Something that rubbed up against big feelings inside of him in a way he'd never felt before.

"What's the plan for today?" he asked.

Twirling out from under his arm, she rinsed out her mug in the sink. "Nothing I can't get out of. Do you need help with anything? You said your place isn't as homely as mine. I can help you pick out a rug?"

"A rug."

"Unless you have some equation to complete, or disease to eradicate?"

He could see the erratic energy gathering in her eyes, hear it at the edges of her words. She was stressing about something. This time he knew it wasn't him.

"Want to tell me what's going on?"

Her mouth twisted. "Family lunch. One which I'm trying to get out of."

Ted's mind shuffled through the times she'd spoken of her family. Sunday lunches had been mentioned. Multiple nieces and nephews. Overbearing older brothers. Fond exasperation.

"Is family lunch a bad thing?" he asked, thinking that, as an only child who missed his father every day, it might have been something he'd rather have liked.

"No." A pause, then, "We eat a lot and laugh a lot. I get to cuddle my zillion nieces and nephews, and spend the rest of the time trying not to get cornered by my brothers, each of whom will take the chance to demand updates on my health, my living situation, my finances, my career, my life."

"What's wrong with your life?"

"Not a thing!" Adelaid's hands came together, fingers twisting.

"Can't you simply say no?"

"To…lunch?" Adelaid laughed. The laughter turning slightly hysterical. Then she clicked her fingers. "That's right. You're an only child."

Truth bomb, he thought, seeing the fight in her eyes.

Only this time he actually did put it down to her ADHD, ramping up due to stress. He'd read into it. Deeply. Since knowing her.

"True," he said, his voice low, gentle. "But I've known Ronan and Sawyer since I was seventeen. When punching each other in the arm every chance they got was their idea of kinship. So I have some idea of what it's like."

Adelaid's fretful hands slowed.

"While a new rug sounds great, consider option number two," said Ted. "Would you like company? A bodyguard? A distraction? Someone to hold your bags?"

"You want to come to family lunch?" she said, her liquid green eyes watching him, carefully. "With my brothers. And their wives. And their kids."

"There will be food there, right?"

"So much food."

"You know how I feel about food."

Adelaid breathed out, her gaze settling. "That's a nice offer, Ted. But I'm afraid my brothers would eat you alive."

"Brad, *Pillow Talk*. Jake, *With Six You Get Eggroll*. Wild Bill, *Calamity Jane*. And Sid, *The Pajama Game*."

Her mouth popped open. "How do you—"

He tapped the side of his head. "Good memory. For

things I want to remember. I may even have watched two out of the four films."

Adelaid's hand went to her heart, her mouth popping open in surprise.

"I've had time on my hands the past couple of weeks," he said, moving in closer and pulling himself up to his full six feet five inches, barefoot. "Thank you for the warning about your brothers. But I can take 'em."

At that she barked out a laugh. "I'm sure you'd put up a good show. You're clearly very strong. And manly. It's just… I've never brought a guy to family lunch before."

She let that fall between them like a stone dropped into a pond, ripples bouncing off the edges of the room.

"They would make assumptions."

Ted took her by the hand and hauled her to him. "Let 'em."

Adelaid's eyes flickered between his, but she gave nothing away. Breathed in. Swallowed. Nodded. Then a smile crossed her face. Like sunshine on a cloudy day. "Are you even free?"

"I'm free."

He wasn't. He was never free. Hadn't been *free* since he'd made a promise to himself, and his "brothers," when he was nineteen years old. Yet he was not ready to leave her.

Not yet.

Not ever, a voice rumbled in the back of his head.

He moved in, curled a wave of her wild blond hair around his finger. Using it to tug himself closer as he leaned down to kiss her. Stopping a smidge before his lips met hers. "What time is lunch?"

"Lunchtime."

"What time is it now?"

"Barely breakfast."

Ted opened his sheet and wrapped her in it.

And that was all it took for her to grab him and kiss him and climb him, and if they made it to lunch it would be a miracle.

CHAPTER EIGHT

ADELAID STOOD ON her brother Brad's porch, her usual bag of marinated chicken wings in hand. She told herself to knock, but her hand wouldn't move. It had been weeks since she'd shown her face at Sunday lunch. What with quitting, and all her part-time jobs, and Ted, it had felt easier, more politic, to stay away.

Ted moved in closer beside her, as if he could feel her rising tension and just wanted her to know he was there. His thumb running down the edge of hers. Calming her. Smoothing down her spiky edges. Only to leave room for a rush of feeling—longing, adoration, gratitude, wonder, disbelief, panic and something deep and sweeping—that made the backs of her knees threaten to give out.

These were not things she needed to be feeling now, right as she was about to enter the lion's den. Her brothers would smell blood, and it would be hell.

She squeezed Ted's hand, then let it go to knock on the door.

Jake, her second-oldest brother, opened the door, a baby on his hip, a toddler wrapped around his leg.

"Thank heck you're here. Take a kid." Jake unwrapped the toddler from around his leg and gave the kid's hand to Adelaid.

She crossed her eyes and curled her tongue at her nephew, till he became focussed on trying to do it back.

Then Jake saw Ted. He reared back and said, "You brought a dude? Bold move." Before promptly handing the baby to Ted.

"Wait—" said Adelaid, wiping a hand already sticky with toddler down the side of her jeans.

But Jake was already gone, calling out, "Hey, everyone! Addy brought a boy!"

Adelaid looked to Ted, to find him holding the baby at near arm's length. His face blank, his eyes wide. It would have been funny if not for the resultant ache in Adelaid's belly. A timely reminder that they wanted different things.

Not that her stomach was listening. In fact, the scent of the chicken had been making her feel funny the whole way over. The sooner she passed it off, the better.

"You okay over there, bud?" she asked.

Ted blinked, his deep brown gaze turning to her. "Yep. Fine." Then some dormant human instinct kicked in and he brought the baby to his hip. "And who is this?"

"Ted, meet Bianca, my brother Brad's youngest." Poor kid had inherited Brad's perma-frown. "There's a dozen more inside. We Adamses are prolific breeders. Still think you can take my family?"

Ted leaned in when the baby lifted a chubby hand towards his glasses, letting her smear and stroke and poke. "I'm currently adjusting my expectations."

Adelaid, on the other hand, was doing everything in her power *not* to adjust hers. But seeing Ted smile and goo, eyes twinkling at little Bianca, her insides fluttered and did cartwheels, before settling into a strange uncomfortable cramp.

He would be such a good father. So patient and focussed. So sweet and kind. So protective of those he loved. She pictured him researching prams and paediatricians. Setting up a creche at Big Think. They had entire spare floors in the building, after all. It really, truly, wasn't fair to humankind that he had cut himself off from the possibility.

Ted glanced over, his expression quizzical.

Adelaid looked away, hoping her yearning wasn't written all over her face. "Come on! No one can hit you when you have a babe in arms, so we couldn't have planned this better."

With that, Adelaid led Ted down the hall, waving to her huge extended family—Brad's wife, Betty, swooping in to relieve Ted of her child, Joey bolting off to find younger victims to poke his tongue at.

They made it to the kitchen in one piece. The room was filled with Adamses. Wives, girlfriends, cousins, kids. Working around one another as they covered the kitchen dining table in more food than any household could eat in a week.

"Everyone, this is Ted," she called. "Ted, this is everyone."

"Hey, Ted," said Sid's girlfriend, Sally, taking the proffered bag of chicken wings, before shooting Adelaid a look of *You go, girl*. Adelaid then motioned for Ted to follow her to the sink. Where they took turns washing sticky kid stuff off their hands.

He turned on the tap. She held out the liquid soap and squelched a bob into his palm. Side by side, they scrubbed their hands long enough they could have performed a surgery. Once done, Ted used the tea towel to dry his hands before passing it to her, smiling down at her, his face close enough she could make out the myriad colours in his hair.

And Adelaid realised how much she'd come to treasure the pockets of time when it was just the two of them, in a bubble, leaning into their attraction, playing "what if?".

And she let herself imagine what that might look like as a reality. As a *future*. Living together, dining together, travelling together, snuggled up on the couch together, him reading his reports, her editing a piece she was writing. It felt peaceful, and warm, and lovely.

But then her twin nephews ran through the kitchen, screaming blue murder at one another, and the spike of joy, of belonging, of longing that pierced her was enough to make her moan.

"Scoot," Wild Bill's wife, Wendy, said, squeezing between them to wash the celery for the Waldorf salad.

Once she moved off, Adelaid turned off the tap with a little too much vigour and twirled the tea towel around both hands, using them as a shield to put a little room between herself and Ted. "Let me know if you're ready to bolt. We can sneak out the back door. So long as they have my chicken wings they won't care."

Ted moved in closer, and leaned his backside against the sink, tipping his head to hers to be heard above the white noise of the busy kitchen. "I get the distinct feeling you're preparing me for failure. Yet I'm not sure how a person fails at lunch. Unless it's by missing one's mouth with one's fork."

It was Adelaid's turn to narrow her eyes at him. "You've never walked into a room, not once, in your whole life, and been concerned at how people will receive you, have you?"

He opened his mouth. Closed it. This time when his eyes narrowed it was out of concern. "Have you?"

"Oh, my gosh. Constantly!" Her arms flew out, the end of the tea towel whipping through the air with a whip crack. "That's the story of my life, Ted. It takes work to hold in my fidgets, and constant effort not to feel overwhelmed. Even then people sense it. And judge. And make things harder. It's why this mob are so protective of me. Why family is so important to me."

Her eye caught on the kitchen doorway as the last of the wives, girlfriends, cousins and kids disappeared through it holding food and the related accoutrements, only to find all four of her brothers standing in the kitchen doorway staring at her.

"Took you long enough," she said, her voice tensing, as if preparing to battle. "Boys, this is my friend Ted Fincher." Only the slightest pause before the word *friend*, but she saw every one of her brothers clock it. "Ted, my sorry excuses for brothers."

Wild Bill, the quiet one, stepped up first, but only because Sid, the youngest, had given him a shove. "I'm Bill."

"Pleased to meet you," said Ted, leaning forward to shake Wild Bill's hand, while simultaneously slipping down against the bench a smidge so as to bring himself down to his height.

"Sid," said Sid, squeezing in to pump Ted's hand hard enough his knuckles turned white. "I'm the cage fighter, so you'd better be nice to my sister, or else."

"Ah," said Ted, "Adelaid already got me with that one."

Sid's mouth twitched. "She's told you about us, eh? What'd she say?"

"That there are four of you," said Ted, diplomatically.

Sid snorted. "Good one."

"We grew up with her, remember?" said Jake, taking his turn to shake hands. "Talks ten to the dozen ninety percent of the time. Doubt that's all there was to it." Jake's arms were crossed over his chest. And was he flexing? Jeez, he was totally flexing.

Adelaid rolled her eyes so hard they hurt. "Stop fluffing your feathers like nervy roosters. Ted is far too savvy to fall for your antics."

"Did you say your name was Fincher?" That was big brother Brad—the oldest, the frowniest and most likely to go full protector. "As in Big Think?"

Adelaid gawped. How the heck—?

"I'm a massive Sawyer Mahoney fan. Just missed out on a signed jersey at a charity auction once. Biggest regret of my life."

Ah. That made more sense.

"I'd be happy to send you something when Sawyer's back in town. Might not have played for a while, but he still loves to give an autograph."

Brad nodded.

Ted nodded back.

"Now," said Brad, "tell us what the heck makes you think you're good enough for our sister."

Jake laughed. Sid grinned. Wild Bill shrank. While Brad cracked his knuckles. Literally cracked his knuckles. And while white noise permeated from the house beyond—kids playing, women laughing—the kitchen was dead silent.

Ted moved in so that his hand was resting on the kitchen bench behind Adelaid's back, his thumb tickling at her spine, as he said, "She invited me here today, and I trust her judgement. Otherwise, I'm not sure how you want me to answer that."

"Are you kidding me?" Adelaid muttered, shooting Ted a glance as she moved away from the bench. His touch not helping. Especially when she could feel him responding to the testosterone leeching through the room.

The last thing she wanted was for him to think he needed to start fighting her battles for her too.

Without thinking about it too much, she followed her gut. Ignoring her brothers and focussing on Ted. She clicked her fingers in front of his eyes. Watched as the fog cleared and his warm brown gaze focussed on her.

Then she shook her head.

He ran his spare hand over the bottom half of his face, his eyes flickering with chagrin. Before he gave her a half-blink. Of understanding. And acceptance. Just like that.

Before she could unpack how that made her feel, how his instant understanding layered over everything else she adored about him, Brad's wife, Betty, called out from the next room.

"Come and get it!"

Adelaid turned to see her brothers leaving the kitchen, noses lifted following the scent like Looney Tunes characters. Food taking precedence over deciding who was alpha gorilla, always.

"So that was my brothers," said Adelaid.

"I like them."

Adelaid laughed. Then realised he meant it.

Ted's eyes glinted as his hand swept around her waist pulling her closer now that they were alone. "They are clearly very fond of you, which endears them to me."

"Fond? Boy, oh, boy, are you an only child."

Rather than calling her out for pulling a truth bomb move, Ted slung an arm around Adelaid's neck and pulled her in for a quick kiss that soon turned into a long kiss.

"I can smell chicken," he murmured against her mouth. "Lead me to the chicken."

Knowing he'd only continue being of use to her so long as he was fed, Adelaid led Ted to the chicken.

Adelaid managed to sit through lunch, but didn't quite feel as if she was really there.

Ted was a dream. The wives and girlfriends all watched him goo-goo-eyed. Her brothers became more and more smitten with him the more Sawyer Mahoney stories he told. And after a while he stopped flinching every time a child screamed.

But every time someone passed a bowl of potato salad or a pasta dish under her nose her stomach turned. Till after a while she started holding her breath any time someone called out "Pass the gravy!"

"Adelaid?"

"Hmm?" she said, and turned to find Betty tapping her on the shoulder.

"Sorry, hon, I said can you take the baby? I really have to pee."

"Of course." Adelaid took baby, Bianca, turning her so

she could face the table, and gave her a napkin to play with. Without thinking she sniffed her baby head, kissed her baby hair and made goo-goo noises into her baby ear.

And then, like a fog rolling in off a stormy sea, Adelaid's feet felt numb, her ears could only hear a strange whooshing sound and she held her breath to hold back the wave of nausea that had swarmed over her.

Passing Bianca onto whoever was sitting at her left, she excused herself and walked as normally as she could through the house.

Her mind now a constant flicker of images of her past few days. Her foggy head. The fact she'd been in bed before nine every night that week. How she'd not been able to stomach the idea of coffee that morning.

She was heading upstairs when she banged into Betty coming the other way.

"You okay, hon?"

"Yep. Bianca is with someone."

"You don't look so good."

"I'm fine." She wasn't. "Look, can I ask you something and you promise you will not tell my brothers?"

Betty's eyes widened in glee. "Please. It's been so long since I've heard any adult gossip I'm nearly dying of starvation."

"Do you happen to have a pregnancy test?"

Betty rolled her eyes. "Are you kidding? You know how often someone in this family pops out a kid. I have a set in every bathroom in the house." Betty looked over Adelaid's shoulder. "Who's it for? Janet? She's looking a little bloated."

Adelaid breathed out, nausea swelling inside her again.

Betty's eyes widened. "Oh. Oh, I see." She grabbed Adelaid by the arm and dragged her back up the stairs and into her en suite bathroom. A quick rifle through a drawer pulled up three different kinds.

"This one is most accurate soonest. That suit?"

Adelaid nodded.

"Don't look so worried, hon. It'll all be okay, no matter what. I know we've just met your Ted, but, Addy, he seems like a dream. And hot. But sweet, you know? As for you, the whole lot of us have been itching for the day we can return the favour and help look after your little ones. You know that, right?"

Adelaid nodded again.

"So, I'll leave you to it, shall I?"

"Thanks."

Four minutes later, sitting on the closed lid of the upstairs toilet, Adelaid stared at the fist gripping tight to the pregnancy test.

Her right leg jiggled. Her mind spun in circles. Had she really said, to Ted, *We Adamses are prolific breeders*? Her ovaries squeezing when she'd seen him smile at her niece. Was it possible she'd manifested her symptoms, so acute her desire for such an outcome?

No. This was not wishful thinking. She wanted a family. But not like this. Not while renting. Working a bunch of casual jobs. And sleeping with a man with whom she'd yet to go on an actual date.

She'd worked hard to make good choices in her life. To manage her condition. To surround herself with people who were kind to her. To create a safe space for herself.

So how had it come to this? Possibly, accidentally pregnant—the flakiest, most reckless, most Vivian thing she could possibly do.

Her breaths started to shallow, her skin prickling, as some of the harder memories of her childhood bled through, the ones she preferred not to focus on. Trying to wake her mum to take her to school, having to pack up and move while the landlord shouted about debt collection and leg breakers, her mum crying at the supermarket while trying to decide between bread or milk for her five babies.

Adelaid closed her eyes, breathed deep. It was not the same thing. She was not her mum.

And she'd done nothing wrong. Nothing bar developed feelings, strong feelings, deep, rich, romantic, soul-deep feelings, for the most excellent man she had ever had the privilege of knowing.

She was in a good place mentally. She was financially stable. At the moment. But if she didn't land on her feet with her shift in career, then that nest egg would start to deplete and fast. But she had a home. Friends. She had support, if she wanted it. For all that her brothers drove her crazy, she only had to say the word and her entire family would step up. For the first time in a long time that felt not like a burden but such luck.

And she had Ted.

Oh, Ted.

This was not what he wanted. Not now, and not in some distant dream future. It was explicitly *not* his plan. Yet, she knew he'd be kind. He'd step up. Not like her mum's boyfriends, who'd all fled at the first sign of trouble. Not like her own father had.

The alarm on her phone went off. Keeping all of the above firmly in mind, her fist loosened. She slowly opened her fingers.

And felt a kind of preternatural calm as she focussed on those two bright pink *positive* lines.

"Holy mother of monkeys," she muttered.

"What? What does it say?"

Adelaid nearly jumped out of her skin as Betty's voice called through the door.

"Can you give me a minute?" Adelaid managed.

"It's positive," someone whispered. "Or else she'd have said so. Right?"

"Is someone else there?" Adelaid asked.

"Ah, it's me. Wendy."

"Betty! You promised you'd keep this a secret."

A shadow bled under the door, as if Betty was right there. "You said not to tell your *brothers*. And they're all downstairs, mooning over your baby daddy."

Adelaid's face fell into her spare hand, and she began to laugh. For it was laugh or cry, really, with her family. And damn sure she wasn't about to spend her first moments with her possible future baby blubbing with tears.

"Are you okay, hon?" Betty asked.

"Yep. I'm fine and dandy."

"We'll leave you to it, okay? Our lips are sealed from this moment on."

"Great. Ta." Adelaid heard the bedroom door swing open and closed and was alone.

Except, according to the two pink lines staring prettily back at her, she'd never be alone again. She was having a baby.

A person of her own. Who would love her, no matter her flaws, just as she'd loved her own mum. No matter what.

Well aware that mental health issues, and conditions such as ADHD, could be hereditary, Adelaid was not concerned on that score. Who better to raise a neurodiverse child than a mother who was informed? If the chips fell that way, she would be the most supportive, open-minded, adoring mother ever.

And then there as the fact that the child would be half Ted.

A teeny person who would inherit his kindness, his gentleness, his scintillating mind, his loyalty, his drive. But probably also the way he forgot to eat, and his anal relationship with time.

A mix of the weird and the wonderful, from both of them.

Ted.

She had to tell Ted. Had to pull the rug out from under him. Change his life for ever.

But not here. Not surrounded by her family. It wouldn't be fair.

None of this was fair. Not the least of which was the fact that they'd only just started getting to know one another. Or that she was about to drop a real metaphorical grenade on the guy that he could not clever his way out of.

Later. Away from here. She'd just have to get through the afternoon without giving herself away.

Hyper-focus could be a burden, but it could also be a gift. Especially when one really needed to finish an article one had been trying to write for weeks.

The evening before, after making it through lunch, Adelaid had felt like she'd been in a pillow fight—exhausted and slightly battered all over. Ted had offered to drive her home and let her get a proper night's sleep.

When he'd kissed her goodnight, turning her to mush on her front porch, it had taken everything she had not to tell him then and there. Or drag him inside.

But she resisted. Not without another test. Not till she was sure.

For it would change everything. Everything. For ever.

After sending him on his way, a kind of mania had come over her, a second wind keeping her up all night, writing till her shoulder ached, till her little finger of her mouse hand had gone numb, and till she could see the shape of the story as if it were a three-dimensional, living thing.

And then it was done.

No wave of relief or pride. Just exhaustion and a bittersweet sense of loss. That the reason they had come together was no more.

Yawning, spent, she'd sent it off at four in the morning—to Georgette, to Georgette's boss and to the Big Think lawyers for pre-approval. After they'd taken their bites, she'd show Ted. Then send samples out into the big wide world, her final chance to lure someone who loved it as much as she did.

Clocks had never held much sway over Adelaid, but now as she lay on the lounge awaiting a different kind of result—after dragging herself to the doctor for a blood test, and pamphlets, and a sample of prenatal vitamins—it was as if she could now hear one *ticking* permanently inside her head.

Leading to what? News? Or an end? Or a beginning?

Her phone pinged. Heart beating in her throat she turned it over.

Positive. Double-checked. Official.

She dragged herself to sitting. Her hand resting over her belly for a few private moments. Eyes closed she sent a message through her arm to the cells miraculously dividing inside of her.

You and me, kid. Anything else is gravy. But you and me? We'll be okay.

Opening her eyes, she dialled Ted's number to set up a time she could see him. So, she could tell him—

He answered all but instantly.

"Adelaid," he said, clearly glad to hear from her. "I just heard."

Her heart beat behind her ears. "Heard?"

"You're finished! Hadley got a ping from contracts. When do I get to read it?"

"Oh. The profile. Now, if you'd like. As soon as you want it."

He laughed, the sound so easy, so free. "I'm so proud of you, sweetheart."

Sweetheart. He'd called her his sweetheart. That was

where they were in their relationship: the bright, beautiful, trouble-free beginning.

"I'm pregnant."

Adelaid smacked her hand over her mouth.

When she heard nothing but silence on the other end of the phone, she murmured, "Ted?"

"I'm here. Did you just say—"

"I'm pregnant. I'm so sorry. I had no intention of blurting it out like that. I wanted to tell you in person, but you were saying such nice things, and I couldn't sit here, feeling like I was keeping something from you—"

"Addy."

Adelaid breathed fast, and deep, diaphragm deep, attempting to clear some of the static in her head. "I made you a promise that I wouldn't get in your way. And I have. I'm pregnant, and that's going to change everything for you. When you were so clear that it's not what you want. I'm so, so sorry—"

"No," said Ted. His voice cutting through the loud grey glitter in her mind like a clash of symbols. "Hell, Addy. You have nothing to apologise for. I—"

She pictured him running a hand up the back of his head. Wished she could curl up on his lap while he did so. And kiss his jawline. And hold him tight. And for him to tell *her* everything was going to be okay.

"Where are you?" he asked, his voice calmer than he must have felt.

"Home."

"I'm coming to get you."

She shook her head, then remembered he couldn't see her. "Please. Do what you need to do today, then maybe come over later? After work. And we can talk then?"

"Okay. And, Addy—"

Adelaid pressed her phone as close to her ear as it would go. "Yes, Ted?"

"It'll be okay. I promise."

She nodded again before hanging up. The words not giving the comfort she'd hoped, for that time the *sweetheart* was missing.

Ted sat on his dad's couch. Leaning forward, his head in his hands. He'd been there for a good half-hour, in the exact same position, working himself up to speak.

"Hey," he said, his voice croaky. For it had been years since he'd spoken to his dad. Longer since his dad had been around to speak back.

Ted ran his hands down his face and leant back in the chair. When he'd first dragged it with him to university, attaching it to the roof rack of his old Cortina, it had his father's impression in the back, his handprint on the arm. Now, it no longer bore signs of anyone's use bar his own.

"Dad," he tried again, "turns out there's a chance, all things going well, that in a few months from now you're going to be a granddad."

Or would it have been Grandpa? Pop. He'd have been a Pop for sure.

While Ted was going to be a dad.

A dad. A father. With a child. A child who would be entirely reliant on him. Him and Addy. Addy, who'd be the most amazing mother, of that he had no doubt.

It was himself he was struggling to picture. Likely because he'd put in great effort never to picture himself that way before.

Would he be like his own dad? His situation was very different. He didn't live in a house with a library, or even a backyard. He wasn't even living with the child's mother. They'd known one another a couple of months, while his parents had been together a decade before he was born.

And his own father had died suddenly when Ted was nineteen. From a disease that still had no cure.

Ted pressed a fist to his chest, and said, "I can picture

you looking at me, one eyebrow raised, waiting for me to explain myself. 'Be careful with girls,' you'd said when you sat me down for the talk. 'Be respectful. And take responsibility.' And I have. Always. This…this was…"

A broken condom. Damaged condom. Out of date condom. Overly hasty putting on of condom. Destiny?

"Unplanned." A beat, and, "Which I'm sure you've picked up on over the years. If you've been listening at all. So, I'm not telling Mum yet, okay?"

Not till it felt more real. Not till, medically, it was more…safe. Till then it was only a possibility. No need for his mother to invest. Emotionally. Not fully. Not yet.

It was early days. And things could change. He knew he was thinking twelve steps ahead of where he ought, but contingencies, playing out eventualities, risk assessment, was his life. It was ingrained.

Things could go wrong.

He knew, from the maternity rotation he'd done at uni, that the first three months were fraught with danger for the embryo.

Then there was concern for the mother. Look at him. He'd broken the mould. A saying that he'd never fully appreciated till he imagined Adelaid in his mother's place.

Flicking fingers to get blood back into his extremities, he moved on. Once born there were choking hazards, broken bones, unforeseen congenital issues. How any parent made it through without developing stress ulcers was beyond his understanding.

In fact, if "pregnancy" came past his desk, seeking funding, he would pass. Far too many variables, so few of them positive.

Pressing himself from the couch so that he might pace the room, his gaze caught on the small yellow pot on the windowsill. Fuzz Lightyear, the quaint little cactus Adelaid had given him. The only furnishing, apart from his dad's chair, he'd ever brought into this room.

Ask him three months earlier if he'd have a cactus, name a cactus, care about a cactus, and he'd have thought you were crazy. But here he was. In a different mental and emotional place than he had been for a very long time.

Because of Adelaid.

He saw the world differently now. Not as mere science, as fact and fiction. But messy, and adventurous, and varied, and in full technicolour. So much so he'd begun to open himself up to the possibility of a future with her. Her strength and determination not a distraction from his mission, but an elevation of his life.

From the moment he'd seen her she'd been inevitable.

Fingers spinning his father's watch around and around and around on his wrist, he said. "You'd like her, Dad. Strike that, you'd love her. I can so imagine the two of you bonding over Hitchcock movies, Mum and I watching from the sidelines, shaking our heads. She's marvellous, Dad. Tender. Hopeful and loyal. She opens her arms to people, even those who might hurt her, which terrifies me. She's—she's the one."

Only his dad didn't respond. For his dad wasn't really there. And never would be again.

Which was why Ted's entire existence had been built on discipline. On rigorously tested fact. While Adelaid's was built on hope. She'd rubbed off on him, for sure.

But was it enough?

Enough was enough. He couldn't continue mulling, hypothesising, talking to his dead father, while Adelaid was out there, no doubt feeling as confused, and shocked, and daunted, as he was.

Work could wait. The time to go to her was now.

Adelaid opened the door to find Ted on her porch once again. Only this time he didn't ask to come in. This time he stepped over the threshold and swept her up in his arms.

And soon they were kissing, and clawing at one another's clothes, as if their very lives depended on it.

"Wait." It was Ted that time, drawing back. "I came here to talk."

"Yes. We should talk."

With a growl, he kissed her again. Kept kissing her as he walked her into the lounge room. And there he put her down carefully, gently, as if suddenly aware how small she was compared to him.

Adelaid sat on one end of the couch and patted the seat beside her. "You look like you're about to pass out. Or throw up. I have dibs, for the next few weeks at least."

Ted sat, a kind of psychic pain flashing over his face.

"I'm joking," she said. "I feel fine. How about you?"

He blanked her, but his mouth kicked up at one corner.

Then she said, "It's yours by the way. The baby."

His expression was priceless. Momentarily baffled, before he burst into laughter. "Hell, Addy. I can safely say I wasn't expecting to laugh like that today."

She reached out and took his hand, moving it into her lap. "I've had a few laugh-or-cry moments myself. This is huge. And unforeseen. And no one's fault. I told you I wasn't on the pill, right? But we used condoms. So—"

He lifted her hand and laid a kiss to the palm, and her nerves seemed to unknot, all over her body.

"Science," said Ted, "is often fallible. How do you feel? Honestly."

"Tired. Queasy. Sideswiped." A beat, then, "Scared."

"Of…motherhood?" The word sat strangely on his tongue. As if he'd have gone with a more scientific term if he hadn't forced himself to be real. Adelaid decided to ignore the red flag. Focussing instead on the fact that he was there, holding her hand.

Adelaid shook her head. "A dozen nieces and nephews. Three sisters-in-law to call on for advice when, or if, I feel the need. I've got this." Her eyes rose to meet his. "I'm scared of everything that must be going on in your head right now."

His expression, the way he was clearly trying to appear strong, and supportive and fine, near broke her heart. For it was clear as day to her that he was holding on by his finger-nails. She shoved red flag number two deep down inside.

"I know you don't want kids, Ted. Or a family. You made that very clear. But you need to know that I… I feel very strongly about going ahead with the pregnancy. For many reasons. Yes, it's unplanned. And yes, I'd prefer to be in a more stable position than I am right now." A job with health insurance would have been nice. "But it's real. And happening. And growing. And I was unplanned. And I'm pretty bloody happy to be here. So…"

Ted shook his head. "If you harboured any thought that I'd ask you to not… Addy, that was never going to happen."

She knew it. But boy did it feel good to hear it. "Thank you. For saying that. Now I also understand if you… If you can't…"

Ted moved closer, slid his big strong sure hand into the hair behind her neck and said, "I didn't want a cactus. But you should see Fuzz Lightyear now."

That's all it took for tears that had been hiding away inside of her to spill from her eyes like salty waterfalls. "What are you saying?"

"I'm saying," he said slowly, "that we go on as we have been going on. With forward momentum. One step at a time. One kiss at a time. One bombshell at a time."

She swiped at her tears, laughter falling from her mouth. "It's a crazy thought, right? You are never home, my hours are all over the place. You're a neat freak, I'm a mess. You're always on time, I'm always late. I'm static electric-ity, you're Mr Cool." She flapped a hand at him, sitting there, proving it.

"We're both pretty determined people, Addy."

He was giving her everything she could hope for, in the situation. And yet, something ate at her. Some third red flag that she couldn't put her finger on. "How are you so calm about this?"

Ted breathed out hard, his hand finally rubbing up the back in his neck in that way she loved so much. "I'm not calm. I'm jumbled and overthinking things and shell-shocked, actually. And I may have spent a good bit of time earlier today talking to my father's ghost." He shook his head. "I just… I don't want to lose this. I don't want to lose you."

"Oh, Ted," she said, before crawling along the couch and into his arms. And whether it was raging hormones, or just simply Ted, she had to have him. Had to show him, with action, what she could not find the words to say.

That she had no clue what she'd done to deserve him, but she'd do whatever it took not to lose him too.

Her hands on his face she drew him to her and kissed him. Hard. Not holding back an ounce of her feelings. This was big, and raw, and scary, but she had Ted, and he was holding her, and he had belief in her. Belief in *them*.

And that was far more than she'd ever had in her life. More than she'd ever dared hope for, in her wildest dreams.

Kisses not letting up, she straddled him, her body sinking over his thighs. Rocking into him as his hands roved down her back before landing on her backside, holding her to him. His tongue slid into her mouth as he rocked up into her, the actions mimicking what was to come.

"Is this okay?" he murmured against her moth.

"I'm pregnant, Ted, not infirmed."

He pulled away, just long enough to swipe her hair from her face and run his thumb down her cheek. And with that he rolled her onto the couch, holding his bulk over her. His eyes dark, and hot, and possessive, he stripped her.

And then, after she asked it of him, he was inside her. Bare. Skin on skin. All slippery heat and gasping sighs.

For a brief spell, there was nothing between them but sweat and breath. No tension, no fear, no uncertainty about what the future might bring.

And afterwards, as they lay snuggled on her couch, Ted caressing her hair from her face, while reading articles on pregnancy on his phone, tossing her little nuggets such as when it was best to tell people, and why folate was important, she didn't have it in her to tell him she was all over it.

She'd remind him she didn't need looking after later. Right now, after the day she'd had, it felt like the nicest thing in the world.

And so things went for the next fortnight.

They'd agreed to tell their closest friends the news, mostly so that they each had someone to click fingers in front of their faces if they disppeared into their own heads too often. Georgette took up knitting "so the kid would have warm feet." Hadley shook her head every time she saw Ted, and Ronan was avoiding him. Forward momentum indeed.

Till one morning, while nursing her morning espresso, Celia introduced Ted to every second person who entered the tennis club, leaving Ted to realise *he* ought to have chosen the venue for their coffee.

"Now," Celia said when she noticed Ted checking his watch for the third time, "what's new with you?"

"I wanted to talk to you about something…personal."

Celia's hand went to her throat. "Darling?"

Ted grimaced, wondering whether either of them would be able to do or say anything out of the normal without their minds going straight to bloody cancer.

"I'm fine. I just wanted to ask you something. If you wouldn't mind telling me what exactly happened when I *broke the mould*."

Celia blinked. "Well, that's rather unexpected. But all right. It was a rare complication. You were a Caesarean birth. A blood vessel was nicked just as the doctor was stitching me up. Nobody knew until my blood pressure dropped dramatically several hours later, my insides filling with blood. It was all rather dire, according to your father, but I remember none of it. A couple of operations and lots of transfusions later and and here we are."

Ted was not squeamish. Medical research was a rather earthy field. Yet he felt his own blood pressure take a dip.

"Is there a particular reason you're asking? Some project you're working on your dear old mum could help with?"

Here goes, thought Ted, readying to say words he'd honestly never expected would come out of his mouth.

"I'm pregnant."

Celia gasped, a shaky hand going to her mouth.

Ted ran a hand over his face to find his forehead had broken out in a sweat. "Well, not me. Adelaid. Whom you met. Adelaid Adams, the writer. We weren't involved when you met her, but have become so. And Adelaid is pregnant. And the… It is mine."

"Ted," she said, so many emotions flashing behind her eyes he could not hope to keep up. "Oh, Ted. I am so happy for you both. Does she know you're here? Telling me?"

"She knows. She's telling her own family now too." He'd wanted to be with her, but she'd insisted it was something she had to do on her own. A rather strong surge in her need for independence a definite side effect of her pregnancy.

"And does she know you're worried about her?"

Ted sat back. "I'm not worried. You're referring to my query? I'm collecting knowledge so as to be prepared for any eventuality."

"Darling, that is the definition of worry. Here's the only piece of unsolicited parenting advice you will get from me. Ignorance really is bliss."

Ted's jaw ticked as he ground his teeth. "That seems counterintuitive."

She smiled. "I feel for your generation with your social media groups and your how-to podcasts. There is such a thing as too much information. For a man such as yourself, your retention capabilities, I'm not sure how you sleep at night."

He didn't for the most part. Then Adelaid had come along, and something about knowing she was out there in the world had settled him. But since she'd fallen pregnant, he was back to his old ways. There were only a few months for him to prepare.

Ted said, "I just want to make sure there's nothing in particular I ought to mention to the OBGYN, regarding your situation."

"You are most welcome to tell him, or her, to take care with their scalpels, but if that's something you feel you need to bring up, then perhaps you ought to choose a different OBGYN."

Celia placed her hand over his. "I know this is like telling the moon not to pull the tides, but stop trying to control it all, Ted. It's simply not possible. Take care of her. Encourage her to rest when she can, to eat well and drink plenty of water. Get some fresh air and sunshine." Celia shrugged. "For all the wonder of science, the basics have never really changed."

Celia clicked her fingers and asked for a menu. Then passed it to Ted.

"Now order something, darling, before you pass out. And you let me know when I am allowed to spoil you all rotten, all right?"

"All right."

The Adams family chat went something like this.

Adelaid: Up the duff. Ted's the dad. Can't make Sunday lunch this week.

Three seconds later.

Brad: Where are you?

Adelaid: Home.

Brad: Don't move. We'll be right there.

Adelaid sat on the front porch, eating corn chips dipped in cream cheese, and watched as three separate utes pulled up outside, one after the other. She pulled herself to standing, braced her feet against the floor, crossed her arms and waited for the onslaught.

Sid, the youngest, and his girlfriend Sally —no kids yet—made it up the path first and held out a fist.

"Is that for me to—?"

He slammed his fist into hers. "Bouya!"

Jake was next. He pulled her in for a manly hug, double back-slap. "Way to lock that down, kid."

"What is happening here?"

Brad was last, as he was unwinding a tarp from the back of his ute, and pulling out what looked like several pieces of hand-me-down baby furniture.

"Stop!" she called, and he stopped. "Can you leave all that for a second and come inside?"

Brad slowly put the high chair back into the tray, then ambled up the path. "What are you wearing?"

Adelaid looked down. "Georgette's overalls. I'm not loving the feel of things touching my stomach right now. Because I'm pregnant."

Nope. Nothing.

Except, "Is he here?"

"If by 'he' you mean Ted, then no, he's having breakfast with his mother, then he has a video link-up with the

UN about some freshwater project Big Think are close to launching."

A grunt. Then Brad followed the others inside, noses lifted to follow the scent of fresh baked muffins in the kitchen.

Couching and spluttering at the sky, which looked serenely back, Adelaid headed in. "Where's Bill?"

"First responder to a four-car pile-up on the M1. He sends his congratulations."

"So you did all actually read my message. Telling you that I am pregnant. While unmarried. Having recently quit my well-paying job."

Again she braced herself, waiting for the fallout. The opinions. The comparison to their mum.

"We like him," said Sid, a mouthful of muffin.

"He's bloody clever," said Jake. "And rich. *BRW Rich List*–level rich. We looked him up."

Brad leant back, muffin in hand, a delighted smile on his face.

A frisson of something that felt awfully like envy skittered down her spine. "What does any of that have to do with this?"

One of them frowned. Or maybe they all did. They'd clearly—as they so often did—become a single wall of opinionated muscle.

"What's with the sass?" asked Jake. "You tell us all the time that we need to stop telling you what to do, that you're a grown-up, that you can make your own choices. We're trying to say you've done good."

Adelaid's mouth popped open. Literally. Her jaw dropping with a clunk.

Her voice was raw as she said, "So let me get this straight. You're finally happy to leave me be, to make my own choices, without butting your big noses in, because

I brought home a big strong man who can do the job you guys have been doing my whole life?"

"That's gotta be a relief, right?" said Jake. "It is to us."

Adelaid stalked over and snatched up the tray of muffins, which got their attention.

"Addy, come on—"

"I have been 'doing good' for years. I graduated high school, winning the principal's arts award, despite barely attending primary. Graduated university, while holding down two jobs. In a highly competitive industry, I hustled my way into a lucrative position with a thrillingly popular digital media company. I have enough money for a deposit on a house. And I've kept a cactus alive for seven months now. I am also growing a life inside of me, which is more than any of you have ever done."

Breathing heavily, blood rising, she said, "I was sure you'd all barrel over here and give me what for, for being single, and pregnant. Like Mum."

"You're not single."

"I am, for all intents and purposes."

Brad frowned, but kept his counsel for once.

Jake scoffed. "And you're not Mum."

Adelaid's gaze whipped to Jake. "What does that mean?"

"She was sick, Ads. Some way, somehow. Mentally, physically, who knows. We tried to get her to see a doctor to find out why. But we were too young to know what else to do. When she died...well, we didn't want to make that same mistake twice. So yeah, maybe we've been on your case. We also made sure you had the best doctors, and therapists, and Brad was onto your high school weekly, making sure they knew how lucky they were to have you."

Brad's jaw ticked. "We know how much you adored her. We didn't want to mar that memory. But just so you know, we've never been concerned that you were like her. In anything but the good bits."

Sid was nearest, so she grabbed him and hugged him like crazy. Then waggled a hand till the others joined them. "Thank you."

"Now can we have another muffin?" asked Sid, his voice muffled.

"Did I have to withhold food? Is that really all I had to do to get you guys to listen? And talk to me?"

Adelaid gave them each a bag of muffins and sent them on their way.

"Can I bring in the baby gear now?" Brad asked. "Betty has had it sitting in the garage for like a fortnight."

"No," said Adelaid. "If I want your help, I'll ask for it. I promise."

Brad sighed, then they were gone. Leaving Adelaid feeling light-headed, flabbergasted and strangely bereft.

She found her phone, then sent Ted a message, telling him she was done. And giving him a quick recap. Then she slumped onto a stool in the kitchen and ate muffin crumbs from the cutting board.

Forward momentum had been wondrous. Her brothers might actually have just washed their hands of her. And Ted… Ted was out there telling his mother that he was going to be a father. All it would take for her life to be pretty much perfect right now was for someone to call and offer to buy her story.

Her feet felt a little numb. Her fingertips lacked sensation. And she found herself having to breathe. Deep settling breaths.

What was a person to do, if after having to fight for everything they ever wanted, one day they looked up and found they had it all?

Later that day, still feeling not quite herself, Adelaid alighted her ride share, kicking at the hemline of the floaty seventies maxidress she'd borrowed from Georgette, as she could no longer stand the feel of anything tight over her tummy, so that she didn't trip over the thing.

About to meet with a book club who'd collected over a hundred thousand dollars' worth of book donations for a flooded library, Adelaid's phone buzzed.

"Hello?" she answered, while tugging at the collar of the dress, which had twisted up in her shoulder bags.

"You, my darling girl, are a genius."

"Deborah?" Her old editor. "Hi! So nice to hear from you! And why am I a genius?"

"Not sure if you heard, but I moved on too, after you left." Deborah went on to mention the name of a publication that made Adelaid's heart stop. "A sample of your Ted Fincher profile fell onto my desk today. What are the odds? I read it, I loved it. I've spoken to everyone here about the wonder that is you, and we'd love to publish your piece."

Adelaid's heart leapt into her throat so that for a second all she could do was squeak. Then, "Oh, my gosh. Deborah! Thank you!"

"We'd also love you to come in and chat about what's next."

Adelaid moved off the footpath when a teacher with a group of kindergarteners all holding a rope wandered up the path. "Of course," she said, watching the little ones wobble and bounce and spin. "I would love that."

"Now," said Deborah, her voice quieting, "I shouldn't be saying this, but what with all the offers you must be weighing right now, go with your gut, push for what you want. Know your worth."

Other offers? *Ha. Ha-ha-ha-ha.* Adelaid said, "You bet. Great advice."

"Then after you do all that, choose us. It would be wonderful to have you on board again."

With that Deborah rang off.

Adelaid's phone began to buzz.

"Ms Adams."

Adelaid tucked her phone between ear and shoulder and rejigged her bags. "This is she."

"This is Daryl Majors from *Imprint*. I've read your Big Think piece and believe its place is right here. With us."

"Thank you so much! That's so nice to hear."

Giving up on her bags, she dumped the lot of them on the verge, and shuffled through her tote till she found paper and pen. Writing down *Deborah* and then *Daryl... Imprint.*

"Any requests—word length, tone, etc.?" she asked.

"We loved it."

"Every word?" she joked.

After a pause, he said, "Every word."

Her pen hovered over the paper.

"I've emailed you a contract. Sign it, send it back and we'll release the funds immediately."

Wow. That was…fast. "I'll have a look and get back to you."

Feeling a tingle up the back of her neck, Adelaid opened her email on her phone to find no less than five more offers for her story.

Seven altogether. So why wasn't she jumping for joy?

Partly because the same dress felt weird, and airy and not at all her. But also, seven offers? After weeks of nothing?

It was a dream. The kind of dream in which you know you are dreaming because it was way too unreal.

She lifted her phone and called Deborah back.

Ted leaned against the picket fence outside the converted weatherboard dwelling in which their OBGYN resided, watching the street for Adelaid's Uber, and unconsciously twisting his watch around his wrist.

Dr Shifarko had a waiting list a mile long, but she had also been an early sensitivity consultant on stem cell research for Big Think, so a quick text and he'd had an appointment that day. Adelaid wasn't the only one who had a fondness for "connections."

Adelaid. Who was late. For their first scan.

It was still early days, so there might not be answers as yet, as to whether the pregnancy was tracking as it ought.

Not that he was *concerned*.

Yes, he felt a low-level discomfort in his gut. But it was the same thing that had driven him all these years. How could he not be feeling something, when according the World Health Organisation nearly a thousand women a day died from preventable causes related to childbirth and pregnancy.

Not that he was *worried*.

Skilled care, before, during and after was key, hence the choice of OBGYN. Despite his mother's advice, Ted believed himself prepared for any eventuality. It was his job to look out for those he cared for.

Speaking of people he cared for, where the hell was Adelaid?

Her habitual lateness was a symptom of her condition. He understood that. But today of all days?

Foot tapping on the path, Ted went to check the time, twisting his dad's watch, only the clasp was unbuckled and it slipped over his hand, landing facedown on the footpath with a dull thud.

Time hung for a second, two, three, before Ted leaned over to pick up the watch. To find a crack had split the face in two. He swiped the pad of his thumb over the face, a sliver of glass cutting into his thumb. The low-level discomfort in his belly rising to a solid medium.

He was sucking his thumb still when a car pulled up and Adelaid barrelled out, a voluminous flowery dress billowing around her, a thousand bags over her shoulder, her hair a wild mass of curls floating about her face.

His heart fair stopped at the sight of her. It hovered in

his chest a good three seconds before kicking like a mule and keeping him alive once more.

And it hit him, like a sledgehammer to the head—no matter what happened in the scan, whether a second heart beat inside of her or no, he wasn't going anywhere.

Adelaid was the one.

"Did you tell them to do it?" she asked, descending on him with rather a lot of energy, even for her.

Ted dragged himself out of his fog of adoration, to find he was still sucking his thumb. Pulling it from his mouth, he directed her towards the doctor's gate, and began walking that way. "Let's head in, yes? And did I tell whom to do what?"

When she didn't move, bar shifting her bags from one shoulder to the other, he went to her, reaching for the straps. Only to stop when she held up both hands, arms straight, eyes wild, halting him where he stood.

"Did you," she said, through gritted teeth, "or did you not call my dream editors with regards to my profile piece, and somehow make it sound as if it was worth their while to offer me the moon?"

"What on earth are you ta—" Something tugged in the back of Ted's mind. A sense of warning, of imminent danger, had him pulling up straight.

Noting his hesitation, she moved closer. Green wildfire flickering behind her gaze. Then growling, she tugged at the dress, some hippie number that made her look like she was about to sport a peace sign. While everything else about her screamed war.

A responding growl built up in his chest. And, doctor's appointment be damned, he'd have dragged her behind the nearest bush if not for the fact there was no denying she was furious. With him.

"Ted," she said, her voice danger soft. "Promise me no editors were coerced into bidding on my story."

"*Coerced* is a strong word."

"I knew it!" She began to pace, muttering under her breath about everyone going whackadoo, when she was the one who was meant to be hormonal.

He wasn't keen on the pink in her cheeks. The rise and fall of her chest. The signs that her heart rate was up. Yes, she suffered a hyperactivity disorder that could bring on such symptoms. But assuming his father was losing weight on purpose had been the death of him, literally.

Ted shook his head. Correlation, not causation. Conflating one thing with another was not going to help. Still, he didn't need to be an obstetric specialist to know stress was not a good thing in the first trimester.

He held out both hands, attempting to stay her. "Settle, sweetheart. Just settle."

She stopped pacing. "Did you really just tell me to *settle*?"

"It was a suggestion. Medically motivated. Can we discuss this afterward?" Ted went to check his watch, then remembered it was in his hand. Broken. He slipped it into his pocket.

While Adelaid shook her head. "I'd had no other offers on the profile. Not a sniff. I'd hoped that my work would speak for itself."

"It will. It does. You are a wonderful writer."

"I know! While you're about to become the thinking woman's muffin overnight."

"What about the *unthinking* women?" He held up a hand the moment he said it. "I did not intend to make light. I only want to do what it takes to get you through that door, so that we can find out if… If the pregnancy is even viable."

She glanced up at the beautiful old building, the oak trees, dappled sunshine. Her throat working. Her hand lifting to land on her belly.

The urge to go to her, to lay his hand over hers, was primal. But something held him back. Some final layer of self-protection, bolstered by the broken watch in his pocket, the unsettling conversation with his mother and finally Adelaid refusing to play ball when it came to her safety.

Too many variables.

Yet he added one more. "Ronan would not have been wrong in knowing how much I want to see you rewarded for all your hard work."

He saw the light flare in her eyes, then dim, before she breathed out, long and slow, her chin falling to her chest. "Ted."

Birds twittered in the trees overhanging the avenue. A light breeze rustled the light layer of fallen leaves. Ted could feel her drawing away from him as if it was a physical thing.

She said, "Can you even imagine how mortifying it was, hearing words of praise from the mouths of people I would give my right foot to impress, while suspecting that they'd been nudged into it. What will they think when it comes out that I am your…?"

She flicked a heavy hand his way, unwilling or still unable to put a label on what they were.

While Ted could think of a dozen. She was his confidante, his friend, his lover, his joy. She was the person he wanted to wake up next to for the rest of his life. *She was the one.*

"They'll think you are a talented writer with connections. How do you think we got so big so fast? We've used every connection we made. Because we believed that what we had to offer had worth. Use me. Lean on me. I will get no greater pleasure than using my influence to help you in any way that I can."

Adelaid swallowed, and he hoped like hell she could see his intentions had been true.

Till she said, "It just feels wrong. Everything feels wrong. These clothes feel wrong. The way my brothers just accepted this as fait accompli, then dropped me like a hot potato, that was so wrong. I liked my life. I liked my hustle. I liked the fact that I was at a point where I put less store in how other people saw me as I'd learned to like myself. Now everything is changing so fast I don't recognise myself anymore."

"Adelaid, that's not—"

"*Fair?* Tell me about it. Some people are born into happy families, some are born into struggle. Some people are given respect from day dot, others leave first impressions they can never break, no matter how hard they try. But despite all that, you can't wrap me in cotton wool, Ted."

A muscle jumped in Ted's cheek. He'd thought he'd imagined all the ways this could go wrong. It seemed he'd missed quite a lot.

"I'd really appreciate it if you'd let me try."

She laughed, but there was no humour in it. In fact, a single tear wavered down her cheek. "I get it. You fix things. You make them better. Because of your dad. It is a noble pursuit. But I'm not one of your causes, Ted. I don't need fixing."

He opened his mouth to deny her claim, then remembered his mother's prophetic reminder that he couldn't possibly control it all.

Letting go a big deep breath, Adelaid reached into her bag, pulled out her phone and dialled. Hand shaking a little she held it to her ear, a watery smile plastered on her face as she said, "Daryl, hi, it's Adelaid Adams. Unfortunately, I'm going to have to pull my piece from contention." Top teeth biting down on her bottom lip as if to stop it from trembling, she listened. Nodded. "Thank you, truly. I'll absolutely be in touch when I have something else lined up. So be prepared!"

When she made the next call, Ted wanted to grab her phone, to stop her from sabotaging herself in that way. But she'd literally just spent the past several minutes making it clear that her sense of self-determination was at stake.

Meaning, Ted had to stand there, feeling impotent and ineffective, as she made call after call. Watching the woman he loved feel pain, in real time, and knowing there was nothing he could do about it, hurt like a bastard.

"What's the time?" she said when she was done. Then, "Where's your watch?"

He pulled it from his pocket and passed it to her.

She took it, saw the break, her face crumpling. "Oh, Ted." Then, "Come on. Let's go inside now. You're right, we'll figure out the rest after."

"I don't want—" he said, his voice croaking. "I want—"

You. I want you. And us. And this...

But most of all he wanted Adelaid to be happy. To feel strong, and fierce, and bright, and proud. To own the space she'd worked so hard to carve out for herself. If he crushed that, if he crushed all the things he loved most about her, he'd never be able to live with himself.

"Dr Shifarko comes highly recommended, but if you want to see someone else, then we find someone else." Too little, too late. "Might I suggest we take this appointment so we can be sure that you are okay?"

Only as Adelaid looked to him, her eyes bruised, did he realise the hum inside of him, that was now ratcheted up as high as he'd ever felt it go, had nothing to do his being a scientist. And everything to do with him being a man.

A man pretending he wasn't deeply daunted by the entire situation. By the terrifying flipside that came with feeling so much. A man forced to look into the face of his own intrinsically hard-wired flaws and not know how to fix himself.

Adelaid tipped the broken hardware into his palm. Then, fixing the straps of her bags, she moved through the gate and said, "Come on, then. Let's get this over with."

And so, they walked into the doctor's office, side by side. The gulf between them interminable.

CHAPTER NINE

"HEY," SAID GEORGETTE, head poking out of the kitchen doorway. "Deborah called. Twice. Sounded super keen to talk to you. You're home early. Thought you'd be off making lovey eyes at your beautiful beast, and— Hey what's wrong?"

Adelaid's bags slumped to the floor by the front door.

"Oh, no," said Georgette, jogging down the hall. "The baby—?"

"Has a heartbeat," said Adelaid with a quivering smile. "A beautiful, perfect, teeny tiny little heartbeat."

Georgette's hands went to her mouth. "Then what am I missing? Is it Ted? Does Ted not have a heartbeat? I knew it. He's a vampire. Or from Krypton or something. No man that big and that beautiful is real."

Adelaid trudged into the lounge, and slumped face-down on the couch. Then remembered what she and Ted had done on that couch. Then remembered she didn't like things touching her stomach. So she pressed her sorry self up to sitting.

"Deborah was calling to offer to buy my story."

"Woohoo! When it rains it pours!"

Adelaid slowly sat forward till her face fell into her hands. "Only because Ted, or Ronan on Ted's behalf, or Hadley on Ronan's behalf on Ted's behalf, put out word around town that anyone who bought my story would be looked on kindly by Big Think. Or something of that ilk."

"Wow!" said Georgette. Then, "That's massive! They're notoriously tight. They don't show favour to anyone, making our job much more difficult. Only...you look like that's a bad thing."

"It is a bad thing! He thought I couldn't do it on my own."

"Ronan?"

"Ted!"

"What? That doesn't sound at all like him. I've seen him read your own stories back to you, he loves them so much."

Well, no, it didn't sound like Ted.

But then again neither had the fact that he'd made her feel powerless.

When she would not, could not, be reliant on anyone. Her brothers, being men, didn't understand how much she feared ending up in the position her mother had. Left behind, overwhelmed by circumstance.

"Look at it this way," said Georgette. "You got your foot in the door with Big Think because of me. Did you feel bad about that?"

Adelaid blinked. "No."

"Because you know I know you're amazing, or because you know I helped you because I love you. Or both."

Adelaid let that sink in.

"As for Ted," said Georgette, "the man's hardly oblivious. The only reason he would have stepped over some invisible line you'd created in your head is because you invited him over that line. In fact, that man would take down the stars, one by one, and place them in your hands, if you asked it of him. Or even if he thought it would make you happy. That's how opposite of oblivious he is."

Georgette tapped her lips.

Adelaid wriggled on the seat. "Do you really think—"

"Stay there. I'm going to bring you a snack. Need to keep your blood sugar up!"

"Not sure that's right," said Adelaid, remembering something Dr Shifarko had said about gestational diabetes.

But Georgette was gone. Leaving Adelaid alone, feeling lost and yearning for starlight.

She grabbed a fluffy orange cushion with big knobbly pom-poms lining the edges and held it to her stomach. Georgette thought it the most uncomfortable thing on the planet. Ted, when it had ended up under his back one time, had yanked it out from under himself, looked at it, then looked at her as if to say, *What on earth is this?*

"It makes me happy," she'd said.

And after showering her with his killer smile, he'd placed it gently on the coffee table as if it was something precious. Purely because it had meaning to her.

"He likes to take care of me." Saying the words out loud, without tone or censure, they sounded like a dream.

When she thought about it, she liked to take care of him too. Keeping food on hand for when he forgot to eat. Gently forcing him to look up from his work. All the ways she'd imposed herself on him, on his sense of order, because she'd seen a need in him. And sought to fill it.

Only he hadn't complained or refused her. He'd made room. He'd let her in. He'd appreciated her inclinations. Her ways of showing him that she…

That she loved him.

She loved Ted. She loved him so much she had no clue where to put it all.

Her love was an inevitable tumble into his warmth, and generosity and wonderfulness. Until, now she thought of it, she couldn't remember a moment of having known him when she hadn't loved him.

Was that what he'd been doing for her, making appointments on her behalf with fancy doctors, giving her career a leg up? Helping carry her bags, because he saw that she was walking funny. Swiping her hair from her face, as if he knew the texture of it would eventually drive her nuts. Showing her that he thought her amazing. Showing her that he loved her. Only in his far more worldly way?

Ted, who'd been cradling his father's broken watch when she'd come at him, a whirling dervish of referred pain, with nowhere to put it now that her Teflon brothers had left her be.

Ted, who'd been shifting from foot to foot, anxious to get her inside to the doctor. Not because of some appointment he'd made on her behalf, but because he'd suffered loss in his life, and wanted to make sure *she* was okay.

Ted, whose face she'd watched for a full minute when the baby's heartbeat was found. Every last twitch inside of her had settled as she'd drunk in the wonder, the delight, and the relief in his expression. Before his eyes had swung to hers, a glint of actual tears therein.

She reached into one of the pockets in her borrowed dress, and pulled out the picture from the sonogram. Nothing but a tiny dark smudge with a tiny white dot in the middle. Running a thumb a millimetre above the image, she thought, *Not nothing. Something. Everything.*

Before Ted her life was fine. Fine if you enjoy paddling a melting iceberg adrift in a warm sea. Since Ted her life had been a billion times better than fine.

On cue, her phone pinged.

Ted: Checking you made it home all right.

Adelaid: I did. Thank you.

Ted: Good.

Ted: Heads-up, I'll check in again tomorrow. And the next day. And the next. Unless you tell me not to.

Adelaid: Of course.

Ted: Till then.

Adelaid waited in case there was more. But it was just enough. Ted, not pressing, only making it clear he wasn't going anywhere. No matter how many emotional grenades she lobbed.

If she could get over herself, he was there for the having. It was all there, for the having. A home, a career, a family. A man who adored her, and believed in her, and loved her for all her quirks not despite them.

Adelaid buried her face in the cushion and screamed.

"Whoa! What did I miss?"

"He loves me."

Georgette blinked. "Between me leaving to get snacks and coming back…"

"I figured stuff out."

Georgette sat, the tray leaning precariously on her lap. And Adelaid handed over the sonogram image.

"Oh, sweet pea. It's a bean. You're growing a bean."

"Ted and I are growing a bean. Together." She could only hope it wasn't too late to let Ted know it.

Ronan stormed into the Batcave, waving his phone in Ted's direction.

Ted looked up from the black-and-white sonogram image he held in his hand, his brain feeling like lead wrapped in tinfoil. "You got my email."

"Hell, yes, I got your email. What's that?"

Ted held up the sonogram.

Ronan looked at it for a full three seconds, before asking, “All well?”

“We have a heartbeat.”

“Hell of a thing. Now what the hell’s with the email? Couldn’t walk into my office and say something to my face?”

Ted lifted himself out of his chair, blinked away the grit in his eyes and said, “I’ll say it now, then. I’m taking a break.”

“For how long?”

“A day. A week. Indefinitely.”

“Ted. Come on. This is ridiculous—”

“She pulled the piece.”

Ronan jerked, uncharacteristically taken aback. “What do you mean—?”

“She received several offers for her story today. Good money. Next looks. Everything she’s been working towards. And she pulled it.”

“Why?”

“Because you called a half-dozen editors and told them to make her an offer!” Ted’s voice echoed back at him.

“Does that sound like something I would condescend to do?”

“Don’t prevaricate. I know you did something.”

Ronan’s jaw released. “Our PR people were prepared for any calls looking for comment. They were given instruction to say that ‘We at Big Think have always been committed to partnering with local talent,’ and that I thought it a ‘warm, humorous, impressively in-depth, well-balanced piece.’”

“Ronan—”

“You intimated that it was important to you that she—”

“I know!” said Ted, throwing out his arm and knocking over a cup filled with pencils. He watched them roll all over the place, a couple tumbling over the edge. And didn’t feel the slightest urge to tidy them up. “I know.”

He'd apprised Ronan of the situation, somewhat. His concern for her stress levels. His wish that more people got to hear her voice. And they'd known one another too long to pretend Ted hadn't known what Ronan would do.

"If it helps any," said Ronan, eyes serious, and curious, "not a word of our statement was untrue. As features go, it was well above par."

"You read it."

Ronan nodded, a slight smile tugging at his mouth. "She pinned you, like a moth to a board."

Ted lifted his hand, the back of his neck itching, but let it drop before he connected. "She has integrity. She worked really hard to get that chance. To get to know me. To write something lyrical, and beautiful, and moving, and quirky, and fresh and true. And now…now she feels as if, by blustering in and stamping ourselves all over it, we took that away from her."

"I refuse your request."

"My—"

"Your request for time off."

"So we're back to that. It wasn't a request. It's a done deal. I've put measures in place, provided Hadley with names, people who will step up. Who already have."

For he'd been stepping back, incrementally, in order to spend more time with Adelaid, and the world hadn't crumbled in his absence. In fact, he was clearer of the head. Actually more efficient, with sleep, good food, fresh air, sunshine and someone taking care of him.

Who knew?

"Are you listening to yourself?" said Ronan. "You do not take time off, Ted. You haven't had a holiday in ever. Ever since this girl came along—"

Ted was on his feet, his hands were fisted in the front of Ronan's shirt before he even felt himself move. Nostrils flared, adrenaline scented the air. And it took every ounce of restraint Ted could gather not to shove his friend against nearest wall.

"Her name," said Ted, "is Adelaid."

Ronan smiled. The bastard actually smiled. "I know her name, mate. I was just checking that you remembered it too."

What the—?

"This entire conversation, you've not said it once. It's a thing you do when in the process of…disentangling yourself. Hence the fact I rarely bother to learn the names of the women you see. Saves time."

Ted uncurled his fingers, and asked, "Are you trying to be an asshole, or does it come naturally?"

"Both, I imagine," Ronan drawled. Then, "You are my friend. And if disentangling is your intention, I stand by you. But…" A rare falter as Ronan looked for the right words. "I have to admit, it would be a surprise. Adelaid Adams might not be the best thing that ever happened to you—for that would be me, Sawyer comes a distant third—but she's close. Since she came along it's been like watching Pinocchio becoming a real boy."

Fanciful words for Ronan Gerard, but Ted knew exactly what he meant.

"Maybe you should be the one to take a break."

"Whatever," said Ronan.

If what Adelaid wanted from him was space, then…

No. Space wasn't what Adelaid wanted. What she wanted was to be seen. And heard. And given the benefit of the doubt.

His work with Big Think was important, worth his best efforts and extremely fulfilling, but it wasn't his whole life. Not anymore.

"So what now?" Ronan asked, still there.

"You want to know how I plan to make it up to my girlfriend?"

"You apologise. Tell her she's right."

Ted didn't even pretend to disagree.

"You should know, PR were also ordered to let Adelaid know that if she's ever keen to write a profile on Sawyer, or..." a beat, then "...or me, then she has an open invitation. Whether you stuff the whole relationship thing up, or not."

As he left Ronan added, "I'll let you have a week. The other zillion weeks you're owed you can save for when the baby is born. You'll need it."

"Wasn't a request!" Ted called, hand cupped around his mouth. "Don't require your permission!"

Then laughed when Ronan said, "Whatever gets you through the night."

Ted sat back in the chair, letting the hydraulics float him about, his mind doing much the same. Then he wheeled the thing to a desk with a computer and pulled up Adelaid's piece.

Odd as it was, reading about himself, he did so again. Only this time, he imagined Adelaid reading it to him.

And as her words, her tone, her humour, her heart, flowed over him, he began to see it for what it really was. Not merely an artful, wry, clever telling of the story of a thirty-something billionaire science geek, it was a love letter. To him. For all the world to see.

It's not about me, Adelaid had said over and over again.

But it was all about her, and had been from the very beginning.

A Bee Gees song jiving through her earbuds, loose gingham dress swishing about her ankles, Adelaid marvelled at the façade of the Big Think Corp building and felt sick to the stomach.

She reached into her tote for a slice of lemon and gave it a quick lick. Both Betty and Wendy had found it the perfect foil for morning sickness and so far, it was doing the trick.

She put the lemon back, beside the container containing the chocolate chip muffin she'd made that morning.

Her phone buzzed. Not the Adams family chat, for it had quieted right down, all but overnight. A wind of change having descended upon the lot of them.

A message from Deborah.

Check email. Sent you a lead on special interest piece. Up your alley. Want?

Deborah, who'd refused to accept the withdrawal of her story. Deborah, who'd recommended she get an agent and sell the bloody thing. Her sample now about to hit social media, before the whole piece went in their online and print magazines.

Adelaid sent off a quick thumbs-up emoji, then scrolled down to her last messages from Ted, sent that morning.

Ted: Sleep okay?

Adelaid: Not so much. I watched Calamity Jane.

Ted: Not a shade on Pillow Talk.

Adelaid: Wash your mouth out with soap.

Ted's reply was an angel emoji!

All but hearing his voice in her head, Adelaid made a beeline for the rotating glass doors. Once through, she saw Hadley talking to the staff at reception. Hadley offered up a nod, then a glance to the glass-fronted staff lift making its way towards the lobby.

"Ted," Adelaid said, the name wafting past her lips on a heady breath when she caught sight of his dark auburn hair, light glinting off his glasses, the sheer size of him compared to the others in the lift.

Adelaid's hand went to her belly. To the teeny tiny smudge therein.

And Ted looked up, as if something had tugged at his subconscious.

Spotting her through the glass, his hand lifted as if he might punch his way through the glass. But self-preservation got the better of him and he waited for the lift to reach the ground floor before he pushed past the poor staffers and jogged across the foyer, his hands going straight to her upper arms as he looked deep into her eyes.

"Everything okay?" he said, the words rough on his tongue. "Is the baby okay?"

Adelaid nodded. Smiled. And whatever he saw in her eyes had him hauling her into his chest. One arm across her back, the other in her hair. And there they stood, simply holding one another for the longest time.

"Your smell," she said, half smiling against his hard chest.

"Hmm?" he said, giving her a little air.

Not too much. Just the perfect amount.

She breathed him in. "I was feeling queasy but then you came, and now I feel nothing. Well, not *nothing*." Another wholesome breath in. "You're better than any lemon slice."

"Thank you?" The words rumbled from his chest to hers.

"You're welcome," she said on a sigh. Had he always smelled this good? This lickable? Good chance. Or perhaps it was a pregnancy bonus. If so, she couldn't wait to see what else it had in store for her.

Adelaid pressed herself back just enough that she could see his whole face. To find his eyes, dark and warm and gorgeous, moved between hers.

"Assuming you did not come here to sniff me, is there a particular reason you are here?" His voice was low. Edging towards a growl. As if he might be high on being with her too.

Adelaid swallowed. For all that she could see how he cared for her, in his messages, even after her flight, in the way he held her even now, this was it. This was her chance to step fully into whatever space he'd made for her in his life, leaving her old defensive ways behind.

"I've come to apologise—"

"There is no need."

She held up a hand. "There is very much a need."

His nostrils flared, and he nodded.

"I was a mess the other day. A perfect storm of every worry I've had in my entire life seemed to wash over me at once. I put it down to so many changes, and wobbles, and— What's the word?"

"Variables."

She clicked her fingers. "Yes. That's exactly it. I was unfair. To you. My expectations impossible. I'm so sorry I put you through that. When all you were doing was being protective, and prepared. Being…you. Considering the hormonal swings, I can't promise there won't be more episodes, going forward. Let's say there will be, just to be on the safe side."

"Going forward?" he asked, his voice deepening, his gaze roving over her face, the hand on her back sliding a little deeper around her waist.

"If that's what you want."

"Is it what you want?"

"Ted," she said, *her* voice now turning raspy, as if it had caught whatever it was that was making his eyes go hot. "I want this. I want us. I want—"

He leaned in and touched his lips to hers. Not shutting her up. More like sealing her words as a promise between them.

"You," Ted rumbled against her mouth, finishing her

sentence as if he'd taken the word from her lips and made it his. "Would you care to hear what I want?"

"Please," she said, the word half whisper.

"I want this," he said, his hand reaching up to tug on a lock of her hair. "And this." His fingers cupping her jaw, his thumb tugged at her bottom lip. "I want every last bit of you. Hormones, mood swings, the lot."

"Thank the gods," she said, her breath leaving her on a whoosh of laughter, "or this whole moment would have been mighty confusing."

She earned a killer smile for her efforts. But she wasn't yet done. She had to make sure he knew how serious she was. No more guesswork. No more stumbling around all her big new feelings.

"Ted," she said. Then, "Theodore Fincher. The truth is, I never saw you coming. So even while you saw me, and accepted me, I was so swept up in you I lost myself. Just a bit."

Ted's eyes flew back to hers.

She lifted her hand to his cheek, to the rasp of stubble along the hard jaw. "But I'm back now. Still a scrappy little fighter, and now a lover, and soon enough, Smudge's mum."

Ted's mouth kicked up at one side. "Smudge?"

She held a hand over her belly. Then reached out for his hand and laid it over the top.

"Smudge," he said, his fingers closing around her hand.

Then his hand slipped a smidge lower, his little finger dipping into one of the big pockets in the side of her dress. She could get used to this, all the same.

"Ted," she warned, realising he had no idea what his scent was doing to her pregnancy-addled hormones. "I think maybe we should take this conversation elsewhere."

"I own the joint," he said, leaning to nuzzle her neck. "I can order everyone out of the building. Just like that. But first it's my turn to apologise."

"Ted—"

"My turn."

Adelaid nodded.

"My work has been my focus for as long as I can remember. And you, more than most anyone, know why. Any time I have paused, taken a breather, I've spent every minute holding my breath, dreading something bad happening to someone I love."

"Ted," she said, her voice gentle, her expression firm.

"I know that I am not the fixer of all things. I know when bad things happen it's not my fault. But I am also aware of the rarefied position I hold, the exceptional confluence of events that have given me the opportunity to enact real change on the world. And for as long as I can remember, I believed that it was my duty to take advantage of every chance I was gifted."

She pressed in closer.

"Then you came along and it was like someone had turned on a light. You showed me I'm no good to anyone if I'm burnt out. If I don't live a life that reminds me what I've been working so hard for."

She may have made a sound. Something between a sob and a sigh. For he tucked her under his chin, his arms wrapped all the way around her.

"You told me, many times, that our getting to know one another wasn't about you. But, Adelaid, sweetheart, from the moment you walked into my office, it's all been about you. I love you, Adelaid. One 'e.' You are worth pausing for."

Adelaid threw her arms around his neck, dragged him down to her level and kissed him. She kissed him till her head spun. She kissed him till she heard applause.

Ted lifted her, bodily, and spun her on the spot. And over his shoulder she could see faces galore looking down from the second-floor balconies. Others had gathered in the foyer, obviously having stopped on their way to and from the lifts. All clapping madly, whistling, cheering.

Hadley stood guard halfway across the foyer, waving her arms and saying something along the lines of "Nothing to see here."

But then Ted, big, quiet, gentle, gorgeous Ted, slid her down his body till her feet hit the floor, then swept her into a Hollywood dip and kissed her. Thoroughly.

And the crowd went wild.

When he brought her upright, slowly, remembering no doubt that her blood pressure might be a little out of whack considering all the magic and wonder her body was currently in charge of creating, Hadley finally convinced the crowd to: "Get back to work, you vultures, and give them some damn privacy! And if I find out anyone recorded a single frame of that—"

Adelaid didn't hear the rest as Ted caught her attention when he started picking up her bags. Bags she'd let slump the floor.

"May I?" he asked, even as he put them over his shoulder. Showing her that he wasn't going to take her stubbornness lying down. That he still fully intended to call her out, when needed.

"How about we go halves?" she said.

"How about we take turns? This is my turn."

Seriously, she was too tired to argue. It was a nice thing he was doing, and it was nice of her to let him too. So, they came out even.

He held out a hand, waited for her to take it, then led her to his special lift. Once the doors closed, the speed of the thing whipping them skyward.

And Adelaid gasped, "Did I even tell you that I love you?"

He kept watching the floor numbers as if willing them to hurry. "I'm sure you did."

"I don't think so."

His gaze dropped to hers. "Then I must have determined as much, based on evidence. You are, clearly, very much in love with me."

"Very much."

He leaned down, pressed his lips to hers.

She knew love wasn't an easy thing. Wasn't hearts and flowers and chocolate. It was messy and difficult.

Some love came without choice. Her brothers loved her. Her mum had too, in her own volatile way. Her love for her child, while still so fraught and fragile, seemed to grow every second.

Ted *had* a choice. He'd seen her at her messy worst. He'd seen her at her most insecure. He'd seen her when she'd floundered, he'd seen her full of fear. He'd borne the brunt of her distractibility, her jitters, her wobbly relationship with time.

And he loved her anyway.

She'd seen Ted hungry, and grumpy, and all impossibly alpha. She'd also seen him cherish his mother, and support his friends, and work himself to exhaustion to save the world.

And she loved him more.

When the lift doors opened, Ted dumped her bags just outside the door, when there was a perfectly good series of hooks and shelves on which to place such things.

Then he lifted her into his arms and kissed her like a man starved.

Knowing how grateful the man was to eat when he was truly hungry, she laughed against his mouth. Then buckled in for the ride.

EPILOGUE

"I'M OFF!" ADELAID CALLED, quickly checking if Fuzz Lightyear and Spikesaurus Rex needed water, but both looked happy on the windowsill next to one another, arms reaching towards the watery sunlight shining through her new kitchen windows.

For they'd found they needed a place with lots of rooms for Adelaid to work in, and near enough to Big Think for an easy commute. A mini lair for Ted so that he could work from home when needs be, and a library filled with biographies of amazing women and Booker Prize winners and romance novels and dense scientific texts so they could snuggle up and read side by side. A nursery, for their daughter, Katie. That had been important too.

Adelaid licked icing sugar off her fingers and bounced out of the kitchen and down the hall towards the front door, slipping on her "new" second-hand brogues. Although she was making better money now, and she'd landed herself a billionaire, she still loved her vintage gear.

Only to find Ted already there, sunlight streaming through the beautiful, colourful leadlight front door, casting a golden glow over his beastly gorgeousness.

Ted turned, wearing her smudged and rarely used pink glasses, having not been able to locate his own. He held an insulated lunch box in his hand, Katie, their teething five-month-old, on his hip, gnawing on his shoulder and leaving pools of drool on the cotton of his button-down shirt.

"For me?" she asked.

Ted pretended she meant the drooly nibbler, but Adelaid ducked out of the way, before leaning in to kiss her arm cheek. Then snatched the lunch box instead. Adelaid opened it up to find a healthy salad, a banana and a blueberry muffin. Good man.

"Who are you meeting today?" Ted asked, hitching Katie higher on his hip. Then he checked his watch—his father's watch, beautifully refurbished after its fall, its new-ish face already scratched from when Katie first learned to roll and Ted had reached out to catch her.

"Oh, only the star of the new Lois Lane movie." Adelaid leaned in and rubbed noses with their daughter, before running a hand over her strawberry blond curls. "She's just been diagnosed with Asperger's, and I have the exclusive."

"Smart girl."

She glanced through the leadlight to find her driver had arrived. "How about you? What are your plans today?"

"Saving the world, cleaning rusk out of my hair."

"So, the usual."

"Yep. Sid is coming over to check on the solar panels and Mum will no doubt find an excuse to pop in. Might put on a movie with this one. Thinking five months is old enough now for her first showing of *Calamity Jane*."

Adelaid mock gasped. "Don't you dare! Not without me."

"Fine."

"Now, Muffin, you give Daddy hell, okay? It's your right and your role as a daughter." The Smudge nickname had gone by the wayside the moment they'd seen fingers and toes, all twenty of which Ted still considered a minor miracle.

For a man who'd seriously never considered fatherhood,

he was a natural. Just as she'd expected. A beautiful calm balance for Adelaid's wilder ups and downs.

"When she's sixteen, maybe," said Ted, laying a kiss atop his daughter's curls. "Till then, let's aim for Daddy's Little Girl."

"Or?"

"Or she can give me hell. Entirely up to her."

One last kiss for her daughter, another for her man, Adelaid walked out onto her front porch, several bags looped over her shoulder.

Dressed for the life she wanted, which also happened to be the life she had.

* * * * *

MILLS & BOON®

Coming next month

FORBIDDEN KISSES WITH HER MILLIONAIRE BOSS
Hana Sheik

Karl said, "Show your grandfather what he can't see. The talent and hard work that brought you this far."

"I'll try." She didn't say it with much conviction though.

He heard it and shook his head. "Make me believe that you mean it."

She breathed slowly and thoughtfully through her nose and then gave it another go.

"I can do it."

"A little better. But it won't cut it because I don't believe it."

Her frustration had been simmering for nearly a day now. All of her flight she'd been wringing her hands, oscillating between being angry at her grandfather to wanting to please him and giving in to his demands. He'd sacrificed for her. Wasn't it time for her to do the same for him, even if it meant her happiness was on the line?

"Make me believe you," he stressed, those dark eyes of his cutting through her.

A switch flipped in her and when she opened her mouth, she didn't recognize the words coming out or the emotion thrumming through her.

"Damn it, I can do this! I'm the only one who can do this, and that should be enough."

Lin hadn't felt the quiver in her hands until the bouquet trembled slightly. Somehow Karl dragged out the fear of losing her grandfather's love and of being abandoned by him and channeled into strength. She burned with the power of belief in herself. Her head rushed with the sensation and her heart was fuller for it.

She needn't look to Karl to see his approval.

Though his face barely dropped its cool guard, he was smiling and nodding, and she didn't think that anything else could have made her feel better in the moment. The swooping in her stomach and the breathless tightening in her chest were just products of the outburst she'd just had…or so she told herself. It wasn't because Karl looked sexier smiling, or that she suddenly noticed how close he was to her, his cologne in the air she breathed and his body heat so enticingly near.

She just had to remember that he was now technically her boss…

Making him very forbidden fruit.

Continue reading

FORBIDDEN KISSES WITH HER MILLIONAIRE BOSS

Hana Sheik

Available next month

www.millsandboon.co.uk